The Stand-in

By the same author

You Must Be Sisters
Close to Home
A Quiet Drink
Hot Water Man
Porky
To Have and To Hold
Driving In The Dark
Smile and Other Stories
Stolen

The Stand-In

DEBORAH MOGGACH

HEINEMANN : LONDON

To Mel

William Heinemann Limited
Michelin House, 81 Fulham Road, London sw3 6rb
LONDON   MELBOURNE   AUCKLAND

First published 1991
Copyright © Deborah Moggach 1991

A CIP catalogue record for this book
is available from the British Library
Hardback isbn 0 434 47349 9
Paperback isbn 0 434 47350 2

Printed in Great Britain
by Clays Ltd, St Ives plc

Contents

Acknowledgements

My thanks to Mercedes Burleigh, queen of stand-ins, and to Tom Hanks's stand-in on *Big* (a delightful man whose name I have, appropriately enough, forgotten). Thanks to John Guare for the Mary Pickford story, and to Stephen Frears for inviting me onto his set. For their help, thanks also to Debbie Stead and Mike Shuster, Dick Hess, Ivan and Susi Sharrock, and Steven Spielberg's mother Leah Adler, of the 'Milky Way'; Rick Finkelstein, Fredi Friedman, Nadia Lawrence, Mike Shaw and Peter Ginsberg. Grateful thanks to Joan M Devereaux of the Bedford Hills Correctional Facility, for her kindness. Thanks to Mel, as always. And, above all, thanks to Susannah York, who sparked off the idea in the first place; and to Maurice Hatton, who introduced us.

Deborah Moggach
1991

LONDON

One

I'm writing this in upstate New York. Outside, the sky is such a solid blue I could touch it. In here it's sweltering; my hair feels heavy as a helmet. Down the end of the corridor they're watching the afternoon movie. I can hear whoops, and the smattering of gunfire.

When Mark Chapman shot John Lennon he said it was like a movie. He said: 'I thought he would just drop. I thought he was going to fall down like in the movies, fall down dead. The guy had five bullets in him.'

Spoken like an actor! When you act you are both within a person and outside them, watching. You slide into a character, like fingers into a glove; you are both concealed and exposed by the person you have become. You watch your fingers and your face move; you're watching the words come out of your mouth. I used to light matches and watch them burn down, until I yelped with pain.

Inhuman, isn't it? At the moment of death, people part from their body, as if they are suspended above it. They look down quite calmly at the throes they are going through. Actors do this all the time.

You hold your wriggling self out on tongs. You hold other people too.

Trev, wriggling.

Lila, wriggling.

Sometimes it frightens me out of my wits. Next time you watch an actress, I bet you get frightened too.

If I shot myself, would it hurt? Or would I just watch myself, taking notes on how convincingly I die?

I can look at myself, nearly two years ago, as if she

isn't me. She's acting in a movie. It opens in a north London street, on a grey day in August. She is thirty-eight. She usually wears t-shirts and jeans but as she's an actress she's wearing silver today. She's mousy-blonde. Slimmish. Goodish-looking. Not enough to stop the cars when she's waiting at a pedestrian crossing; not that sort. Not like Lila.

I see it like a movie; I suppose that's part of the trouble. And only I know how it will end.

I'd had a humiliating night with Trev, and my thighbones ached. They ached from the making-up part of it, which had gone on till dawn. Down in the street a car alarm had suddenly wailed; we had fallen apart, damply, like two opposing teams giving up when the umpire blows his whistle.

Trev was my inflammation; he was my illness. Him and his smug smile. I was prodding him about his past.

'Just some bird I once knew,' he had said.

'Hasn't she got a name?' I demanded – suddenly, ludicrously righteous on behalf of some long-ago female. He was so cocky. Him and his smug cock, that wept when I touched it. That could make me weep.

We had been together for eighteen months and I was getting worse. I was jealous of everything he had handled. I could be jealous of an old kettle he hadn't got any more, how's that for insanity? I didn't tell him, of course. Not the extent of it. Alone, I could work myself up to fever-pitch – I could even be jealous, in anticipation, of all the women he might sleep with after me. He was only twenty-seven; one day he was going to slip through my fingers.

Him and his stubble. My face felt sore; in the mirror my mouth looked blurred. Flinching, I sponged Number Five over my chin. I was performing in *Gertie and the Giants*, a kids' show about the disappearing rainforests. Most of the others were students from the Central. We were dressing up as multinational companies – property, timber, McDonalds which felled the forests for grazing land. Martin, who was unhappily in love with Adrian, was climbing into an adapted oil drum; he was appearing as Toxic Waste.

We were called First Aid Theatre because we drove around in an old ambulance. Once, after a party, I had caught Trev kissing Natalie in it, but he just said he was giving her mouth-to-mouth resuscitation.

They were more Trev's age, really. I was thirty-eight; the oldest. I was playing the Fairy Godmother who guides Gertie through the forest. I give her three wishes and together we save the trees. It was all a bit worthy but I believed in those sort of things then.

Outside it was a grey, still morning. Through the window I could see the amputated arms of a plane tree; the council had lopped it. I zipped up my silver, fairy godmother's dress from the Oxfam shop. If only I could give myself three wishes, I would keep them all a secret.

Outside the door, children were waiting in the community centre hall. I ought to be pausing, and thinking myself into my role. Pulling on my tights, I hopped on one leg and knocked against the washbasin. At my age I ought to be in a TV series, shot entirely on film, with a plangent oboe soundtrack. Adapted from a forgotten feminist novel of the thirties, it had fetching period costumes, dove-greys and plums, and a row of BAFTA awards. I should be in the West End, appearing in a new play Tom Stoppard wrote especially for me, rather than for Felicity Kendal. I should be playing Viola before it was too late. I should be having a baby.

'Seen my leaves?' asked a tree.

'Seen my plaits?' asked Gertie.

Rob, who played a Big Mac, paused and said: 'They seem strangely quiet.'

We looked out of the door. The children had gone.

Earlier, I had not noticed anything unusual. It was a terraced street in north London, one of thousands. Why it had been chosen, I never knew. Months later I remembered that moment when I stepped out on to the pavement, in my silver dress. It seemed unnaturally quiet; the air was still, as it is when you are a child and everyone is hiding.

The street had been closed off. I looked up. The houses had eyes; there were faces at the windows. People leaned out, watching. The end of the street was blocked with vans, and lights flared on the last few houses. They looked freshly painted, and I thought for a moment that the council must have restored them.

Then, of course, I realised that they had just been smartened up for some filming. Fat black cables snaked across the street; I stepped over them. Watching the filming was a crowd of people; among them was my lost audience, the children.

Filming is ridiculously alluring. People had been drawn towards the magnet of those bright façades. Temporarily their street had a new identity, as if they had dreamed it. Yesterday the corner shop had been an ordinary newsagent's, one window boarded up and the other filled with cardboard boxes of disposable nappies. Now it had been transformed into a proper corner shop, the sort you don't see any more. It had a freshly painted sign and sweet jars in the window. It looked lurid and yet nostalgic, like the memories of a boozy uncle.

Beside me a small girl picked her nose. A man moved us all back, like cattle.

'What're you filming?' I asked. I wanted to add: I'm in the business too.

But the man was muttering into a walkie-talkie. A woman with a pram whispered: 'It's called *Sexbusters*.' She looked at her watch. 'And I've got a chicken in the oven.'

Minutes passed. Somebody bumped into me; the children were fidgety, but I knew I had lost them. It was the summer holidays, after all. Nobody was forcing them to see *Gertie and the Giants*. I thought of Rob, pinioned between his buns; he would be prising himself out of his Big Mac costume by now. So much for the rain forests.

And then somebody told us all to keep quiet. 'When you're ready!' came a far voice. A hush fell.

The corner shop door opened, a bell tinkled, and out came a couple.

They dazzled in the light. They were laughing, soundlessly, in the glare. The man held a toffee apple. Outside the shop, they paused. He tenderly passed it to the woman. She took a bite. And then they walked along the pavement, arm-in-arm, and out of shot.

'She's smaller than I thought,' whispered somebody.

'Who is she?' asked somebody else.

'Lila Dune, dickhead! I told you.'

More minutes passed. A smell of curry drifted from the unit canteen; it was nearly lunchtime.

The next take was ruined by a plane passing overhead. The next one by a scuffle which broke out among some boys. 'Get those kids away!' shouted the man with the walkie-talkie.

Vaguely bored, I shifted my weight on to the other foot. My thighs still ached; it was the same ache I had had as a child, when I had been riding a horse for hours.

I didn't recognise the actor, but Lila Dune was famous. Well, recognisable. She specialised in daffy, slightly tacky blondes. I had only seen her in a few films; one was a romantic comedy with Nick Nolte, another was something with Burt Reynolds and a lot of cars. She had a supporting role in that one. They were instantly forgettable. They were the sort of movies I only watched when they happened to be repeated on TV.

In the months to follow I re-ran that moment, my own personal re-take, over and over in my head. It was the moment I first saw Lila Dune. A blonde, very pretty woman, dressed in a white suit, came out of a corner shop. Shapely. Surprisingly small, but then weren't they all? A frisson, yes. But everybody, even another actress, feels a frisson when they see somebody famous, in the flesh, in a street roped off as if there had been an accident. Besides, Lila Dune was American, and this made her more of a star.

I felt nothing else, I'm sure. And nothing else would have happened if I hadn't recognised Eric.

7

The unit was breaking for lunch, and I was about to leave. Just then a stocky man, dressed in a white coat, came out of the corner shop and lit a cheroot. He was playing the shop-keeper and I knew him because, years before, he had played a dentist in a sit-com for Anglia TV and I'd had a tiny part. Besides, we shared the same agent and had met once or twice at her Christmas drinks.

He was chatting to the walkie-talkie man when he saw me and waved. I threaded my way through the crowd.

He pointed to my dress. 'Where's the ball, Cinders?'

I told him about Gertie, and turned to the other man. 'You stole my audience.'

'This is Jules Sampson,' said Eric. 'Terrific actress. We have the same agent, Maggie Fitch.'

The man shook my hand, and apologised for stealing my children.

'It doesn't matter,' I said. 'It was our last show, anyway. The council's been rate-capped; they've cancelled our grant.'

'So much for the British theatre,' said Eric. 'So what're you going to do, sweetheart?'

I shrugged. 'Re-paint my flat.' Trouble was, I had just re-painted it.

'How can you tell if somebody's an actor?' asked Eric. 'When they go for a crap they take the phone off the hook.'

'In case Columbia Pictures calls,' I said.

'Or even a dogfood commercial . . .'

'Or even an Allied Carpets commercial . . .'

'Or even a voice-over for dogfood,' I said.

Eric barked. Then he looked solemn. 'Let us not denigrate the humble voice-over. Repeat-repeat-repeat . . .'

The man, whose name I hadn't caught, was gazing at me. 'Anyone told you something?' he asked.

What could I reply to that? 'What?'

'You look amazingly like Lila.'

I raised my eyebrows. 'So I could be a film star too?'

'Same build,' he said. He looked me up and down, as if inspecting a piece of masonry. 'Similar bone-structure.'

I should have felt more flattered. After all, Lila Dune was gorgeous. In darkened cinemas all over the world, men throbbed for her. She was the archetypal bleached blonde, who looked as if she had just got out of bed. She had the snub, kittenish face that is both helpless and seductive.

But any comparison is a form of theft. For some reason, I felt more diluted, as if he had stolen from me my mousier hair, my heavier features, the Jules-ness which didn't match up to Lila Dune.

Perhaps I was more flattered than that. Probably. By now I can't tell; hindsight has confused my memory of that moment. Standing there in my fairy godmother's dress that sultry August day, I had no idea of the wishes that would be granted not to Gertie but to myself, and how powerless I would be to resist them. Nor did I realise that the granting itself would be a form of theft, for nothing is given without something else being extracted. All human beings deal in more-or-less disguised exchange, and we only realise that we are both the robbers and the robbed when the most important thing of all is stolen from us.

I didn't think of any of that then. Two summers ago I wasn't a simpler creature, just a less aware one. I went to the pub with First Aid, and the pram woman must have gone home to her roast chicken, and all the children dispersed and I never saw any of them again. And in a hundred homes that evening somebody told somebody else that they had seen Lila Dune, and nobody told anybody that they had seen me.

That sounds egocentric. It is. But when I say *me*, I also mean *you*.

Two

Of course I should never have got involved with Trevor. Nor, as it turned out, should he have got involved with me. Funnily enough I can picture him quite clearly now, but for months I kept his face a blur, on purpose, so our eyes couldn't meet. It still helps, slightly.

He was utterly, and devastatingly, charming. It was as simple as that. I bet he would have charmed you, too, unless he was knocking off your wife, and even then you might have eventually forgiven him because somewhere, underneath it all, you both knew that he was one of the boys. A man's man. A bloke. One of the lads.

He could sell anybody anything. In fact that was how we met, when he sold me some chimney pots. I put them on my balcony, for plants. I later discovered they were double the price I would have paid anywhere else, but by then it was too late.

He wasn't tall – hardly taller than me. He was slim and wiry and twice as alive as anyone I'd ever met. That might be a strange word to use now but it's the nearest I can get. As if, within him, wires stretched tight, tingling. Dark hair, bright eyes, wicked grin. Impish. And always restless – jangling his van keys, fidgety, alert. Like many attractive people, one knew exactly what he'd been like as a child. Graceful, elusive, utterly unselfconscious. And when suddenly he fixed his eyes on you, it was such high voltage that your bones melted.

Oh, I don't know; it doesn't really capture him. I'd simply say that, wherever he was, that was the place things happened. Once, on a motorway, I followed a beautiful sports car just because I wanted to be near it. I felt it knew, better than the rest of us, just where it was going.

In many ways we weren't suited at all. For a start, he was hardly an intellectual. My father was a deputy headmaster. His father was a builder. He worked for his local council, modernising old properties in north London. He would tear out Victorian fireplaces and install central heating. Trev, still in his teens, realised that half a mile away the middle classes were gentrifying their homes, so he would load the fireplaces into his Dad's van and flog them to the Laura Ashley crowd. He was a wood-stripper and a wife-stripper; he was streetwise and skip-smart. Once he sold a woman some panelling her next-door neighbour had thrown into a skip right outside her own front door. And, as he so charmingly put it, got his leg over into the bargain.

When I met him he was twenty-six, and moved in a swarthy netherworld of junk shops, men with vans, men with dogs, men with mates who could get you anything. Dealers, fixers, men who lived as instinctively as foxes. He disappeared for days with them on mega-piss-ups. Brought up on *Blue Peter* and piano lessons, I found it all irresistibly dodgy.

I was eleven years older than him and he liked to point out my period features. But every love-affair is a form of barter; as one acquaintance said: 'You want him for his body and he wants you for your head.' He said I had class. He was impressed by my collection of books and by the fact that he had once seen me on TV; it was a short-lived drama series on Channel 4 and I had played a probation officer. I suppose, in a minor way, he must have found this glamorous. I wasn't well known, and most of the jobs I'd had were in small fringe theatres that put on undiscovered European classics and which were only reviewed in *City Limits*. With my looks I was frequently cast as a repressed, intelligent wife – Dorothea Casaubon, for instance, in an adaptation of *Middlemarch* that a now-defunct company staged above a kebab house in Tufnell Park. *Leave it to Soak*, a BBC daytime series on household management. That sort of thing. Like most working actresses

I have never had a big break but I just about earned a living doing just about anything – voice-overs, school workshops, a video on *Forgotten Women in History* for the Open University. And though I didn't have many close friends I knew a lot of people in the business. It's a tight, enclosed world, and not as bitchy as people think. In fact it's loyal, because nobody in the world is as insecure as an actor, and nobody knows quite how they feel except another one.

And there is nobody as insecure as an actress in her late thirties, who sees the good roles slipping away to younger women and her own period features, inexorably, appearing.

From the moment he met me, Trev wanted to be a writer. Not 'to write', but to be 'a writer', which meant doing deals about something more interesting than furniture. He pictured lunches in Soho brasseries with husky-voiced female journalists who asked him about his working methods. He pictured signing his books, like a pop star, for a queue of groupies. He pictured status. Money, of course. Above all, possibilities. Overnight, he thought, his life could change. Columbia Pictures could call – not for me, but for him.

He had a bedsitter in Islington. He started to write, at night. I lived a few miles away in Belsize Park, a creamy, stuccoed, middle-class sort of neighbourhood. In the evenings, in thrall to him, I would truss myself up in a suspender belt and stockings because he loved to touch my skin there. I spent a fortune in Fenwicks; I made solitary, sensual pilgrimages there and, under the stern, *dominatrix* eye of the Austrian assistant, laced myself into basques so tight I could hardly breathe. I felt like a starlet. My body was ageing, but he aroused it in ways I had never felt before and I wanted to suffer for my pleasures. Under my misleading clothes I was his harlot. Pathetic, wasn't it?

My journey to Islington was punctuated by traffic lights. At one, I would tilt my driving mirror and apply lipstick; at the next, Caledonian Road, I would brush my hair. Heart thumping, I would prepare myself for him in my exposed little dressing room. I delayed these preparations until I was in my car. That passers-by could share my final touches made the whole thing highly erotic. I have always liked to be watched.

Of course he sponged off me. It was me who brought along the food and wine, who lent him money and who ended the evening with an empty cigarette packet. But I didn't even admit to myself that I noticed. I just cooked him dinner, and when he moved near me my mouth went dry. For months, like a student, I didn't even know what was on the TV. In his disgusting, peeling kitchenette he touched me and I opened up to him like a flower. We would eat first because he was so hungry; then he would put on a Ry Cooder tape and pull me on to his bed. He liked screwing, slowly, to slide guitar music.

In the small hours I would drive home, damp, flushed, my skin burning and my blouse buttoned up wrong. When I breathed heavily, I could smell his scent on my face. I would pass through the same traffic lights in reverse order. Those shabby intersections were stupidly dear to me. Intimate, momentarily, with the darkened houses either side, I would take out my brush and tackle my matted hair. I'd always wanted to be really messed-up by a man. By the time I reached Belsize Park I still hadn't got out the tangles.

I felt buffeted, bruised, heavier. Liberated. I felt wonderful. Trev was the sort of jerk who, seeing some angry feminist, could say that all she needed was a good fuck. I told you I despised myself.

When I arrived home I would have a long bath and rejoin my other self. Back in his bedsitter he would work. Once he started he wrote fast, and soon he had written several rather derivative short stories and a stage play. This was called *Use Me*, and it was about a middle-class woman who was in masochistic thrall to her plumber. It was extremely explicit, and a lot of it took place on her kitchen table. Stripped pine, of course.

I'll try to be objective about this. It wasn't exactly a good play – its plot was hopeless, and I told myself the woman was unconvincing. I didn't like to think about her too much. But he had two talents that many better writers don't possess. He wrote exactly as he spoke – direct, slangy and rude. And, more important – though it shouldn't be – he knew how to sell.

He used me, of course, just as he used my car and my washing machine and my slavish, older body. He used my contacts in the theatre, and after nearly a year of re-writes, phone calls, boozy lunches and relentless charm, he got an acquaintance of mine, a radical producer, a likely lad himself, to put together a production above a pub in Tottenham.

It opened that August. I thought I would be offered the lead, but the part went to the director's ex-wife because she was being bolshie about access to their kids and he wanted to soften her up. Of course I acted as if I didn't mind. Trev never guessed. But then he never guessed what a terrific actress I was. Nobody did.

Trev's bedsit was revolting, but he never suggested leaving it and moving in with me. It was on the ground floor of a house in a busy one-way street. The only sign of neighbours was when the car-clampers appeared and the cry went from flat to flat 'Clampers, clampers!' as if the recruiting officers had arrived. It faced a furniture superstore. All day, happy couples double-parked outside, and reappeared carrying household items. He groaned at the baby-seats in the back of their cars and said, 'Catch me changing nappies.' Stroking the inside of his thigh, I murmured, 'Catch me.'

His mattress was on the floor. When I climbed to my feet, my back ached. I'm too old for this, I thought. Naked, I filled the kettle at his sink. I kept my back to him so he couldn't see my slack belly. It was Saturday afternoon. Outside, two children rattled something metal along the railings.

One of them said, 'I can swallow my burps.'

'So fucking what?' said the other.

The street was veiled by the previous tenant's net curtains; Trev was no home-maker. I switched on the kettle. I should be at my dance class. When I saw them I would have to lie, yet again.

But then I was good at lying. The night before I had told Trev that I couldn't see him because I was going out. In fact I had eaten toasted cheese and watched *Bergerac*. However, I wanted him to think that I had another life; more than that, I wanted to convince myself that I still had some sort of life within myself, and that I could last an evening alone. And I had lasted, hadn't I?

Trev came up behind me. Sometimes he licked my spine. Sometimes he made up an alphabet of all the parts of my body. Sometimes he wrote in Pentel on my buttocks, words I couldn't see until I found a mirror. Once it was affectionate; once it was a recipe for hot cross buns. He had invented it, of course; he was hopeless at cooking. Today he was blind, and tried to find out who I was.

'Mmm . . . female,' he said, burying his face in my hair. He ran his hands over my shoulders, and cupped my breasts. 'Thought so. Right first time. Intelligent nipples. You're a barrister.' He groaned. 'Black high heels, severe skirt . . .' I shook my head. He ran his hands down my waist. 'Hmmm . . . prose-bearing hips. You're one of those novelist birds. You write about adultery amongst the quiche-eaters and you want to be shagged by Melvyn Bragg.'

'No fear. And quiche is passé.'

'No? Wrong?' He ran his hand lower. I tensed. He paused, his fingers damp. 'Ah,' he murmured. 'Now I know.' He whispered to me, his breath warm in my ear. As he whispered, my body opened like a mouth. I turned to him, my legs buckling. He pulled the bathroom door shut behind me, and pressed me against the panels. I was still wet, from the last time. Whimpering, I gripped him as he slid into me.

'Hayley!' A woman's voice, close. 'Throw it away!'

A child cried. A car revved up and I smelt exhaust smoke. Saturday was humming along a few feet away. The door rattled as I bumped against it.

15

He put his hand behind my head, to cushion it, and smiled into my face. As a lover he could be surprisingly, and temporarily, considerate.

And all the time I was watching myself move and listening to my own high cries. Inhuman, those noises, aren't they? I played them to him, and to all the audiences I had never reached. The people leaned forward in their seats.

Glued together, we slid to the floor and finally ended up on the bed. The kettle spouted steam on to the wallpaper. Afterwards he laughed, stroking my cheek with his finger. I got up and began making the tea all over again.

'Guess who I saw yesterday,' I said, opening the fridge. I took out the milk and sniffed it. 'Lila Dune.'

He groaned. 'Lila Dune!'

'She's in London, making a picture.' I paused. 'Probably earns as much as the council's entire arts budget for the year.' I turned. He was lying on the mattress, his eyes closed. 'What's the matter?'

'Lila Dune,' he murmured. 'I'm getting another erection.'

'Why?' I looked down at him. 'Anyway, you're not.'

'Remember her in *Touch and Go*?'

I nodded. 'Lousy film. You must've still been in nappies.'

'I was a throbbing teenager. Remember when she came out of the swimming pool, all wet, and – '

'All right, all right!' I searched for the packet of tea bags I had bought him. 'Anyway, she's ancient now.'

'Only your age.'

'She's older!' I paused. Probably not, actually. When caught on the off-beat, my own age could surprise me. Thirty-eight was what other women were, women I saw shopping.

'You should be grateful I like mature women. With my incredible sex drive and their experience . . .' He closed his eyes again. 'I had this photo of her up on my wall, from *Time Out*, she was poured into this dress, and I'd go to bed and – '

'Spare us your jejeune masturbatory fantasies – '

16

'Her, and Angie Dickinson in that cop thing – '

'Angie Dickinson! You really are a gerontophile.'

'A what?'

I was scrubbing out his mugs. I looked inside them. 'These are grotesque.'

I wanted him home with me, drinking out of my own clean tea cups. I wanted him to want to live with me. I wanted his socks and his underpants in my cupboard, under my own tight roof. I wanted him to have never known any woman but me. I was humiliatingly jealous, and it was getting out of hand. Usually I disguised it. When, for instance, he mentioned some long-ago holiday in Spain, I tried with various veiled assumptions to prove that his companion was female. She was, of course – I found that out when the subject of topless beaches came up. I felt a sort of curdled satisfaction, a bitter sediment in my stomach. I almost relished my own distress. Pornographically, I aroused myself with visions of them in a hundred hotel beds. It was insane, of course; I knew that. However young they are, everybody has a past – *I* had a past, for Christ's sake, and eleven more years of it than he did, but he never seemed that interested. My efforts to inflame him only made him amused, and left me feeling flustered and juvenile.

Trev didn't reflect on the past or anticipate the future. I suppose that was part of his attraction for someone like me, who schemed and brooded. He lived simply, in the present, like an animal.

Once I went to a wine bar where an ex-girlfriend of his worked. Her name was Dawn. Like a lovesick schoolgirl, I found myself writing her name down the margin of a script I was learning. *Dawn. DAWN.* The wine bar was in Battersea, the other side of London. For my own equilibrium I convinced myself I needed to go to that area anyway, to look at some bathroom fixtures. I almost convinced myself with my own performance, spending all the morning looking at bidets. Then I lingered outside the wine bar, casually, like somebody on a first date. She was dark, and very pretty. I went in and sat down; as she passed, I gazed at her mouth and her breasts with such attention that I alarmed myself. Obsession, I guess, is a form of desire; when I paid, my hand was trembling. I went back at night, and watched. When I looked at my watch, I had been there forty minutes. I felt like an assassin, waiting for a celebrity. I sat there, night after night.

I'm telling you this in case you understand it. By now I can't tell how normal I was – in some way, you would know better than I would. I have had to remodel my own past, you see, in the light of what happened. It's the only way I can make sense of it, but by doing this I have lost the exact reality. It's as if there has been an explosion in my kitchen; I've returned to find my saucepans buckled. The blast has altered my possessions for ever; I can never knock them back into their former shape – not quite.

A girl in my class at school was later killed in an air crash. When I think of her she isn't Anna-the-schoolgirl, but Anna-who-was-soon-to-die. When a tragedy occurs you don't only lose the person concerned, you also lose your accurate, unclouded memory of them. It is doubly sad, for you lose out not once but twice.

Three

The following Monday I had a phone call from my agent. At first I couldn't grasp what it was about. A man I hadn't heard of had phoned from a film company.

'For me?' My stomach churned.

'He met you on Friday,' said Maggie. 'Don't you remember?'

'Friday?'

Maggie, my agent, didn't sound too excited about any of this. In fact she almost sounded diffident – not a word that sprang to mind when her clients described her.

It was the movie *Sexbusters*. No, it wasn't exactly a part. On the other hand, it was work. Lila Dune's stand-in had been beaten up by her ex-husband.

'Whose ex-husband?'

'Not Lila's, darling. Her own. Anyway, she's gone into hospital and they need another stand-in right away. Like, tomorrow. They've got three more weeks of filming and, well, darling.'

Well, darling, meant well darling we've not got much else on the cards, have we? Well darling beggars can't be choosers, £400 a week's not to be sniffed at, darling, and my other phone's ringing.

I said I'd think about it, darling, and phone her back.

I finally tracked Trev down at Look Back in Ongar. This was a second-hand furniture shop, down the Essex Road, that belonged to one of his mates. Trev was using the phone; he was always using people's phones. He loved the telephone like an American.

Look Back in Ongar specialised in the sort of chintzy

suburban furniture that used to belong to people's aunts but was now high style. I sat down. Going out with Trev didn't always make me feel old. In many ways it was rejuvenating. Besides, when we were alone we could simply be a couple – lips, bodies, fights. Alone with somebody, you adjust to them and they to you; there is no third person to mirror back to you your discrepancies.

It was his friends who reminded me of my age. With them, I realised that Trev was practically another generation. They seemed cocky and yet unweathered; they seemed young. In their company he took on their colour, chameleon-like, and it seemed as if he had always been this way. This disturbed me so much I pretended I didn't notice.

They polished up the sort of furniture my parents would have thrown out. They dressed like dudes and put gel on their hair. They played the juke box in reconstituted Soho bars and discovered, for themselves, the Buddy Holly songs that I knew from my childhood. One of them had even asked me, respectfully, what it was like in the sixties, as if I were a museum specimen. I had replied, tartly, that in the Flower Power year of 1967 I was still only seventeen. Trev had sucked his thumb and said, 'And I was only six.' This gave me a jolt, as if I were sitting in a train and it suddenly shunted backwards. Or, indeed, forwards. This happened quite often, with me and Trev. Depending on my mood I found this piquant, irritating or disturbing. Sometimes I just found it gratifying.

I waited until Max, the owner, had gone out of the shop. A TV company was hiring a three-piece suite and he was loading it into a van. I moved next to Trev and told him about the stand-in offer. I wanted us to be like a real couple, and for him to join in the decision-making. Besides, I was curious to see his reaction. With a thump, I realised I didn't know him well enough to guess how he would answer.

He was seeing his agent later that day and he'd had his hair cut. He wore his wide, peacock-blue shirt and his red leather tie. He looked like an advertisement for Coca-Cola. I gazed at his legs, spreadeagled. It hurt to look at him; instead I gazed at the shelves of hideous plaster odalisques. I didn't really mind about the stand-in job, you see, one way or another. At that moment I simply ached with pain, from wanting to have his baby.

'Think of the contacts!' he was saying. 'Once you're in with those guys.' He fished for one of my cigarettes.

'Know what you do?' I said. 'You just stand there while they set up the shot. While they light you. You're just a dummy.'

'Listen, dummy. It's the first step. Where's your matches?'

'You're not even an understudy. Christ, you're not even an *extra*!'

'Look, you'll be on a film set. Big geezers with cigars. Anyway, I want to know what she's like. Hey, I'll get to meet her!'

'Trev, I'm an actress! I've played Hedda Gabler.' Well, above a pub I had. In Cardiff.

'Listen, prune-face.' He ran his finger down my cheek. 'Play your cards right and next stop Hollywood. Maybe she'll be run over by a bus and you'll take the lead.' He lay back, exhaling smoke. 'I'd be quite happy with Laurel Canyon.'

'Ah, Laurel. The starlet with the big knockers who so admires your work.'

He opened one eye, looked at me and closed it again. 'Imagine it. Socking great swimming pool. Some uniformed berk bringing us Bacardi cocktails. Crumpet coming out of the woodwork.' He sighed. 'You lying there, scripts dangling from your painted fingernails like Faye Dunaway.'

'I don't want to go to California. I want to work at the National Theatre.' I picked at a hole in the sofa upholstery. 'Neil Simon said it was paradise with a lobotomy.'

'The National Theatre?'

I dug him with my elbow. 'You're not interested in my career. You're not even interested in the bloody theatre.' This was true. He preferred going to the movies; practically the only play he had seen was his own. 'You just want to be rich and famous.'

'Don't you?'

'I want to play Cleopatra, with Peter Brook directing me.'

But I wasn't playing Cleopatra, was I? And then I had to explain who Peter Brook was, because Trev had never heard of him.

On the way home I bought some fruit. It was a sunny day and I was wearing a halter-neck dress I had just made. For the first time in my life, however, the greengrocer didn't call me 'love' or 'darling'. He called me 'Mum'.

For some reason, this decided me.

And that's where my story really begins. Although you could say it began eighteen months earlier, when I first glimpsed Trevor in that architectural salvage yard, surrounded by his priapic chimney pots.

Four

I come from a silent household. Perhaps that's why I find the fluster of filming so attractive. My father became the deputy head of a grammar school that was merged into a comprehensive. It broke his heart. He was a bookish, inward man who wasn't good at what is called relating – a word he loathed. I don't remember him ever touching me, or indeed my mother, with affection. The only way I could tell he was pleased with me – when I got my A-level results, for instance – was when he went to his bureau, fetched his camera and took my photo. When he died, years later, I went through his things. He had kept all my letters in separate plastic folders, each dated in careful typing. I should have been touched – I was, momentarily – but I was also repulsed by his secretiveness, and angry at the sheer waste of all that feeling.

I was disturbed, too, because I recognised something of myself in it. My early efforts to attract his attention met with so little response that I retreated to my bedroom where I sat in front of the mirror, watching my brooding face with spasms of self-pity. I would mouth into the mirror my carefully prepared speeches, and his longed-for replies. With practice, I had him perfectly – his nervous cough, his deliberate pauses, the way he ran his finger over his moustache, touching his lips as he did so. I became a repressed, secretive child, closing myself off into my own fantasy world where I could re-run everything and make it all right. When I was alone, of course, it always worked. From the age of twelve I wanted to be an actress.

My mother was a pretty, under-used woman who at some point must have realised that her marriage wasn't up to much and who simply gave up. She was the last generation of middle-class women who didn't work. Accompanied by her droning companion, the vacuum cleaner, she made the rounds of our house in Arundel each morning and in the afternoons took to her bed with a series of small ailments which were her last, and largely unsuccessful, attempts to get my father to notice her. In fact he found illness embarrassing and boring. I was more intelligent than my mother and realised that. Excellence was the only thing that pleased him. A staunch liberal, he had groomed children to excellence in his old grammar school days, and when I went to drama school I studied with his picture in my head, like a framed painting of the headmaster he never quite became, telling me to try even harder. If I failed he was not angry but disappointed, which of course made it worse.

The only time I had him to myself was when I was up on stage. He came to all my productions, even terrible, amateurish ones in arctic community halls. When I apologised, he said that schoolteachers functioned best in a draught. Afterwards we actually had some proper conversations. We would go to a pub and he would buy me a drink – I would always have a scotch because that was what he drank. He loved going over my texts – he had taught English and knew a great deal about plays, even contemporary ones. He would come alive then; I realised what a terrific teacher he must have been. Teaching, of course, is easier than fatherhood because you can be more detached. In fact you have to be. But once you're detached you can, strangely enough, communicate better – it's like telling somebody on the phone all the things you are too shy to tell them face to face.

My mother would twitter on about how pretty I looked. He would simply pause – he didn't even pay her the compliment of sighing – and wait until she had finished. And then we would get back to what absorbed us both, more than anything in the world, which was words.

Every actor performs for somebody. They have to. It might be the director, or – more rarely – the producer. It might be their drama teacher, if such a person has been potent for them. It might be some mythical film scout, who they imagine in the audience to psyche themselves up. It might be the reviewers, and always one in particular, the one they admire – the after-effects of this can carry on long after the first night. It might be their lover, for whom they display themselves erotically. It might be the playwright, though this can be unnerving. It might simply be some imagined member of the audience, someone just like themselves, a soulmate who knows and appreciates exactly what they are trying to do and would do it that way if only they had the talent. It might be several of these in succession, particularly in a long run when the actor needs to stay awake. It might be none.

In my profession I've heard people mention all of these. But I've never described the face in my own darkened auditorium. It is my father's. I always performed for him; in a sense, I still do.

Arriving at a film unit when it is halfway through shooting is like arriving at a new school in mid-term. In my case it was even worse. As I had suspected, a stand-in was certainly not a member of the crew – a bunch of men in anoraks who were, as always, a law unto themselves. They either looked surprisingly young, with tight jeans and highlights in their hair, or else leathery and preoccupied.

Nor did I feel like a member of the cast, who that first morning were nowhere to be seen, though I presumed they were in the make-up trailer. People rushed past me; I hung about, feeling both invisible and yet in the way. It was a chilly morning; I shivered in my sweater. They were setting up an exterior shot, in a smart Kensington street, outside the scientist's house. What scientist?

Finally I found the lowest of the low: an extra. She was a woman with a poodle who eerily resembled my own mother, though dressed as a Kensington shopper.

'He's got an irritated bowel,' she said, gazing at her dog. 'Perhaps I shouldn't have had him clipped.'

We drank a styrofoam cup of coffee together, leaning against a garden wall.

'It's a re-make of an old forties film everyone's forgotten,' said the extra. She had a high, refined voice. 'It's a comedy about an eccentric old scientist who'd invented a pill that can change a person's sex.' He was being played by an alcoholic stage actor who was having a sunset success in the movies. His younger American wife was being played by Lila Dune. 'I don't know anything else, except that Miss Dune is supposed to be having a thing with the director.' The extra looked at her watch. 'Hotpoint's coming this p.m. to mend my washing machine. Does p.m. start at one, do you think, or two?'

'Twelve,' I said. 'Post meridiem.'

The woman frowned at me for a moment, and then wandered off.

Suddenly the assistant director was there, the man with the walkie-talkie. He clasped me around the shoulders as if I were his long-lost niece, and told me to step this way.

Films are shot in such a fractured fashion that it is hard to piece together their story. It is like being shoved up against various items of furniture – a table-leg, a cupboard – and never being able to stand back and see what the room looks like. I had hardly ever been in a real film; I had only appeared in student movies or else in low-budget TV dramas that were shot in the studio. *Sexbusters* was the full works – a big feature with scores of technicians who had moved in on the street, blocked it off and set up their equipment as if major surgery was about to take place.

A girl led me to the wardrobe trailer. She gave me a blue coat and a wig. It was a long, blonde wig; not mousy like my own hair but brassy yellow like Lila's. It was too tight.

'Sandy's head was smaller than yours,' said the girl. Her breath smelt of peppermints.

I looked in the mirror. In the wig I looked phoney and skittish, as if I had rifled someone else's dressing-up box.

'Do I have to wear this?' I asked.

'Jock's finicky,' said the girl. She pointed to a taxi. It was parked in the street, outside the scientist's house. 'You sit here, Joyce.'

'Jules.'

The girl looked at her watch and shouted to somebody. I put on the coat and climbed into the cab. Its back seat was full of Harrods carrier bags. In the front sat the cabbie, a middle-aged Jewish actor I vaguely recognised. He had played Moses in a children's serial I had read for, but failed to get.

'What's up?' he said. 'Rex is in a filthy temper.'

'Who's Rex?'

'The director.'

'I don't know. I've only just arrived. What am I supposed to be doing?'

'Search me,' said the cabbie. 'You've been shopping, I suppose, and you're coming home.'

The assistant director wound down the window. He explained that once they had set up the shot I had to get out of the cab and carry my bags up the front path to the house. A maid would take them from me.

I did as I was told. I sat still for what seemed an age. The wig felt like a thick rubber band around my skull. When instructed I got out, with the bags, and walked up the front path to the house. But it was an odd sensation, as if I were invisible. The sun came out. The lighting crew weren't looking at my face, they were calling out numbers and adjusting their lights. I was simply a blue coat, with legs; I was a solid, with a shadow. I stood on the front steps, with all those eyes on me and yet none of them seeing me at all. It was curiously exhausting. Somebody shifted a tub of geraniums to one side. Somebody asked: 'Where the hell's Russell?' Beyond the houses, which rose up in front of me, white as icing, the Knightsbridge traffic hummed.

Minutes passed. People seemed to have forgotten about me. They all seemed to be in a bad mood. Every film unit has its own character, which is formed in the first few days of shooting. It comes from a chemistry of egos, weather, and a hundred other things. But the most pervasive of these is the director who, like a headmaster, sets the morale of the whole group; and the morale of *Sexbusters* was low.

I didn't discover this until later. All I noticed was that the actress who played the maid, arriving at the door for the shooting rehearsal, sighed at me and rolled her eyes heavenwards. And then I was told to move off the set. I tried to find the extra, but the woman had already been positioned at the far end of the street; she was working, now, and out of bounds.

Film stars, like royalty, have a habit of suddenly appearing from nowhere. When I turned, there was Lila. She had come out of the house; she seemed to be arguing with a tanned, muscular man who wore a lumberjack's cap. This, I deduced, was the director, Rex Benson. He was grinning. Lila stood on the doorstep and blew her nose. Rex patted her shoulder; she smiled sweetly at him. A make-up girl approached her with a brush; she smiled sweetly at her. Then she walked down to the taxi-cab. She was wearing an expensive-looking blue coat and high heels. She looked sensational.

I didn't get to meet her until after the lunchbreak. They were doing all the exterior shots of the house that day. Due to some hold-up with Lila, however, the cab scene had over-run, and people were scuttling about in a frenzy. There was no chance for me to introduce myself.

Instead I ate lamb chops in a double decker bus. I sat next to the actress who played the maid. In front of us sat the group of extras who, like extras everywhere, ate twice as much as everybody else, as if stoking up for a siege.

'Rex is a shit,' said the actress.

'Why?'

'Jumps anything that moves. He keeps telling me to bend over more when I'm doing my dusting.'

'Ah,' I said, 'one of those *droit de seigneur* ones.'

'Pardon?' She lit a Silk Cut and blew smoke over the hair of the people in front. 'No wonder she's cracking up.'

'Who?'

'Lila. He's been screwing Lorraine right under her nose.'

28

'Who's Lorraine?'

The actress sniffed. 'She doesn't come here any more.' She gestured around the bus. 'Too good for us, I suppose. And she's only got this teensy-weensy part as the gerbil-keeper.'

'Gerbils?'

'In the lab.' She explained the story. 'It's a wacky comedy,' she said, rolling her eyes again. 'This old geezer, the scientist, he's invented this sex-change pill. His wife, that's Lila, she's wooed by this handsome rival scientist. But when she finds out that the rival scientist is only using her to get the secret formula she blows her top, and gets her revenge by feeding him the pill and turning him into a woman.' She stubbed out her cigarette in her apple crumble. 'He's a woman now, right? So he gets his revenge by falling in love with Rory.'

'Who's Rory?'

'The scientist's son by his first marriage. So Adelaide – that's Lila – she turns him back into a man.'

There was a pause. 'And why not,' I said. The extra with the Hotpoint appointment looked at her watch and got up. I wondered idly what she had done with her poodle. *The Lady with the Little Dog* . . . I felt a wave of homesickness for Chekhov. Why was I sitting here, choking in the cigarette smoke of people I didn't know? Where was Trev, and was he thinking about me? I remembered the night before, when he breathed into my ear and licked my elbows. Outside, a shadow passed over the houses; voices shouted in the silenced street. Last night I had dreamed I was standing, naked, on a stage. I was playing Hermione in *The Winter's Tale* and I had forgotten my lines. Suddenly, with a hiss, I melted. Then I woke up, sweating.

After lunch the atmosphere improved. Or perhaps I just felt more at home because I had eaten a meal. The AD, whose name was Malcolm, actually paused for a moment and outlined the afternoon's scenes. He added that they had to get three scenes into the can, including one where the rival scientist appeared at the house in drag. The actor, Tony Chandler, had spent all morning in wardrobe and make-up.

Besides, I was no longer the newcomer. The morning's extras left and new ones arrived, plus a Sunlight Laundry van, which was to make a delivery to the house. Two more members of the cast appeared – the eccentric scientist and his screen son Rory. The director was seen with his arms around both of them, laughing.

'It won't last,' whispered the actress who played the maid. She had finished shooting for the day and was waiting for a minicab. 'It just means he's made it up with Lila.'

'Rex has?'

She nodded. 'He goes into her trailer and she gives him a blow-job.'

'Really?'

'She's dieting, apparently, and it's very low-calorie.'

I was only being used for one of the scenes. I had to stand at the bedroom balcony, watching my ex-lover, now female, arrive for a date with my stepson. The sun blazed. I pulled on my wig and gazed at the upturned faces. I imagined myself the Juliet I had never played, and now never would. *Wherefore art thou, Trevor? Thinkest thou of me, who swelters seen yet unseen, the effigy of another?* I closed my eyes and pictured him, loaded with chimney pots, climbing up the drainpipe to my balcony.

Tony Chandler was a newcomer. Apparently he had started as a model, made his name in a lager commercial and was now breaking into the movies. I had been introduced to him earlier; he was handsome in a delicate way, like an etching. Now, from my balcony, I watched him drive up in his Morgan and rehearse climbing out, swinging his legs in their high-heeled sandals. He wore a red, curly wig and a full-skirted dress. One of the cameramen wolfwhistled.

Later, off the set, I watched Lila acting the scene for real. I felt a tweak of resentment. That balcony was so familiar to me by now – its warm railings, its wisteria – that Lila seemed the usurper. I myself had stood there for an hour, but now I no longer existed; I was simply the servant who kept the throne warm for the queen's arrival, for the radiant smiles and flashing cameras.

From a distance, I watched the first take. Lila leaned over the balcony, her hair golden in the sun.

'Rory's not at home,' she shouted down. 'And, honey, green's not your colour.'

I picked up somebody's newspaper and sat down on the garden wall. My blonde Lila-hair fell in my eyes and I pushed it back. Another cancer ward had been closed, I read, for lack of government funds. A Labour MP said that Britain was becoming a two-nation country: the rich were getting richer and the poor were getting bled.

I smelt perfume. For a moment I thought it was the garden flowers behind me; then I looked up and saw Lila.

Lila was just a few feet away. She was with the AD, Malcolm. They stopped. Malcolm turned to me.

'Have you two actually been introduced? This is Julia Sampson.'

'Hi. How're ya doing?' Lila shook my hand.

Malcolm beamed. 'Lila's been telling me how great it is, that you could join us so quickly.'

I beamed at Lila. I suddenly had an absurd desire to please her. 'Terrific story, isn't it?' I said.

'Think so?' said Lila. 'I think it's kind of dumb.'

I blushed. 'Well – it's fun anyway.' Tony passed by, in his dress; we watched him take off a high-heeled sandal, groan and rub his foot. 'A real *Tootsie* role,' I said.

Lila turned to me eagerly. 'Know where I can get them?'

'What?'

'Tootsie rolls?'

'Pardon?' I said.

'I've searched all over,' said Lila. 'I'm a junk-food junkie.'

Malcolm took her arm. 'I'm sure we can find you some, Miss Dune. We'll get it sent to your hotel. Leave it to us.' And he steered her away.

Do you know, my heart was thumping? When I unclenched my fingers, my palms were damp. It was ridiculous. She was

31

only a woman. And yet, when I lifted the newspaper again, my hands were trembling.

She was incredibly pretty, of course. Beautiful, really. I wasn't prepared for the effect she would have on me, close up. It's hard to describe her – as Tolstoy nearly said, all beautiful people are the same, but the rest of us are not-quite-beautiful in different ways.

Despite the thick make-up she was more fine-boned than I had expected, more delicate. Her arms were slender and honey-tanned; her eyes wide-spaced, and she had the most wonderful mouth – full and inviting. Her mascara was slightly smudged; she looked just slightly awry. On her cheek, just where it should be, was a beauty spot.

Though she had the vulnerable face of a young girl, she also looked her age; this, I'm sure, had improved her, it made her face more defined and interesting. There were faint laughter-lines around her eyes, and at the corners of her mouth.

Next to her, I felt drained and colourless, a foolish imposter in my Lila wig. I felt like a foliage plant next to a lustrous, over-scented hothouse bloom. There was something slightly sluttish and over-ripe about her, something very sexy.

But it was more than this. She was famous.

I had met well known actors before, but Lila was different. She was a star. Second-division, maybe, but still a star. It's the perfect word: star. It implies that they exist above us, breathing different air. It doesn't even imply – it takes for granted.

Oh, it's beyond reason. I mean, I didn't even particularly admire her work – give me Vanessa Redgrave any day, now there's an actress's actress. Lila had been so-so in the takes I had seen; she had no range. She didn't even appear in the sort of films I liked.

I couldn't really explain it. I just felt uncomfortable, as if I had slightly betrayed myself. Why had I sucked up to her, telling her what a terrific story it was? I was probably twice as intelligent as Lila, yet I felt so stupid. I suppose, just for a moment, I was star-struck. What a cliché. Like, when I describe her it comes out a cliché – honey-tanned, wide-spaced eyes. I'll be going on about her spun-gold hair next.

When you are in love you speak in clichés. *He swept me off my feet. Our hearts were one. I felt I'd known him all my life.* Tired, battered old phrases you have despised for years; suddenly, in a rush, they are yours, you welcome them back like lost possessions.

My father despised clichés. He hated sloppiness. He admired precision; he sought words which knocked together and produced sparks. But then my father had never lost control; he had never dared to love.

That night, in bed, I told Trev that I'd shaken Lila Dune's hand.

'I'll touch you,' he said, 'and then I'll never wash again.'

He took my hand and pushed it down between his thighs.

That night I dreamed that I was trying to reach my father, but he couldn't hear my cries because I was trapped between two doors. Then I realised they weren't doors, they were two sides of a bun. *All that gristle*, he said. *It's disgusting*. And he turned away.

When I woke I tried to tell it to Trev. But I wasn't really speaking to him. Telling a dream is entirely selfish; you are just trying to fix it in your mind, like dipping a photograph in the chemicals of speech and waiting for the picture to appear.

The one thing I'm glad about, now, is that my father died before any of this happened. He is the one person I couldn't have faced.

Five

For the next couple of days I hardly spoke to Lila. By the
nature of my job, in fact, I found myself working more closely
with the crew than with the other actors. I became friendly
with Nobby; he was one of the grips and had rosy cheeks and
a beer belly. He was the only person who seemed to know I
was an actress.

'Saw you on *Grange Hill*,' he said. 'My kids were watching
it. Didn't you play some school inspector?'

I nodded. 'Twenty lines, and they cut them to five.'

He ruffled my hair. 'Never mind, ducks, it might happen one
aay.' He lowered his voice. 'Anyway, *Grange Hill* is bleeding
Von Stroheim compared to this.'

'It is kind of dumb,' I agreed, and then I suddenly realised
that this was what Lila had said.

I had to stand in a shop. We were filming in Burlington
Arcade. It was a scene where Adelaide, the scientist's wife,
was buying her lover a Burberry. By now I had been given a
copy of the script; I guessed that Adelaide should be played
flirtatious and excited, as she was at the corner shop the week
before. Such considerations, however, were none of my business. I was simply a shop accessory, as lifeless as the racks of
coats, to be placed in the composition and framed by Jock, the
cinematographer. He was the finicky one who had demanded
the wig.

I felt as inert as a banana in a still life. This should have
been restful, but I ached with frustration. I was at work, and
yet wasn't working at all. I was simply standing there, with
my mind wandering – do I need more bin liners? What do I

have to video tonight? This battled against my instincts as an actress, which were to empty myself of my own preoccupations and think myself into Adelaide's: I am guilty; I am married to an old man of whom I am fond; I am spending too much of his money on a raincoat for my lover. I am acting in a deeply silly film.

'OK. Thank you, Jules. Call Miss Dune.'

There was a stir in the crowd. For some reason I didn't want to see Lila. Perspiring from the lights, I moved out of the shop. As I walked down the arcade my sweat dried and I became just another shopper. I pulled off the wig and paused outside Fortnum & Mason. In the window, jars of caviar were stacked in a pyramid. *Sexbusters* was being filmed in a London that was unknown to most Londoners. With an eye on the American market its scenes were being shot in the corny tourist areas – Bond Street, St James's Park. The unworldly old scientist happened to live in a million-pound mansion, with a butler and maid. His wife had a tryst in a corner shop that was straight out of Dickens, complete with toffee apples. What rubbish! I gazed at a leather suit in a shop window. It cost six times my entire salary for *Middlemarch*, the show that nobody came to see.

Half London, however, wanted to see Lila Dune. Apparently she had recently starred in some ghastly American mini-series on TV. When we finished she was engulfed by a crowd of autograph hunters. Her blonde hair matched the wig that hung like a dead mammal from my hand. A limo was waiting, its engine running. It filled the street with exhaust fumes. Lila, still signing, was ushered away by her secretary – a square fierce Hungarian called Irma. The limo drove off. On the pavement the murmurs subsided, like diminishing ripples on the shore of a lake when a sailing ship had passed by, and out of sight.

As I turned to go, I felt a hand on my arm.

'Weren't you in the film too?' asked a woman.

I paused. 'Sort of.'

'What's she like?'

'Who?'

'Lila Dune,' said the woman. 'Do you get to speak to her?'

I paused. Then I shrugged. 'Of course.'

'Really?' the woman breathed.

'We're quite close,' I said. 'You get close, of course, when you're working with someone.'

'Gosh,' said the woman, bright-eyed. She hesitated, then took out the sheet of paper with Lila's signature on it. She tore a piece off the bottom and passed it to me.

'Go on, do us a favour.'

'What?'

'Sign your name.'

I paused. Stupidly, I blushed. 'Of course,' I said graciously, and signed.

'The camera loves her,' said Nobby. 'It's as simple as that. Some women have it, like Marilyn Monroe, and some don't. It's, like, a glow from inside. Nothing to do with looks. Nothing to do with acting ability. But put her in front of a camera and – pow!'

'Do you find her attractive?' I asked.

He thought for a moment. 'Bit out of my depth.'

'Too glamorous, you mean? Too spoilt?'

He shook his head. 'She's amazingly unspoilt, considering who she is. I mean, too screwed up.'

'Is she?'

'Don't you ever read the magazines?'

'Not that sort.'

Tempers were short that day. Malcolm, the AD, was setting up the afternoon's shoot. Rex, the director, was noticeably absent. Officially he was having a meeting with the producers, who hadn't liked yesterday's rushes. But Lorraine, the young actress, was not around either. Lila was kicking up a fuss, apparently, about a dress that didn't fit; Natasha, the dresser, was in tears. Or perhaps it was Lila who was crying. Nobody seemed to know what was going on. Irma was stomping

36

around, demanding fresh orange juice for her employer. She kept telling everyone that in New York you could get fresh orange juice anyplace, day or night.

We were shooting interiors in the lover's house, a luxurious mews cottage just off Belgrave Square. Malcolm was in a flap. He was gangly and curiously asexual, he didn't have Rex's charisma. He wore a sweat-stained t-shirt, with the title of another movie he had worked on, *Hell to Pay*, printed on the front. We were supposed to be shooting a showdown scene, when Adelaide accuses her lover of treachery.

An actress, who was playing the lover's ex-girlfriend, had arrived. She sat outside in the cobbled street, knitting a long and unseasonable scarf. I seemed to have been hanging about for hours. Film-making, I had long ago realised, was mind-numbingly dull, with odd pockets of panic. Orson Welles had said: *Anybody can be a film director, as long as they can stay awake*. It was hot. I sat, my back against the warm wall of the cottage. I heard the robot chatter of a walkie-talkie. Nearby the unit photographer was swopping recipes with the continuity girl. On film shoots people talk about food all the time.

'I pop it in uncooked,' she said. 'But I take the bones out first.'

'My flatmate cooks it with mozzarella.'

'Mozzarella?'

And then I was summoned indoors, to sit on a suede settee. I wondered what was happening between Lila and Rex. Like Lila, I didn't trust the director. You couldn't rely on a middle-aged man who wore such tight jeans that his crotch bulged. And that lumberjack's cap! Lila was a star; surely she could do better than that?

Tony Chandler's stand-in sat down beside me. Minutes passed; everybody was restless. It was a large, open-plan room, lavishly furnished with zebra-skin rugs and glass tables.

I whispered, 'So this is his pad? Looks more like a porn king's hideaway.'

'Listen, toots, if it's verisimilitude you want you're in the wrong movie.' He was called Rod. He had a mid-Atlantic accent, like a disc jockey. He passed me a wad of gum. 'We all are.'

'How's Tony getting on with Lila?'

'She hates his guts.'

'Why?'

He shrugged. 'Because he only fancies boys.'

I chewed. 'I see.'

'She seems to take it personally.' He chomped for a moment. 'She is one insecure lady.'

'How could she be? She's got everything.'

'What difference does that make?'

'Doesn't it help?'

He turned to me. 'Lila's a junkie. She wants every man in the world to fall in love with her. And then some more.'

'They probably do.'

'But when they do, she thinks they must be crazy.' He blew a bubble, and cracked it back into his mouth. 'So she can only get her rocks off with real jerks, like Rex.'

'Ah.'

'When it comes to men, she's as screwy as all getout.' He smiled faintly. 'But then, I suppose, so am I.'

More minutes passed. Then we heard the sound of a car, stopping. The door slammed; high heels tapped on the polished floorboards. Lila came in, flanked by Irma and Malcolm. She wore a tight yellow dress with a flounce around the collar. As she drew nearer, I saw that her eyes were pink and her face heavily made-up.

'Honey, you're my size.'

I jumped. Lila was looking at me.

'You'd wear an outfit like this?' Lila asked. She turned her back. 'My ass looks like a Minnesota meat-packer's.'

I shook my head. 'You look great.'

'Get this – they wanted me to wear yellow pantyhose!'

I laughed. 'Like Malvolio.'

'Huh? What they want me to look like, scrambled eggs?' She closed her eyes and sat down in an armchair. Her hands were trembling. 'Jesus, do I have a headache.'

'Darling – ' Irma moved closer.

'Aw, get off!'

Irma moved back. Hurt, she turned and glared at the clapper-loader.

Malcolm diffidently suggested they start working. I went outside and sat down on the cobbles. The sun, for once, felt even hotter than the lights indoors. I pulled off my wig.

The knitting actress had gone to make-up; the enclosed little street was quiet, just for the moment. The only sound was the hum of the generator in the lighting trailer. Leaning against the wall, I fingered the yellow shawl that they had put around my shoulders for the colour reading. I had this flimsy, fabric link with Lila; it gave us a spurious closeness.

Once I had a crush on a girl at school called Jo-Jo. One afternoon I stole Jo-Jo's games skirt and took it home. That night I had slept with it on my pillow. When I woke I found that I had stuffed a corner of it into my mouth. The serge was damp. I had felt as ashamed as a boy, waking up after a wet dream.

You're my size. Lila, swooping close, suddenly intimate. In fact, Nobby was the only person so far who had remarked on our resemblance. 'You do look alike,' he'd said, his head on one side. 'Much more than Sandy did. I know – you look like her long-lost cousin, the family swot.' 'Thanks a bunch!' I had retorted.

The cables, bound with tape, lay heavily on the cobbles. If I narrowed my eyes I could imagine them pulsing. I closed my eyes. Trev's flesh was in my mouth, and my jawbone ached. *It's very low-calorie.* I thought: I hate him. I'm besotted.

I thought of Lila, temporarily twinned with me in yellow. Lila was irritable as they zipped up her dress; in despair, she snapped at Irma. *She can only get her rocks off with real jerks.* Perhaps Lila and I had more in common than we guessed.

Six

It was the Cotswolds that brought Lila and me closer. Earlier shooting there had been disrupted by rain. Now that the long-promised heatwave had arrived the *Sexbusters* schedule had been rearranged. Cast and crew were going to a village called Much Wallop for two days' filming.

'Much Wallop?' Trev laughed. 'So it's a spanking picture, is it?'

It was Wednesday, the night before I was due to leave. I had picked up Trev after a performance of *Use Me*, which was into its second week and playing to poor houses. To comfort him I had blamed the weather. Theatre people always blame the weather for poor houses – it's too hot, it's too cold, it's too rainy, it's summer, it's winter. When a play is doing good business this never crosses anybody's mind.

He unlocked the door of his bedsit and we went in. I hoped he would ask me to stay the night; in fact, I had secretly packed my things in the boot of my car, because I had an early start. As we entered the room I glanced at his answerphone. It was on 4. But he never played back his messages when I was there. I didn't mention this; I mustn't be cramping, I mustn't be possessive. Most days I didn't know where he was. We lurched from night to night; sometimes the thread between us had snapped and I had to start getting to know him all over again. Even in my company he could be absent, slapping his pockets, looking at his watch, searching for a lost phone number. Sometimes I felt as if I had taken in a stray dog, a beautiful one like a whippet. One moment he was licking me, the next scratching at the door.

Tonight he was preoccupied. I tried to get his attention.

40

'You're right,' I murmured. 'It *is* a skin flick. I didn't want you to know. And it features me.' I came up behind him and slid my hand between the buttons of his shirt. 'We did this scene today, there was this house full of fur rugs, zebra skins, and I'm wearing these boots . . . they're long, black boots, shiny boots, right up my thighs . . . ' I rubbed against him, breathing into his ear. Under his shirt, I stroked his chest. 'I'm wearing this tight leather dress, very expensive, Bond Street . . . but then *I'm* very expensive, I'm the star of this picture because nobody can do it like I do . . . you know that . . . nobody in the world . . . ' I rubbed myself against him, pulling off his shirt.

Abstracted, he patted my buttocks in a 'there-there' kind of way.

'Haven't you spoken to the producers yet?' he asked.

'I haven't even met them. I don't even know who they are.'

'Can't you get anyone to come and see my frigging play?'

Hurt, I moved away. He went to the fridge, took out a can of lager, cracked it open and drank.

'Think of their budget!' he said. He'd had to sell his van to help finance his play. 'It's diabolical.' He passed me a can. 'It's immoral.'

I laughed. 'People always call money immoral when they're not getting any.' I went up to him. 'I'm sorry.' I stroked his back. He had the most beautiful back of any man I had known, smooth and hard as wood.

'My play's worth ten times your escapist crap.'

'Not mine. Theirs. Of course it is.'

'Get someone to come and see it, Jules. We've only got a week left.'

'Even if I have to give the director a blow-job in my trailer?'

He walked to the window. 'Yep.' But it was too dark to see if he was joking.

Much Wallop was greatly in demand for film shoots. It was a picturesque old stone village that rambled up and down a hill.

'Unchanged for centuries, it's been preserved in aspic for TV costume dramas, historical romances and brown bread commercials,' intoned Effie, the continuity girl. 'They're so bleeding blasé here. The locals make a fortune as extras. In fact, they're either on the dole or else employed at the brake-linings factory, but they're so used to becoming professional yokels that they subscribe to *Screen International* so they know what films are going into production. These darling, quaint old shops've had their names changed so often that nobody can remember what they're actually called.' We were sitting outside the pub, in the sunshine. 'Isn't it a hoot?' she said. 'When the estate agent sells a cottage, he just shows an old movie clip of it.'

Effie was a plain, bouncy, upper-class girl, the sort of person who said 'beg your parsnips' and 'mind you own beeswax'. I liked her because she knew everybody's secrets.

Away from London, the atmosphere had changed. For a start, the unit seemed smaller, and most of the cast weren't needed for these two days and had been given time off. The rest of us drew together; we were staying at the pub. Although we were working there was a feeling of truancy; just to get out of London, in a heatwave, made the whole enterprise feel like a jaunt.

It was one o'clock. Across the lane the horse-chestnuts stood, heavy and dusty in the sun. It was a golden, late-summer day; wasps dawdled dozily around the table, attracted by the damp beer patches.

'May I join you charming young ladies?' Sir Joshua Broome sat down, mopping his brow. He carried a large scotch. Taking out a packet of Players, he asked, 'Gasper, anyone?'

Sir Joshua was the old stage actor who played the scientist. With a few drinks inside him he was a fund of anecdotes about the good old days, about Wolfit and Larry, about long-dead actresses' indiscretions, and about eccentric theatrical land-ladies in whose digs he had stayed when he had toured the country, playing Shakespeare and Shaw in the days before the TV set, as he put it, had become a twinkle in anybody's lounge. Though repetitive, he was listened to with a certain respect by the crew. To film people, overpaid and compromised, there is something admirable about the theatre. It spells integrity. Struggle. Art. I myself had even felt this; 'How do you manage?' I had been asked, twice already, when it was discovered that I mainly worked in the theatre.

Broome jerked his head towards the pub. 'Sweetlings, you could cut the atmosphere in there with a knife. Our friend Rex is giving Miss Dune a post mortem on this morning's performance.'

'In bed?' asked Effie.

'My dear girl, no doubt that is what they nowadays call the sub-text. Young men in jeans on Channel 4. I am speaking of her acting ability. She's not, how shall I say, focused.'

'Rex keeps criticising her,' said Effie. 'She's instinctive. He's handling her all wrong. He's humiliating her.'

'As long as she doesn't hit the bottle.'

'What happens then?' I asked.

'Don't know yet. She's on the wagon. Doctor's orders.' He lit his cigarette. 'There'll be trouble ahead, you mark my words.' He looked up at the blue sky. 'Blow, winds and crack your cheeks! You cataracts and hurricanes, spout till you have drench'd our steeples, drown'd the cocks!' He started coughing. 'Drown'd the cocks!'

'Drown them at birth,' I said. 'They're nothing but trouble.'

That evening I had my first real conversation with Lila. What Effie called the nobs were having dinner elsewhere, guests of one of the producer's friends who had a knighthood and an enormous house nearby. I had eaten in the pub, with various members of the crew. Afterwards I went upstairs. To my surprise I met Lila in the corridor. It was 9.30; she looked as if she had just come out of the bath. She wore a black and gold bathrobe, and had bound up her hair in a turban.

'Honey,' she said, 'you got anything for sunburn?'

'I thought you'd gone out.'

Lila shook her head. 'I need some sleep.'

'I've only got Nivea.'

'I got Nivea. Irma has some other stuff.' She sighed. 'Do I need her tonight.'

Irma, her secretary, had succumbed to the changeable English climate and had stayed in London, suffering from flu.

'I'm feeling real stressed; I get lonely when she's not around.' Lila paused. Her face was scrubbed clean. Without make-up, her skin was pale and surprisingly freckly. She looked bare and defenceless, and even more lovely.

'Take a look at my hands.' She lifted her hands; they were trembling.

We paused for a moment in the pink corridor. I felt like a teenage boy. Should I ask her into my room?

'Irma's been with me for fifteen years. She was my masseuse, I've always had this back problem, that's how we started. I'm all she's got.' She suddenly looked at me; her eyes narrowed. 'You have anything in your room?'

'Only Nivea.'

She laughed. 'Liquor's what I mean.'

'Oh. No. Sorry.' I felt like the school goody-goody, in the dorm.

Lila sat down on the window seat. She looked at her hands again, as if they belonged to somebody else. 'My granny, she was an old lady. Real old. She was Polish. She had this loose skin on her hands and she let me push it around. She didn't give a damn.'

I looked down at my own hands. 'Ours aren't quite like that,' I smiled. 'Not yet.'

There was a silence. Perhaps I had been too presumptuous, to link my age with Lila's; to link myself at all. Below, I could hear muffled laughter and the bleep of a video game.

'I always wanted to come to Britain,' said Lila. 'Know this is the first picture I've made here? It's so – historical, isn't it?'

'You've only seen the historical bits.'

'I thought, I'm thirty-eight and I'm still playing dumb blondes.'

'I'm thirty-eight too!' I said. 'Snap!'

'My agent, he said Lila, you can't play bimbos for ever, you've got to develop as a comedienne. You'll be playing a woman in her prime, she's honest, she's funny, she's sensitive, she's gutsy. He said, you'll be working with Rex Benson. He's one of the best, he made *Hula Hoop* and *The Big Thrill* . . .' She sighed, then smiled. 'And he's made Suzy and Annie and Lorraine. . . . That shithead, he needs a revolving door in his bedroom.' She stood up. 'It's been great talking to you.' She flashed me a smile and disappeared down the corridor.

I sat down on the window seat, its fabric warmed by Lila. I felt stirred by my sudden status as confidante. Then I thought: perhaps she calls me honey because she can't remember my name.

Lila's relationship with her director was visibly deteriorating. Without Irma to protect her she seemed more vulnerable, though I hardly had a chance to speak to her the next day. By the nature of my job, I saw little of Lila on the set. We simply exchanged places – when I was there, during the set-up, Lila was absent, and when it was time for Lila to come on I was sent away. In fact, I had realised by now that I was more a member of the crew than the cast. I was not an artist; I was a technician.

Besides, film stars are seldom alone. If it wasn't the make-up girl or the hairstylist with Lila, it was Joshua Broome who had become an avuncular figure; he sympathised with her and, a heavy drinker himself, regaled her with anecdotes about boozing with Richard Burton. If it wasn't Broome it was Malcolm, the AD, who was growing increasingly harassed and attentive. If it wasn't Malcolm it was a publicity photographer who wanted to take stills of her in various picturesque rural settings, or a local newspaper reporter who wanted an interview. I didn't know where Lila ate; when we broke for lunch she disappeared. The sound man said she binged on chocolates; Effie said she was popping pills. She was bingeing, she was dieting, she was putting on her face pack, going to bed and reading all her old press cuttings. Screwing Rex was also suggested, but he was discovered sitting in his Mercedes listening to the Test Match results. When famous people disappear it is like a lamp fusing; the room becomes dimmer. I thought: if I disappeared, nobody would notice that anything had happened at all.

In fact, Lila had been phoning. After lunch, I went to my room to fetch my book and met Lila halfway up the stairs.

'Your British Telecom,' she said. 'Know how many times it took me to get through to New York?'

'I'm sorry.'

She laughed. 'It's not your fault, honey.' She sighed. 'Gee, you're nice. Why can't I ever meet a man who's as nice as a woman?'

I blushed. 'It's only because we're always saying we're sorry.'

'You're so right!'

'We're masochists.' I suddenly had a vision of the woman in *Use Me*, being slapped by her plumber.

'I was telling my therapist, only the damned operator kept interrupting, I was telling him why do I always get involved with assholes?'

'Why?'

'I know why,' she said. 'It's, like, I'm trying to get closer to him.'

'To who?'

Lila looked at me, puzzled. People had listened to her for so many years that she no longer knew what they did or didn't know about her. Her life was so public that she could no longer distinguish what was private about it. I had my first inkling of this, on the stairs that day.

'My father, he left me when I was small,' said Lila. 'I can only have relationships with older men who'll dump me too, on account of losing my father. My therapist, he says it's the only way I can stay close to him.'

'Your father, or your therapist?'

Lila laughed. 'That's some question. Know something? You're in the wrong job.'

I felt myself blushing, deeper.

'I have these dependencies,' said Lila. 'I'm trying to work through them. You look like a grounded person.'

'Do I?'

'I'm sure as hell not.' She smiled. 'Martin Luther King, you know him?'

'Of course.'

'He said, "I have a dream." Know what mine is?'

'What?'

'It's this guy, who loves me for myself. Who doesn't get off on all this shit.' She gestured at the staircase, vaguely. 'The money, all that shit. Who doesn't get off on, like, I've screwed Lila Dune. And *I* don't get off on him despising me.' She closed her eyes. 'And then, when I find him, we'll settle down together and we'll have a kid. I'd really like a kid. Kids are so great, aren't they?'

I nodded.

'You got any?' Lila asked.

I shook my head. On the landing, the grandfather clock chimed twice.

'Me neither,' said Lila.

The next day, Friday, we were going back to London. I was sorry to leave; I was already feeling nostalgia-in-advance for these two golden days. I scrunched across the gravel to my car, which was parked behind the pub. It was 10.30. I looked across the hedge. Already the roses had been unpinned from the porch of the neighbouring mansion; its dream life was being dismantled. Its owner was washing his BMW; life was returning to normal. By teatime it would be as if we had never existed in this village, and all that remained would be two signed photos of Broome and Lila, joining the celebrity collection in the Ploughman's Bar.

There was only one more week's filming left, indoors on

47

a sound stage. By next weekend it would all be over. Trev's play, too, would be closing. Its set would be struck, its furniture disposed of, the long-suffering kitchen table returned to its owners. There would be nothing left except a few reviews, one of which (*Blitz*) called it 'promising'.

Trev and I would be back to square one. So much for big breaks. I hadn't even met the producers of *Sexbusters*, let alone spoken to them; the director hardly knew my name. Lila had confided in me, but then Lila seemed profligate with her confidences. Everyone from her hairstylist to her driver seemed to know about her problems with sleeping, her fluid retention, her cravings for candy and her painful and irregular menstrual cycle. Depending on whether they liked her or not people found this either relentlessly egotistical or endearingly indiscreet.

I climbed into my car and turned the key. The engine groaned. I tried again. I pushed the choke in and out, fast – an old trick. The car wouldn't start. After ten minutes the battery ran down.

I got out, kicked the door, opened the bonnet and looked inside. The engine was its usual mass of furred pipes.

'You have a problem?'

I turned round. I had seen Lila's limo – long and shiny – parked the other end of the car park. Now I saw her walking towards me. She was dressed in her public disguise – dark glasses, with a scarf wrapped around her hair.

'It's done this before.' I kicked it again. I glanced from my car, a Renault 5, to the limousine.

'You travelling to London?' Lila asked.

I nodded.

'Want a ride with us?'

Did I want a ride? What a question!

Know what I did? I just took my car keys to the pub and gave them to the man behind the bar. I told him to phone a garage. It was because I had Lila beside me. I felt so bold, you see. I drew my strength from her. I knew the publican would agree to do this, simply because I was standing beside a film star. She made me powerful.

And he did, with a smile. Just for a moment, I felt special.

Lila's driver had already put my suitcase into the boot of the Daimler. I knew I should be staying in the village and seeing to my car; I would have to come back for it another day. What the hell.

It was like falling in love. The sudden recklessness; the half-lies. Wasn't that ridiculous?

I sat in the back with Lila. The door closed. I smelt perfume and warm leather. We slid through the village. Lila stretched out her legs. She was wearing white slacks, a pink blouse and, as always, one too many gold bracelets. When she shifted, her necklace tinkled. I thought: she's like a field of oilseed rape. So dazzling that she hurts your eyes. The rest of the countryside, the rest of us, we're dimmed into obscurity.

'That sonofabitch says he's got to visit his mother in Cheltenham. Think he's lying?'

'Lots of people have mothers there,' I replied. 'That's what Cheltenham's for.'

She touched my knee. 'You're so sweet.' She took away her hand, her bangles chiming, and looked out of the window. A row of stone cottages slid past, then a steep field of cows. 'It's all so pretty. It's so small! You feel, like, it's on account of it's an island. You've got to fit it all in. I used to see the map and I'd think, they'll all talk like somebody in a Shakespeare play. I'll find myself a real gentleman there.'

'Not any more you won't.'

'You're darned right.' She laughed. Then she looked at me. 'Neat pants. Where did you buy them?'

'I made them myself. I make most of my clothes.'

But she wasn't listening. She said, 'That fink, know what he said? He said she's had an operation so he's got to stay

49

overnight. And then he's got to be at the studio tomorrow, all day, with the set designer. What's he think I'm going to do?'

'You must know lots of people in London.'

'Why?'

'Well . . .' I shrugged. 'You just must.'

'Honey, when I have a call I go to bed early. I have this problem with sleep, see, so I take these pills. They're the strongest you can get, they'd knock out a baseball team. And if I don't have a call, like tonight . . .' She shrugged again. 'You're so damned polite, you British.'

'You mean standoffish?'

'It's like, you don't want to intrude.'

'Katherine Hepburn, apparently she lived in London for two years and she got lonely. Nobody liked to talk to her in case they seemed to be sucking up.'

'Sucking up! What a great word.'

Suddenly I felt like a radiator. The heat rose up the stem of my neck and spread over my face. I turned to look out of the window. 'Why don't we go out tonight?'

'Huh?'

'I could show you London.' I cleared my throat. 'It might be fun.'

'Hey, we could visit Covent Garden, everyone says it's great, they have these little shops.'

'Not that London.' I took another breath. I had an idea. My heart thumped. A field slid by; it was steep and green. At the top stood two horses, nose to tail. 'I mean, no offence, but you haven't seen the real place at all. The real countryside, the real London. You've just seen what the tourists see, what the Americans see. Cashmere sweaters and shortbread. You've just seen a set of picture postcards.' I paused, breathing heavily. 'England's not like that any more. In fact, it never was.'

'So where do we go?'

'I've just heard about this brilliant new play. Not one of those star-studded revivals, not one of these safe, West End jobs. But a real play, with no Japanese in the audience. Let's go and see it.'

'Gee. What's it called?'

I paused, as if trying to remember. 'Ah yes. It's called *Use Me*.'

Seven

It was Trev's birthday today. I realised this when a man came in to mend the faucet. A man! I've forgotten the smell of them. The bulk. The stubble. What a surprise! He said, would you believe, '*Have a nice day.*' I said, '*Thank you, and you have a nice day too.*' But I said it in an American accent. Otherwise he would have started all those questions.

I went outside just now. Three women were sitting in the watery sunshine; two black, one white. They were all overweight – gross, in fact. This seems to be an American problem. They need to comfort themselves, all the time. It's a gargantuan need. I, on the other hand, have gotten thinner (note the *gotten*).

They were doing nothing, just sitting there. They didn't know Trev's birthday had come and nearly gone.

My last birthday, nobody knew either, or the birthday before. I spent all day in a hotel in Los Angeles. You can never get out of Los Angeles, there seems no end to it. I could see a faint ridge of hills, a smudge in the smog, but there was no reaching them.

I sat beside the pool doing nothing, like these three women here, and I watched people getting in and out of their cars. There were two shabby palm trees and the scaffolded back of a hoarding: beyond was the sliding glitter of the freeway.

Dusk fell. Lights were switched on in the rooms, one by one. Shadows moved behind the blinds; someone laughed, high and hysterical. Through the bushes came the Babel chatter of twenty different TV channels. Other cars arrived and left; lights swung over the building. I sat there until it was dark. Some machine that was aerating the pool bubbled and burped. Earlier in the day the water had been as warm

52

as mucus. There was a faint hum from somewhere, like the hum of a generator when you're filming. I felt conscious of the machinery of my veins, and my moist cunt that nobody had touched. I looked up; for once it was a clear sky, with the stars in arrangements that nobody had explained to me. I didn't know what any of them meant; besides, above California the stars were different. Stars – up there, breathing a different ether. I thought of Lila's thighs, smooth as satin.

I brushed past a bougainvillaea; its thorns scraped my leg. And then I was in my room. I took off my clothes – shorts, t-shirt, briefs. I was glowing from my birthday sun. I lay down on my bed and I started stroking my small, spread breasts that had never suckled a child.

Then I got up and lit a candle. I had bought it earlier that day – I believe in ceremony, don't you? And then I lay back, my head flung over the edge of the bed, my throat stretched. Blood rushed to my cheeks. I started touching myself as Trev had touched me. His face was pressed against the window, watching me. They were all watching me – Lila, Roly, my father whose finger moved to his moustache, who coughed his little cough but who then attended. Because I had got him now; I had got them all.

Scrape-scrape went the cicadas, outside in the bushes. I was both inside and yet I was outside, looking in. Their sound was the sound of the cameras, whirring. I began in earnest. I heard my own rasping breaths, and as I heard them I breathed more heavily, the heat was spreading and I was burning. I started crying out, little yelps for my audience, as if I wasn't really alone – and I wasn't, was I? Just then, just for a few moments. And then, in a spasm, my back arched and my nimble finger made me shudder so sweetly, again and again, and there seemed no end to it until I was gasping, beached on my bed like a porpoise. And only then did I hear the hum of the air conditioner, and I felt the sheet bunched up beneath me, pulled half off the mattress. My candle had sunk and was starting to gutter – it was only one of those cake candles, it hadn't lasted long.

So that was my birthday present to myself. I lay back, my cheeks burning, my father turning his face away. *I thought you would be a great actress*, he said, but I could hardly hear him now, he had buried his face in his hands. I didn't listen; I just heard the murmur of the freeway.

I can hear the traffic now. But it seems so far away; it seems to come from another country.

I should be feeling homesick; I've been in America two and a half years now. I have a mother and a brother in England. But I feel nothing. No – not quite. I feel detached, as if I'm standing on the opposite bank of a river from myself. My past is simply the sound of that traffic, murmuring in the distance. I inspect my feelings, like a mathematician looking at a graph, and only I can juggle the figures.

I told you it's inhuman, didn't I? I think I talked about John Lennon. Only yesterday, but already it seems a long time ago. And when on earth did he die? Can you remember?

Time is elastic. Time is what you need it to be. In your hands it can shrink and stretch. When you are driving to a new destination the journey seems endless; when it is a familiar route you are there almost before you have begun. The beat between *I've got something to tell you* and the dreaded news itself – in that beat your life replays as if you're just about to die. But if the person is simply opening the newspaper, then time is as transparent and tasteless as water.

Ah, but when it thickens.

I'm thinking, now, of that moment when Lila's limo dropped me off at my flat. She sank back, just a woman in dark glasses, though the car made her special and a neighbour I had never spoken to paused, and glanced at me again. I took my suitcase upstairs. In my sitting room the plants had wilted. I counted the hours until the car would pick me up again.

I showered. I had a beautiful bathroom. Spotless. Blue-grey tiles. Lila might have a limo but I guessed she wasn't finicky. I pictured her shower cubicle, long blonde hairs blocking the plughole. There was something sluttish about her that appealed to the Trevor in me.

I didn't phone Trev – not yet. I plucked my eyebrows and gazed at myself in the mirror. Compared to hers, my lips looked thin. Trev once went out with a girl who had lips as full and soft as marshmallows. He said he could come, just looking at her mouth.

I pouted. I held up a hand mirror and inspected my profile. Strong nose, heavy chin. From the side I didn't look like Lila at all.

I phoned the garage at Much Wallop. My car would be ready the next day. I sat on the sofa and looked at my sitting room. When you live alone, everything is as you left it. Depending on your mood, this can either be reassuring or unnerving. My room looked neat and unremarkable, as if anybody could live there – a wall of books, two posters from the Jeu de Paume in Paris, a Habitat dining table and chairs. It looked like the sort of room people rent out. It looked as if I had never lived in it.

It was up on the first floor, with a big window and a balcony. In the summer my view of the houses opposite was blocked by a lime tree; it greened and shadowed my room, giving it an oppressive feeling, as if it were under water. The tree dripped sticky stuff on the cars below. My neighbours wanted it lopped, but I coveted my six months of secrecy each year. I've never liked real people looking in; imaginary ones are so much more interesting, aren't they?

I can see my flat quite clearly today. There must be somebody else in it now; if I went back I would hardly recognise it. My possessions have been put into storage. Perhaps the chimney pots have been thrown away, who knows?

I can remember that Friday afternoon. I wandered around, doing nothing at all. My flat existed in a vacuum, like a stage set. I feel, now, that I was emptying myself, preparing myself for something important. I was preparing myself for Lila. But maybe I was just exhausted from a week's hard work, not acting.

You might ask: why didn't I tell her that the author of the play was my boyfriend? It was for Trev's sake. I wanted her to think we were going to see a terrific new play, by a terrific new playwright. I didn't want her to think I was only taking her along because I was involved. I think my motives were as pure as that.

At six o'clock I dialled Trev's number. When the ringing stopped and there was that pause, my heart sank. I hated speaking to his machine; it made me feel that we had nothing to say to each other. When the beep went I suddenly wanted him, badly.

'Hi, it's me. I'm back. Listen, I'm bringing Lila Dune to *Use Me* – who says I'm not supportive? Don't come. I want her to see it on its own merits.'

I put the phone down. Five minutes passed, and then I dialled again. I misdialled, once, because I couldn't concentrate. I got the Texas Pancake House. I tried again.

'It's me again. Do come.' I paused. I didn't say *I love you*. I said, 'I'd love you to meet her, but pretend we hardly know each other, OK?'

I put down the phone. It was the greatest mistake of my life.

Lila was an hour late. I sat waiting, my hair brushed. Had she forgotten? When Trev was late – he usually was – I seethed, because he had stolen an hour of the time we would have together. I feared his priorities. My mind raced with alternative scenarios, which grew more lurid as the minutes passed. My guts shrivelled. But I always kissed him lovingly, I never let him know.

Waiting for Lila, however, I simply felt nervous. I had changed three times, and had finally settled for my blue jacket and the trousers Lila had admired in the car. I hadn't booked a meal because Lila had said this was her no-food day, but I had bought some juices and drinks which I had put into the fridge. I had polished a couple of glasses; they waited on the stage set that grew more unreal as the minutes passed. I had put on the Mozart Requiem; the voices were singing now, all over again, a second time. I wanted Lila to come in when it was casually playing.

Perhaps I should play something lighter – show songs? I hadn't got any. Perhaps Lila wasn't coming. The more I thought about it the more unlikely it seemed, that I should take a film star to a grotty pub off Tottenham Lane. Lila wore backless dresses and went to premières. Maybe she thought even Belsize Park wasn't safe.

Our moment of intimacy on the journey had drained away; Lila was simply a film star again, unknowable, with a suite at the Park Lane Hotel. She was like royalty. She wore the invisible envelope of the famous; she moved in a driven network of accompanied visits to Bond Street, her London wasn't my London. She probably hadn't stepped on public transport for years, except for a shoot.

Suddenly the bell rang. I clattered downstairs. At the door stood the driver. He was an ex-jockey called Pat. Behind him the limousine was double-parked, its lights winking like a police car. The man in the basement flat, who was putting out his rubbish, straightened up and looked across at the long black car blocking the road.

I ran upstairs, got my things and rejoined them, panting. I was a fool – of course Lila wasn't going to see my flat. I stepped into the back of the car, like stepping into a room.

'You guys use the Ouija board here?' asked Lila.

I shook my head.

Lila said, 'It's nifty. Irma, she hid it in the closet. She thinks I listen to it better than I listen to her. You think it's garbage?'

'No. I just like to make my own decisions.' That sounded priggish. I said, 'I think women ought to take their lives into their own hands, rather than listen to a bit of cardboard.'

'That's just what it told me, the Ouija board!'

Lila was wearing a yellow jacket and slacks, with high-heeled sandals. Underneath the jacket, her knitted top was appliquéd with rhinestones. She wore the curiously fashionless clothes of somebody who dresses for men. She seemed different tonight; fresh and alert. Her perfume filled the car.

'I look OK?' she asked, taking off her dark glasses.

'You look fine.'

'This the kind of stuff to wear?'

'Sure,' I said, copying her accent.

We drove through the streets. We passed shops and shabby buildings, ruddy in the sunset.

'This is fun!' said Lila. 'It's great of you to ask me.'

She had closed the windows. They were tinted, one-way, so outsiders could not see in. As the car stopped at some traffic lights a group of youths jostled and peered. I met their blind eyes. I smiled at them; they could just as well be watching me. I re-crossed my legs, slowly; I wished I were wearing a skirt, so it could move up my thighs.

The Three Crowns was a gaunt pub next to a funeral parlour. It was embellished with graffiti. Two black youths leant against its wall. Nearby, a green light flashed above a minicab hire office. Above it stretched the suffused sky.

I said, 'You'd better not expect merry cockneys and toffee apples.'

We got out of the limo. As we did so, a flashbulb popped. I swung round; a man had come out of the pub. He took another photo. I hurried Lila past him.

Trev was in the bar. He looked so unfamiliar, after two days, that my heart lurched. He had slicked back his hair with gel; he was wearing his black leather jacket and a black leather tie I had never seen. He looked studiously mafiosic. The director was with him; he must have come in specially.

I introduced them. 'This is Trevor Parsons, the writer. And Reece Bendien, the director.'

They all shook hands. Various drinkers, mostly old Irishmen, paused to gaze at us, their glasses halfway to their lips.

We went upstairs; Trev even stood aside to let us, the women, go first. Next to Lila I felt both proud and anxious, as if I were accompanying a precious piece of porcelain. Even the girl taking the tickets, who was usually cool, included me in the smile she gave Lila.

The room was half-full. As we entered, a hush fell. Then a ripple ran through the audience. Some of them, I guessed, recognised Lila. The rest just saw a very sexy, rather over-dressed woman. She must be famous; hadn't they seen her somewhere?

The four of us sat in a row near the front. Without her attendants, without even her driver, Lila was my responsibility. Was it too stuffy? Too cold? Was the seat too hard?

I whispered to Lila, 'Sorry about the photographer. Nothing to do with me.'

'Sorry about what?' In fact, I was to learn, Lila hardly noticed. Clicking cameras were as familiar to her as the beat of her pulse; she no longer knew an ordinary reaction.

Reece was sitting the other side of Lila. Next to him, Trev seemed beyond my reach. And when the curtain rose, the play seemed miles away.

I had already seen *Use Me* a couple of times. Tonight it seemed to be played down the wrong end of a tele-scope, in mime. The actors mouthed, they moved, I heard the echoes of what they must be saying. The woman was married. The plumber came to her house to mend the boiler, and then she begged him to stay because there were so many more things for him to do. Each night she undid his handiwork – she broke the pipes, like a goblin in a fairy story; she fused the lights. Each day he had to return and repair them all over again. As he did so she told him about herself and her husband, in greater detail, and each day she wore less and less when she opened the door to him.

I sat on the hard seat. I had stomach cramps; I felt suffo-cated. On the stage the plumber was kneeling on the floor, fixing something with his screwdriver. The actress came in; she was wearing a black negligee and high-heeled slippers; she stood behind the plumber and just touched him with her pointed toe. She started speaking about her wedding night but

59

I didn't hear. My face was burning. Why had I brought Lila to this place?

Lila's perfume dizzied me. On stage the woman took a spanner from the plumber and started stroking it. Then they were on the kitchen table and she was straddling him. I closed my eyes and the curtain fell.

There was a smattering of applause.

'Holy shit,' giggled Lila. 'You guys are kinkier than I thought.'

'He's what's called rough trade,' I said. 'He comes with our class system. Middle-class women are supposed to be over-educated and frigid. That's why they go for men like that.'

'Billy Hurt, he was in this picture about a janitor. But he was Billy Hurt.'

Down in the bar Trev had ordered a bottle of champagne for the interval. *Champagne!* Lila, however, drank orange juice.

'Your play,' she said. 'It's so powerful!'

Trev, for once, had bought his own packet of cigarettes. He offered one to Lila, and then one to me, with the courtesy of a stranger.

'I'm trying to show that it takes two to be used,' he said.

'How's that?' Lila asked.

He lit Lila's cigarette, leaning close to her. 'For every sadist there has to be a masochist. It's a collusion.'

'On account of her wanting it?'

'Exactly!' He grinned at her, moving closer. My skin prickled.

Reece joined in. 'Every relationship is a form of manipulation.'

Lila sighed. 'Boy, you're so right.'

'Trev's play shows how none of us is free of guilt,' said Reece. 'Outward liberation means nothing if we are still, inside, crippled by our patterns of behaviour. In *The Duchess of Malfi* she *needs* to be used by Bosola, the self-destruction is inbuilt from the start. And you know how that ends.'

'How?' said Lila.

Reece ran his finger across his throat. Lila shivered, and pulled her jacket across her shoulders.

60

In Act Two the woman has kicked out her husband. The plumber had moved in. Once installed, however, he becomes her master and she his slave. He ties her apron so tight that she cries; he forces her into crippling, higher heels. She serves him meals, she sponges his brow. She lies naked, spreadeagled on the table, as he sits smoking a cigarette. It is his turn to speak now. He describes his sexual conquests, he tells her that she is worse than the lot of them, she's a slut. He taps his ash into her belly button. The play ends when she murders him.

Pat, the driver, was waiting in the bar, drinking tomato juice. With Lila's imminent departure, Reece moved in for the hard sell. 'Pinter understood the pornography of class, of violence.' He put his arm around Trev. 'This bloke, we predict his impact's going to be even greater.'

Trev simpered – a new sight for me. I glared at him. With his sleek hair, he looked like a water rat. I realised that I hated his play.

Lila said, 'You guys, you're all over Broadway now. There's been this sweet show, *Me and My Girl*.'

'We'll get there,' said Reece. 'You wait.'

I turned to Lila. 'They're working on this really terrific show already. It's about two young pseuds.' I smiled. 'It's called *Me and My Gel*.' Before Trev could react, I ushered Lila away. For some reason, I wanted to get her away from them both.

We drove back to Belsize Park. In the car, Lila sat huddled in her jacket.

'Does that guy have talent!' she said. 'You're lucky.'

'Why?'

'I don't get to hear that kind of talk.'

I was just going to apologise for its pretentiousness. I stopped.

'All I hear is the gross,' said Lila. 'All I hear is dollars. Twenty million, domestic. Forty million, worldwide. They don't say, is she crippled by her old patterns of behaviour?'

'What do they say?'

'They say, What did her last picture do?'

We slid through the dark streets in our dark car. Illuminated signs passed us by . . . *World of Sarees* . . . *Nicolette Sauna and Massage* . . . We passed the *Five-Star Tandoori.* Behind its curtains, red light glowed. A waiter stood outside, ready to usher customers into his little theatre.

'They don't even ask, can she act?' said Lila. She looked out of the window. 'I never went to college. I never had those conversations. We were real poor. I had my big break when I won this beauty contest. And I'll tell you, hon, when you're Miss New Jersey Dairy Products there's nobody talking about *The Duchess of Malfi.'* She laughed. 'The only motivation they know is whether they can get their hands on your ass.'

We sat for a while in silence. Finally we stopped outside my flat. Lila leant across and kissed me, impulsively. Then she turned away, and put on her dark glasses.

The next day it felt unreal, as if it hadn't happened. I once fucked a man in a bus shelter in Sidmouth. It was so dark I hardly saw his face, and the next morning it seemed so unlikely I couldn't believe it had ever taken place. I only had my grazed backbone to remind me, and the sound of the sea in my ears.

I felt like that on the Saturday morning. All I had was a headache from the champagne. It was partly because of our behaviour – Reece so pretentious, Trev so unctuous, me so diffident. Well, unctuous. None of us had seemed ourselves. She had made us false. She didn't mean to, but she did. It was beyond her control, and she noticed nothing because that was how everybody behaved in her vicinity. Besides, the thought of her amongst those Irish alcoholics downstairs and those creaking leather jackets upstairs was so ludicrous in retrospect that I couldn't connect it up. Why did I feel like this when she was only human?

In those early days of knowing Lila I veered wildly. Shopping in Sainsburys I thought I couldn't possibly have anything to offer her. Back home in my book-lined flat, misting my ferns,

I felt strong and intelligent; I felt I could conquer the world. Just then, she was lucky to know me.

Trev came to supper. It was a warm, sultry night. I felt curiously aroused; maybe it was the weather. I wore a dress I had made from Liberty cotton; underneath it, my legs were bare and smooth. I felt intensely female and for once he was with me, full-beam. He was alert and playful; he even scrubbed the potatoes. Why was he being so helpful, all of a sudden? I gave him poached salmon. I wanted to lock the door and keep him there; I wanted to feed him up and have him all to myself. Outside the window I heard the rumble of thunder.

'It was weird,' he said. 'Just for a moment, when she came in, I thought it was you, all tarted up.'

'Really?'

'You never said you looked like each other.'

'Do we?'

'Then I realised.'

I almost asked: was she more beautiful? I didn't speak.

He speared a lettuce leaf. 'She's older than I thought.'

I smiled, pleased. 'That's because she's stayed the same in your dreams. They have to stay the same.'

He sipped his wine. I wanted to ask him more, but I didn't dare.

'To tell the truth, it made her sexier,' he said. 'Her face. She wasn't so perfect.'

'You going to hog all the salad?' I asked, abruptly.

Later, in bed, I turned my back to him. He stroked me, and breathed into my ear. After a few moments he turned away, sighing.

I spoke into the darkness. 'Have you ever pretended I was someone else?'

'All the time. How else could I get it up?'

'Have you?'

He nodded. 'Tonight you're Mrs Thatcher. Can't you tell?'

'Have you?' I persisted. 'When you can't see, but you can only touch?'

'I'll touch you if you'll let me.'

'Have you pretended I'm someone else?'

'Oh shut up!'

'You have!' I stared at the glimmering rectangle of the window-blind. The thunder rumbled.

'Listen, nit-face . . .' He stopped.

I lay rigid.

'You're an impossible bloody woman,' he said.

'You had those photos up.'

'What photos?'

'In your bedroom. When you were young.'

'That's different.'

'Is it?' I asked.

'For Christ's sake, Jules.'

I didn't speak. After a moment his breathing deepened. I realised he had gone to sleep. Outside the rain began, drumming against the chimney pots on my balcony.

I dreamed I was back at home in Arundel, but the house was six storeys high. I was in my nightie, leaning over the banisters. Down at the bottom of the stairwell, a long way below, lay Lila. Her backbone must be broken; she stirred, feebly. She was a small figure, squirming, in a white dress. She looked like a butterfly, and somebody had trodden on her. I knew I should be going down to help her, but I couldn't move.

Some time later Trev, only half-awake, started coaxing me with his hands. I turned, blindly, and we made love without a word, our mouths glued together. Afterwards I gripped him tightly, my arm numb under the weight of his shoulder.

'Stupid bitch,' he murmured. 'It's you I want. Can't you tell?'

That was the first night I betrayed him. I didn't wear my diaphragm, you see. I wanted to get pregnant.

The next morning, in the Sunday paper, there was an item in the arts column. A photo, too. It just featured

Lila. There was no sign of me; they must have chopped me off.

Use Me, a play by former antiques dealer Trevor Parsons,
had an unexpected visitor on Friday night. It was the film star
Lila Dune, currently in London shooting the Carvalle-Reichman
comedy Sexbusters. *Miss Dune was visibly moved by the play,*
which is showing to packed houses amidst rumours of a West
End transfer. 'He is one hell of a powerful writer,' she said. 'A
new Pinter. Use Me *is the most interesting new play I've seen*
in London.'

I lowered the paper. I stared across at Trev, sitting unshaven in my dressing gown.

'How could you? She never said all those things! You just used her. And what's all that crap about a West End transfer?'

He smiled smugly. 'She won't mind. She'll be flattered.'

'She hasn't even *seen* another play.'

He gestured, vaguely, with his knife. 'Sounds quite intellectual, doesn't she?'

'Christ, you're an ambitious bastard.' Breathing heavily, I glared at him across the littered breakfast table. 'You'd sell your own grandmother for ten bob.'

He smirked at me. 'It's decimal coinage now.'

'What's she going to think, me taking her to a play just so we can prise a quote out of her? She'll never speak to me again.'

'She'll like it. You see.' He leant over, stole my piece of toast and popped it into his mouth. I flinched; I hated him doing that. Munching, he said, 'You don't know her as well as you think.'

And he was right. On Monday, when I saw Lila, she mentioned the newspaper item.

'Irma showed it to me,' said Lila. 'Did I sound OK?'

Eight

The unit was working at high speed – *Sexbusters* was behind schedule and had to wrap on the Friday. By now Rex and Lila were hardly on speaking terms. The atmosphere was so bad that the crew – like most film crews, not a curious bunch – had detached themselves and worked on automatic pilot, counting the days until it would all be over. Despite the activity, an ominous air hung over the studio; another, subtler script was playing alongside the one currently in action on the sound stage.

Lila seemed distracted, and had lost her concentration. Rumour had it that she was cracking up, as she had cracked up in the past. The question was: would they get the movie finished before it happened? Filming on location, the outside world is only too distracting. In the studio, on the other hand, you are so closed off that normal life ceases to exist; it is stilled until you rejoin it. Whatever you are feeling, it can grow out of proportion, like a monstrous plant in a greenhouse.

In this sealed space, vast as a hangar, I felt claustrophobic and itchy. Effie was too frantic to talk. Nobby, my only other confidant, was feeling lousy; he had some recurring stomach bug from filming in Africa. Already people were absent, for one leaves in spirit days before the actual departure. Some of the crew were going on holiday, some on to another film. One of the sound men, who had worked with Fassbinder and who had a death wish, was going to race his motor bike on the Isle of Man.

I went outside for some air. The studio was in an industrial park in Wembley. Across the road, a fork-lift truck was loading washbasins into a lorry. From one of the buildings came the sound of a tannoy, calling somebody I would never know. Clouds scudded across the sky, swiftly, as if somebody was reeling a backcloth. In the car park loomed Lila's motorhome. It had black tinted windows and a TV aerial. As I stood there Irma came out of its door, carrying a lunch tray. She wore a fitted suit, as always, and sensible shoes like a hospital administrator. She looked severe – in fact, fierce. She looked like Lotte Lenya in that James Bond film; when Bond approached, two knife blades sprang from the toes of her brogues.

When she had gone, I looked at the motorhome. It was large, ribbed and creamy; it dwarfed the cars. With its black windows it looked sealed and mysterious. Lila was in there, unassailable. It was Thursday. Soon she would be gone, back to America, back to the blurred and glamorous life that I could only imagine as a sequence of magazine stills – *Miss Dune leaving a night club; Miss Dune sharing a joke with Michael Douglas*. It was like the circus leaving town. All that is left is an empty field, tyre tracks in the mud and everyone suddenly looking drab.

Was this how I felt? Not quite. I don't think I was that obsessed with her, yet. I envied her, of course, though I could see that her fame was a kind of imprisonment. I felt superior to her, because I was more intelligent. I felt resentful that for seventeen years I had worked hard at my craft, only to end up as a piece of scenery, whilst she effortlessly earned tens of thousands of dollars being an inferior actress to myself. I felt attracted to her because she was beautiful, and in her vicinity I too had a spurious glamour. I felt drawn to her because she resembled myself, but re-dreamed: she was myself in the bathroom mirror, when I was younger and narrowed my eyes until my reflection blurred; when I pretended. She was the me I longed to see. She was a reminder of the treacherous inequality of life, and luck, and fate. One tiny rearrangement of features can make a beauty; one extra chromosome can make a killer.

I liked her. I know that. I hadn't started to hate her, not yet.

Friday was the last day. It's easier to tell you about that part.

'I've got blasted cystitis again,' said Effie. She had put glitter on her cheeks.

'Is this real champagne?' asked Sebastian from wardrobe.

'Did I ever tell you about Oliver Reed and the clothes peg?' asked the designer's assistant.

'Yes,' said Effie. 'Twice.'

'I went to a party in LA,' said Tony Chandler. 'Swifty Lazar gave it, and nobody drank at all. Just club sodas. Dead boring of them. Dead Californian.'

It was Friday night. The wrap party was being held at the Retro Grade Club. This was a converted VD clinic near Leicester Square; three floors of thudding music.

'It's not champagne,' said Effie.

There was a silence. The crew and cast had spent three months working together, but now we were standing there with nothing to do except talk we couldn't think of anything to say. Like awkward people everywhere, we looked as if we were wearing borrowed clothes.

I had put up my hair. Drink in hand, I listened to Connie (make-up) tell two of the sparkies a slanderous story I had already heard about Michael Winner. I glimpsed Rex talking to three men (one short, one bald, one both) who I now knew were the producers. Lorraine was there, wearing a dress that was seemingly made of kitchen foil. The unit typist started dancing all by herself. People shuffled their feet and fell silent. It was like demob day in the army; seeing each other in their civilian clothes, everyone felt suddenly shy. Somebody even asked me, 'What are your plans for Christmas?' – the sort of thing one asks, in desperation, one's hairdresser.

I felt stupidly bereft. Maybe Lila wasn't going to come. Big stars seldom come to wrap parties. They have either long ago left for some other project or else don't fancy drinking lukewarm Asti Spumante and making small talk to members of the crew whose names they never knew anyway. Half an hour passed. She wasn't going to come, and I would never see her again.

In fact, I was just about to leave when she made her entrance.

Everyone stopped talking. This was not just because she looked stunning – her hair was piled on top of her head and she wore a red satin sheath dress that revealed her shoulders. It was the way she walked, with the steadiness of the unsteady.

I stopped and watched. Rex was dancing with Lorraine, whose Bacofoil was unwrapping at the back. Lila went up to the producers, smiled sweetly as they kissed her, and chatted with them for a moment. Then she turned, and took a bucket of ice from a passing waiter. She removed the champagne bottle and put it on the floor. Then she took the bucket over to the dancers, walked up to Rex, turned the bucket upside down and poured the contents over his head.

The ice cubes bounced on to the floor. There was a surprising amount of water at the bottom. Rex cowed, staggering; he was drenched. Lorraine squealed. The crowd moved back.

'You low-life cocksucker,' said Lila, and walked carefully away, in the direction of the bar.

People moved apart for her. Somebody giggled; Rex had not been a popular director. Joshua Broome clapped Lila's performance but she didn't seem to notice. She was very drunk; or maybe it was drugs. Everybody else seemed too embarrassed, or surprised, to do anything at all.

I went up to the bar and stood beside Lila.

'You can do better than that,' I said.

'Huh?' Lila turned. She looked flushed and hectic; her lipstick was smudged. 'What'dya say?'

'I said, you can do better than that. Give me five minutes.'

Lorraine had disappeared. Pretending I wanted to phone her up about something, I got her number from the make-up assistant, who had been her best friend on the set. Then I asked the club manager for a piece of card and some Sellotape and rejoined Lila at the bar. 'Follow me,' I said.

She came, obediently. We pushed open the back door and found ourselves in an alleyway. It was chilly. I took out the card. On its blank side I wrote, with Pentel: *Play out your fantasies with Young Actress, Lorraine. Tel: 388 7991.*

'What're you doing?' asked Lila. The drink had made her slow-witted.

'Just follow me.'

I led her to the end of the alley. A phone booth stood there. It was plastered with cards. *Busty Lynn's Massage, Madame Vanessa, Leather Equipment for Sale, I'm Susi! Young Model.* They all had phone numbers.

I realised, with surprise, that I was holding Lila's wrist. I stroked the skin, just for a moment. 'Watch this.'

I broke off a piece of Sellotape with my teeth and stuck up Lorraine's card. We stood back and looked at it; Lila staggered, and steadied herself against me.

'You going to leave it there?' she asked at last. It had taken her a while to understand what I was doing.

'Sure.'

Lila's eyes widened, then she laughed.

I smiled. We stood there for a moment. A police siren wailed. Beyond the alley, in the lit street, people passed to and fro, out for a good time. They looked suddenly innocent. Neon signs glared: *Wendyburgers, TICKETS ALL SHOWS.* Lights chased around a sign for *Minicabs Day and Nite.*

A breeze rustled some rubbish, heaped in a doorway. I realised that a man lay sleeping there.

Lila hiccupped, then shivered. 'I sure as hell wouldn't like *you* for an enemy.'

I just grinned.

The next day Lila and Irma flew back to America, and I presumed that an episode in my life was over.

But it wasn't, was it? In fact, it had only just begun.

Nine

Filming is like being in hospital. You are in a sealed world with its own food, its own peculiar routines starting at an unearthly hour in the morning. It has its own cast – people you will never see again. While you are in there nobody knows what is happening to you. There are vast stretches of boredom. You come out of it into a city that seems unchanged by your absence, though the trees in your street might be more heavily in leaf. You feel bereft, that it is all over and there is nothing to show for it – it might never have happened. Life resumes its normal course and yet, though those weeks seem an illusion, a dream, you are not quite the same. You have been tinkered with; there has been a small shifting, within, but you have been sewn up again and have emerged into the outside world seemingly the same.

I have always felt this – with stage shows too, as well as the small amount of filming I have done. In the past, though, this has been a professional sensation – I have learnt something I can work on, I have inhabited a character that has expanded me, that I can use again. I have learnt, through various directors, how to express myself in ways I didn't know I possessed. I have been, to some extent, taken over by another person who didn't exist until I made her flesh. Even with less happy experiences, with unsympathetic directors, I have also gained something – how to manipulate, to battle or, *in extremis*, how to fake in rehearsal and then rediscover my character on stage. How to pretend to everybody – even, sometimes, to myself.

With *Sexbusters*, though, I had learnt nothing. This wasn't just because I had simply stood there while they stretched a tape measure from my head to the mantelpiece and shoved a

71

light meter in front of my nose. For the first time in my life I had dipped my toe in the big movie business and what had I found? A foolish re-make of a foolish film that never should have been made in the first place – how bankrupt can the imagination get? A feeble script and unconvincing characters. Glossy and inappropriate locations. A second-rate director who thought from his groin. The cynical use of a bankable star, and a distinguished but wrecked old stage actor, to give the whole shabby enterprise some sort of clout.

I should never have got involved with it. I had just done it for the money, and some sort of prurient curiosity, and I felt soiled. *Gertie and the Giants* seemed a long way away now, in another life.

I felt changed, but it was nothing to do with my work. Some wound had been opened, and I didn't want to locate it. I had stitched it up carefully so that I wouldn't notice the difference. It's ironic, really. I would spend weeks in workshops and rehearsals, getting under a character's skin, exploring and analysing. But then work is easy, isn't it? Even when it's difficult, it's easy.

The day after the party a motor bike messenger rang my doorbell. He gave me a box. Inside it was a big bottle of *Je Reviens* perfume. With it was a note. *'To the best "Me" around! Thanks. See ya! LILA XXX.'*

A month passed. I wasn't pregnant yet. It was a humid September. Outside my window the lime tree sweated. Indoors I waited for the phone to ring. I wasn't out of work, of course, I was just waiting for work. One phone call – today, next week, next year – and I must drop everything. One missed period, and my life could change.

Meanwhile I existed in a state of suspended animation. I went to my body workouts and my French conversation classes. I read reviews of plays in which I had not been invited to take part, whose directors were becoming younger and less known to me. I noted, sourly, that an actress who had played my fellow supermarket cashier in an afternoon soap (parts for which we were both miscast) had joined the RSC and was rehearsing Imogen.

I wore the perfume, but not for Trev. I didn't want my skin to remind him of anybody else. When I was spending an evening alone I dabbed it on; with my wet finger I touched my pulse points.

I felt sluggish and yet unsettled. Trev visited – he was always a visitor, it was always greetings and farewells with Trev. Sometimes I resented him when he arrived, because then I could no longer anticipate him. Each arrival was simply a countdown to his departure, every moment was one step nearer to my renewed solitude. At night, unknown to him, I urged him to make me pregnant – me, a liberated woman, was using the oldest trick in the book, wasn't it shameful? The hope inflamed me; I was slippery with passion. 'Blimey,' he said afterwards, and felt over his body for broken bones. In a film we would end up marrying, and in the closing reel we would kiss and I could have him to myself for life. *Kids are great, aren't they?* said Lila. She was thirty-eight too; time was running out for both of us.

At the end of September a script arrived from my agent. It was a play about the homeless; somebody was going to stage it at a community centre in Brixton. It was a worthy piece about life's injustice and I agreed to join the cast. My character had a speech about the haves and the have-nots, and as I read it I thought about the Daimler, and how behind its black windows anybody could re-create themselves, and how I had despised myself for play-acting.

Rehearsals were due to start in the middle of October. I was to play a social worker – a role I had been cast in twice before, which must be a sign of something. This social worker, Marion, was a particularly mature specimen – the stage directions, florid pieces of writing, called her *'menopausal and malcontent'*. Juliet had slipped from me for ever. Now I was destined to shrivel, or to thicken, into character parts. Ahead lay a wasteland of aunts. Or, in feminist venues for an even tinier salary, lesbian careworkers of abused children. Play your cards right, as Trev might say, and in twenty years I could end up as Lady Bracknell. In Slough.

On Tuesday, the week before rehearsals, I was just going to the launderette when the phone rang. I rushed back, up the stairs.

'Darling,' said Maggie, 'listen to this.'

'What's happened?'

'I think we made a bit of an impression last summer.' She paused. I heard the click of her lighter. It must be something interesting, for her to light a cigarette. 'I've just had the casting director of Maizin Productions on the line. It seems that our friend Lila Dune has asked for you personally, to stand in for her on her next picture.'

'Me?'

'There's been a bit of an argy-bargy with the unions, of course, but there it goes.'

'There what goes?'

'She's the star.'

I paused. 'She wants me?'

'It's a picture called *Bump In The Night*. They start shooting next week.'

'Next week?'

'In New York.'

'New York?'

'You going to go on repeating everything I say?'

I walked to the launderette on weightless legs. My skin felt stretched. I sat down next to an old lady who had fallen asleep and I watched my clothes curve and fall, curve and fall. I saw them through the window of the dryer but they no longer belonged to me.

I felt nauseous. It wasn't exactly unpleasant. It was more

74

like that turbulence when some longed-for boyfriend has just phoned, and afterwards you settle down to recall, in luxurious detail, every word he said.

She wanted me. More than that, she had made a fuss to get me.

The dryer stopped. The woman next to me woke and said, 'Shame about his birthmark, isn't it.' Then she coughed into a handkerchief and went back to sleep.

I pulled out my clothes and started to fold them. My face felt hot, as if I had just been summoned by royalty. What was I going to wear?

I knew, of course, that I should refuse.

Trev, who was like a child when it came to gadgets, had got a new answerphone. It had a ten-number memory, with a little window for the names. I sat in his armchair and pretended not to read it. Number 1 was his agent, Dominic. Number 2 was Max, his best mate, who ran Look Back in Ongar. Number 3 was myself. I sighed. I least I was earlier than his parents; they were 7 and he had given up after that.

I told him about the offer. It felt like a repeat of last August's conversation, with Trev my Mephistopheles all over again.

'What about *Plight*?' I said. 'I can't let them down.'

'Two weeks playing to a bunch of old dears who thought you were their raffia class?' He put on the kettle. 'You ever been to New York?'

'No!' Didn't he know anything about me? Had he never asked?

'Nor have I.' He put on the tea. He was being nice to me today, as if I had suddenly become an important visitor.

'It's not my world.' I said. 'It's another dumb picture.'

He sat down on the floor, between my legs. He had just washed his hair; I stroked his wet head. Today he felt like my labrador dog, which had been playing in a pond. I often

75

compared him to dogs. Sheaves of typewritten paper lay all over the carpet. He was writing a novel, but he wouldn't tell me what it was about. This made me feel flattered but uneasy, as if he were monitoring my movements. On the other hand, maybe it wasn't about me at all. That would be worse.

I stroked his hair and wondered, yet again, if he were a natural writer or just a second-hand dealer, who banged other people's words together, sanded them down, polished them up and flogged them as genuine.

I didn't want to know the truth; I was too besotted. Nor did I dare ask if he was figuring on coming to New York.

The next day my period started. I sat on the lavatory and thought: I seem to spend my whole life alone in bathrooms, looking at myself in the mirror.

So I ditched the community play and decided to go to America. I lied to the theatre company, and told them my mother had died. I told them with such conviction that my own eyes moistened. When I put the phone down I felt a small charge of electricity shoot through my veins; just a buzz. Lying always energised me.

A contract was faxed to Maggie, my agent. It was terrific money – $750 a week plus hotel accommodation. Like most actresses I was chronically badly-off; it had taken me ten years to afford a place of my own.

Now, looking at my contract, I felt greed stirring within me like a foetus I never knew I was carrying. I told myself I would never buy those stupid leather suits in Bond Street, I wasn't like that; I didn't want a limousine with a driver. All I wanted was the money to forget that money was important; I wanted to possess the insouciance of the fortunate. Lack of money is like being a cripple; every step achingly reminds you of your bad leg. It makes you petty; it stops you thinking about anything interesting.

*

That's not quite the truth, is it? That's the old me talking, the other Jules. Remember *Belle de Jour*, where the respectable housewife leaves her home each afternoon and works in a brothel? Catherine Deneuve. I dreamed that film again, after I saw it. In fact I dreamed it several times, with variations.

The Thursday before my flight I went shopping. I went to a shop I had seen once, just off Marylebone High Street. It sold a wide range of exceedingly tarty dresses – red sequins, dripping silver, slippery silk . . . backless, frontless. The sort of dresses I had never imagined buying – the other me, that is, the Jules who bought material at the Liberty's sale.

I bought one with my Barclaycard. It was made of bronze satin, and it was slashed one side to leave a shoulder bare and the other to reveal a thigh. It was the sort of dress Lila would wear. In my stuffy, curtained booth I stood in front of the mirror and turned slowly, holding my gaze. I re-applied my lipstick. Then I took out my eye pencil and, licking the point, painted myself a beauty spot, just where she had it.

I pouted at myself and then I gradually pulled the skirt up, a little higher. Between the curtains there was a gap. Two Arab men were standing in the shop; they could see me. I smiled at my reflection and then I peeled off the dress, oh so slowly. As I did it, I watched them in the mirror.

I didn't show the dress to Trev. For some reason, despite our games, it would have confused him. After all, it confused me.

Trev was going to come with me, but at the last moment he backed off.

'Listen, love,' he said, 'I've had a phone call from BBC Scotland.'

'Really?' I felt suspicious when he called me *love*. It was too sincere.

'Straight up. This bloke, he's interested in *Use Me*, but I've got to do more work on it.'

'What do you mean?'

'I can't go with you.'

I didn't reply. I looked at him, sharply. His face was bland. What the hell was going on?

'What bloke?' I asked.

'Bill Bryden.'

I turned away, so he couldn't see my face. I started scrubbing the draining board, vigorously. My skin felt boiled.

'I'll miss you something chronic,' he said. 'But it's only two months.'

I knew I should be delighted for him. His big break and all that. I scrubbed harder.

'I'll phone you,' he said. He turned me around and ran his finger down my nose. 'I'll phone you every day.' He lifted up my damp, red hand and kissed it. 'I'll miss your careworn hands. I'll miss your funny face.'

'Funny?'

'Gorgeous face. I'll miss this little bit here.' He touched the corner of my mouth. Then he leant forward and kissed it gently. 'I'll miss this little bit here,' he said, sliding his hand up my skirt.

I didn't trust him. I turned away to dry my hands.

'Hey, why don't I look after your place?' he asked. 'My heating's packed up. I'll water your plants.' He grinned. 'I'll keep your bed warm.'

Bitterly I thought: the only time he suggests moving into my flat is when I'm moving out. I didn't say anything, however. I smiled sweetly and showed him the spray for my ferns and how to work my newly-repaired washing machine. Just for a moment we seemed unexpectedly domestic. It felt intimate, to show him my fusebox.

'Remember, it's my bed,' I warned. 'My sheets.' I paused. 'Just remember that.'

He crossed his fingers. 'Scout's honour.'

I looked at him sharply. 'You've never been a Scout.'

And so, on a bright morning in the middle of October, Trev drove me to the airport – he was borrowing my car too. Now

I was leaving he was suddenly ardent. The Renault squealed along in third gear, he drove with one hand on the wheel and the other up my skirt. Whimpering, I cried, 'Clutch!' He pressed the clutch and I shifted the gear stick for him, into fourth. I rested my head on his shoulder.

'You smell gorgeous,' he said.

'Just perfume.'

'New.'

I nodded. It was Lila's.

The motorway sign flashed past: HEATHROW AIR-PORT $^1/_2$ MILE. Now I was leaving England, the scruffy fields beside the road suddenly looked poignant. Three months ago I had worn a silver dress from Oxfam; it had cost £2. By chance, I had stood on a street with wishes in my head but nobody to hear them. Now I was flying to America. In my suitcase was a bronze dress that cost a hundred times more, and what were my wishes now?

At the airport I felt ridiculously nervous. My bowels growled. Trev, self-conscious now, gave me a dry kiss on the cheek. He suddenly seemed young and bereft. I clasped him awkwardly at the entrance to the departure lounge. Then I walked quickly through the gates. When I turned round he had disappeared into the crowd.

An hour later I was boarding the 11 o'clock British Airways flight to JFK. As I stood in the cabin, wedged between two businessmen who were stuffing their Burberrys into the luggage compartments, I smelt Lila's perfume on my skin. I pictured her wild loopy writing: *'To the best "Me" around!'*

NEW YORK

One

I was waking up, slowly, from an operation. They had cut me open and removed something vital. I lay in my bed, drowsily, my mouth dry as cotton wool. Far away I heard a clanging; somebody was banging shut a rubbish bin, again and again. Inside the bin, organs steamed like meat.

My eyeballs smarted. Traffic was passing, way down below me. It came from the bottom of a well. I ran my fingers across the starchy sheet and spread my legs like a starfish. The mattress was too wide for a hospital bed. Something clanged again, down in the street. I had been back at primary school, banging the cymbals in the band, except I had never had a go on them, it was always Louisa something who had been given the cymbals to play, marching up and down the stage with her smug plaits swinging. I climbed out of bed; I felt swollen and heated with jet lag, as if I had flu. It was only midnight. I was in a strange hotel room with heavy beige drapes at the window. Parting them, I looked out. Opposite me, buildings rose up, high as cliffs, blocking out the orange sky. Between them I glimpsed more huge buildings, banked up; some were spotlit and seemed to be steaming in the dark, breathing out white mist.

In the windows opposite, empty offices were lit as brightly as stage sets, waiting for something to happen. Through the double glazing, sirens from a thousand cop shows wailed down the canyons of the streets. I felt utterly alone; I felt exhilarated.

I dressed, put on my coat and boots and went down to the lobby. I walked, most of that first night in New York City. The clanging, I discovered, came from a loose manhole cover out in the street; tinny yellow taxi-cabs rattled over it as they passed. Opposite, glowing pink neon, was Dianne's Discount Body Waxing. The blind was pulled down. *'Full Leg'* it said. *'Bikini Line. Back. Priced Accordingly.'* Behind the blind, light still glowed.

I walked up E 39th Street and across Lexington. I didn't call it Lex, yet. Everything was new to me. The air was sharp; I breathed lungfulls of it. Smoke steamed from manholes as if Hell was down there, exhaling. Long black limousines slid past, their windows dark. A man, dressed in rags, stood next to a lamp-post. His head was tilted, listening to it. Then he argued back, his voice rising. 'Siggy didn't wait for me!' He paused, waiting for a reply, and then shouted back. 'They told me personally!'

I walked past lurid shop windows; *Camera Barn. Radio Shack.* I didn't know how far I had gone, but the shops were growing shabbier. Headless mannequins stood behind the glass, wearing dusty shirtwaisters. In doorways, sleeping shapes stirred and muttered. I could smell the river. One man, his head bandaged, came up to me with his palm outstretched. I gave him a dollar bill. He saluted. 'See you in paradise,' he said; he started tittering, and sank away into the shadows. I passed a barricaded shop window, heavy with padlocks. *Chiropractor*, said the sign. *Come on in! Get your spine in line!* Outside a warehouse a white Cadillac waited, purring, a plume of smoke rising from its exhaust.

I went into an all-night coffee shop and sat down on a plastic chair. I couldn't think what meal I should be feeling hungry for. A man beside me muttered at a bowl of ketchup sachets: 'I ain't going to no wedding in no tux.'

The waiter brought me a plate of toast and luminous jelly. As he put it down he looked at me and frowned.

'Ain't I seen you someplace?' he asked.

I jumped. 'No.'

'TV show maybe?'

I paused, then I shrugged. 'Maybe.'

Did he mean he recognised me from some movie, from

Touch and Go, when I rose from the pool all wet and gave the teenage Trev a hard-on? Did he really think I was Lila, or was I just a nobody he had stood next to one day, queuing at the bank? I pursed my lips into Lila's pout. At the counter, rows of grapefruit were displayed. Each was cut in half, with a moist cherry in the centre. They were lit as glamorously as film stars. And outside the streets were full of nobodies confiding in pieces of metal; vouchsafing, to lamp-posts, their private catastrophes. Each of us carries our own dramas, but where does the spotlight fall?

I didn't feel lonely that night, not then. I felt dislocated, and excited, and feverish with jet lag. Back in my hotel room I pulled off my boots and lay down on the bed, my legs aching and my senses alert. I flipped through the TV channels on my remote control. A blurred hand stroked something furry. *'Niteline Escorts,'* breathed a voice. *'When you're all alone and don't want to be.'* A girl lay on a bed, her legs spread. *'This is my friend Bambi, she specialises in cocksucking.'* Phone numbers flashed on the screen. You could even use your credit card. One number for *Fuck*; another for *Tits*. *'Six nasty girls are waiting for your calls. Live talk 24 hours a day.'* Outside the sirens wailed; indoors the TV moaned. A couple appeared, naked. Her head was flung back as she mimed ecstasy, sliding her tongue across her pearly actress's teeth as if she were playing a harmonica. Faster and faster she gasped, to a background of airport departure lounge music. Suddenly I remembered Lorraine in her Bacofoil. Maybe strange men were still ringing her up, muttering obscenities.

'I sure wouldn't want you for an enemy,' said Lila to me, her eyes wide with alarm. But I wasn't her enemy, was I? I was only her stand-in.

I was woken by the phone ringing. All of a sudden everything seemed unreal – the single, long warble of the phone, the unfamiliar room, my walk last night. I was lying in bed and it was two in the afternoon.

'Welcome to New York,' said a voice. 'Was your flight comfortable? How do you like your hotel?' It was somebody from Maizin Productions. Did I have my shooting schedule? My call sheet? They looked forward to seeing me the first day of principal photography, a car would collect me the next morning.

A car! They were treating me like a star. Maybe Lila had fixed it. I ate some afternoon breakfast in a coffee shop round the corner, bought a map and walked uptown towards Central Park. It was a beautiful, sunny Sunday, though the deep wells of the streets were in shadow. I flung back my head and gazed up at the sheer, dizzying faces of the apartment blocks. At the top, the penthouses caught the sun. I glimpsed tufts of bushes, whole trees sometimes, up there; a balcony, an awning. Lives were being lived in the sunshine; the rich and famous would be anointing their tanned limbs whilst down here in the street, where the wind blew chilly through the funnels of the cross-streets, the rest of us were buttoning up our coats. Skyscrapers cast whole neighbourhoods into darkness. I started to realise, that day, how New York is two cities, sliced horizontally. The top slice is in perpetual sunshine and peace; they even have their own birdsong up there, I found that out later. In their offices and apartments they breathe a different air. Occasionally they descend into the frenzied, sunless rat-runs but only to slip into something long and comfortable and purr to their destination. My blood throbbed; deep inside, something in me responded to this schizoid city.

Perhaps I didn't realise it then. I don't know really what I thought that day when I was still suspended between two lives, with no part to play because I was still invisible. To some extent we all perform, all of us. With nobody to mirror back our image we don't exist – or we exist, utterly freely, just for ourselves. Nobody – except one stranger on the phone – even knew where I was staying. I walked into that amazing, theatrical park a free spirit, perhaps for the last time in my life. For the next day it was all going to begin.

The trees rustled, gold and bronze. Huge boulders jutted

from the ground, breaking its surface like primeval creatures the city had tried to bury. A black man on rollerskates was pushing a supermarket trolley from one trash bin to the next, pulling out cans which he stored in his trolley like a squirrel hoarding nuts. There were real squirrels too, scrawny as rats, and the disco thump of radios, and couples embracing on the bleached grass. A chilly wind blew. Around me, people acted out their dramas in the open air, singly or in pairs. I criss-crossed the paths, heady with my own invisibility. Above the thinning trees rose apartment blocks, heartstoppingly high, as preposterous as painted backdrops. On one side of the park they were in shadow; on the other they caught the pearly light of the dying sun. Their windows were lit, flashing orange as if they were on fire within. I gazed up at their penthouses. Lila had told me she lived on Central Park West; which building might it be? The light was fading; I must have been walking for hours.

Then I stopped. Ahead, set into the grass, was a mosaic plaque. I peered closer; the lettering said IMAGINE.

'This is Strawberry Fields, honey,' said a large woman, surrounded by carrier bags. She pointed across the park. 'That's the Dakota, know that? That's where he was gunned down.'

I gazed at the plaque, Lennon's memorial. What had Chapman said? *I thought it would be like the movies.* Imagine what? Being someone else? Someone different? Actresses have to imagine all the time, they have to inhabit another skin, sliding into it as if they are sliding into a glove.

Through the dusk, I gazed up at the lit buildings. Lila might be up there, at this very moment. She wasn't thinking of me, but I was thinking of her. That's fame for you.

Imagine being Lila. When I turned, her soft hair fell across my cheek. When I turned, everybody looked.

Two

Movies arrive in clusters, like London buses. *Sexbusters* was one of those transformation pictures that were popular a few years ago – gender-benders like *Tootsie*, age-benders like *Cocoon* and *Big. Bump in the Night*, on the other hand, was one of those extra-terrestrial family comedies, there was a spate of them too, remember? In *Bump* Lila was playing a divorcée who falls for a man her teenage son hates. One day, to ingratiate himself with the boy, the man takes him to a Disneyland-type Space Park, where in the Mars Capsule something goes wrong and the boy emerges with extra-terrestrial powers. He uses these to sabotage his mother's love-affair – misdirecting her car when she is driving to her boyfriend's apartment, playing tricks on him and destroying their trysts with special effects. The movie was going to be shot entirely on location in New York City. And for the first time, Lila was playing not a romantic lead but a mother.

People's looks change, just slightly, in another country. Lila looked somehow more fragile, here in New York; she seemed to have lost weight. Maybe it was the make-up, they'd had to age her up a few years. Maybe it was the way they had dressed her hair for the part; it was swept back off her cheekbones, her skin looked taut and pale. The divorcée she played, Mary-Lou, was a real-estate broker; Lila wore a slim blue business suit which revealed her wonderful legs. We were up Columbus Avenue, roped off from the crowd like circus animals, shooting a scene outside a gourmet pasta shop. I had walked in and out of its doors about twenty times already, wearing a blue jacket over my skirt. Everyone was hectic, that first morning. Lila had just said, 'Hi, how're ya doing?', kissed my chilly cheek and disappeared into make-up. I trod the pavement for her, sorry sidewalk, again and again, trying to remember the names of the crew. Mart, Bob, Don, which was which? A lot of Bobs; there are always lots of Bobs, in crews.

During the lunch break I walked a block to Central Park and sat for a few minutes in the sun. I had finished my English cigarettes by now and had bought some Winstons. I sat on a bench, my eyes closed, inhaling the American tobacco and wondering what on earth I was doing here.

Somebody was breathing on me, boozily. I opened my eyes. A withered black woman was looking into my face. I jumped. She wore a yellow wig; Heidi plaits hung down on either side of her face.

'You tell them what I said,' she whispered. 'You tell them what I said. See the fuckers' faces then.'

The cinematographer on this film was pernickety, too. That afternoon they put me into a blonde wig, swept back like Lila's hair. I sat in the make-up trailer having it fitted by someone called Rodney. He was a distinguished-looking gay with silver sideburns.

He glanced down at the book I had been reading, a paperback of *Washington Square*. We started talking about books. One of the more curious facts about film shoots is that, despite the interminable longueurs, nobody reads. They barely even glance at a newspaper.

'You've got a good, strong face,' he said. He looked at me, his head on one side. 'Enigmatic.'

'Is it?'

'Asks the lady, enigmatically.' He smiled. 'You British, I never know what you're thinking. It's like you've been trained in some secret service.'

'It's called a middle-class upbringing.'

He took a pin and fixed up a trailing strand of my wig. 'You're smart. The Thinking Guy's Lila Dune. Lila, she's a sensational-looking woman but she has the intellect of an azalea.'

89

Suddenly, we both burst out laughing.

Outside the Plaza Hotel, it smells of dung. There are these horse-drawn carriages there, waiting for out-of-towners like me. That evening I hired one, for a twenty-dollar clop around Central Park. The driver was a young, friendly chap; he touched the horse with his whip and we jolted forward. We left the traffic behind, it was reduced to a faint roar. Amongst the trees it was hushed and primitive.

'Like to stargaze?' he asked.

Thinking he was going to point out the constellations, I nodded insincerely. But he was pointing to the pinpoints of lights way up, at the top of the apartment blocks.

'Diana Ross, that's her apartment,' he said. 'When she's in town.' He hummed *Baby, baby, where did our love go?* 'You like Woody Allen?' He pointed. 'He lives there, that's his, he has the whole penthouse floor and Mia, she's across the West Side. I'm a movie nut.'

I swung my head. Through the trees the buildings looked spectacular, some of the old ones were floodlit. They rose, crenellated cliffs of them. They looked even more improbable at night, like tricks of the camera.

'That's a landmark building.' He pointed to one of the apartment blocks. 'Lila Dune, the film star, she lives there.'

I didn't reply.

'You seen any of her movies in England?' he asked.

'No. Who is she?'

'Who's Lila Dune? You don't know? She's, like . . .' He lifted his hands from the reins and made an hourglass shape. 'Blonde. Drop-dead sexy. Done a lot of TV work. Plus fifteen movies, maybe twenty. Kind of so-so, most of them. But with a bod like that, who's worrying? Career went down the tubes for a while, she had some problems. She ain't so young no more, either. But the buzz is it's picking up.'

'I don't know her,' I said, steadying myself as we clopped around a corner. 'I'm kind of busy. I have two little kids, they lead me a merry dance.'

'Boys? Girls?'

'One of each. And then in the evening I have to go to the theatre.'

'You an actress?' he asked.

I nodded. 'Heard of Paul Scofield?'

'Sure.'

'Lovely man.' I gazed at the black branches of the tree, tangled against the sky. 'I played Cordelia to his Lear.'

'No kidding!'

I told him about my triumphant Stratford season, and my following year at the National. I told him about my house in Holland Park and my huge, boisterous dog that knocked down the postman but meant no harm. It was so dark that he couldn't see my face. I spoke to the jolting branches.

Tell them, said the woman with the custard-coloured plaits. *See the fuckers' faces then.*

Those first few days, my feelings about New York City veered from one extreme to the other. Sometimes it seemed the most glamorous city on earth, at others an asylum for the terminally insane. I felt precariously balanced; one tiny push and I would tumble down some chute, into chaos. I would join those people shouting in the dark. I felt alert, alive, as poised as an animal sniffing danger. I felt this from the beginning, long before anything started happening. I can remember it, I really can.

My hotel was midtown; most mornings I had an early call and took a cab to wherever the shooting schedule sent me, uptown, downtown, wherever. I have a good sense of direction – something that is not a great deal of use to me here. I started to plot out the shape of Manhattan. I bought some trainers – Reeboks – like everyone else; they were comfortable and noiseless. At night I walked. One night I walked right down to Wall Street, fifty blocks or more, I felt as lithe and silent as a panther. I looked into lit lobbies, where night porters sat at their desks, where fluted marble columns cast a suffused glow and where elevator lights blinked, rising and descending with their invisible cargo. Once, when I was passing, the doors of an elevator slid open and there was just emptiness inside. Up in the sky, lives were being lived and I felt intensely alone. Even the street sounds are different, with tall buildings on either side; there's a hollowness, an echo.

I missed Trev, my body ached for him, especially when I got back to my hotel room, but I knew that he was missing me, he said so on the phone, and our temporary separation felt so sweetly painful that I almost relished it. I wanted him to be impressed with my growing familiarity with the streets and my insouciant use of newly acquired slang. I was starting to call lorries 'trucks' and queues 'standing in line'. I knew how to buy subway tokens. The things I was beginning to take for granted, I was sharing them with him in my head. He was always with me. In a strange way we were becoming habitués together, if only he knew. I wanted to teach him about the city. I loved being the older, experienced woman. I wanted him to notice what I was noticing, because what was the point, otherwise? I would be impressed with myself, if only he were here to see. Sometimes I felt pleasantly dreamy about him; sometimes I felt angry, that he wasn't with me. Feelings about somebody can fluctuate even more in their absence. My normal input was cut off; I was like a hospital generator, fuelled by my own manufactured energy. I sent him packets of Hershey Kisses, and a book of James Dean photos from a shop called Mythology. I missed his laughter, desperately. I missed that almost more than his body. I sent him silly postcards.

Lila was busy with costume fittings, those first few days, and I hardly saw her. But she was nice to me when we met. In some curious way she seemed to like me – curious, because we were such an ill-matched couple. We may have looked similar, once my wig was fitted, but we had so little in common. Even more curious, she seemed to need me. She asked me into her trailer and we sat there, drinking some disgusting ginseng tea she had been told was fabulous for the pores. She lay back, wrapped in a satin robe, her eyes closed, while her little white dog snapped at my ankles. She said her personal life was at an all-time low, she had no relationship at present.

'My therapist says I'm getting too dependent on Orson as a displacement-substitute,' she said. Hearing his name, the dog leaped onto her lap. She caressed him, her long red fingernails sinking into his fur. 'He's a placebo or something.' She leant forward and kissed him. 'I'm trying to get my act together without goddam men. Men are the pits.' She had just read something about the willing victim syndrome. Lila was full of half-digested information like this – from her shrink, her diet doctor, her friends, Tarot cards, magazine articles and How-to-live-a-meaningful-life type manuals. She told her latest theories to anyone who would listen – which, as she was a film star, meant a lot more people than you or I would get.

I loved it when she asked me into her trailer, it made me feel special. She sat there at the mirror, her afternoon's lines propped up in front of her. She inspected her face anxiously, and asked for beauty tips. I didn't have any, of course, but she didn't seem to mind or even notice. She never really listened to anyone else. We sat there, sealed off from the outside world, listening to her syrupy country and western tapes until Irma tapped on the door and interrupted us, glaring at me as if she were Lila's mother and I some teenage boyfriend.

Lila was also generous to me on the set. 'Jules here's the best stand-in they ever gave me,' she said to the director, Chuck Cox. He smiled at me, benignly. With Lila telling him, he had to listen. Somebody was calling him to the phone, and Walt from props was showing him two ashtrays and asking him which one he wanted Lila to throw. We were shooting a scene in a restaurant. Extras were everywhere, trying to get to a phone, weaving their way back from the coffee machine with plastic cups balanced precariously, or sitting at the tables writing their own movie scripts. Even my cabbie that morning – a rare, chatty one – had told me he was writing a movie script.

'It's just, like, you know how I would do it,' said Lila. 'It's

93

kinda weird.' She laughed. 'Maybe we met in another life, I like the idea of that.'

I smiled. 'Maybe we were swapped at birth.'

Chuck was called away. Lila lowered her voice. 'Seen my lines for this? This is some asshole script. What I'd give for a good writer. Where are they? Where are those guys?'

I didn't understand, at the time, the significance of this remark. When actresses complain about scripts it is usually because their part is too small. They don't analyse a script, the way my father used to take apart English texts and reappraise each word. They don't have time to talk about motivation or character development, they are too busy being shunted around. Once a film is in motion it's a series of escalating crises, phone calls, and massive reorganisations because it's suddenly started to rain. I soon learnt that nobody discusses the script. It's just *fabulous*. It has to be fabulous, doesn't it, or else why else were we there, busting our guts?

Besides, Lila said that she had always wanted to work with Chuck – he was a fine, respected director, he'd done terrific stuff with A-list stars like Jessica Lange and Meryl Streep, actresses who were really taken seriously. Despite her fame, Lila was deeply insecure. This was something else I realised, as the days passed. It's hard to believe, isn't it? You see this beautiful face, up on the screen, and you think she's got it all. You sit there, envying her until it burns. And, all that time, she's burning too.

Rodney, the hairdresser, emerged from his trailer and we sat together, watching Lila throwing the ashtray at her lover, who she suspects is two-timing her. (He isn't; it's just some Martian mischief-making.) At each take, Lila played it more ferociously. I watched, awe-struck, as she lunged at him. Half her hair was falling down; she looked like a madwoman, one of the women I saw in Central Park. She stumbled through the restaurant, knocking over wine glasses and scattering chairs. Suddenly I remembered her in the Retro Grade night club, her eyes wild, her mascara smudged, emptying the champagne bucket over the man who had betrayed her. Even the extras looked startled – unless, as was likely, they were over-reacting to catch the director's eye.

The floor was mopped for another take. Rodney, wielding his sprays and combs, fixed her hair. Then he came back to me and sat down. We watched.

'You bastard, you bastard!' screamed Lila.

Rodney lifted my hand. 'I meant to ask you. How did you do this?'

I've never told you, have I? There's this long scar across the back of my hand. The pinpoints of the stitchmarks have long since faded, but the raised purplish weal remains. Will remain, I guess, for ever.

'I was attacked,' I said. 'I was doing drama therapy with some disturbed kids and one of them attacked me.'

Rodney was watching Lila. 'Know something?' he said. 'That's what she is. A disturbed kid.'

I didn't know, then, just how disturbed she was. I knew she was fragile and volatile and insecure, a prey to her wildly swinging moods. I knew that fame can unbalance its victim, distorting reality and turning other people into sycophants and liars. But I didn't yet know anything about her past – the father, the broken marriages, the mental breakdowns. I had read every magazine interview I could find, but they usually just plugged her latest film. All that came later.

At that stage, you see, I just thought it was Lila who was disturbed. That's what I thought.

Something else happened that first week. It seemed unimportant at the time. In fact, I hardly noticed Lila's remark – not until I needed it, months later.

She had joined me on the set of that afternoon's shoot, the lobby of her lover's apartment. I had done my bit and we were hanging around while the riggers repaired something. We sat in the canvas chairs; out in the street, faces pressed against the glass doors as people watched us. Maybe, just for a moment, they were confused. Two blonde actresses, sitting under the bright, white lights. Which was the star? Which twin had the

Toni? From the back, who could tell? Except one canvas chair said MISS DUNE and the other said ARTISTE.

Lila and I were talking about Rex, the English director. This was another topic that drew us close, as apart from Irma I was the only person on the set who had ever met him.

'The motherfucker,' she said. 'The lousy worm. He used to tie me to the bedposts, I had to put a whole lot of guck on my wrists the next day. Guess I was into self-denigration then. I've come through that now.'

'You seemed quite spirited at the time,' I said. 'You and your ice.' I started giggling. 'Wonder if that phone number's still up in the telephone box.'

'Huh?' She looked at me, her eyes blank.

I stared back at her. Then I explained what had happened. She asked me to repeat it, to make sure. She had genuinely forgotten the whole incident.

'And you want to know why I quit drinking?' she said. 'See, I do things I don't remember later. I wake up in these weird places and I don't know how I got there. It's real alarming.' She shivered. 'Once, I was in this guy's room in a Ramada Inn. A Ramada Inn! How the hell did I get there? He used to play a cop in *Hill Street Blues*, that's the only way I recognised him.'

I didn't reply. I had never known any real alcoholics, I didn't know what to say. We went on to talk about something else. But I must have remembered this conversation, because of what happened later. I must have stored it somewhere in the back of my brain, like a hammer which you don't remember you have in the cupboard until you suddenly want to kill someone.

That night, I dreamed Lila was Karen Black in the movie *Five Easy Pieces*. I often re-dreamed movies. Not so strange, perhaps. After all, dreams are our nocturnal cinema visits, our sleeping screenings for which we need no entrance tickets. Nor was my re-casting inappropriate, for Lila had that same cheap, dumb-blonde sexuality that Karen Black exuded. Jack Nicholson was fucking her, remember that scene? Striding with her from room to room while she yelped with pleasure. And when he finally flung her onto the bed he pinioned her to the bedposts, tying her wrists and then her neck with leather thongs. Twisting under him, she struggled; first her blonde wig came off and then her head. It rolled onto the floor, breaking like a wine bottle, and he was fucking a body, it could be anybody's, it could be mine. I tried to re-cast the movie, struggling awake, but I couldn't wake up. I knew what was going to happen, you see. For when he finally lifted his head, and I saw his face, it was Trev, grinning.

Three

A pattern emerged, on the set. During a long shoot a pattern always emerges – a running gag amongst the sound crew, the setting up of a fall guy, shifting alliances, a temporary love affair between the grip and the make-up girl, a tension between two of the actors. Actors, however, come and go. The rest of us were constant. Being a stand-in, I was neither crew nor cast but something in between. In some sense I was isolated; in another I could be the confidante, the recipient of gossip and grievances, from either side. I was adrift in the no-man's-land between the mechanics of film-making and the creation of characters.

Here, however, my Englishness enhanced my peculiar status. Though mute when working, though merely a body to be shunted around, when I opened my mouth I was everybody's darling. They loved to hear me speak. 'Say to-ma-to again,' they urged, copying my English accent. I told them that I was an actress, I could do American accents too, lots of them. I gave them my three Barbra Streisands, my six Meryl Streeps and (bitchily, because I was jealous of her) my one-and-a-half Diane Keatons. I could do a Marlon Brando, that slid, through *The Godfather*, into nasal incomprehensibility; I could do both the male and female Dustin in *Tootsie*. I was a terrific mimic. Unused for so long, my voice limbered up. I made people laugh – a refreshing sound I hadn't heard since playing in *Bedroom Farce* in Hornchurch.

Lila, you see, couldn't be anyone but herself; as an actress her range was pitifully limited, utterly one-note. I was a chameleon, a ventriloquist – I was an actress. But by one twist of fortune, nobody knew this. When *Bump* came out, it would be Lila there, up on the screen. Mine would be a name glimpsed by nobody, a name rolled on as the cinemas emptied, one name lost amidst dubbing editors, stand-by gaffers and plasterers. It would be Lila who would be interviewed amongst the popping flashbulbs.

Lila, I think, recognised my expertise. In those days she was anxious to learn. I sat in her trailer hearing her lines – she had a memory like a sieve. We ran through scenes together, with me playing her lover or her son. 'Mom,' I whined, 'is that fink coming to dinner again?' 'He's no fink,' she replied, 'he's the man I love.' I helped her with the interpretation of her part, the struggle between her motherly and romantic impulses, her son and her lover, developing them from the wooden and hackneyed script, fleshing them out.

I showed her how to improvise. 'You're Mary-Lou,' I said. Mary-Lou was the name of her character. 'Now let's see you being short-changed in the grocery store, what will you say? You're stuck in an elevator between two floors, how will you deal with it? Your mother's come to stay, what's she like, how do you relate to her?'

She was so fascinated that she even turned off Tammy Wynette. She had never gone to drama school, she'd never had discussions like this. Her looks had propelled her straight from beauty contests into showbusiness, from New Jersey Dairy Products to a long-running TV soap, and there had been no time for anything except intensive grooming and a series of disastrous love affairs with her leading men, most of whom had since turned out to be bisexual.

So I became the resident intellectual. Sometimes I felt like Professor Higgins in *Pygmalion* and she was my willing Eliza. On the set, I was considered clever just because I used to read. One day Lila picked up my copy of *Middlemarch*. She looked at the author's name.

'What's he like?' she asked. 'He a good writer?'

I told her that George Eliot, in fact, was a woman. She clapped her hand to her mouth.

'Don't tell them,' she hissed, indicating the camera crew,

who were drinking coffee nearby. 'They think I'm an air-head.'

Another time, during a break, Chuck spotted me reading my Penguin Ibsen. He paused beside me; he was a small, muscular man, as fidgety as a monkey; like all directors he was an egotistical bastard – they have to be, to do their job – but I liked him.

He said, 'I'd be doing *Hedda* if I didn't have three sets of alimony to pay.' He shrugged. 'But come to think of it, maybe Ibsen wouldn't have written *Hedda* if he'd had three sets of alimony to pay.'

Lila was sitting nearby, selecting shoes. When he had gone she whispered, joking, 'Now you're going to tell me this guy Ibsen, he was a broad too.'

I laughed. 'Hedda Gabler was.' I took out a packet of Salems, offered her one, and told her the story. I said Hedda Gabler was an underused, intelligent woman who ends up shooting herself. I said that I had played her myself.

Lila asked to borrow the play-text. She was an eager pupil, she wanted to learn. She said she would read it that night. But later that evening, when I switched on my TV set, there was an item on the WCBS News. Some new movie, I've forgotten its name now, had just opened and there were shots of celebrities arriving for the première. Among them was Lila. Her hair was piled up and she wore a fur coat. On her arm was a chubby, elderly man who I later learnt was her agent. In the spotlights she looked dazzling; she flashed a smile at the camera, at the jostling crowd, and was gone. So much for Ibsen.

It was during my long evenings that I missed Trev the worst. Sometimes it seemed ludicrous, that he was only living in my flat because I wasn't there. I couldn't decide if he was more likely to misbehave on my territory or not. On the one hand he would feel more guilty, my rows of maidenhair ferns chastising him; on the other hand, my flat was so much more salubrious than his (not a hard task) that it would certainly make a more seductive venue in which he might, as he put it, get his rocks off. As I lay on my hotel bed switching TV channels, my imagination festered. When I phoned he was often out. I pictured him in the Coach and Horses, scribbling down girls' phone numbers on his packet of Rizla cigarette papers. I pictured him padding, naked, across my spotless bedroom to join some hateful little scrubber, fifteen years my junior, under my duvet.

When we spoke I tried to paint a glamorous picture of my life in New York. 'Come over,' I said. 'I'll pay.' I lay there, in my jeans and t-shirt, and murmured, 'You'd love what I'm wearing. It's this leather corset, laced so tightly, and this lacy black suspender belt, mmm, and silky stockings . . .'

But he said he couldn't, this project was just coming to the boil. It was ever so hush-hush, he said, ever so exciting. He said he missed me; he made some dirty suggestions down the phone, things he was going to do to me when I got back, and that was that.

Lila and I had the same days off, of course. Remember that song, *Me and my Shadow*? That was me, bound to her. When she was released, so was I. Usually, however, when we finished for the day she just disappeared – to her fancy apartment, I guess, or to one of the battalions of experts who serviced her psyche and her muscle-tone. Maybe she had lunch with producers in places like the Russian Tea Room, places I'd read about. Maybe she lay blindfolded, plastered with mud packs. Maybe she sat, bingeing on bagels and watching re-runs of *M.A.S.H.* while Irma gave her a pedicure. God knows. Her life was so different to mine that I couldn't imagine what she did with her time. What did film stars do? I longed for us to be intimate but there were always people who spirited her away, a car was always waiting, its engine purring, its driver listening to the baseball commentary and smoking Marlboros.

And then, one day in November, two weeks into shooting, Lila said she would take me shopping. We were sitting in her movie brother's gym – *Bump* had an unconvincing sub-plot

101

where Mary-Lou's keep-fit fanatic of a brother was training to be an astronaut – and the next day they were shooting scenes that didn't include us. I was sitting on what looked like a surgical examination couch, trying to work the levers.

'Honey, you look like Orphan Annie,' said Lila. She fingered the cloth of my skirt like a Jewish tailor, tut-tutting. It was an old denim skirt from Fenwicks. 'Let's go shopping, huh? I want to show you my city, like you showed me yours. How about it? Shall we have some fun?' She sat down next to me. 'I meant to have gotten round to it sooner. I'm feeling more together now.'

In fact, she looked more together. Her eyes were bright; her face radiant. Something must have happened. At the time I just thought she had met somebody, some man, or maybe she just felt better about her character in *Bump*, thanks to our sessions in her trailer. I didn't know, then. Besides, I was too pleased to care. She said we'd go shopping and take in some lunch somewhere. *Me*, out to lunch with Lila Dune! It was one thing to be close to her on the set, but quite another to accompany her into the outside world. I felt stupidly flattered, and then contemptuous of myself.

'OK,' I said, casually.

A Maizin limo arrived the next morning, very late – Lila was always late. She was wearing a silky pantsuit and dark glasses. Around her head she had wrapped a scarf, her public disguise. It made her both more ordinary and yet curiously tantalising, like those snapshots of the incognito Marilyn Monroe. She was in good spirits, flirting with Randy, the driver, and telling us about the first time she came to New York, as a teenager, how she had hitched a ride with a girlfriend and they walked arm-in-arm down Broadway looking at the lights.

'One day, I told her, I said one day my name's going to be up there.'

'What happened to your friend?' I asked.

'She married a pig farmer in Idaho and they had three kids. Three little girls.' She sighed. 'My gynaecologist says my tubes

102

are all fucked up, the way I've abused my body. There was this time, see, when I'd swallow anything. They called me the Walking Laboratory.'

'You look very well on it,' I said, before I could stop myself.

'My whole life's one big fuckup,' she said, gazing through the tinted windows. 'But yesterday I went to see this woman, she's highly respected, she has politicians, everyone. So she read my cards and there were these conjunctions, one was the High Priestess, she says something very positive's going to happen.'

So that was why she was looking so well. Lila was a feminist's nightmare. It was as if she didn't exist until she was told something – by her astrologer, her nutritionist, her agent; by the script which gave her the lines she had to speak. That's what made her so attractive to men, I suppose. Despite her fame and wealth she was helpless, she was an empty vessel to be filled. She was intensively female. In the eighties there weren't many women left like her, she was an endangered species. Most of the women I knew were strong and independent, or pretended to be, clomping around in Doc Martens and demanding everything from gay rights to multiple orgasms.

And where was I in all this? I thought I knew, I thought I was strong and independent, but nobody is quite as simple as that. I felt myself pulled, seduced, by something in Lila. Maybe she was starting to feel just a little affected by me. Maybe.

It was a glorious sunny day, dimmed by our dark windows. We slid along Madison Avenue and stopped outside the Ralph Lauren shop.

'This is so damn British,' she said. 'You're going to love it.'

We left Randy outside, leaning against the limo and chewing Lifesavers. Lila and I went in. The store gave me the strangest sensation; it was like stepping onto the stage set of an English country house. It was like going back home to Sussex. Rooms were laid out with brass beds and fireplaces; there were old

Persian rugs on the floor. Gymkhana rosettes were pinned to the walls; I could have won them myself. Polished oak furniture displayed photos of people's ancestors in silver frames; one of them strongly resembled my Uncle Charles. I almost expected to see my old Famous Five books on the bedside table.

Lila pulled out a Shetland sweater and held it against me.

'I don't want to be English,' I protested. 'I want to be American.' I suppose I meant: I want to be more like you. 'Take me somewhere *you* go,' I said.

So we drove down to Saks. I can hardly remember the drive. I was concentrating on amusing Lila, entertaining her. The whole thing seemed so unlikely – the film star sitting beside me, the Ralph Lauren shop so phonily confronting me with my own past. The limo smelled of Lila's perfume; it was not the sort she had given me, it was sharper today. What had Nobby said? *You look like her long-lost cousin, the family swot.* Me, with my mousy hair and my home-made clothes.

We went into Saks and she took me up to the lingerie department. She said she was a sucker for lingerie. When she took off her dark glasses people turned to stare – Americans are less inhibited about this than the English. She was no Jane Fonda but she was famous enough, particularly over here, where she had done a lot of TV work. I stood next to her proudly, rifling through the racks of lacy underwear. An elderly assistant, with a hairy mole on her chin, came up and hovered ingratiatingly.

'You need any help, Miss Dune?' she simpered. 'We haven't seen you in a while.'

'I've been in London this summer,' said Lila. 'This is my pal, Jules Simpson.'

'Sampson, actually,' I said.

The woman smiled at me unctuously, as if mine were a famous name too. Lila selected a silk slip, in cream and peach, for herself. I looked at the price tag; I suddenly thought of *Gertie*, and our grant being cut.

Lila turned to me impulsively. 'You'd look great in aquamarine,' she said, and grabbed one from the rack. It was the palest blue slip, as light as dandelion fluff. She laid it over my arm; I stroked it, lovingly.

We went into two cubicles. Through the wall I heard Lila moving around as she undressed. I felt curiously aroused. I knew, then, that there was something of Lila in me, the part of me that flowered for Trev, the part of me that nobody else knew. The *me* who threw aside her jeans and t-shirt and trussed herself up in satin and stockings. I didn't want to think about it. I undressed and wriggled into the slip.

'Can I come in?'

The door opened and Lila appeared. Standing together in the cubicle, we inspected ourselves in the mirror.

I felt short of breath, as if I had been running. I looked at her reflection. She was ravishing – tanned and somehow riper than I had expected. Womanly. Though she was fine-boned, her breasts were surprisingly heavy. There was a sheen of perspiration in the cleft of her cleavage. Close-up, I could see the freckles on her shoulderblades when she turned to look at herself from the side. I could feel the warmth of her skin.

'You look fabulous,' she said.

How could she say that? Next to her, I looked pasty. She drained me. It was too cruel. Next to her fruity, slightly over-ripe sluttishness – she even had a ladder in her tights – I looked lean and sexless. Next to her snub, kittenish face my own looked pinched. My mouth seemed to have shrunk. Maybe she was thinking the same thing, because she said, 'Barbara Hershey, she had silicone shots.'

'What?'

'In her lips, when she played Mary Magdalene.' She grimaced. 'Sounds ikky, doesn't it?' She peered closer at herself. 'I'll need some tucks soon. This guy I know, he's divorcing his wife. I said to him, "Has she had plastic surgery?" And he said to me, "Sure, I've cut up all her credit cards."' She laughed, and turned to inspect me. 'No, that looks really fabulous. You're going to drive some guy nuts in that. Wear it when you get into the sack. You have someone special in London?'

I was just about to reply when she gave a little yelp, and moved closer to the mirror.

'Holy shit!' she wailed. 'Just take a look at this zit. What the fuck am I going to do?'

She started talking about her skin, and how a zit could play hell with continuity. Weight gain was even worse.

'On *Three Steps to Heaven* I was involved in this destructive relationship, my personal life was falling apart, so I started eating. One scene, I opened a door weighing 120 pounds and came out the other side at 135. See, there was a month between the shots.'

With Lila, conversation was a one-way business. So I never got to reply to her question; I never told her about Trev. At the time I didn't mind; in fact, I needed to keep a part of myself separate. Trev was my other life and I wanted to hold onto it, to stop it draining away and becoming Lila's. Besides, she would find out that he was the author of *Use Me* and that would be embarrassing.

Call it chance, call it what you will. Blame it on the pimple. For if she hadn't seen the pimple, I might have told her about Trev. None of this would have happened, and I wouldn't be here.

Lila bought me the slip.

'You can't!' I protested.

'Don't be a *dork*,' she laughed.

She bought several things for herself. Making a purchase put her into top gear, the shopper's high. Gathering momentum like an alcoholic after the first drink she swept through Saks, buying shoes and blouses for herself and putting them on her charge card. I followed in her slipstream, the recipient of her rhetorical questions: 'Isn't this just *darling*?' 'You think tartan drowns the features?' 'Maybe this is too goddam straight, too Mary Tyler Moore?' 'How about these hokey little hats?' She never listened to my answers.

Others were swept along too. Celebrities are like the Pied Piper, a procession gathers behind them. Soon she had the floor manager, an anxious assistant, a bearded paparazzi photographer alerted by God-knows-who to her presence in the store, and a fellow customer who wanted Lila's autograph for her sister in Pittsburg. Once you are famous all the world's a stage, and you can never be alone. You are watched from all sides; pick your nose and it's in Suzy's column in the *Post*. Even when people don't stare they become stagier, inspecting the racks of clothes with extra interest, a-bristle with self-consciousness.

I noticed this even more when she took me to lunch. We went to a fancy place called Chez Hortense, up on 63rd and Lex. Canopy, carpet on the sidewalk, trees in tubs, the lot.

Lila was welcomed like royalty. The maître d's face wore the same glazed simper with which I was becoming familiar. The restaurant was packed; in fact, there was a queue for tables. As we proceeded, however, the waves parted for us as they did for Moses. The staff grovelled. Maybe some customers were flung out in the middle of their meal, because miraculously an empty table materialised. A waiter, flicking his wrists ostentatiously for our benefit, spread a new pink tablecloth, laying it with a flourish, a courtier's bow, like Walter Raleigh laying down his cloak. There was a hush amongst the other diners, who then went on talking with heightened animation. Lila's presence made everybody artificial. She took off her dark glasses and shook out her hair. The maître d' came over with the menus, his face perspiring.

'Hi, Jacques,' she said. 'How're you doing?'

'Very well, madame,' he said. 'It's a pleasure to have you with us.'

As he passed me the menu he bowed, slightly; despite my low-key appearance he presumed I must be important. Glamourised by my companion, I was included in the magnetic field of fame. I felt warmer, sexier. We all warmed ourselves at the fireside.

Lila, I'd long ago realised, knew nothing about food. Diets, yes, but not food. She carelessly ordered a Caesar salad and lit a cigarette. I ordered turbot glazed with a *velouté de morilles et oseille*. For a moment I felt the superior; sometimes our relationship shifted like this. Sometimes it was I myself who rose on the see-saw.

The place was full of rich women nibbling at their lunch and leaving most of it on their plate. They looked like Trump Tower inhabitants: the eat, drink and remarry brigade. They had lacquered blonde hair, bamboo-thin arms and the stretched, vulpine look of the face-lifted. Lila drank Diet Coke and I drank half a bottle of chilled Chardonnay. The fish was delicious. Lila told me a slanderous story about Micky Rourke and as the meal progressed we grew giggly.

'I wish I had a sister,' she said, sighing.

'So do I,' I said. 'I've only got a brother and he's a boring accountant in Hull. He's a closet gay but he hasn't even got the oomph to come out. He was terrified of my father, but even though my Dad's dead now I think he's lost the nerve. He sublimates it with DIY. He channels his emotions into grouting. My family, we're experts on sublimation.'

'You're the nearest I've got to one,' she said.

A sister, she meant. 'Really?' I asked, blushing.

'You make me laugh. You're a pal.'

I took out the pack of Salems I kept for her, and passed her one. The waiter pounced with a flaming lighter. He lit her Salem, and then he lit my Winston. She blew out a jet of smoke and turned to me. 'I only had dolls. I only played pretend.'

'So did I,' I replied. 'Maybe that's why we're actresses, we both played pretend.'

Just then, somebody came up to our table. In New York, people are bolder about interrupting. She was a bony, over-dressed woman, rattling with gold like a jailer. She asked if Lila could autograph her menu.

'I just adore your pictures,' she gushed. 'Know my favourite? It's *Heads you Win*, when you played the cheerleader who had that accident. When they put you in the back-brace I cried like a baby.'

How strange it was to be famous! Nobody talked normally to you; instead, they offered you information about yourself. They offered homage, they fed Lila their own versions of her, their reflections of her in a distorting mirror. Lila was given this weird, warped view of reality; no wonder she sometimes freaked out. Nobody offered their own lives, or their real opinions.

I was thinking this when the woman turned to me. 'Hey, you guys related?'

Suddenly I put on a hick, Appalachian accent – one of the favourites in my repertoire. 'Sure,' I said. 'Can't you tell? I'm her kid sister, Loralee.' *Let's play pretend*. I turned to Lila. 'We growd up together, didn't we, sis? Our Lila, she was always the good-lookin' one, you couldn't get her away from that damn mirror, she was always mussin' up her hair this way and that, and boy did she get the fellas, they was around our place like bees round the honeypot, did she play them local hillbillies along!' I paused, for breath. Lila was staring at me, her eyes wide. She clapped her hand to her mouth, her chunky rings glinting. 'It was poor ol' me who had the zits,' I said, gathering speed. 'Poor ol' me, her little sis. Some people, they said she was crazy, she'd get into nothin' but trouble, I mean one day she took all my dolls and she pulled off their heads 'cause they were prettier than she was, she didn't want no competition.' I took a breath. 'But there was nobody in the neighbourhood prettier than our Lila, boy was I jealous!' My voice rose. 'Sometimes, you know somethin'? Sometimes I wanted to kill her!'

There was a silence. Startled, the woman said, 'Well, how about that?'

When she had gone, Lila turned to me. 'OK,' she drawled. 'You got the part. Now let's fuck.' We both collapsed with giggles.

When we left the restaurant, she linked my arm. 'Know what?' she said. 'You're really good!'

'I know,' I replied.

'Loralee,' she whispered in my ear, spluttering with laughter.

When Randy opened the door of the car he raised his eyebrows at me. 'What you two been doing?' he hissed. He thought she had been hitting the bottle again.

As the days passed I helped Lila more and more with her part. She and I had few moments together, but when we did I said we should work on our feelings about motherhood. Neither of us had kids; both of us wanted them. How could we perform, as mothers? (Note the *we*; I was involving myself in this, why not?) I had only once, briefly, played a mother: I had twin boys in a commercial for instant mashed potato, but you can't explore a lot in thirty seconds, especially when the twins and I loathed each other on sight.

Lila adored kids and animals. In fact, I think she preferred them to men, they didn't threaten her or mess her up. However, she only had the most vague and sentimental idea of motherhood, culled from watching too many afternoon soaps. She had guested, once, on an appallingly sickly mini-series about a couple whose kids all seemed to suffer from incurable diseases, but she hadn't been able to do much work on her part as she was having a nervous breakdown at the time.

In *Bump* her screen son was played by a precocious brat called Forrest. He had just played Harrison Ford's son in a highly successful weepie about child custody and he was bumptious as hell. He upstaged Lila, showing off to the crew; he crept into her trailer and nicked her secret supply of Fudge-Covered Oreos.

'Explore your ambivalent feelings towards him,' I urged her.

'My what?'

'Use your aggression. He might be your son but he's making your life purgatory. Listen, Mary Lou, he's trying to ruin your chance of being a woman, of fulfilling yourself. It's very Oedipal. It's not just your candy he's stealing, it's your chance of happiness with another man.'

Those last weeks of November we were filming in Mary Lou's apartment on Riverside Drive. Maizin Productions had

110

rented two adjoining flats, one for the cast and crew, the other for filming. We all mingled more easily here; the stars weren't separated from the rest of us, out of bounds in their trailers. Lila and I had more time together, sitting in her dressing room overlooking a spectacular view of the Hudson River. I started inventing bits of business for her to do, during the scenes with her son.

'When you're crossing to the kitchen,' I said, 'and his robot toy's lying on the floor, why not give it an irritable kick?'

When they shot the scene, that was what she did. Chuck, the director, was delighted.

When she went for a costume change she whispered to me, 'Hey honey, what'd I do without you?' I blushed with pleasure.

The next day I had an even better idea; it was so bold that it surprised even myself. They were going to shoot a breakfast scene between Mary Lou and her son; I had been sitting at the table as they set up the shot, and the idea came to me whilst I was staring vacuously at the cereal packet.

When they let me go I hurried across to Lila's dressing room and knocked on the door. Irma was sitting beside Lila, going through her morning's mail with her; Rodney was teasing Lila's hair into the screen equivalent of a rumpled, early-morning look – in other words, it appeared as if Lila were just off to the opera.

Orson, the dog, growled at me. Irma glared at me and turned back to Lila, showing her a letter. 'Darling,' she said, 'they want you to open a shopping mall in Tucson.'

I leaned over to Lila and whispered in her ear, breathing the fumes of her hairspray. 'Before they call you, I've got an idea.'

I met her in the corridor. When I told her, she gasped. I said I'd had the idea from the champagne incident, the one she had forgotten. I told her not to do it in rehearsal but during the first take. 'Watch their faces then,' I smiled, and added, 'Think angry. Think of him stealing your Oreos.'

They rehearsed, and then they set up for a take. Down went

111

the clapperboard and Lila began the scene as expected. She poured milk onto her son's Cheerios whilst Forrest said his lines. They were having a conversation about her boyfriend.

Forrest said, 'He only wants to date you because you're rich.'

'He doesn't,' replied Lila. 'He wants to date me because I'm me.' (It was that sort of script.) Her voice rose. 'Will you stop standing between me and my one chance of happiness!'

And then she did it. She lifted up his bowl of Cheerios and emptied it over his head.

Forrest gasped, spluttering. He was dripping with milk. The crew froze; Chuck stared, and then frantically gestured to the cameraman to keep rolling.

Genuinely upset, Forrest struggled to his feet. 'What the fuck are you doing, you stupid bitch!' he shouted, close to tears. Lila just shrugged, and went into the kitchen.

'Cut,' said Chuck. He turned to the AD. 'Print it. We'll use it.' He beamed – a rare sight. The crew let out its collective breath; someone laughed.

The table was mopped; Forrest was mopped. Lila came back from the kitchen and Chuck put his arm around her. 'That was truly great, Lila. Beautiful. Risky, but that's what we're about.'

They couldn't do another take anyway, because wardrobe would have had to launder Forrest's clothes. Lila apologised to him, and started picking Cheerios out of his hair. He pulled away. Rodney came up to him.

'Let's get that hair washed,' he said.

Forrest muttered, 'Anybody told her she's getting old age spots on her hands?'

Each day of shooting, like each day of school, has a different quality. Lila wouldn't have noticed this sort of thing; she only noticed what affected her. I, however, am one of life's observers, and my job on *Bump* gave me plenty of time for that. Something shocking energises a crew, it revs them up. The rest of that day's shooting went wonderfully, there was a buzz in the air and a new feeling of respect for Lila. She was obviously a more inventive actress than they had thought. Nobody knew it had been my creation, not hers.

And it was Lila who posed for publicity stills – Lila who got all the credit. The unit publicist had made some phonecalls, and somebody arrived from the *News* to interview her, soon after we wrapped. I paused, listening, on my way out.

'I've been exploring my ambivalent feelings,' she said into the outstretched microphone. 'See, Mary Lou has this dichotomy about being a mother and being a lover, and that makes her express it aggressively towards her son.' I looked at Lila, but she didn't see me. I genuinely think that she had forgotten the whole idea was mine. 'I've been putting in some work on motherhood, I've gotten to understand a lot about myself, how to face up to these feelings. On the other hand, I'm very instinctive, as an actress, so I knew I had to express them the only way I knew how – violently.'

I went out, slamming the door behind me.

I felt restless and angry that night; maybe I should have analysed my own ambivalent feelings. Lila had betrayed me. Or, to be exact, she had rubbed me out. My scalp itched, from wearing that damn wig; every night I had to wash my hair. I needed to talk to Trev but, when I dialled, all I got was his voice on my answerphone. 'It's silent here, silent as the grave, but if you want to speak to me just leave a message – '

I slammed the receiver down on him in mid-sentence but this was only marginally satisfying. Cursing him, I wondered what he was doing. I had a horrible suspicion that this hush-hush project was female. I had been away a month – an eternity for a bloke like Trev. I had never known a man so highly sexed. He once told me that if he swallowed a couple of tablets of speed and six pints of scrumpy he could screw non-stop for forty-eight hours. When I closed my eyes I saw him fucking a spreadeagled girl, his cock grown as long as a broom handle.

I paced around my room like a caged animal. My surroundings were utterly featureless: a blue armchair, a reproduction desk with a cigarette burn on it. They had put me in the most anonymous hotel in New York. I don't think I could even find it again, if I looked. It was somewhere on E 39th Street. My few clothes were shut away in the cupboard. It was as if I didn't live here, as if I didn't exist.

I was the ghostly presence through which other lives were lived; I was like a piano tuner, toiling away unseen so that a virtuoso could play my instrument to tumultuous applause. Rage rose in my throat, choking me. I felt ridiculously hurt. I had a shower, washed my hair and dried it, dressed up in my one good suit and went out.

During the past month I had been taken out to a few places. One of the make-up girls had invited me to her birthday brunch at the Carnegie Deli; I had looked up an old friend of Rob, the guy who had played the Big Mac in *Gertie*, and he had taken me to a Mexican place in the Tribeca. An ex-colleague of my agent had taken me out for sushi, an experience I didn't care to repeat. Tonight I wanted to pamper myself; after all, I had the money. So, on impulse, I hailed a cab and went to Chez Hortense.

I went into the restaurant and looked around. Fringed pink lights glowed at the tables; it looked more seductive at night. A pianist played *Ain't Misbehavin'*. It was only seven o'clock and the place was still nearly empty.

Just then the maître d' hurried up. It took me a moment to realise that it was the same man as before; his features seemed rearranged. He glanced at me coldly.

'You have a reservation?'

I shook my head. 'Can I have a table for one – '

'We're fully booked.' He turned away, brusquely. He hadn't recognised me.

Just then the waiter passed, the one who had been so friendly before; he looked straight through me. Stung, I turned away. Without Lila I was a nobody. Worse – I was invisible.

I walked slowly down the street. It had been raining; a bus thundered past, splashing my legs. No wonder New York was a city full of paranoids. No wonder lone men in parkas took pot

114

shots at celebrities. There's a bank somewhere on 6th Avenue which has a curved steel door; at the end of the day it rolls around closed. The whole city suddenly seemed to do that, to revolve around and close me out, presenting me with its reverse side, blind metal. The other side of that open, eager welcome I had when accompanied by Lila.

I caught the first bus that came along. Inside it resembled a day-release centre. Everyone seemed odd, but in a mild, tranquillised way. Some buses were like this. A woman wearing knitted cobwebs swivelled her head from side to side, making clicking sounds with her tongue. A bald man, who stank of wine, was measuring two pieces of string and arguing to himself. His feet were bandaged in about eight pairs of socks. Why do lunatics always wear so much on their feet, I wondered? Or else nothing at all.

I got out when I recognised the Flatiron building, a landmark I remembered. I walked for a while along the lower end of Broadway, the dark end without the theatres. Buildings vast as warehouses loomed up on either side; I was in the wholesale garment district. Through windows I saw shadowy racks of clothes, waiting for women to put them on and pretend to be someone different. My feet ached.

It was that night, when I seethed with bitterness, that I first wondered what it would be like if I dressed up as Lila. It was just a passing fancy then, nothing more. But I remember the moment. I had gone into a late-night grocery store to buy some cigarettes – I had been smoking heavily recently. I stood behind an old black guy who was buying a coffee. When he took it, he produced a bottle of Brut aftershave from his pocket, poured some in, and left the shop.

'What's he doing?' I asked the store owner. But he was Korean and didn't respond; maybe he didn't know what I was talking about.

It was one of those nights in New York when you only meet loonies. I walked along, feeling part of some vast, crazy detritus. It can happen so fast, in that city. In the morning you're working on a $20 million movie, giving

115

advice to a world-famous movie star. A few hours later you are flotsam.

At that point I became aware of some stretch limos parked across the street. I was somewhere near 13th Street, and over the road I could see a roped-off doorway guarded by heavies. There was a long line of people, waiting to either be admitted or turned away. Later I learnt that it was some night club – Nell's, I think. Looking across the traffic I thought: what if I wore my Lila wig and arrived in a limo, would I get in? What if I used my Lila voice – girlish, but with that gravelly edge of a smoker? I had practised it, you see. I had been watching her. I had been watching all the cast and crew, in fact. I could do the location manager's Southern drawl, the publicist's Bryn Mawr, the warm brown tones of one of the actors, Joss Ridley, an up-and-coming guy who had just worked with Dennis Quaid and told everybody what hellraisers they were together. But mostly I had been watching Lila.

I ended up in a place in the Village that served Cajun cooking. I hadn't a clue what Cajun meant, then, but the place looked friendly and I needed that. Nobody told me it was fully booked; in fact it was practically empty. There were checked tablecloths, and black-and-white Marlene Dietrich photos on the walls. Out the back was a yard; a spotlight shone on the slimy fallen leaves.

A waiter called Clayton served me. He told me his name early on; most gays, I've noticed, seem to be nice towards a woman on her own. Maybe because they know what it's like to be lonely. He had a neat, blond moustache. He brought me something pan-seared in a burning sauce, and asked what I did. For a moment I thought of pretending – I could be anything in the world – but that would have made me feel lonelier. Besides, he said he was an actor, resting between jobs, so I told him.

'It's a tough business,' he said. 'This is a tough city. If you've made it, it's the most exciting place on earth. If you haven't, you don't exist.'

He said his last job had been the voice-over for a llama in

an ad for the Bronx Zoo. Before that he had been in a mini-series called *High*, about a detox clinic up in the Rockies.

'I played a heroin addict whose mother was an alcoholic lesbian,' he said. 'They cancelled the second series.'

'Actually I'm only standing-in,' I said. 'For Lila Dune.'

Several of his friends were stand-ins, he said. Some were failed actors; some were budding actors, hoping to be spotted. 'But who spots a stand-in? It's kind of a dead-end job but it's also seductive, because the money's good.' He knew Tom Hanks's stand-in, and Charlie Sheen's. 'They get to become some kind of doppelganger,' he said. He was an intelligent bloke; he'd majored in philosophy, he told me, in Athens, Ohio, before getting stage-struck. 'They think they're going to get buddy with the star, they're going to go to all the parties. But some stars, they don't say a word to them all through the shoot, they wouldn't recognise them in the street.'

'It's not like that with Lila,' I said. I gazed out at the yard. A single tree rose out of the greasy sediment of leaves. I said, more to convince myself than him, 'We're getting to be pals.' I thought of our giggly lunch at Chez Hortense.

'That's what a girl I knew thought, with Faye Dunaway. She used to buy her cigarettes for her, she used to run errands.'

'This is different!'

His voice rose to a camp falsetto. 'Lordy Lord, we're talking one of my all-time favourite movies! We're talking *All About Eve*!'

I looked out at the tree-trunk, glistening in the spotlight. Beyond the high brick wall a siren wailed. Every minute of the night, it seemed, sirens wailed.

'What do you think of Lila?' I asked.

Like most people in the profession he had a poor opinion of her acting ability; in fact, he said, she couldn't act at all.

'I can,' I said loudly.

He didn't hear my boast; he was fetching me a coffee. When he came back we played that game where you think of what sort of car, or animal, or book somebody would be. We did it with Lila. I thought: it must be strange to be

117

famous, because people who haven't met you can play games about you.

'Car?' I asked.

'Pink Cadillac convertible,' he said.

'With something wrong with its gaskets.'

He laughed. 'Animal?'

'Warthog,' I said. 'Just kidding.'

'I know, she's a Saluki.'

'Isn't that a motorbike?'

'That's Suzuki,' he said. 'Movie?'

'*Sunset Boulevard*,' I said.

'Bitchy bitchy,' he said, smiling.

Give her a few years, I thought, and she would be cracking up like Gloria Swanson. She would be lying on her couch with liver-spots on her hands, Forrest had noticed them already. She would be surrounded by photos of herself, hundreds of celluloid lies.

'We're just a teeny bit jealous,' he said. 'Aren't we?'

He sat down next to me. 'Mary Pickford had a stand-in. She had her for years and years. She was more than a stand-in; she was a friend, secretary, confidante. One day Mary Pickford's offered this part but they want her young, that's how her public sees her. Face-lifts were just starting then – this was back in the forties. So Pickford sends her stand-in to a clinic in Beverly Hills, to have a face-lift. In those days it took six weeks; it was a difficult operation. So the stand-in had the operation, and after six weeks . . .' He paused. 'They took the bandages off.'

'What happened?' I whispered.

'It was fine! The stand-in looked wonderful! So Pickford goes to the clinic and has the operation herself. And after six weeks they take off the bandages.'

He stopped, sighed, and looked around the empty res-taurant.

'What happened?' I yelped. 'Go on.'

He looked at me, pausing for dramatic effect. He lined up the tabasco bottle, next to the salt.

'For Christ's sake!' I nudged him.

'When they unwound the bandages,' he said, 'they found that they'd severed a nerve in her face. Just one side. For the rest of her life Mary Pickford had a kind of half-smile, like this.' He did a rictus grin. 'She became a recluse. The stand-in stayed with her and looked after her, until she died.'

I walked back along Christopher Street. Like stars, the gays come out at night. It was eleven o'clock and the pavements were crowded with men in black leather trying to pick each other up. They glinted like beetles in the street lights. Nobody looked at me. I was not just invisible as an actress, it appeared, but as a woman too. Men wearing Nazi caps jostled each other significantly; the street was criss-crossed with eye contact, like search lights in some war of which I had no part. A bondage shop declared, '*Come in! We're Open!*' In the window, dummies wore chains and masks; their black leather jockstraps were stuffed with newspaper.

I suddenly missed Trev, painfully. When I got back to my hotel room I phoned again, but I just got the answerphone. In England, it would be five in the morning. I undressed and climbed into bed. I missed his body but I missed the talk too. Clayton's story had disturbed me. It had lodged in me, like something bulky I couldn't digest. I wanted to talk to somebody English. Thoughts spring into your mind, don't they? Silly things like: what's happened to rissoles? Does nobody eat them any more or do we just call them something else, like *quenelles*? Or a man on the bus looks just like the little old geezer in *Last of the Summer Wine* and there's nobody to remind you of his name.

Things like that. I wanted to be reassured. I only had an inkling, then, of how homesick I would become. It just caught me at odd moments; I felt breathless, as if I had been winded. That was all. It passed soon enough. I turned off the light and went to sleep.

It doesn't pass, now. I feel it all the time. Sometimes it gets stronger, like one huge wave in a heavy sea, and then I'm engulfed. Everyone sits here like zombies; I suppose I do too. But inside my head it's chaos. There's no distractions, nothing to disperse it, so I sit here with my thoughts winding tighter and tighter until I want to scream. I want to scream out to her, that Jules of two years ago. She is lying on her hotel bed. In the cupboard hangs a bronze dress, not her style at all but she had bought it. She is already beginning her slow metamorphosis. She is wearing more make-up nowadays, too. She is starting to say 'candy' instead of 'chocolate', have you noticed? I can hardly remember Clayton now, but he mentioned *All About Eve*. I don't know about that. Sometimes it seems more like Jekyll and Hyde.

She gets up, unbuttons her jacket and climbs out of her skirt. She folds them neatly; she's always been obsessively tidy. People don't guess that, but then they don't guess a lot of things about her.

She stands there for a moment, in her Saks slip. The glow of the city, through the window, drains the colour from it. She strokes her breasts slowly, feeling the silk. She steps out of her briefs. In front of the mirror she piles up her hair and turns her head one way and then the other. She doesn't seem to care that the window blinds are open and the curtains tied back; she doesn't mind who is watching. In fact it turns her on. It always has. That is when she comes alive. That is why she's an actress. She strokes her belly, then she slides her hand down between her legs. She touches herself, through the Lila-silk. Nobody can see her; opposite, the offices are empty. She is alone in a vast, indifferent city. Danger lies ahead of her, but she has no idea what it is. I want to shout out to her: Get out! In this city of disguise and slippery illusions, in this violent, schizophrenic place where anybody can become anything, she is heading for disaster. I want to shout: Go back to England, before it's too late!

120

Four

I had violent dreams that night and woke up with a sense of foreboding. It had suddenly turned cold; even in my overheated hotel room I could feel it. There was a change in the air.

Down in the lobby two businessmen with early flights to catch were checking out; one of them looked at his watch and said, 'It's six below in Chicago.' He was enormously fat. I remember everything about that morning: the stiff new arrangement of gladioli, slanted like spears in their vase; the icy blast when the porter opened the door to take out their luggage.

Out in the street it was freezing and grey. The air clamped down like a steel lid. People walked by, muffled up anonymously; we lose our personalities in the cold. The bundles puffed past, exhaling breath. Steam rose up from the manholes, thicker than ever today. I walked briskly, up towards Lex. Between the offices, the Chrysler building slid into view. Sheathed in steel, it resembled a giant's hypodermic syringe; its needle was shrouded in mist.

Today we were filming in Rockefeller Plaza – a scene where Lila arrives in a cab to collect her son, who is ice-skating. When I arrived a crowd had already gathered. Dwarfed by the surrounding buildings, a row of flags hung limply around the sunken expanse of ice, which looked smooth and milky. For some reason Rockefeller Plaza made me uneasy; the four walls of buildings blocked me in, I felt both confined and exposed. Extras, wearing skates, sat around the rink nursing plastic cups of coffee; steam rose between their gloves.

I had my wig fitted, then I went into the wardrobe trailer.

Kelly, the wardrobe mistress, wrapped me in a thick, chestnut fur coat. It was fox or something, I didn't know anything about furs.

'Isn't it adorable!' she said. 'The furrier's getting a credit at the end of the picture, so I told him to send us two.' She grinned at me. 'See, someone thinks about you.'

Outside, an icy wind had started to blow. I pulled the fur around my face. Everywhere I looked, people stared; they even watched from the office windows. I huddled into my collar. After two weeks in the cocoon-like privacy of Mary-Lou's Riverside Drive apartment I felt unnerved, coming out into the open. I glimpsed Lila, hurrying into her motorhome. She was dressed in an identical fur coat. For once we didn't just look vaguely similar, we looked the same. In fact Bob, the AD, called out to me, 'We don't need you yet, Miss Dune!' before he suddenly realised his mistake.

The taxi-cab was parked near the rink. I was to get out of the cab and go over to my mark, beside the rink, where I was to wave at my son, trying to get his attention.

As simple as that. I climbed out of the cab, walked the few steps to the rink and stood there. A gust of wind blew my phoney blonde hair across my face. The sky had darkened; maybe it was going to snow. To one side of me the crowd was shunted back as the camera, on its crane, was wheeled back a few feet. I remember that. There were cops, too; they were stopping the traffic, way over the other side of the Plaza. The air was heavy yet blustery, a Tab can rolled past my feet. I remember the lights, shining on my face. They had to adjust them, because the sky had darkened. It was 9.30; the minutes ticked by. That morning I felt more like Lila than I had ever felt before. Maybe it was the fur coat wrapped around me, luxuriously tickling my cheek; both of us under the same skins. I remember the AD calling out, 'Raise your arm, honey.' I raised my arm, as if I was waving, and they shifted the second camera to get my face into shot. Beyond the buildings the traffic rumbled; it sounded like distant thunder.

And then, a split second before it happened, I saw something. It was just a tiny movement in the crowd opposite, on the far side of the rink; a tiny stir, like a finger in an ants' nest. I was aware of it, momentarily, and then I heard a faint, sharp crack. I had never heard it before, in real life, but the moment I heard it I knew exactly what it was.

It passed by me, very close. I cowered, my arms around my face. I heard the whistle of it, and then a curious, resonant sound, almost a plop, like a pebble dropping into a pond. The bullet had entered the rear end of the taxi-cab. Over the other side of the rink, somebody screamed; there was a scuffling in the crowd. I saw a cop, running, and then another.

Over our side it took a minute for anyone to realise what had happened. In real life it always takes much longer or shorter than you think; time is thrown out of joint. I think I was the only one who knew what it was. I turned and looked at the cab. The yellow metal was pierced by a small, scorched hole. I thought: it looks like an anus, and then I started giggling. I was shaking so much that I slid to the ground, I literally crumpled.

Maybe I was hysterical; maybe they thought I had been shot. I remember wondering if I was acting it well enough. Would I fall this way? I saw myself shot again and falling, more gracefully this time, getting it right. Were they going to let me do it properly?

Somebody had tried to shoot me, somebody in the crowd. Suddenly I felt furious.

What an impertinence! It seems a funny word to choose, but that was what I felt. Fancy shooting at me! I giggled more wildly. Poor old stand-in, I thought. The only time I can get shot is when somebody uses a fucking gun.

I suppose some of the crew had realised what had happened, by now. Bob hurried over.

'You OK?' he asked, helping me to my feet. I felt as ungainly as a new-born calf. The row of extras was staring at me, from the rink.

'Sure you're OK?' he asked again. A cop was running

towards us; he seemed to be miles away. Bob's face shrank and blurred, and I felt myself bumping against him as I slid down, between his arms.

The next thing I remember, I was sitting in the production trailer. The continuity girl, Corey, was gazing at me, her jaws working. I smelt the spearmint of her bubble gum. I laughed, weakly. I decided to play it jokey and noble.

'Some people'll do anything to get noticed,' I said.

'Huh?'

'You know, hiring a gunman – '

'Honey,' she replied, 'he was after Lila.'

It took a moment for this to sink in. Actually, it wasn't such a surprise. I guess I had known it all along.

I looked round. There were other people in the trailer, watching me curiously. Bob, Rodney, Kelly. Lila was there, too. She was sitting in a cloud of smoke, hunched in her fur coat. She looked like a hunted animal. Her face was grey, her mascara smudged.

'Jesus Christ!' she said. 'You OK?' She sat down beside me, wedged on the seat. She put her arm around me. 'Want one of these?' she asked, fumbling in her other pocket for her cigarettes. Her hand was trembling.

'I'm fine,' I said.

'You look terrible,' she said. She put the cigarette tenderly between my lips. Kelly leant forward and lit it. I leant against the thick fur of Lila's coat.

'Jesus Christ,' said Lila again. Her voice was flat; she was in a state of shock. Irma came in, then, and took her away. Somebody told me later that she had gone on a crisis visit to her shrink.

Filming was abandoned for the day. The cops asked me some questions. A reporter arrived, but when he heard it wasn't Lila who had narrowly escaped death, just a stand-in, his interest evaporated. I learnt, later, that the would-be assassin had been caught trying to leave down the subway. He was just some nutter who had escaped from a mental hospital, just a

124

screwball with a grudge against the famous. America breeds them; they flourish in the darkness of obscurity like poisonous fungi. They fester with the injustice of it all. Seething, they lie on their hotel beds whilst outside the window other people's names are up in lights.

IMAGINE, said the plaque. One pot shot and you can alter history. Squeeze the trigger and, hey presto! Instant fame!

Back in my hotel room I pulled off my tights and washed my grazed knee. Nobody had noticed that I had hurt myself when I fell. They seemed far more worried about Lila and how it would affect her. Once he had seen I was the wrong person, watch the Magic Disappearing Journalist! Lila wasn't trembling for me, but for herself.

Patting my legs dry, I suddenly boiled with fury. The dumb cow, the egocentric bitch! Didn't she realise that out there, in Rockefeller Plaza, it might have been me who had died for her? Me, Jules – the ultimate stand-in?

I took a cab down to the Village. It was lunchtime, and I needed to talk to somebody. I would go to the Cajun place and tell Clayton about my brush with death. Funnily enough, I suddenly felt manic. Everything sprang at me, vividly, as I looked out of the window of the cab. I started giggling, making up little Manhattan haikus. *The Lebanese taxi driver hawks and spits as his passenger tries to make herself understood.* I watched the passing office blocks. *Handsel, delivering pizzas, loses his way in the forest of an atrium.* We bounced over the potholes; inside the cab, somebody had torn a hole in the plastic seat, revealing its fluffy entrails. Over the driver's impassive shoulders I grimaced at his photo, hanging from the dashboard on his licence card. Above his printed name: MOHAMMED IBRAHIM SHABAZZ, his swarthy face glared. How differently would you react, I thought, if I were Lila? But Lila was stupid, *stupid.* Why should her loss to the world be any greater than mine? Why should it get the headlines? She couldn't make up haikus, she couldn't notice anything beyond the end of her own stupid snub nose. I had more intelligence in my little finger.

125

I got out at Greenwich Avenue and walked past a row of shops. *The ash lengthens on the Korean grocer's cigarette as he hoses his salads.* I turned up Christopher Street, past a homosexual gauleiter festooned with chains. *Under the rusting fire escape a lone gay whistles for a mate.* I sauntered along, swinging my handbag. I had acted well that morning, hadn't I? I had acted being shot. Now I was being shot for real, the camera panning around the street and then tracking me as I walked along, my haikus in voice-over. I was a kookie Village resident, a poetess fought over by six men. All around the block the traffic had been stopped. Trailers jammed the side streets and the lights flared on me, just me.

By daylight the Cajun restaurant looked smaller and shabbier, as if I had dreamed it. I went inside and sat down. I couldn't see Clayton. A waitress came up. When I asked her, she said he had gone.

'He had a call from LA,' she said. 'He flew out this morning. He's doing a Diet Pepsi commercial.'

My back was covered with hair. It had been growing for weeks but I hadn't noticed it till now. A girl was bending over me. 'Quick!' I hissed to her. 'Pull them out! I'm appearing in a movie with Lila Dune, what's she going to say?' Pink light glowed; the blinds were pulled down. 'She hasn't got any,' I said. 'She's all smooth.' I lay, a monster. I was a werewolf. The sign said *Dianne's Discount Body Waxing.* The girl was wrenching out my hairs with a huge pair of pliers but it didn't hurt. Even as she pulled them out, I could feel new ones growing. Inside I was filled with a knotted, evil wad of hair and it was poking out all over my body, like the entrails inside the taxi seat.

When I woke it was dark. By the frequent clangs of the manhole cover I knew that it was the rush hour. My mouth was dry. It took me a while to come to my senses. I lifted the phone and dialled London, but Trev wasn't in. The bastard, he was never in. It must be eleven o'clock, over there. I had eaten lunch at some point, and before that somebody had tried to shoot me. There was nobody to listen to me.

126

I got up unsteadily, had a shower, and dressed in the silk slip and a tight woolly dress I had bought at Bloomie's. I did consider the bronze dress but I hadn't the nerve. I put on my high heels and made up my face with care.

I outlined my lips and then filled them in with glistening crimson. Barbara Hershey had plumped up her lips, for Mary Magdalene. Pouting at my reflection, I layered on the mascara. Then I fetched my diaphragm and inserted it. I remembered Kelly, stitching one of Lila's dresses and telling me about hotel bars. 'You should start a relationship in the Warwick, because it's so sexy,' she had said. 'Dark and sexy. And when it's got to end, go to the Plaza because it's so damn public he can't start beating up on you.'

I took a cab to Sixth Avenue, got out at the Warwick and went into the bar. She was right; the place was so dark that I stumbled as I entered. All I could make out was the black bulk of businessmen and some spotlit bowls of peanuts. It's changed now, they have redecorated it. But it was like that, then.

I sat down and ordered a vodka and tonic. Piano music played faintly from some place or other, I didn't care to look. I took out a cigarette and lit it with a steady hand. My heart pounded. I knew it was only a matter of time. I felt miles away from my body.

A man was looking at me. He was sitting at the next table. I couldn't make out his features but that was probably all for the best. I held his gaze, smiling at him. I willed him to come over. I could do something, couldn't I? I could do this. Tonight, in the dark, I was as desirable as Lila. I could make a man do anything.

He smoked. That was a promising sign, he must be from out of town. Hardly any men in New York, except film crews, smoked any more. I watched him stub out his cigarette, and pause. He tapped his finger on his briefcase, beside him on the seat. He was thinking. I finished my drink.

I willed him, with all my concentration. He waited a

127

moment, then he picked up his briefcase and walked across to my table.

'Hi,' he said. 'You waiting for somebody?'

I shook my head.

'May I join you?' he asked.

I was perspiring in my wool dress. But then so was he. Now he was beside me I could see that he was a broad, fleshy man. Not too bad-looking, in fact. While the waiter fetched our drinks he introduced himself. 'Marvin Scales,' he said, shaking my hand. Then he chuckled. 'But there's nothing fishy about me.'

'I'm Jo-Jo,' I replied, without thinking. I knew a Jo-Jo once but I didn't have time to remember who she was.

He sold hearing aids. He called them audio facilitators or something. It was all microchips nowadays, apparently. He had some in his briefcase the size of pinheads. He came to New York five days a month and stayed at the Warwick. He called New York 'the Big Apple'.

'And what's your line of business, Jo-Jo?' he asked. 'Let me guess. You're a model.'

I smiled mysteriously. 'I do whatever I'm asked.' I spoke with an American accent; I didn't want him to know anything about me.

Thank God he was a drinker too. There aren't so many of them left, either. He ordered another bourbon for himself and another vodka and tonic for me. I began to feel swimmy. He told me how many thousands of miles he had travelled that year, you needn't know how many, I didn't listen. He said he wasn't paid for his job, he was paid for sitting around in goddam hotel rooms all by himself for nine months a year.

'That's a pretty dress, Jo-Jo,' he said. He stroked my arm. 'You're a very attractive woman.' He put his hand on my thigh, heavily. Through the wool, he felt the knob of my suspender clip. His hand lay there, massaging it thoroughly. 'Very attractive.' His voice was husky; he cleared his throat.

I smiled at him. In the dark, under the table, I took his hand and slid it under my skirt, up my thigh. He drew in his breath, sharply. His finger stroked my bare skin, above my stocking top.

'Boy, is this my lucky night,' he whispered, hoarsely.

We made our way across the bar. In the lobby, the light was bright. He was shorter than I thought, with a bulging belly. We avoided each other's eye as we waited for the lift. It seemed to take for ever. Finally there was a ping and the door slid open to reveal two couples in evening dress. They filed past us, smiling politely. We stepped in and stood like dummies, rising together to the twelfth floor. I could smell his cologne; it was sickly-sweet. I stared at the framed inspection certificate screwed to the wall, willing my lust not to drain away. We walked along the corridor to his room and he fumbled for the key.

Inside, I was relieved to see, the room was nearly dark. A recessed light glowed above the unmade bed. The curtains were closed. He hurried across to the bed and pulled up the covers; he must have taken a nap before he came downstairs. On the floor was an F.A.O. Schwartz carrier bag; perhaps he'd bought a present for his kids. In a few weeks, I suddenly realised, it would be Christmas.

'May I use your bathroom?' I asked.

'Please. Go ahead,' he said. We were both very polite.

In the bathroom I peed and then washed my hands, looking at my flushed face in the mirror. The woman I saw bore little resemblance to myself. She was breathing heavily; she looked coarse, and her mascara was smudged. In front of her, in a glass, was a strange man's toothbrush, orthodontic probe and another unknown instrument. This guy was heavily into dental hygiene.

I went back into the room. He was lying on the bed, stripped to his jockey shorts. He looked large and bald. His hand was on his cock; he rubbed it as he watched me. Maybe he didn't have a wife at all. Maybe anything. I paused, suddenly panic-stricken. Then I rallied, and tottered towards him on my high heels. I sat down on the bed.

'Allow me to introduce Marvin Junior,' he said in a tight, high voice. 'He's mighty pleased to make your acquaintance.'

For a moment I thought that his son was in the room. I swung round, but he pulled me back. A hand pushed down my head; his stout cock rubbed against my eye socket. I shifted, and took it into my mouth. It tasty faintly sour, but talcy too; he must have showered before he went down to the bar. Way behind me, he grunted. His buttocks rose rhythmically against my face; gagged by his cock, I could hardly breathe. He shifted, and there was a click as thank God he switched off the light.

American men were obsessed with oral sex; I had read enough Updike novels to realise that. My jaw ached as I worked away; my dress was hitched up around my waist. Inside my briefs his finger probed me in a desultory way; he wasn't much bothered with me. With his other hand he pushed my own hand around his balls, clamping it there, squeezing. His balls were large and surprisingly furry.

'Attaboy,' he yelped, in his baby voice. 'Attaboy. Go to it, go to it.' He spoke faster and faster, like a train gathering speed. Already he was whimpering, in spasms, as he regressed into baby talk. I manhandled him over so that he lay on top of me. He was very heavy. My dress was up around my neck now, half-smothering me; I spread my legs as he buried his face in my breast.

'May Marvin Junior pay a little visit now?' he asked, muffled.

I pressed his buttocks; his cock slid in, at last. At least he didn't want to kiss me; he sucked my breast loudly, breathing through his nose.

He gnawed my nipple until it hurt and I pushed his head away. He started fucking very fast, for a few moments I was plunged into oblivion. I ignored what he was whimpering; it sounded suspiciously like 'Mommy'. I just squeezed my eyes shut in the darkness and moved underneath him, I was muscular and vigorous, I was the best whore in New York. The cameras whirred; the crew was transfixed. Everyone was watching my supple body as I arched and fell beneath him. He was moaning helplessly, he was in my power.

I climaxed, in disappointingly faint waves, but he took no notice, hammering away until I started getting sore. Finally he came, groaning loudly and shouting, 'Dirty boy! Dirty boy!' He collapsed, his face buried in the pillow. He was suddenly, crushingly, heavy.

'Boy, will I sleep well tonight,' he muttered.

I paused for a moment, then slid out from under him. He was asleep already, his lips making small rubbery noises against the pillow.

I pulled down my dress, put on my shoes and crept out of the room, brushing my hair as I went. I took the lift down to the lobby. I was so shaky that, when it stopped, my legs buckled and I staggered for a moment before I regained my balance.

Lila didn't show up the next morning. I wondered what she had been doing the night before. Maybe she had freaked out; maybe she had gone on a massive bender. Maybe she had disguised herself and gone out into the city, to some anonymous bar, and picked up a strange man. Somebody who didn't know she was famous; a nobody, like the rest of us. And she had drunk so many vodkas she couldn't remember it the next day. Who knows? She was an unstable woman, and the shooting had thrown her off balance. It only took a little thing to topple her over.

I had one hell of a hangover, but I was sane and strong, wasn't I? *I* was reliable. So I took over her part – me, Julia Sampson. While the PA made frantic phone calls I was summoned to rehearse. I was the understudy, beckoned onto the stage because the star was indisposed. After all, they could trust me by now; it had even filtered through to Chuck that I had been helping Lila. I had made sure it had filtered through; I'm not stupid.

We were shooting a scene in Mary-Lou's lover's recording studio. He was a rock star, have I told you that? The movie had to be peppered with his dreadful songs. This was because

131

Grover Cain, the co-star, was a superannuated rock singer who was trying to make it in the movies. After all, Cher had done it. She'd got an Oscar too.

Anyway, he was recording a song and I had to barge in and accuse him of infidelity. I'd seen him with another woman (a hologram, in fact, courtesy of my son's interplanetary powers). It was a big scene. Totally asinine, but a big scene. Even the writer had turned up.

I knew the lines anyway. I knew the entire script by heart – what else do you think I had been doing, those long evenings? I had acted each scene, pacing my hotel room and gesticulating at the bedside table. I had spoken into the mirror, making my reflection weep. I had argued at it, like that bum had argued at the lamp-post. I had stood at the window, declaiming to the suffused jostle of skyscrapers, glimpsed between the slices of the buildings opposite; I had mouthed my anguish to the neon sign, way below, saying *Dianne's Discount Body Waxing*. I knew the part a bloody sight better than Lila did.

Chuck treated me with some deference that morning. For the first time he needed me – the acting me, not just a solid bulk to be positioned and lit. I was introduced to Grover, who had never taken a blind bit of notice of me until now. He shook my hand, his brown eyes spuriously sincere. They took me outside the door and I readied myself, breathing in Jules and finally breathing out Mary-Lou. The rusty old machinery turned, my God how long it had been. My skin tingled; for the first time in six months I was truly working.

'Cue the song,' called Chuck. 'And action!'

I strode through the door a tough businesswoman but suddenly vulnerable, a wounded woman afraid of losing both her lover and her son.

'Who was she?' I spat out. 'Who was she, you worm?'

Grover, in mid-song, stood at his microphone. 'Who was who, honey?'

'You know who I'm talking about!' I barged over, pushing him against the soundproofed walls. 'That woman you were jogging with in Central Park!'

'I wasn't jogging with nobody!' he protested.

Suddenly I ad-libbed, I couldn't bear not to. 'Don't you double-negative me!' I yelled. 'What do you mean, you runty little shit-head, you *were* with somebody!'

Grover stared at me, but then we heard Chuck laughing – an unexpected sound. They cut there and he beckoned over the writer, a small Jewish guy whose chief claim to fame was rewrites of *Miami Vice*. Chuck said to him, 'We'll use that.' He turned to me. 'I liked it. A whole lot. I loved that energy!'

I replied, 'What nobody understands is that Mary Lou is a strong, independent woman who's despising herself for her own impotence.'

He grinned. 'The *Hedda Gabler* of Riverside Drive.'

I smiled back at him. 'I knew you'd do her in the end.'

Soon after that, Lila arrived. Nobody seemed to know where she had been. She was hustled into make-up while we rehearsed the scene again, incorporating the new dialogue and building it up into a nice piece of screwball comedy, touching and playful. Even Grover, who had the acting ability of a bathroom sponge, surprised us all by making up a bit of business for himself. Just for a while there was a real creative fizz in the air – a rare sensation, on this project. The crew even overran their coffee break by a few minutes. I hadn't enjoyed myself so much for ages.

Then Lila came on. I had to move aside and let her get on with it. She took the amended script and inspected it, frowning.

'What the fuck's this double-negative?'

Drinking my coffee, I called over, 'It's like: I wasn't shooting at nobody.'

'Whadd'ya mean?' she asked.

'Which means, I must have been shooting at somebody.'

She stared at me. 'Why're you saying that?'

I shrugged. 'Just an example.'

We finished early that day and Lila dragged me off to her

133

nail salon. She seemed tense; she said she didn't want to be alone. It was down on Murray Hill, near my hotel; she said she had been going there for years and had a favourite girl called Timmi. It calmed her down, she said, having her nails done; it was so therapeutic.

Pinky's Fingernails was down on 37th, next to some fancy new condos. The sign said *Nail Sculpture*. We got out of the car, and Lila told me I should get my nails done too.

Inside it was hot. There was plastic panelling on the walls and trolleys of enamels in every shade of pink and crimson; they looked like miniature blood transfusions. At each trolley sat a Korean girl, waiting for custom like a concubine. They wore panne velvet and a lot of jewellery. They were chatting and giggling with each other; they were hardly older than children. 'These girls,' said Lila, 'they know the dirt about everybody.'

I pictured celebrities' mistresses, having their nails filed so they could tear their rivals' eyes out. They would claw each other like cats. Lila greeted Timmi affectionately and sat down. I was put into the seat next to her, and a child-bride called Marni or something asked me if I wanted linen or silk wrapping. She said it would make my nails beautiful and strong.

'You been in a fight?' she asked in her sing-song voice, lifting my hand and looking at the scar. Another girl came over. They sighed, like wind through dry grass.

'Silk's finer, honey,' said Lila, leaning over. 'But linen lasts longer.'

She had silk and I had linen, like some fairy story where she was the princess and I the serving maid. Marni filed my nails and then glued on featherlight squares of linen, layer after layer on each nail, building them up. As she worked on my hands I listened to Lila. She was talking to Timmi, who obviously adored her. In fact, the giggly female atmosphere seemed to suit Lila; deep down, I suspected that she preferred women to men – they were less harmful. Besides, she was like me, she didn't have much of a family, and these girls seemed

134

like little sisters to her. Lila was no snob; I'd noticed already that she was at her most relaxed with working-class girls – beauticians, make-up assistants. After all, that's where she came from herself – untwist fate and that's where she would have remained. She would be working in a beauty parlour and married to a Toyota salesman.

But she hadn't, had she? She was famous, and it had nearly cost her her life. Timmi was listening as Lila told her about yesterday's shooting, a drama from which I was by now totally excluded.

'These psychopaths,' she said, 'they're nuts. Jesus Christ, do they freak me out. Jodie Foster, Olivia Newton-John, all of us, we all get it. Like, these letters. Irma throws them in the garbage before I read them, but I know they've come, just by the look on her face. Some of them, they call my answering service. These fruits – sometimes they even got my personal number! I have to change it every few months. There's all that hate out there, you wouldn't believe.'

'Who could hate you?' asked Timmi, painting blood-red enamel onto Lila's nails. She mopped a drop that had smudged, because Lila's hand was unsteady.

'Someone out there, he wants to kill me,' said Lila.

'But you said they've taken him in.'

'If it's not him, it'll be someone else,' she said. 'There's always someone. Trouble is, you don't know who they are.'

She waited for a moment, until her nails were dry. I sat beside her, listening to my own girl's tinkling bracelets as she worked on me. Then Lila reached for her bag.

'From now on,' she said, 'I'm taking no chances.' She undid the clasp. 'This morning, Irma and I went shopping. I bought something that's going to make me feel a whole lot safer. A whole lot.'

Timmi looked in her handbag and gasped. I leaned over. Amongst the mess of make-up tubes and hairbrushes, half-buried in Lila's sluttish debris, nestled a pistol.

'Pretty, isn't it?' crooned Lila, as if it were a baby.

It was indeed pretty: a small, shiny Smith & Wesson. Its

handle was mother-of-pearl; it had a snub little shaft. So this was why she had arrived late for work.

'From now on,' said Lila, 'it's going to be right here, in my purse. And that's where it's going to stay.'

Some of the other girls came over to look. They sighed and tinkled. I remember thinking how indiscreet Lila was being – she would show anybody anything. That was her nature. They clustered around, ogling the gun; Lila looked like Snow White, surrounded by her dwarfs. She demonstrated the safety catch, clicking it open and closed. They tittered fearfully.

Lila closed her purse and I sat back in my seat. Marni asked me what colour I would like my nails. For a moment I didn't hear. My jaw was aching. I suddenly realised that last night I had been technically unfaithful to Trev.

'Choose a colour, honey,' said Marni.

I started, and looked at Lila's blood-red nails. 'The same as hers,' I said.

Five

The days passed. I got a card from Trev, postmarked Edinburgh. I couldn't read the date, it was smudged. The painting showed a skating man, from the National Art Gallery of Scotland. '*Pissing with rain. I'm pissed too. Robbie likes idea but he's pissed as a newt. Taking "carry oots" to his place. Miss you, my brainy little sassenack (?).*'

Why the *(?)*? Was he doubting his affection, or his spelling? Or my brains? Who was this Robbie, so suddenly intimate? Trev wouldn't go to an art gallery with a BBC producer. He wouldn't go to an art gallery at all, unless some girl took him. Besides, wasn't the BBC man called Bill?

My suspicions festered, but I was helpless. I wanted him here with me in New York, waiting in my hotel room at the end of the day. I wanted him to laugh with me at the dogged joggers and at the tracksuited fathers I saw in Central Park. They pushed strollers, briefly bonding with their babies whilst their wives stayed home, ordering up some brunch and kvetching to their girlfriends about co-dependent relationships. I missed the way he said 'diabolical'. I remembered how we had gone to a restaurant once, when he was wearing a borrowed suit for somebody's wedding. No waiters had appeared so he had pretended to be the maître d', ushering in customers. He had strolled round the tables taking orders.

Was another woman getting all this now? Something was up; I knew it. His postcards were too brief and bland; his absences from my flat too prolonged and unexplained for somebody who was supposed to be working on a script. But I was four thousand miles away; five time-zones separated us. When I managed to get him on the phone I put on a

137

cheery voice and asked him no questions. I just told him my news.

We shot scenes in Irving Place, on the Brooklyn Heights Promenade, outside the Apollo Theater in Harlem. We shot a night-time chase sequence through SoHo. All over the city traffic was stopped for us, as if for some fatal accident. I felt full of coiled energy, as if I were a jack-in-the-box with a weight straining to hold me down. Maybe it was the sharp, exhilarating air. Coming from a sluggish English autumn I wasn't prepared for the nervy bite of a November in New York; it hit my veins like heroin, it ran through me like quicksilver. Way up at the top of the buildings, inching higher as the days passed, the sun shone; windows flashed messages to each other. Dizzyingly high, up on the roof of apartment blocks, tufts of bushes stuck out, as surprising as pubic hair. Each building pushed up higher than its neighbour, greedy for air. Some were tinted glass; some were sheathed in a thin skin of mirrors, making narcissists of the neighbours with which they were competing.

Down below I paced the echoing, hooting streets. I was adrift, floating on the windy currents that blew up the side streets. I walked for mile after mile, warmed, momentarily, by the blasts of hot air from the doorways of stores that sold training shoes and bagels and compact discs. I was both powerless and powerful, restless and focused. I paced the streets, mouthing the words of overheard conversations and practising my accents. I sat in public plazas, on the cold concrete rims of fountains or tubs filled with bark chippings, and watched people. I watched, all the time. Men and women passed me without a glance. But I noticed them. When it grew too cold I went indoors, into the vast, glazed public spaces that create a city within the city. I sat under the stars of Grand Central Station; I sat, half-hidden by glossy rubber plants, in the lobby of the Hyatt. I sat on a spindly chair in the lobby of the IBM building, where clumps of bamboo transformed typists, munching their lunch, into women of

138

Chekhovian melancholy; amongst the greenery they ate tubs of coleslaw. I rode up and down the escalator in the Trump Tower, past a Babylonian waterfall splashing down mottled, blood-red walls. I wandered its marble floors, mesmerised by the energy so throbbing I could almost touch it with my new linen fingernails.

I thought the Trump Tower was the most hideously vulgar place I'd ever seen. I said to Lila: 'This book I read, it described it as the inside of the stomach of someone who's eaten pepperoni pizza.'

Lila, however, adored it. 'But last time I went, I couldn't move on account of all the people staring at me,' she said. 'And now I'm totally freaked.'

It was the end of November. We were sitting in the wardrobe trailer, the washing machine humming beside us. Kelly had fetched us coffee and doughnuts. Like all wardrobe mistresses she was enormously fat; whilst clothing others, it seems, she had given up on herself. But she was motherly, and we had some of our best chats there. Lila thrived in a harem atmosphere, where we all sat around and said what a lousy time we had with men.

'Sometimes I wonder what it'd be like if I was just a normal person,' said Lila, her mouth dusted with sugar. 'Just a regular guy. I could just go anyplace and nobody'd notice.' She took a bite of her doughnut. 'It must be strange.'

I said, 'It's *your* life that's kind of strange.'

The machine started its spinning cycle; the engine whirred and it started rocking, as if people were struggling inside. I took a gulp of coffee and looked at Lila. She wore a pink tracksuit – we had just shot a scene in the Sheeps Meadow. I leant over and wiped a blob of jam off her chin.

'I've got an idea,' I said softly, licking the jam off my finger.

I said she should become someone like me.

'Let's try it,' I said.

We borrowed this mousy wig from make-up. Our next day

off I took Lila back to my hotel, for the first time. She wore the wig and the desk clerk didn't recognise her. This gave her a terrific buzz. We scuttled into the elevator, laughing.

'Can I go through with this?' she asked, removing her shades as we stopped at my floor.

'Don't be a sissy,' I said.

I opened the door and let her into my room. It was its usual neat and featureless self. The first thing everyone does in a hotel room is go to the window and look out. On the ledge was my pair of binoculars. I haven't told you about them, have I? She picked them up.

'What are these for?' she asked.

'Watching things, of course. You ever seen *Rear Window*?'

She shrugged off her fur coat and wandered around my room like a child, idly curious. I sat on the bed, watching her as she opened the fridge and looked at the bottles of miniatures. It was strange having her there. I thought how film stars resemble children. They are kept purposefully retarded. Everything conspires to stunt their growth. They are pampered and yet exploited; they are told lies, people tell them only what they expect to hear, they are protected from the windy outside world. Away from her familiar surroundings Lila seemed more vulnerable, lost and mousy in her lank wig. For once, I felt more powerful. We were on my territory now.

'First you've got to scrub that stuff off your face,' I said. 'Then I'll lend you some of my clothes. We're pretty much the same size.'

I opened the drawer, where I kept my t-shirts. Half-hidden amongst them was my store of Salem cigarettes – five packs. I didn't smoke them but I kept them for her. I covered them up; I didn't want her to see them.

'Make your choice,' I said, pulling out t-shirts. There was one saying *Stop Global Warming*, another one saying *Protect the Rainforests*; their commands clamoured at me quaintly, from my old days. I pulled out another one. It said *First Aid Theatre*. 'I was working with them when I first saw you,' I said.

She was in the bathroom, wiping off her make-up. She didn't know anything about my former life; she wasn't interested. Was that fair? After all, I was interested in *her* life, everybody was. In interviews they asked her opinion on everything from night-replenishing creams to surrogate motherhood and listened, gleamingly, to her banal replies.

'You want to hear about me?' I asked. 'Me, meaning you.'

'Holy cow, do I look flaky,' she said, wincing at her reflection in the mirror.

'Touché,' I said.

Her bare face gazed at my reflection, over her shoulder. 'Huh?'

'Nothing. Now, you've got a small flat – not apartment, flat.'

'I've got a small flat,' she repeated, trying out her English accent.

'In Belsize Park. And a large mortgage. And you've got three videotapes which you re-use all the time, and an A-reg Renault that keeps breaking down. Remember it? You saw it once.' I spoke faster. 'And you hand-wash clothes that say Dry Clean Only, and you buy milk in bottles not cartons because it's a penny cheaper, and you pull all the fluff out of your Hoover bag so you can use the bag again – '

'What's a Hoover bag?'

'Exactly,' I said. 'And your heart thumps when the mail arrives, not because it's some nutcase who's in thrall to you but because it's your bloody bank manager who isn't.' I paused for breath. She looked startled.

'Why are you shouting?' she asked.

'I'm not. I'm just trying to explain.'

She moved away from the mirror. 'Sometimes you have this crazy look in your eyes.'

I went into the other room. 'I'm perfectly normal,' I said. 'There's nothing wrong with me. Come and get dressed.'

I laid out jeans, t-shirt and sweater on the bed.

'It's just an interesting exercise,' I said. 'We used to do it at drama school. Role reversal, role-swapping.'

She adjusted her wig. 'Sometimes you spook me.'

She stepped out of her slacks. Underneath she wore creamy pantyhose, with a ladder down the thigh. I passed her the jeans and she pulled them on. They were slightly too tight; I was leaner than her.

'My name is Julia,' I said.

'My name is Julia,' she repeated, in an approximately English accent.

'I'm a remarkably talented actress.'

'I'm a remarkably talented actress,' she repeated.

I corrected her. 'Rem-ar-kably talented.'

'Rem-ar-kably talented.'

'My hobbies are making origami out of old magazine interviews with Lila Dune and fucking strange men in hotel rooms.'

She looked at me. 'You kidding?'

'We're all liars, aren't we?' I smiled at her. 'Give us our lines and we'll say anything.'

She unbuttoned her blouse and took it off. She wore an underwired bra – beige lace. 'You're making me nervous,' she said. 'You have any valium?' She pulled on a t-shirt and my blue sweater.

I stood back and inspected her. She looked back at me. She did, in fact, look surprisingly nervous. Maybe she felt insecure, looking so ordinary. Maybe she was having second thoughts about the whole enterprise. Funnily enough she didn't really look like me, despite the clothes. I could manage the transformation much better, the other way round. I could act like her because I knew her mannerisms and I could copy her voice. That was because I was a real actress. She just looked lost – an unremarkably pretty woman who didn't know what to do with her hands. Her beauty was somehow dissipated.

'One thing we're getting straight,' she said. 'I'm not going to smoke your goddam cigarettes. They have a high tar content.'

I laughed and we went downstairs. We walked down the street, towards 3rd Avenue. Nobody looked at us.

'It's like I'm invisible,' she whispered.

'Join the club.'

'It's neat!'

'Think so?'

We walked past the key-cutting booth and the *Golden Brioche*; we turned the corner and walked past *Pinky's Nail Sculpture*. She paused at the window. Timmi was squirting the glass and rubbing it down.

'Hi Timmi!' She waved. But Timmi didn't recognise her; she just went on rubbing.

We walked along 3rd Avenue, past the scruffy stores and Szechuan restaurants. Lila hadn't walked around New York for years; she was like an invalid re-learning the use of her legs.

She said, 'This guy, this fan, he came up to me once and he says *Do you know who you are?* I said *That's a good question.*'

Laughing, I gave her a lesson in English vocabulary. 'Biscuit not cookie,' I said. 'Lorry not truck.'

But she wasn't listening. She was too entranced by her sudden freedom – the freedom of the nonentity. It was rather touching really. Fame is a prison, and she had been let out for an afternoon amongst the hoi polloi. The seedier the area the better; 3rd Avenue was unknown to her, it was another country. Celebrities have their own network, their own exclusive grid. They travel in their limos between Mortimers and their apartment in the Upper 60s, between one First Class Lounge and another, places where they are welcomed discreetly, cushioned from gawpers and where they only meet people like themselves.

That was another reason why Lila wasn't recognised. Famous people are not just identified by their faces but by their environment and their props – the stretch limo, the fancy neighbourhood, the fur coat. Shed that and they are halfway to resembling the rest of us.

She turned to me. 'You can do this all the time!' she exclaimed. 'Where do you go?'

I shrugged. 'I have some friends down in the Village,' I said.

'Actors, writers. Some of them live in lofts in SoHo. We play word games and eat Cajun cooking.'

'I love words,' she said, as if she was saying *I love guacamole*.

Walking along the sidewalk, I realised that it was not just myself who made a fantasy of her life. She made one of mine. London was a theme park of toffee-apple vendors and Penhaligons, as phonily convincing as a Ralph Lauren store. My life consisted of smoky debates among the literati. My father was a brilliant professor and my mother a Home Counties aristocrat. Lila had reconstructed my life, she had polished it up and simplified it, just as I had hers. On the rare occasions, that is, when she thought about it.

We stopped at Toni's Deli, a place I occasionally frequented. It was famous for its overstuffed sandwiches.

We ordered pastrami, to go.

'So who's your friend?' asked Toni, a large Italian.

'She's my cousin from London,' I said.

'I have an apartment in Belsize Park,' said Lila.

'She means flat,' I corrected.

'I mean flat,' she said, stifling her giggles. 'And go easy on the to-mah-to.'

He looked at her curiously. 'Haven't I seen you someplace before?'

'Nope siree,' I interrupted. 'Not unless you've seen *Leave it to Soak*. That's the high spot of her career so far. She thinks she's a remarkably talented actress but in fact she's a nobody.'

He wrapped the sandwiches. 'I can see you're a nice happy family,' he said.

'She's just jealous of me,' I replied. 'She finds it hard to cope with her competitive feelings.'

Out in the street we burst out laughing. We strolled along, munching our sandwiches. I suddenly felt close to her. Just for a moment she was mine, all mine. The sky was aflame with the setting sun. Just for a moment there was nobody else around to pull us apart – no Chuck, no Irma, no multitudes of adoring fans. We were two ordinary women in jeans and sneakers, laughing together and licking mustard off our chilly hands. A guy delivering crates of sodas stopped and whistled.

But then, when I turned, I saw that he was whistling at Lila.

It was dusk when we got back. A white Lincoln Continental was waiting outside the hotel, gleaming in the street lights. It had come to fetch Lila to a meeting with some producer; she was late. We hurried up to my room where she changed, like some reverse Cinderella, out of my clothes. It was only then that the driver recognised her. She bundled the wig into the pocket of her fur coat and kissed me goodbye, hastily, in the street. She was going to a meeting about some new project, some film in LA. Our strange interlude was over; she was suddenly Lila Dune again, with a separate life I could never touch. She was a film star with twenty movies behind her and two ex-husbands; with a house in Hollywood and an apartment in New York that I would never see. I stood, choking in the exhaust smoke as the car drove off. It rattled over the manhole cover, the punctuation mark of my countless dreams, and was gone.

I took the elevator back to my room, went in and shut the door. I picked up the t-shirt and pressed it to my face; it smelt of her perfume. The clothes were empty; she had dissolved away, it was as if she had never been here.

I walked a long way, that night. It was bitterly cold. I passed a row of benches. Each one was occupied by a mummified bundle, faintly snoring. I saw the white breath issuing from them. I passed a late-night bar, with LITE illuminated in the window. Far away, I heard a police siren. In a doorway, something stirred inside a large Toshiba box. All over the city, people slept in boxes like caddis fly larvae. A man approached me, his hand outstretched. His hair looked matted with glue. 'God bless America,' he said to me, and collapsed at my feet.

In America, crime pays. I saw my lawyer this morning; you

wouldn't believe the offers I'm getting. Films, books, TV. Three companies – CBS, Columbia and something else – are bidding for the screenplay rights to my story. God bless America. I'm famous, you see. I always knew I would be famous one day.

Six

We finished shooting in early December. The movie had been brought in on schedule and under budget and everyone was in high spirits, especially Lila. She glowed. Maybe she was taking some new vitamin shots. Maybe it was just due to the festive season. I didn't guess the reason, then. I was supposed to fly back to England but she said I should stay on for a few days.

'New York, it's so neat this time of year. The stores and everything, don't you just love it?'

We were at the wrap party, which was being held in a new night club down in the meat district. It had been converted into a temple to the internal combustion engine. Bits of cars were built into the bar; sawn-off Cadillacs lined the walls, for seating, and downstairs there was a huge room crammed with open convertibles facing a drive-in movie screen. In honour of Lila they were going to show one of her old pictures, a comedy caper called *Smackeroos*, about a quarrelling couple who pulled off a bank heist and then couldn't agree how to spend the money.

I didn't have time to answer Lila because suddenly she was whisked away. She was always being whisked away – by Irma, by her agent Roly, by the unit publicist Corrina. For six weeks I had hardly been able to finish a sentence; I would find myself talking to the air.

Brushing past a jutting radiator grille I went into the bar. Grover, her co-star, was performing in front of a video camera and a crowd of party guests. He was singing about how great it had been, working on *Bump*. The list of names he warbled, needless to say, excluded mine. I wore my bronze dress, for the first and possibly the last time, but nobody had remarked on my Cinderella transformation and my arms were cold.

'Hey, sing us a song!' I swung round, but of course it was Lila they were pulling out of the crowd.

'I can't!' she cried, laughing and struggling.

'Come on, Lila!'

She cowered, in her blue leather dress. It's strange, about actresses. Give them a part to play and they will do anything, in front of an audience of thousands. But ask them to just be themselves in front of their mates and they collapse in embarrassment, they are as hopeless as everybody else. I had never heard Lila sing. She had starred in a sudsy bio-pic, once, about a doomed country and western singer but that had been dubbed. She looked around for help. Suddenly I realised she was searching for me.

'Hey, Jules!' she cried. 'Get your ass over here, I'm not doing this alone.'

People stood back and I stepped over to her. She put her arm around me, whispering in my ear.

'What the fuck are we going to give 'em?' she hissed.

Ridiculously, the only song I could think of was *I'm a pink toothbrush, you're a blue toothbrush*. Lila and I stood there, paralysed. The car headlights dazzled us, as if we were rabbits. I felt dizzy. After all these months of impersonating Lila, here I was, her partner.

'Stand by,' called Chuck, 'and . . . action!'

Lila and I stood there, dumbly. I heard the crunch of plastic glasses as people milled around. Then Bob, one of the grips, called out to me, 'Hey Jules, what's that tune you're always humming?'

'What tune?' I asked.

'*Me and My Shadow*.'

I stared into the lights. I didn't even know I hummed it.

'Do I?' I asked.

He called back, 'You do a whole lot of things you don't know about.' He laughed. 'We've been watching you.'

I blushed. Then I turned to Lila, and linked my arm through hers.

'You know the song?' I asked. '*Me and my shadow,*' I sang, '*strolling down the avenue . . .*'

Arms linked, we sauntered across the floor, twirling imaginary canes and tipping our top hats like Jack Buchanan. '*Me and my shadow, all alone and feeling blue . . .*' Lila's voice was high and breathless; mine was stronger. I've got a good, clear voice and I had taken lessons, years before, when I had auditioned for *A Little Night Music.* We sauntered up and down, hip against hip, moving smoothly in step.

'*and when it's time for bed, we climb the stair, we never knock, there's nobody there . . .*'

Lila's voice echoed mine, hesitantly. I smiled into the headlights, tossing my hair. At last I was stopping the traffic. I felt strong and confident in my shimmery dress, slit to the thigh. Tonight they were gazing at me, just at me. I out-Lila'd Lila. Who was the shadow now?

We finished with a flourish and they applauded. Lila, panting, put her arm around my shoulder.

'Aw shucks,' she laughed. 'It was nothing.' She turned to me, affectionately. 'Let's hear it for Jules. Seriously, I'd just like to say how much I appreciate her coming over to work with us on our picture. She's been more than a lighting stand-in, she's brought something very special to *Bump,* like, a touch of British class.' She squeezed my shoulder. 'Furthermore, she's been more to me than that, she's been real supportive, it's been a learning process for me, too, and I hope it's been a two-way experience, like, that she's learnt something from us.' She stumbled to a halt.

I smiled at them all. 'She'd put it better,' I said, 'but I haven't helped her learn her lines.'

Everybody laughed. I realised that I was perspiring, heavily. When I went off to find a drink I heard someone say, 'Yeah, but she's got better legs.'

Who did they mean, Lila or me? Which one of us? I never knew.

It was a good party. The presence of a film star – even when you have been working with them for weeks – gives a gathering an unmistakable sexual throb. The star doesn't notice it, but the rest of you do. I looked fondly at the now-familiar faces of the crew – Vinny the clapperboard loader, Bob the standby plasterer, or was it Don? It was too late, now, to find out. Rodney, who was wearing too-youthful chinos. I was going to miss them.

I chatted with Grover's stand-in, Joseph, a young actor whose father had been a stuntman. By the nature of my job I knew him far better than I knew Grover for we had stood together, chilly and immobile, all over New York, making small talk to each other while the technicalities were interminably adjusted.

'Lila's right,' he said. 'She wouldn't have gotten Mary-Lou together without your help. She was starting to give her real depth, by the end. I saw some rushes last week.'

I glowed. It's curious; people don't tell you things until everything is over. It's like neighbours only starting to talk to you once your house is up for sale. A film set is like a factory floor; its workers are both busy and yet disengaged. They do their job, they crack jokes, they complain about the bacon butties and the traffic jams on the way to work. They clock-watch; they talk about their diets. In America they talk about their diets all the time. The one thing they never talk about is the film. Those conversations took place long before, during script conferences with the writer and Perrier-drenched lunches with the actors. Most of the film crew haven't even read the script, except the parts that concern them.

And then, some time before it's over, they all start talking about their next project; what film, what star. They talk about it with more interest, and in much greater detail, than they ever talked about the movie they happen to be making. Kelly was flying to Europe to work on some Scorsese picture. Rodney was going to work on a TV series called *The Menoporsche*. It was about a Wall Street broker with a mid-life crisis. Rodney's assistant had gone to do a TV commercial and the next day I was booked on a flight to London.

In fact, I wasn't that keen to hurry back. Trev had gone away for a few days; he said his sister was ill, and though such brotherly concern was deeply uncharacteristic I had to believe him. I didn't really want to return to an empty flat. Nor was there any work in the pipeline. I had phoned Maggie and she'd got nothing for me. As I wandered down to the drive-in movie I thought about Lila's words. When applied to New York, 'neat' was a pitifully impoverished adjective – I pictured my father's contempt – but she was right, it would be wonderful to stay on for a few more days.

That's all I was thinking, idly, as I went into the drive-in movie. I opened the door of a Chevrolet and sat down in the passenger seat. The film had started and various members of the unit lolled around in their automobiles, moaning that they had nobody to neck with. In the doorway stood Irma, her face rapt and illuminated as she gazed at the screen. She wore a black dress with a white lacy collar, like a nun; she watched her beloved Lila as if she were undergoing a religious experience. It was pathetic, the way she worshipped Lila. I knew she distrusted me, and I certainly distrusted her. She hadn't spoken a word to me during the entire shoot. She was jealous, that was why.

I had seen *Smackeroos* before, on TV. It was not one of Lila's more distinguished efforts. Under the sixties flick-ups she pouted and simpered. In those days she was just a starlet.

Just then the real Lila came in and climbed into the neighbouring convertible with Roly, her agent.

Staring at herself on the screen she said, 'Holy shit, take a look at that hair!'

'We're not taking Orson,' said Roly. 'I'll get an asthma attack. Why does he always want to sit on *my* lap? The damn dog's got some sort of radar.'

Lila was watching the movie. 'Eek! I look like Sandra Dee!'

'Sweetheart,' said Roly, 'just leave him in New York. Your maid can look after him.'

Lila was next to me, in the driving seat of her car. I

151

watched her younger self, squeaky-clean in a summer dress, running through a meadow while banknotes fluttered from her handbag.

'I remember that!' said Lila. 'I had these menstrual cramps. I was blown up like a frigging balloon.'

I yawned. Catch Lila thinking I was engrossed in her old film. I lifted my wrist, in the darkness, and looked at my watch. Tomorrow night I would be whole again, sleeping in my own bed.

Lila was talking to Roly. He replied; I couldn't hear what he said. Then she turned to me, gripping the rim of my door.

'Hey Jules!' she said. 'I have a proposition for you.'

At first I didn't take it in. She said something about flying to LA the next day, she was going with Irma and Roly. Why didn't I take another week in New York, do some shopping, see some shows? I could check out of my hotel and move into her apartment.

'What?' I asked.

'Stay in my place for a week. You'd be doing me a favour. See, I don't trust my maid to look after Orson. And he gets kind of lonely at nights.'

I sat very still. Up on the screen the celluloid Lila sat at a kitchen table, counting a mountain of banknotes. '*Boy-oh-boy-oh-boy,*' she gasped.

I turned to Lila. 'Say that again?' I asked.

Seven

The next morning I checked out of my hotel and took a cab up to Central Park West. Lila had already left for Los Angeles. It was a wonderfully sharp, sunny day; the air hissed into my lungs. I knew her apartment building, of course; I didn't need her instructions on how to get there. Weeks before I had found out her address; I had sneaked a look at the casting assistant's file. Since then, many of my midnight walks had drawn me, magnet-like, in that direction. I haven't told you about those walks, have I? I used to vary the route. I consulted my map and took different streets to keep myself stimulated and delay the climax of arrival. Sometimes I walked up Madison, past the Ralph Lauren mansion where she and I had browsed amongst the sweaters. From there I would cross Central Park, fast, avoiding the shadows moving behind the trees. Sometimes I cut diagonally along Broadway, that junk-filled arterial vein, jostled by panhandlers and teenage runaways who loitered under signs blazing *Hot Male Sex Acts*.

Then I would cross Columbus Circle and walk up Central Park West, until her building hove into sight. Sometimes, on purpose, I would delay looking up. I would pause and pretend I wasn't interested. I would watch the passing taxi-cabs bouncing down the street – all the traffic bounces, in New York, there are so many potholes. Then I would look up, slowly, to the top floor of her apartment building, the penthouse floor, and see if her lights were on. There was a row of windows up there – tiny glowing rectangles. I came to know every combination of light and dark windows, a geometric puzzle whose clues were locked into her evening's unknown activities. Once I brought along my binoculars. (I'd stolen

153

them, in fact; I didn't tell you that either. I stole them from a store on 47th Street, from under the nose of the assistant.) Once I brought along my binoculars and saw a tiny figure emerge from her balcony. I saw the blonde hair. My heart thumped, as it had thumped long ago when I had watched Dawn in that wine bar.

Sometimes I went right up to her building, which was a few blocks from the Dakota. It faced the park. I paused under the canopy and gazed into its lobby. It was vast, with red lacquer walls and a lot of mirrors. There were armchairs and lamps, and vases containing Japanese arrangements of tortured, polished branches. There was a desk and two doormen, and a sign saying 'All Visitors must be Announced'. I had gazed through the glass, into the theatre for which I had no ticket.

Today, however, I was admitted. One of the doormen gave me an envelope with the keys inside. The other carried my bags to the elevator.

I thanked him coolly. 'I can manage from here, thanks.'

I was already becoming a different person, rich and blasé. Stepping into that elevator I felt my metamorphosis begin; it was like stepping into my bronze dress. *Stock Liquidation*, say the signs all over New York. *New Season's Stock Arriving*. Old buildings disappear overnight and new ones rise up in a matter of weeks; the city makes amnesiacs of its population, nobody can remember what anything was like before. On the 31st floor the doors slid open silkily and I emerged a new woman.

Fidelia, the maid, opened the door. She was small and Spanish. Orson snapped at my ankles; he and I disliked each other on sight, and it was a mutual feeling that intensified during my stay.

I walked into the living room. It was huge and luxurious. There were white sofas scattered with cushions, and brass tables with glass tops. There were boldly patterned, swagged curtains tied with ribbons, and photos everywhere in silver frames. It was not quite as vulgar as I had expected; she must have had an interior designer in to help her.

I went over to the windows. The view was breathtaking.

154

Manhattan rose below me, cliffs of buildings knife-sharp in sunshine and shadow. The city was laid out at my feet. I had never seen it as a whole until now. Downtown rose sky-scrapers, tall and slender and thin-skinned in glittering glass; some were tinted dark and some rose in spires, reflecting the sun. The AT&T building was the colour of bleached liver, its top was carved in a niche, like a piece of Chippendale. Across the park stood the sandy-blonde apartment buildings of the Upper East Side, topped with bushes and copper-green roofs. Beyond them rose up block after block of buildings, growing hazy in the distance. Smoke gently steamed from their roofs. Unknown to its inhabitants below, the whole city was breathing.

I turned round. Fidelia had put on her coat; she was waiting to leave.

'How often do you come here?' I asked.

'I come each morning from nine o'clock to noon,' she said.

'Why don't you take the rest of the week off?' I said.

She stared at me. 'But . . .'

I smiled at her. 'I'm fine by myself,' I said. 'I'll manage.'

'But what will Miss Dune – ?'

'Don't worry,' I said. 'I'll call and tell her.'

So began the most extraordinary week of my life. Looking back, I can't remember what I did for the first day or so, except walk from room to room. I seldom went out, except to take the dog and his accompanying pooper-scooper to the Park. At night I slept in Lila's bed, under satin sheets that smelt of her perfume. Her bedroom was decorated in a French Provençal theme, all ruched drapes and little flowery cushions. She had a walk-in closet the size of my bedroom back in London; it was filled with jogging suits and spangled evening dresses. She had a pink marble bathroom with gold taps and a sunken jacuzzi. I explored everything, of course. I opened the bathroom cabinet and inspected her many medicaments – she was even more of a hypochondriac than I had suspected. I sniffed her bath gels and rubbed her moisturiser into my shins. I pulled open the

155

drawers in her bedroom, while Orson darted at my heels with little playful nips. Her maid had kept things outwardly tidy, but Lila was sluttish. I had guessed that. In her dressing-table drawer I found a hairbrush choked with hairs and a powdery sediment of half-squeezed make-up tubes. In another drawer lay a charnel-house of used plastic razors. Repelled and yet fascinated, I sifted through the debris.

She had masses and masses of underwear; silk, lace and even plain stretchy cotton. I opened the closet and felt her rows of dresses; I stroked her sable coat. From the walls her face gazed at me; in the bedroom, nearly all the photos featured herself at various stages of her career, it was a shrine to her narcissism. There were framed publicity stills – Lila with Walter Matthau, Lila with Johnny Carson. There was a poolside snapshot of her with an unknown, muscular man, maybe one of her husbands. There was a blurred photo of her as a little girl, standing outside a trailer-home. She looked like me, when I was young; she really did.

I leafed through her correspondence, promising myself a more thorough inspection of that later. There were a couple of shelves of books, mainly the kind that people leave behind in hotels: Danielle Steele, Judith Krantz, *Women Who Always Say 'No'*, or maybe it was *Women Who Always Say 'Yes'*, I can't remember. *Victoria Principal's Workout Book*. A set of leatherbound *Giants of Russian Literature*, inscribed 'With love and respect, Craig' and obviously never opened.

There was another bedroom, decorated in blue. In the corner was an unused-looking exercise bike. There was another marble bathroom. There was a huge, country-style kitchen with shiny wooden counters; they looked unused, too. There was a freezer crammed with Häagen-Dazs ice-cream and a fridge full of vitamin pills, apricot kernels and suppositories. At the bottom was a forgotten bag of salad; it had rotted into blackened slime. I flung it into the garbage. There was a glass-fronted cabinet crammed with brand-new electrical appliances: a soda-stream, a waffle-maker. Like many New Yorkers, she obviously never cooked.

Wrapped in her bathrobe I sat eating breakfast whilst the TV babbled and the ice-maker periodically grumbled in the bowels of the fridge and haemorrhaged ice-cubes. For a few hours Lila had slipped into my life; now I had slipped into hers. For a week I could live the pampered life of a film star. IMAGINE, said the plaque. Imagine being Lila. I swallowed some of her vitamin C pills and made myself some redwood-blossom tea. I smelt her opened packets of cranky infusions. Her junk food was hidden away, like pornography. In a cupboard under the counter I found her hoard of M&Ms, Snicker bars, Marshmallow Puffs and Chocolate Pinwheels.

In the evenings, when it grew dark, I fixed myself a drink and wrapped myself up in her sable. I sat on the balcony, next to her rusting barbecue, and gazed at the fairytale view. Lila couldn't possibly have appreciated it the way I did. The Citicorp building breathed out frosty white light; the skyscrapers were topped with winking red beacons as if they were sending secret messages. Turrets and façades were dramatically spotlit, like the backdrop to some gigantic opera. The neon sign on the Hitachi building said TODAY'S WEATHER: COLD. I heard the clackety-clack of helicopters and the faint hooting of the traffic far below. I trained my binoculars on the penthouse windows of my rich neighbours in the sky, watching shapes moving across rooms and switching on TVs. They were oblivious to me, but I could see their faces as they talked.

I felt curiously blank, those first few days. It was like the period between reading a script and beginning rehearsals; I was empty, and waiting to start filling out my role. I felt utterly detached from everything. I remember dragging the dog out onto the balcony one day, and showing him the cabs down in the street. They scurried like beetles.

'Your namesake in *The Third Man*, know what he said?' I lifted him up by the loose skin of his neck and pointed him down at the street. 'He said would you feel any pity if one of those dots stopped for ever?' Orson whimpered. 'You've never heard of *The Third Man*, have you? Wonder if your mistress has.'

And each night I lay in Lila's bed, touching myself under her sheets.

After a couple of days I reckoned that Trev would be back in London. Lying in an Eau de Jonquil bubble bath I phoned him, but all I got was the answerphone. In my huskiest voice I left a message.

'I'm having a jacuzzi, honey, in my million-dollar penthouse here on Central Park. I'm soaping myself oh so slowly, I wish you could join me. Sweetheart, I'm up on the thirty-first floor and I have two bedrooms with ensuite bathrooms and a lounge the size of a ballroom. It's so *neat!*'

When I put the phone down I thought: why should he believe me? After all I was always lying to him on the phone, spinning him a fantasy. It was one of our games.

Hearing my own voice gave me a jolt. With no maid around, the only creature I had spoken to was the surly and unresponsive Orson who lay, a white ball of fluff, on his mistress's bed for most of the day. The only way I could get him to jump off was by feeding him M&Ms; he had a passion for the yellow ones. He gobbled them down, slobberingly, glaring at me from under his shaggy eyebrows.

After my bath I dried myself, then I sat at Lila's dressing table. It was a sumptuous altar, loaded with bottles. The mirror was surrounded by theatrical lights. I started making up my face, dabbing on Lila's blusher and outlining my lips into a thick curve. Behind me the TV babbled; it was some 24-hour cable chat-show, and a teenager was delivering a homily about his crack-abuse. '*Like, it made me a different person,*' he droned. '*I felt, like, I was capable of anything.*'

I pinned back my hair and took down her wig from its stand. It was a long, blonde wig, identical to her own hair. She'd told me that she wore it sometimes when her own hair was out of condition. I put it on. I swirled my head from side to side, watching the blonde hair swing

158

against my cheek. *'I felt I was these two persons,'* said the TV.

I felt a shiver of stage-fright. I was sitting in my dressing room; at last they had called me to go on stage. Hushed in the darkness, my audience was waiting.

I went to the closet and chose myself one of Lila's most glamorous dresses – a red, sequinned Bill Blass. Slowly I unsheathed it from its dry-cleaning bag. I stepped into it and zipped it up; it held me like a skin. I had already put on her underwear and stockings, I forgot to tell you that. For an actress, the appropriate underwear is very important; it makes you move differently, it makes you become one with your character. Shoes help, too. Bette Davis said: 'I think upwards from my feet.'

Wriggling my hips, I wandered around the apartment. I tossed my hair, and came to a halt in front of one of her innumerable mirrors.

My breath stopped. It was Lila, standing there. Lush, pouty lips; sooty eyes. I watched myself as she twined a strand of hair around her finger; Lila often did that when she was perplexed.

'Holy shit, is that a zit?' she asked, frowning at her face in the glass. She wrinkled her nose. 'Am I failing to relate to men on account of my father fixation? Why can I only get it together with assholes, who increase my low self-esteem? It's so goddam self-destructive.' There was a pack of Salems in the inlaid cigarette box. She took one out of its pack and lit it with her silver table-lighter, inscribed affectionately from Mike Ovitz. She blew menthol smoke out of her nostrils. 'I'm feeling kinda insecure. Shall I crack open a bottle of bourbon or call my analyst?' Lila sighed. 'That Jules, now she has taste. She's real cultivated. Like, I buy books by the yard but she reads the damn things. What she's got you can't purchase. I'm talking class, I'm talking intelligence. Sometimes I'm so damn jealous I want to strangle her. Maybe I should call my analyst after all.'

159

Suddenly the phone rang. I jumped.

It was Lila. 'How are you, honey?' she said, her voice faint and crackling. 'How d'you like the apartment? Is everything OK?'

I pulled off the wig guiltily. 'It's lovely,' I said. 'Just beautiful.' I rubbed off my lipstick with the back of my hand – God knows why, it was only lipstick. 'I'm having a wonderful time.'

She sounded in terrific spirits. It was 90 per cent humidity, she'd got a heat rash, but the project they were working on, this new picture, it was real exciting, and somebody wanted her to endorse a new brand of spaghetti sauce.

'Listen kid,' she said. 'Can you do me a favour? It's my Mom's birthday tomorrow and I haven't done a damn thing about it. In my desk I have the number of this flower store on Columbus, could you get the number and I'll get some sent to her?'

I sat there on the bed, gazing at the phone – it was one of those fiddly white-and-brass reproduction jobs, the sort of phone people have in Totteridge. I paused, and then I said, 'Why don't I take them to her? Then I can give her your love, in person.'

It was simple curiosity, I guess. Just a jaunt. It would get me out of New York City, I could see New Jersey. I could see where Lila came from. It wasn't so strange, was it?

I bought some flowers, charging them to Lila, and hired a car from a Hertz place near the Lincoln Center. Singing lustily, I negotiated my way through the traffic, crossing Amsterdam Avenue and heading for the West Side Highway. I've always loved driving. The English Jules had pottered around in a Renault and campaigned for the reduction of noxious emissions. But there was another Jules waiting to be released. America had released me, just as Trev had released me all those months before, opening me up in the dark. We all have doubles, the voices inside us which dare to say the unsayable, which shout out swearwords in church. We have

160

our own stuntmen, who boldly perform our fantasies for us, heedless of danger; who shoplift from department stores and fuck strange people in hotel rooms. I once knew a woman who picked up messages from Neptune through the fillings in her teeth. She had ended up in a locked ward in the Maudsley, poor cow. Didn't she understand? Our voices don't come from outer space, they are much more interesting than that. They come from the movie running in our heads, parallel to our own disappointing lives; any time we can switch it on and become as macho as Mel Gibson or as seductive as Lila Dune. They are inside us, waiting to be activated. There was a Lila Dune inside me; over the past months I had come to know her well. She was tackier and prettier than me; she was more vulgar and sexy. Scratch the surface and she was there, like the mess inside Lila's dressing table. She was simpler, too; more generous and impulsive. And now I was going to visit her mother.

I drove through the Holland Tunnel and emerged on the New Jersey Turnpike, blinking in the sunshine.

'. . . *here is the news, sponsored by First Investors Fund for Income . . . handgun conviction appeal quashed . . . hostage in Lebanon . . .*'

I wound down the window; my hair whipped the side of my face, stinging my cheek as I drove. I put my foot down, speeding past *Interstate Exit* signs, past an out-of-town shopping mall marooned in a sea of parked cars. I felt exhilarated, driving into the heartland of America, into Lila's past. I felt like a detective.

'. . . *come visit our Savings Adventure!*' urged the radio.

For the first time in weeks I thought about my mother. Since coming to New York I had phoned her, once, but we really lost contact long ago. Like a local radio station she had gradually grown fainter and fainter, until I was no longer within her transmission area. We had never had much in common, and since my father's death we had even less. After someone dies, or leaves, their partner reverts to type, as if for all those years they had been holding themselves back. She had become even pettier, if that were possible, wittering on about how she must remember to take her library books back, and where did she leave the Baby Bio? It's extraordinary, the amount of things a really boring person can find to talk about. You would think they would run out, at some point. Her prattle was as seamless and exhausting as the disc jockey on my radio, a loop cyclically returning again and again to the First Investors Fund, the weather and the unchanged trauma of the news. My mother understood nothing about my dreams and aspirations, and if she herself had any, there was too much babbling interference for me to hear.

I had driven twenty miles. I passed trailer parks and roadside diners, gas stations and *'Krazy Vin's Nite Spot'*, marooned in a parking lot. There were no villages, no towns, nowhere you could call home. Where did Americans come from? As time passed I had the sensation that I was simply driving between two rows of studio scenery: the passing façades of furniture stores and clapboard houses were propped up beside the road, and behind them was nothingness. I have since discovered that most of the States is like this, but at the time I felt airy and disorientated. Who was Lila? Was she born out of nothingness, like a genie out of a bottle? Was she just a collection of movies, wigs and a closet full of clothes?

'. . . so lightly carbonated you can shake it without taking a bath . . .'

Lila had given instructions. I took the exit at *Ortho Pharmaceuticals*, a long factory ranged behind swelling lawns. The manufacturers of my diaphragm, I realised, as I drove past its bushes nestling between its landscaped, breasty curves . . .

'. . . you want any Pontiac, anywhere? Look in the Nynex Yellow pages . . .'

I thought of my own past, my own unborn possibilities. The children I had never had, the roles I had never played. I switched off the radio. Lila's own past was a collection of interviews and clippings which I had found stuffed into a filing cabinet back in her apartment. Accounts of her early life were somewhat confused. According to *MS*, she was brought up in Plainfield, NJ. According to *Star Secrets* it was Plainville, Conn. Her father's original Polish name

162

was variously misspelt, ranging from Dunnacovicva through to Dunacovika. One clipping gave her a baby brother and another gave her four ex-husbands instead of two. Most agreed that she was born in rural poverty, a Steinbeckian poor white scenario which featured a trailer home, struggling mother and a truck-driver father conspicuous by his absence. According to *People* magazine: '*Lila Dune, smouldering siren of hit pictures* Touch and Go, Prime Heat *and formerly Jade in CBS's long-running TV weepie* Beverly Boulevard, *grew up under the spell of her father, a charismatic haulage contractor who first idolised then abandoned his doting daughter.*' According to a yellowing clipping from the *Detroit Examiner*, '*Teenage sizzler Lila Dune worked at her local Howard Johnsons to support her mother, and attended dance classes in the evenings.*' The *National Enquirer*, however, had it that she worked as a sales clerk at J.C. Penneys whilst posing for pin-ups on her days off. It added: '*Mauled by killer pit bulls at age sixteen, budding beauty Lila Dune would have grown up scarred for life were it not for the bravery of her neighbor, gutsy retiree Karl Sudenberg.*' But as this item was flanked by one story about a headless ghost spotted in a police patrol car and another about a woman with three breasts I couldn't vouch for its accuracy. An eighteen-year-old newspaper clipping hinted at a whole cupboardful of skeletons in her past. '*Rising young starlet Lila "Beverly Boulevard" Dune's husband Vince, sueing for divorce, is claiming substantial alimony checks, or else threatens kiss'n'tell revelations concerning her steamy off-set affairs, her spells in the 'nut house', and secrets from her scandalous teenage years.*' This first husband, Vince, was variously depicted as a high-school drop-out, a local hero, a minor felon and a drag-car racer. Perhaps all of them.

No doubt these confusions stemmed from journalists' casual relationship with the truth, surpassed only by Lila's own somewhat shaky hold on reality. After all, she had been reinvented so often. Like learning her lines, she could re-read her own myths and start to believe whatever past she had been assigned. Even I had constructed a past for her, in Chez Hortense, and look how our visiting fan had lapped it up, decapitated dolls and all. I could construct a past for myself, complete with stage triumphs and stormy affairs with famous leading men. What is the past, after all, but our own shifting wishes and interpretations? It is a series of line drawings, waiting to be coloured in with whatever crayons we have to hand. We needn't even make up new events; we can just pick and choose – a shading here, a highlight there, a few judicious rubbings-out.

Certain facts I knew, from Lila herself. She was brought up in a trailer, an only child. Her father drove long-distance trucks. He drank heavily, and when he came home he beat the shit out of anyone who got in the way. How different from my own father, the master of self-control and icy contempt! Her drinking problems and instability were no doubt inherited from him. Finally he got into some brawl and left home for good. Like myself, Lila had grown up trying to get him back, trying to attract his attention. In her case she did it from the screen. Meanwhile, at eighteen, she had made a hasty and unsuitable marriage to Vince, the local boy who raced cars. Her second marriage had been to an older man, probably a father substitute. He was a nightclub promoter who now owned a string of clubs out West. This marriage had come to grief too. When it came to long-term relationships, Lila's record was as woeful as mine.

I drove through a suburban sprawl of gas stations, rusting pick-up trucks and tract homes. My heart beat faster. That sunny winter's morning, before everything changed, I was simply motivated by curiosity. What was Lila's mother like? What would she tell me? I was feeling generous too. Here I was, driving thirty miles to deliver birthday greetings and a bunch of lilies to somebody else's mother. I was a surrogate daughter.

Suddenly I started chuckling. That's what I was: Lila's stand-in! Not just on set, but in her family too. But then it's easier being a stand-in daughter than being the real thing, isn't it?

*

164

And I was. I charmed Mrs Dunnacovicia, I could tell from the start. I gave her the armful of lilies. I acted the loving and attentive daughter – something I had never quite managed to do in real life. In fact I warmed to the part and felt myself filling it out. Besides, it was nice to talk to somebody again, after my silent days in Lila's apartment, mouthing at the mirrors.

Her mother was called Margosia. She asked me to call her that. She was small and plump and surprisingly youthful for somebody who had just turned sixty-one. I could see traces of Lila's features – the snub nose, the wide eyes – in her soft face. She lived in a brand-new cedar-shingled house with an ornamental flamingo in the front yard, and white-painted tyres filled with last summer's dying flowers lining the path. There were hanging baskets in the porch.

'Lila had this built for me,' she said, gesturing around. 'Isn't it just beautiful?'

The trailer-home had long since gone, so I couldn't see Lila's old bedroom or imagine her father staggering about, roaring drunk and banging against the aluminium walls. Her childhood had vanished.

I stood in the living room. On the giant TV set a game show silently played, the figures waving as if underwater. There was an orange settee and a flame-patterned rug. Along one wall was a hideous veneered sideboard filled with coloured glasses and topped with a baroque display of ornaments. Lace doilies hung over the chairs in a vaguely Eastern European way, and on the wall hung a plinth supporting a plaster statue of the Virgin. I realised that, however lapsed, Lila was a Catholic. I thought of my father's dry atheism and how, when I was young, I lit joss-sticks and hungered for a faith. How hard I prayed, with nobody to hear!

Margosia came in, stuffing the flowers into a fairground vase. 'Can't fit them all in,' she said. 'My, what beautiful lilies! How did you know they're my favourite flower?'

I smiled. 'I just knew.'

I looked at the painted plaster figure. What had I prayed for

– fame? Beauty? Love? An Oscar on my mantelpiece, instead of the Virgin Mary?

She returned with another load of lilies stuck into another vase. Their perfume filled the room.

'Happy birthday,' I said again, and kissed her. Her skin was so soft that my lips sank into her cheek. She smelt of face powder.

'She doesn't have time for her old Mom any more,' she sighed, putting the vase on the table. 'The only time I see her's on the TV set. Still, I'm so proud of my little girl. I always knew she was something special.'

Mothers always say that. To them, of course, it's true. But what about the rest of the world?

The trouble with fame, it upsets the balance for the rest of us. It's like when somebody takes an exotic holiday. When they return home, tanned and full of adventures, our own life thins. Perfectly acceptable a moment before, it is suddenly drained of interest. Fame does that. Lila had drained the colour from me. But we were all special to begin with. To our parents, we were. Every little girl is a potential film star. My father expected great things from me. And what had happened? What was my most lasting claim to fame? The woman who extinguishes her cigarette in a British Caledonian in-flight safety video.

Margosia was prattling away in the kitchen. She was a simple woman, and delighted to have some company. She said she had been married again to a good, kind man, but he had died. She talked about some made-for-TV movie Lila had starred in, playing a high-flying attorney; she asked if Lila had given up smoking yet. She said there was something wrong with the furnace downstairs, and did I like decaf? I stood in the lounge, trying to catch up with all this and connect her to Lila. I wanted to ask her a hundred questions, but just then she came out of the kitchen and stopped dead.

'Oh my!' she gasped.

'What is it?'

'Just then, I thought it was *her*, standing there!' She gazed

166

at me, over the coffee tray. 'Anybody told you there's a resemblance?'

'That's why I got the job in the first place,' I said, smiling.

I had told her what I did.

'You know something?' she said. 'I've been to watch Lila filming, but I've never noticed no stand-in being used.'

'Nobody does.'

I ate a cookie and she showed me the framed photos on the sideboard. One featured Lila in a phalanx of drum majorettes; she looked a fresh, all-American girl, with her white teeth and shapely legs. Another showed her in her high-school prom dress, looking lush and blonde. She didn't look exceptional – just a small-town, pretty girl. One of millions. I inspected them greedily. The final one showed an infant Lila being held by a handsome, gypsyish man wearing a plaid work-shirt.

'Wasn't she an adorable baby?' sighed her mother.

'Adorable,' I said.

'A real little tomboy,' she said.

'Really? So was I.'

She rubbed the photo frame with the edge of the pinafore thing she wore, over her slacks, and put it back. We sat down with our coffee, while blurred contestants grimaced on the TV screen.

'Were you a happy family?' I asked.

'She was the apple of her father's eye.'

'Does she still see him?'

She shook her head. 'He never came back. Not even to visit. Except that once – ' She stopped.

'What once?'

She fiddled with the packets of sugar. 'It's nothing,' she muttered. 'Know something? These newspaper people come here, people from the TV, they ask me all these questions. They're so darned inquisitive. Can't she have no privacy? Can't she make no mistakes? Can't she live like a normal person?' She stopped, and looked up. 'I don't mean you, honey. I mean the others. Some of the lies I've read, I can't recognise my own daughter!'

There was an awkward silence. She had an orange smudge on her nose. It was pollen, from when she smelled the lilies. I leant over and rubbed it off for her.

She smiled. 'You're different,' she said. 'I feel, like I can trust you. Like you're almost one of the family.'

I smiled. 'Really?'

Would you have dressed up in Lila's clothes? Would you, if you were slim enough? I was slim enough; in fact I was slimmer than Lila because I didn't binge on Snicker bars. I had grown to love her apartment, with its sensational views, and pranced around in it sheathed in her shiny evening dresses. They reminded me of my bronze dress I had bought in that moment of madness. My favourite of hers was a gold, pleated number from some boutique in Rodeo Drive; I imagined collecting my Best Actress Academy Award in this, shimmering bashfully up to the platform. I had never known a woman with so many outfits – suits, jackets, glitzy evening wear, leatherwear; designer outfits by Oscar de la Renta, Cardin, Bill Blass, Ralph Lauren. Some of it looked scarcely worn. Lila was a greedy shopper. Like most Americans she had a huge and insatiable hunger for more, more, more. In movie theatres, people gorged themselves from popcorn tubs the size of dustbins. *Buy,* urged the babbling radio; *eat* urged the babbling TV. Cars had grossed-out into stretch limos, long as tugboats, that jammed the traffic and blocked the streets, parking for hours with their engines running while the driver sat in the back watching evangelical preachers braying for dollars on colour TVs. At night, when I dragged Orson out for his walk, I watched the monster garbage trucks gobbling rubbish while inside fast-food joints vast men, pale and plump as capons, stuffed themselves with junk and left a mountain of litter behind them. Skyscrapers thrust upwards, each one higher than the next, and down below the streets were a Sodom and Gomorrah of gluttony and gratification. Orson's nails scraped as I pulled him along, accompanied by the sounds of police sirens and the night-bird whistles of the doormen outside the Waldorf Astoria and the Pierre, calling for cabs. The store windows were crammed with Christmas displays, goods heaped to the ceilings. Their aisles were crammed with shoppers. F.A.O. Schwartz was filled with plush mechanical animals, giant giraffes and elephants nodding to the bleeps of the cash tills.

Back in England I had been a different person, dutifully recycling my *Guardians* and growing spider plants in my old yogurt pots. I had worried about the ozone layer and campaigned for worthy causes. I had a modest wardrobe of clothes and six pairs of shoes. Like my father, I switched off the lights when I left the room. New York both horrified and fascinated me; its brash sexual greed stirred something inside me, something that had lain largely dormant. Looking back, I suppose that my one-sided love-affair with Lila was really a one-sided affair with America herself, a country so childish and wasteful, so rich, tacky and greedy, and filled with such a raw energy that my scalp tingled.

It tingled when I wore Lila's clothes. Even her mother had pointed out our resemblance. For some reason, her words had a profound effect upon me. I honestly hadn't thought of doing anything about it until then. She wasn't a clever woman, and she hadn't realised what she was saying – indeed, she was as egocentric as her daughter, and had remarked on the resemblance more in wonderment to herself than to me. But it was then that something had clicked.

The idea came to me when I was walking Orson in Central Park, the morning after my visit to New Jersey. Lila wasn't due back for another couple of days. It was another sharp, sunny, winter's morning. A gay dog-walker strolled by. I recognised him; he was flanked by large poodles and afghan hounds which rose and fell like carousel horses as they loped along. I'd come to recognise some of the homeless by now, too, laden with their plastic bags and muttering their exhausting grievances at the bare branches. A few remaining leaves fluttered to the ground as Orson relieved himself beside the Imagine plaque. Whilst excreting, he always held my gaze. If his bowel movement was particularly loose, or copious, there was a triumphant gleam in his eye, challenging me to scoop all *that* lot up. We had grown to loathe each other, and engaged in various one-upmanship manoeuvres of some complexity.

Avoiding him, I gazed idly at the plaque. *Imagine*, I thought. Imagine picking up a man in a hotel bar and bringing him back to Lila's apartment. I would hide Lila's photos and pretend it was my place. We would fuck each other senseless between Lila's sheets and then, the next time he visited, I would have disappeared into thin air. The doorman would coldly ask: 'Apartment 31B? Who were you wanting, sir?'

Then I thought: Imagine dressing up as Lila. I would put on her wig and sally forth into this steaming, seething city. I would pick up a man and bring him back to the apartment. He would think he was shagging a film star. And when Lila returned he would be shown up and she'd have the shock of her life.

This idea, though amusing and mildly arousing, seemed logically impossible. But it was just then, whilst I blenched at the smell emanating from Orson's direction, that I remembered the dry cleaning ticket.

I had seen it on her desk, pinned to a note for Fidelia. The note itemised various small tasks to be performed during Lila's absence – buying dog food, calling the janitor to mend a dripping faucet, cancelling her Personal Fitness Program trainer, who apparently visited once a week to monitor her low-impact aerobics and to bully her onto her bike. I had carried out most of these instructions myself. All that remained was the collection of Lila's dry cleaning.

When I returned to the apartment I went over to her desk and picked up the note. Her loopy, immature handwriting blurred. For a moment I couldn't understand why, then I realised that my hand was shaking. Wasn't that ridiculous? I hadn't done anything yet.

The idea was so bold that I felt breathless, and sat down in her soft white settee. Why not dress up as Lila, and collect

170

her cleaning? Why not see if I could pull it off? After all, I was convincing enough in the mirror. Why not go one small step further?

Think of it purely as an acting exercise, I told myself, gazing at the tubs of dried-out cypress trees on her balcony. Would I be good enough to get away with it?

I didn't have the nerve to do it in daylight. I would have to wait until dark.

If you appear on stage in the evenings, people think your days are free. Nothing could be further from the truth. Agreed, you can sleep in late. But from midday onwards you are tensing yourself for curtain-up. As the hours pass you gradually drain off your normal life, you empty yourself in preparation for the role ahead. You may behave as usual but in fact you are a walking husk, an empty shell filled with nothing but anxieties. You are like a person who is just about to make a journey. Long before you have climbed into the plane, long before you have been waved off at the quay, you have already departed. Long before dusk Jules had disappeared. It was Lila now who stood under the shower, rubbing foaming gel over her limbs. She towelled herself dry, chatting brightly to her dog. At her dressing table she made up her face with care, darkening her eyes and outlining her mouth with crimson lipstick. How wide and luscious her lips looked now! When she pulled on the wig Orson started whimpering.

'I'm just going out for a while, honey, to collect my cleaning,' she told him. 'That putz Fidelia forgot to do it for me.' She scratched his coat with her long red nails. 'If my Mom calls, say I'm real sorry I couldn't make it for her birthday, but next time she buys some pasta sauce I'll be right there on the jar.'

She went into her walk-in closet and selected a green jogging-suit, the sort of outfit she'd have been wearing all day when she'd just ligged around her apartment making phone calls, leafing through a pile of scripts Roly had sent over and watching the video of some TV series Lorimar wanted her to guest in.

She dressed in the jogging suit and slipped on a pair of cream Gucci loafers. They were a little tight – that was weird, maybe her feet had grown. She combed her long blonde hair. Later that evening she was taking a meeting with some publicity guys who were working on the promotion of her new picture *Sexbusters*, due to open in the spring, and then she was invited to dinner with Guber and Peters, studio heads at Warner, or was it Columbia, to discuss a new project that was in development. Kevin Costner was joining them. He was going to play her young lover who is suddenly afflicted with blindness. Or was it AIDS? She's too damn dumb to remember.

She slid into her sable coat, wrapped a scarf around her head and put on a pair of shades – her street disguise. Then she collected her dry cleaning ticket and a large tote bag, containing some clothes belonging to Jules, her sweet little stand-in.

Orson was jumping up and down now, growling. My, was he acting funny! She closed the door on his muffled barks and left the apartment, walking down the hall to the service elevator. She wasn't taking the main elevator to the lobby, no way! On the set one day she had told Jules about this freight elevator. It didn't lead to the lobby, see, it led to an exit door on the ground floor, round the side of the building. Fire regulations stipulated there had to be an emergency exit – one-way only, on account of security. You could get out – there was one of those push-bars on the door – but you couldn't get back in. This guy had used it, this TV celebrity she was having a relationship with, what a fuckup that was. Anyhow, he had used this exit to get out of the building in the middle of the night – he was married, see, and famous, and if the doormen saw him it would have been kind of deleterious to his image as a regular family guy. Asshole.

In contrast to the mahogany-panelled residents' elevator, this one was just a scruffy metal box. Freezing cold, too. Nobody saw her get in. Lila's ears popped as it descended to the ground floor. She stepped out, crossed a hall past the garbage chute, and pushed open the door to the street.

The wind whipped her face. Jesus, was it freezing! Huddling

in her fur, she walked up the street, past the brownstone walk-ups. It was 6.35. Lights came on in the windows.

What does she think about? God knows. But her heart is thumping. Inside her jogging suit she's perspiring. The noise on Columbus batters her. DON'T WALK, says the sign, but she is blundering across. Stay calm, she tells herself.

She knows how to walk, she has practised it often enough. Lila walks with a little Monroe wiggle. She walks two blocks up the street, without mishap. One or two people look at her, but she can't tell why. When you're famous, you no longer know why people stare. In one sense, fame is sexy. In another, it's the most de-sexed situation there is. See, you don't know if people are staring at you because you're attractive or because they recognise you. She realises this, for the first time. Are they looking at 'me' or *me*?

She's calmed down by now, thinking of this. Lila doesn't think of it, but Jules does. She arrives at the cleaners, and stops. There's a customer in there, a woman. Lila waits outside. Her sable coat is fabulously warm; nothing beats a real fur. She's never heard of the anti-fur lobby, or if she has she doesn't give a fuck. In fact she's got two other furs back at the apartment, a ranch mink and a red fox. Why the hell not? Leave it to Jules to care about those sort of things. Jules couldn't afford a real fur anyway.

The woman comes out. She doesn't register Lila, standing there. Lila goes into the shop. Hot air blasts her face. The man behind the counter is small and bald. He gazes at her for a moment, and then his face breaks into a smile.

'Well hi, Miss Dune,' he says. 'How're you doing?'

'Fine,' she replies with Lila's voice. She's a ventriloquist.

'Haven't seen you for a while,' he says. 'Been away?'

She shakes her head. 'Just filming, here in New York City.'

'If only Florrie was here!' he says. 'She'll kill me when I tell her. They showed *Honolulu Honeymoon* last week on TV, did you see it?'

Lila shakes her head. Her shades have slid down her nose; she pushes them up.

He says, 'She wanted to know, was it you who shot those rapids?'

Lila swallows. Her hands are sticky. 'No,' she says. 'It was a stunt man. Woman.'

'Florrie, she cried at the end, when he was knifed.'

Who was knifed? Lila hasn't a clue. It's some old movie of hers. She replies, recklessly, 'So did I.'

'So did you?' He bursts into laughter. 'My, that's rich!'

Lila fumbles for her dry cleaning ticket. It's somewhere in her pocket. The man is still chuckling.

'Wait till I tell Florrie *that*!'

Lila's head spins. What's she said wrong?

'You cried when he was knifed?' says the man. 'After what happened in the chopper?' He shudders with renewed laughter. 'After what he did to you in the *hotel*?'

Lila finds the dry cleaning ticket and hands it over. She'd better keep her mouth shut. He takes the ticket and turns to rifle through the hangers. A moment passes.

'I told your maid we might not be able to get it out,' he says, pushing the clothes to one side. He inspects the ticket again, and goes on searching. 'What was it, may I ask?'

'Huh?' she replies. What the hell is he talking about?

'She didn't know,' he says.

'Who?'

'Your maid. Looked like vinaigrette.' He finds the corresponding ticket, pinned to an outfit, and lifts the hanger. 'Well, we did our best. Tried two stain removers.'

He lifts the cellophane. It is a creamy silk blouse. She pauses. She doesn't know where the stain should be.

'Can't see it,' she murmurs.

He smiles. 'That's OK then.'

It is dark in Central Park, and freezing cold. A siren wails in the distance, in the humming canyons of the streets. Here it is quiet. The ground is frozen hard as steel. Underfoot, the leaves crackle as she steps across the grass. Lamps cast pools of light onto the criss-crossing paths; she avoids them and heads for a clump of bushes. A man moves behind the trees but there seems to be no one else about. Maybe tonight it's too cold for muggers. Even for murderers.

Hidden in the bushes, she gets to work. She pulls off the scarf and the wig and stuffs them into the tote bag. She takes off the fur coat and bundles it in too, squashing it down. Swiftly, she dismantles Lila. She starts giggling. My God, she tells herself, this dressing room is even more freezing than the previous record-holder, Wigan Rep.

For some reason, she feels hysteria bubbling up. She fluffs out her hair and buttons herself up in Jules's grey overcoat. With an icy knuckle she rubs off her lipstick. And in a few minutes she walks into the lobby of the apartment building, smiling a greeting to the doorman as she heads for the elevator.

I felt utterly exhausted that night, and triumphant too. I had pulled out the plugs that connected me to the rest of the world, and now I was running on my own batteries. I felt emptied, as if I had played the leading role in a play whose lines I had finally mastered. After all, there had been enough rehearsal time.

I was too revved-up to sleep. I turned restlessly in Lila's bed, listening to the wailing sirens far below. Orson was fidgety too; I heard his nails scratching on the hardwood kitchen floor as he prowled around.

I had pulled it off! I had done it! For an hour I had used my acting skills to the full; those dormant muscles ached. I hadn't just impersonated Lila. I had taken over her part, I had become her, sliding under her skin like fingers into a glove. And the dry cleaning man had bought it; he had believed in her too.

The mattress creaked as I turned over, burying my face in the pillow. I smiled. I even smelt like Lila; I had sprayed her scent onto my wrists and my throat. Where did she end and I begin?

Eight

Sometimes I see magazines here. Not often, and not those that I would have chosen. They are usually TV Guides, or unreadably downmarket women's weeklies from which somebody has always cut out the recipes. Yesterday, however, I chanced upon a copy of *Newsweek*. It described some Trevor Nunn production of *Othello*, where Ian McKellen played Iago. The English names gave me a jolt, then a patriotic glow. I'd met McKellen once, years ago. In this production, apparently, he had realised that Iago's strength lay in his indispensability. *Newsweek* said he gave an electrifying performance. Othello was as simple a soul as Lila. He had no idea how deeply he was in Iago's power, simply because Iago had made himself indispensable – quiet, efficient, and watchfully anticipating Othello's every need. When the play opens, Iago is as humble as a stand-in. But though he starts out as Othello's servant, he ends up as his master. That's because, like me, he has brains.

I'm thinking about my role in Lila's life, and wondering how indispensable I had become by the time I was staying in her apartment. I was certainly pretty useful. I had helped her in her work, drawing out and developing her acting skills. I had become her confidante and adviser. I had given her a crash-course in world drama. I had stepped into the breach and taken over her daughterly duties in New Jersey. I had looked after her dog and her apartment. I had dealt with her phone calls – not many, admittedly, because her answering service had been told she was out of town. I had read the various scripts that had arrived, and had my comments ready should she ask my advice. I had moved various objects

176

around her apartment, with more flair than either she or her decorator possessed. I had replenished her meagre supplies with virgin-pressed olive oil and Coopers marmalade. The day before her return I laundered the sheets and, practically bankrupting myself, filled the rooms with fresh flowers. I had even collected her dry cleaning. I hadn't become an Iago yet – that would come later – but I was undeniably useful. Verging, indeed, on indispensable.

So when she phoned, the evening before her return, the news was not as utterly unexpected as it might have been.

'Hi hon!' she called. 'How're you doing? How's that whacko dog of mine? Orson?' Her voice rose, 'Orson, you hear me? You been a good boy?' She seemed to be in terrific spirits; almost manic. She went on to say that the project she was involved in, some re-make of *Jane Eyre*, was going into production early in the New Year. 'How about coming out to LA to work on it with me?' She said they would fix it with my green card, with the unions, all that shit. 'I told them, *Jane Eyre*, it was a British picture, right? Wasn't it *dynamite*? I told them it would help, like, with you being British, it would help me. They'd fixed me up with another stand-in, she's OK, I've worked with her before, but we don't have, like, a *relationship*. So I told them I'd check on your availability. How about it?'

I said I would think about it, calm as calm. I probably sounded non-committal. I sank back into the armchair. My first reaction was a warm rush. She wanted me! Lila Dune, the big star!

My second thought was Trev. I missed him more and more. The bastard was never in when I phoned, and I was at fever pitch. Could I get him to come out to LA? Would the sun and the glamour rekindle his lust for me? I could pay his fare; for the first time in my life I had money to spare. Surely, whatever he was doing, coming to LA would be both a tremendous jaunt and a leap forward for his career. Think of the contacts! A budding writer would give his right arm to be involved in a big movie production.

I tried to phone him again, but of course there was no

answer. He had recorded a new message on his machine, which added: 'Please give the date of your call.' He must have gone away. But where?

I was an idiot, of course. Looking back, I can't begin to comprehend what an idiot I had been. I guessed something might be up. But I didn't want to know what it was and I thought it would all be over when I returned. I was in America, remember, and utterly sealed off. America is a foreign country; the longer you stay there the more you realise this. Nobody mentions Britain; it's our illusion that they do, but it's a lie. America is blind to anywhere else. Besides, I had been working on a film. Nobody outside the business can understand how totally enveloping it is, how cut-off you are, both engrossed and exhausted, when you are making a movie. Even if you are just a stand-in. You are all in it together and nothing else matters. You have a whole new family and set of relationships. You eat the same food and breathe the same air. No wonder marriages collapse. News from the outside world scarcely trickles through. War can be declared, and all it means is that some items disappear from the catering wagon. You are inside a huge ego, perma-sealed.

I did guess something was up. But I didn't guess the truth.

The morning of Lila's return I packed up and went back to my hotel. That evening, I was going through my things and found, in my handbag, the keys to her apartment.

It was a fine, frosty night and I decided to walk uptown to her apartment building and give them back. I would either give them to the doorman or go up and see her. It would be a good excuse to say hello and re-establish contact. I didn't have anything else to do that evening. Any evening, for that matter.

I had a bite to eat, first, in my old coffee shop around the corner. My solitary candlelit dinners in Lila's apartment, with the spangled city at my feet, were already taking on the unreal glamour of a dream. Munching my toast I thought: did I really live there? For a week I had literally stayed amongst the stars. New York is a vertically snobbish city and just for a few days I had climbed that ladder.

I had conflicting feelings about all this, of course. Why did I get a charge from something I despised? Why was I in the thrall of some peroxide airhead? My little toe had more intelligence than Lila. It was ridiculous. I was being sucked into something that was utterly alien to me.

I remember that half-hour when I sat in the coffee shop amongst the solitary diners, the pitiless strip-lighting showing us all up for who we were. No lighting cameraman had Vaselined his lens for *us*. A woman at the next table was muttering, 'Baby didn't come for them shoes. I had them for her in a box.' I remember my walk through the streets, the store windows winking with Christmas lights. It was December the tenth.

Maybe I wouldn't go to Los Angeles, I thought. I would simply go back to London, burdened with Christmas presents, and put all this behind me. In this chaotic city there was madness up there amongst the rich and madness down below amongst the poor. I had glimpsed both, and they scared the hell out of me.

I walked up the park side of the street. As I neared the apartment building, a limo drew up outside. It was a white stretch job, one of the extra-long ones. I paused on the other side of the road, gazing at it idly. It was so long that it had two lozenge lights between each window.

The wind blew against my face as I watched the doormen, both of them, hurrying out. The back door of the limo was opened, and Lila stepped out. Her hair was piled up on top of her head and she wore a fluffy coat I hadn't seen before.

The traffic was heavy, and I couldn't cross the road to greet her. I waited for the lights to change. Just then I saw that somebody else was getting out of the limo. It was probably Irma, I thought, or Roly.

179

Lila was laughing. It was a man who got out and took her arm. He wore a leather jacket, and just then he turned around. Under the lit canopy I could see his face quite clearly.

It was Trev.

LOS ANGELES

One

I had lost weight. I noticed it, with fleeting surprise, when I was lying beside the pool. My skin was greyish-white, it looked grubby in the sunshine, and my hip-bones jutted up. Over the past month I had stopped taking care of my body; it was simply something that had to be fed and washed. It was like an invalid's body; it ached all over. Maybe I was still in shock.

The hairs had grown on my legs, too. I supposed I ought to do something about that, now I was in the land of bronzed pulchritude. I was starting work the next day. But where could I find a razor? Where could you find anything in Los Angeles, without driving twenty miles along the freeway?

I lay there, my fingertips smudgy from leafing through the *Los Angeles Times* Sunday edition. It had arrived, a massive weight; now it lay spread around on the concrete, slabs of it, like some rifled tomb. I hadn't been able to read a book for weeks; I hadn't the concentration.

I had been looking at the Real Estate section. It was full of homes in Santa Monica and Pacific Palisades and Brentwood. They had maids' rooms and libraries and spas and pools; they had gated security. If you were rich here, you lived in a fortress too; just like New York. They were built in the Dutch style, or Georgian style, or Classic Spanish. I scanned the columns. Bel Air . . . Pasadena. My heart jumped whenever I saw the words *Beverly Hills*. Lila lived in Beverly Hills. I knew the address. I had even bought a map – $1.50 from a slot machine in the lobby. But I had only arrived the day before and I hadn't got a car.

You can't get anywhere in LA without a car. There was

another film crew staying at the hotel; I had seen their equipment stacked in the corridor. In the elevator I had spoken to a tubby little guy who said he was a juicer; in LA crewspeak that's a sparks. I said I was new here and he said the same two things everybody says: that LA's got no centre, it's just 100 square miles of suburbs. And that it takes an hour to drive anywhere.

'Just arrived in Tinseltown?' he asked. He said he was here to make a made-for-video picture. 'It's a whore movie.'

'A whore movie?'

'A horror movie.' I hadn't understood his pronunciation.

He said it was about a man who had screwdrivers for hands. 'He goes round fixing up divorcées' homes and then he mutilates them.'

I lay beside the pool. The hotel was built around it, three sides of white walkways and railings like an ocean liner. The fourth side was a fence, lined with bougainvillaea bushes and oleanders, and something else I didn't recognise, in terracotta pots. Beyond that was the parking lot. Every few minutes the air would fill with exhaust fumes as somebody revved up their car; then they would drive off, pausing to put their token into the machine. People went on leading their lives, this was the curious thing. All over the world they drove around in their cars, they behaved as if nothing had happened.

Was it Colonial, her house? Did it have a butler's pantry, hardwood floors and a security system? Was it Mediterranean-style, with 180-degree views of mountain and ocean? I flung aside the Real Estate and leafed through the Entertainment Section. MGM/United Artists was shooting a musical tale: '*A prematurely deceased German shepherd dog checks out of heaven and, hoping to find the pit bull who had him murdered, returns to the jazzy canine underworld of 40s New Orleans.*'

Pit bull meant Lila. Hadn't she been nearly torn to pieces by one, long ago? *Beverly Hills* meant Lila. Even *West Hollywood* meant Lila, because my map showed that it was the adjoining residential area. An advertisement for *Acorn Inns* meant Lila, because she had a pair of gold, acorn earrings. Everything I read or touched reminded me of her. Have you ever been jealous? So jealous that you feel ill with it, nauseous all the time? An obsession that grips you clammily, worse than sexual desire? It feels like something solid and curdled, lodged in your stomach. It blocks your lungs; sometimes you can hardly breathe. When I pictured her I felt winded, as if I had been punched in the belly. I felt hot and feverish, all the time. Oh, I can hardly start to describe it. However obscure the connection, I made it. The word *Paramount* gave me a sick jolt, because she had made pictures for them; *Nick Nolte*, because she had worked with him. *Richard Gere* because she had nearly worked with him once – maybe she had never even met him, it didn't make any difference. Now I was in the heart of the film industry, every sentence in the newspaper was a minefield.

It didn't even have to be about movies. An ad for *Salems*, the mention of *Oscar de la Renta* in a gossip column. *Lancôme* because she used their make-up. *Revlon* because she didn't. Even the sun was tainted, up there in the eternally summery January sky, because an hour's drive away she was warmed by its rays too. She hadn't just taken Trev away from me, she had stolen my world.

No, not stolen, exactly. Tainted. Everything had her festering inside it like a cancer. She had seeped into my landscape like some noxious chemical leaking into the water-system; wherever I looked, the trees were starting to turn brown.

I hadn't seen her, or Trev, since the month before when I had spotted them outside her apartment building. The day my life had collapsed.

Maybe you understand what I went through. Maybe it has happened to you. First the shock. Then the slow, sick realisation . . .

I can't describe it. Not just now. I'll tell you another time, when I'm feeling better.

I'll tell you about the phone call I received, the next day.

I had lain awake all night, dry-eyed, as cold as lead. I had slept a little in the morning, and at midday the phone woke me up. It was Lila. She sounded breathlessly excited; I had never heard her so happy. She babbled on for a bit about her new project and how they'd had problems with the script. How they needed a British angle, seeing as it was *Jane Eyre*.

'Remember that guy in London? You took me to see his play? So, well, I call him and he comes over to do the re-writes! Where did you *find* this guy? He's fabulous! Boy, does he understand women. You remember that terrific scene where she, like, needs him to dominate her? Well, he's bringing that into this script, that quality.' She paused for breath. 'Hon, I'm so grateful. If you hadn't taken me to see that play . . .'

She had babbled on. My heart was hammering. For a few minutes I thought, wildly, that this was purely a professional relationship. Then I thought: what the hell was Trev doing, going into her apartment?

Besides, there was something in the tone of her voice. I knew, before she told me. 'It's all happened so fast,' she said, her voice confiding. 'It's, like, it's never been like this before. And know something? He's Scorpio – that's my complimentary alignment! Isn't that neat? You've got to come over, we're gonna take you out to dinner.'

I had managed to mutter something polite, and put down the phone. Then I had packed my things, gone to the airport and taken the first flight back to England.

He hadn't told her. *She didn't know.* She thought he was just a friend of mine.

The shit. The bastard. *The shit*.

My flat in Belsize Park had been left surprisingly tidy – no doubt he had cleaned it up, out of guilt. He had even asked the woman downstairs to water my plants. He had left no note, nothing. The bastard.

I had spent Christmas in Arundel with my mother and my brother, whose hair had receded another two inches. I had behaved perfectly normally – in fact, my mother commented on how well I looked. 'Svelte and slim,' she said. I told them amusing anecdotes about the New York film community, dropping famous names because she enjoyed that. I made most of it up, of course. She thought I was having a marvellous time. I used my acting skills to the full; I couldn't let them know the truth and start to feel sorry for me, that would have been insupportable. My mother would have smothered me in sympathy; she was anxious to please, to be of use. She was so suffocatingly kind. She was the sort of woman who asks the Jehovah's Witnesses in for tea.

On Boxing Day Trev had phoned me. I was back in my flat, lying on the bed with the curtains drawn.

'Jules?' he said. 'Listen, hon, I want to explain what's happened – '

I slammed the phone down. He didn't phone again.

As there was nothing for me in England – no job, no man, nothing – I had flown out to Los Angeles.

Why the hell shouldn't I come? Was he going to steal away my expenses-paid trip to California and my $800-a-week job too, on top of everything else? Like hell he was.

By the time I arrived, on January 5th, I was still in the early stages of grief, loss and fury. I hadn't worked anything out, yet. I had no plan. I just felt utterly empty, and seething. Of course I should have forgotten all about it, washed my hands of the whole sordid affair and stayed in England. I know that now.

But I had to come. I needed to be near them. With horrified fascination I had been drawn to the West Coast, irresistibly.

Round and round my head went the same old questions, blunted with endless reuse. How could he have betrayed me? How long had it been going on? Why didn't he tell her about our relationship? How could anybody, even Trev, be such a bastard? Or had he told her, and she didn't care?

I lay there in the sunshine, frying in my own fury. I lit a cigarette; I was smoking heavily, too, and I cursed them for damaging my lungs. Next to me, a man sat talking into a portable phone. His back was felted with black hairs. He even had tufts of hair on his shoulders.

187

'If we're talking Michelle Pfeiffer,' he said, 'we're talking Alice in fucking Wonderland.'

How could she do this to me, a woman who had everything? She had beauty, money, fame, success. She had the whole bloody world at her feet. She had a million-dollar apartment in New York and a house in Beverly Hills. I hadn't minded about thinks like that until recently – in fact, I had despised them. But now I minded, desperately. She had everything the world desired, and on top of that, the bitch had to have Trev too.

I pictured them in bed. It played endlessly in my mind, like a pornographic TV channel. Sometimes I couldn't switch it off; I was paralysed. I couldn't move. I watched their limbs moving together; I watched Lila's lush, bruised lips parting as Trev slid his tongue into her mouth.

'When I get to the office,' said the man nearby, 'this mother's using my phone. He's sitting in my desk, waiting for his calls to be returned. I say to my secretary, who the fuck does he think he is? Ray fucking Stark?'

They were fucking like rabbits. Trev drew back from her, sitting up straight, grinning down at her just as he had grinned down at me. I knew all his tricks. He rocked teasingly from side to side, his cock locked into the wrong woman. He ran his fingertips over her spread, fuller breasts. Was he touching her in the same places, opening her up like a flower?

Disgusted, I swung my legs over the sunlounger and got up. There were only a few people around the pool. They were unmistakably film people – you can always recognise film people – but I didn't know if any of them were attached to my project. A group was sitting around a table, which was spread with papers; a couple of men in shorts were making phone calls. Despite their minimal attire they all looked hard at work. In fact, as I was to discover, movie people in LA work all the time. Even when they are sitting around a pool they're talking business. If they're not doing deals together they are either on the phone or driving their cars – frequently both at the same time. Phones are clamped to their ears like a fungus.

Pasty and English, I felt utterly alien. I had no idea I could feel so lonely amongst people who, after all, spoke my language. When I walked past the tables nobody looked at me. I was just a stand-in, a nothing. In the movie I was invisible. I glanced at the men. They had a sleek, polished look; their faces were handsome but somehow uninhabited, as if they were listening to invisible Walkmen. I noticed this more, as time passed. People here looked like suntanned Mormons. Or maybe it was just my own emptiness in their faces. I don't know.

I stood still, breathing in a scent. It reminded me of Lila's perfume. I was gazing at a bush, weighed down with blooms. A hibiscus, or something. Its blooms were dewy, deep-red trumpets; their throats were velvety and yet moist, too.

'Call Elliott,' said somebody, 'and check on her availability.'

How available was her cunt, moist and welcoming! It opened up for him, when she parted her legs. How he loved to yank my legs up, wrapping them around his neck!

Somebody was staring at me; I must have been standing there for a long time. It was a Mexican gardener, in dark-green overalls. He had paused, in the middle of sweeping up fallen petals.

I went up to my room, got dressed, and went out into the street. The hotel was just off Santa Monica Boulevard, in a nowhere place of palm trees, telegraph poles and scattered buildings. Like most of LA, nothing distinguished it from anywhere else. It was 3.30 in the afternoon, and very humid. Beyond the buildings I could see the smog lying, a brown smudgy layer that looked solid enough to touch.

Cars whizzed past me along the six-lane highway. Beyond was the fainter hum of the freeway, and the wailing of a police siren. Funnily enough, despite the huge sky, I felt more trapped here than I had ever felt in New York. There was no sign of human life. Walking up the road, jet-lagged and benumbed, I started to feel like the only living person on

189

earth. New York had assaulted and excited me – a loud jostle of humanity. Now, in this nowhere place, I had been deserted not only by Trev but by the whole human race.

I walked past a Travelodge motel, swamped in its acres of cars. Looking for a pharmacy, I walked another block and passed a courtyard apartment block, built around a tropical grotto of foliage and a dried-up fountain. I passed a closed Chinese restaurant. I passed another apartment building and heard the jabber of TVs, but saw no sign of life. My legs were aching. I passed a Car Wash and a huge plastic sign saying *Hickory Hut*. I paused at intersections, waiting for the bleeping WALK signal. Nobody else waited beside me. Lila had emptied my world; she had sucked it into her and left me dry and gasping.

I passed a liquor store, barred and fortified. Finally, after six more blocks I arrived at a small shopping mall. It was an L-shaped courtyard of shabby buildings dwarfed by its plastic signs: RAIFA REAL ESTATE. COCKTAILS. KEYS, SCISSORS SHARPENED. I negotiated my way through the parked cars. KODAK COLOR STUDIO. ACUPUNCTURE. NAIL SALON.

Hot and exhausted, I finally gave up. The sun was sinking. In London I would have just been waking up – or was it the middle of the night? The air was clogged with exhaust fumes. Cars were streaming past; it must be the rush hour. When the signals changed to red the traffic stopped and in a moment the street was jammed with BMWs, Jeeps and battered Nissans. The sun flamed against their windows; their radios thumped pop music and Spanish babble. A black girl sat in an open Corvette, tapping the dashboard while Carly Simon belted out *You're so vain*. How many millions of people lived here? What if Lila passed – or *he* did – and saw me all alone? PALM READINGS. CABARET, DANCING, GO-GO GIRLS. Above, the sky was stained red as the sun went down.

If only I had told her about Trev, that day in the changing room at Saks. If I had told her, none of this would have happened. She would never have stolen him from me purposefully – *surely*?

I walked wearily back the way I had come, pausing at the newspaper machines. One sold the *Wall Street Journal*, the next sold *Singles: America's Most Respected Publication for Singles*. They stood there in a row, ready to excrete newsprint in exchange for quarters. If I put in my money I could discover '*How to Hire a Porn Star for Your Party*'.

Night fell swiftly. I walked the streets, dazzled by headlights. A couple of cars slowed down, but then they revved up and drove on again. Maybe I looked strange. Maybe I was talking to myself. I can't remember now. Who knows, if I don't? I saw one other human being, an enormously fat woman dressed in rags. She was rummaging in the garbage bins outside McDonalds, and muttering to herself.

'Gross, gross, gross . . .' she was saying, as she stuffed something into her mouth. She was an old film star, talking percentages. She was Lila, grown vast.

It took me an hour to reach my hotel. In reception I found that my call sheet had been delivered, for the next day. At 7a.m. a car would take me to the location.

I sat down in the coffee shop. There was nobody else there; all the other guests had obviously found somewhere better to eat. I lifted the plastic menu; it was shaped like an avocado and printed with alien names: *Parrilladas, Enchilladas, Tex-Mex Salsaburgers with melted Swiss Cheese, Empanadas Chaperoned with French Fries*. A thousand years ago I had been sitting in Belsize Park, eating at my own kitchen table. My throat felt fuzzy; was it breakfast time or what? I remembered my first morning in New York: the swollen glands, the fevered dislocation. But the hope, too.

To stop looking lonely I pulled out another section of the *LA Times*. A column printed TV soap updates. Pushing some iceberg lettuce around my plate I learnt that, in *General Hospital*, Victor choked on a heart-shaped jewel and died. Across the room the waiter was speaking Spanish into a phone. Outside the traffic hummed past. I sat there with my new companions Thorne and Stacey . . . Ridge and Marge . . . Jerry, who drowned after he jumped off the Capwell yacht.

Later I went up to my room. It was on the fourth floor, and overlooked the parking lot. Beyond that rose up a multi-storey car park: five floors of concrete spaces, lit by fluorescent lights. The cars looked tethered to their meters; their radiator grilles grinned like teeth. As time passed the cars were driven away, one by one, until the place was empty. I leant out of the open window. I heard the eternal hum of the traffic, flowing like blood through the veins of this alarming, alienating, endless suburb. Down below, some insect scraped in the bushes.

What were they up to now? Were they wining and dining at Morton's, prior to a night of tempestuous lovemaking? I could hardly even form the words, they hurt so much. Lila was filming tomorrow; she had told me she always dosed herself into oblivion with sleeping pills and had an early night. Would she be asking Trev to hear her lines and tuck her up? The thought of them being companionable was suddenly, unbearably, painful. Worse than the sex.

I sat down heavily on the bed; its sateen cover sighed. I felt sick with loss. I missed her, you see. I realised it, that night. She had not only stolen Trev; *he* had stolen *her*. He had stolen my friend, my surrogate sister, my glamorous alter ego. However much I resented Lila, I was bound to her. It was like some grotesque soap, more grotesque than anything dreamed up by the makers of *Guiding Lights* or *One Life To Live. Talented struggling actress Jules has discovered that her toyboy Trevor has been two-timing her with beautiful film star Lila Dune. Murderously, Jules plots her revenge . . .'

Except she couldn't even buy a bloody razor to slit his throat. Or her own. Or both. Or shave her legs. She couldn't do a bloody thing.

Two

There had been several attempts to re-make *Jane Eyre*, the most popular love story of all time. After all, why should only Joan Fontaine collect on the residuals? This particular version had gone through four or five metamorphoses.

It had begun some years earlier, in the mid-eighties, when a producer called Monty Leach had had the bright idea of updating it into a dance movie. *Flashdance* had grossed $95 million in 1983, and everyone was trying to cash in. Leach had developed a script with a couple of writers who had come to him with a pitch for another story but who had ended up writing a scenario where Mr Rochester was an old movie star, a virtual recluse, who lived in a Long Island mansion (they were going to use the *Great Gatsby* locations). His wife was a former starlet who had been disfigured in a motor accident and had locked herself away. Jane Eyre was a young dance teacher who had been brought in to train the young Adèle and the movie would be punctuated with dance numbers, including one where Jane, wearing a leotard, sang to Mr Rochester's answering machine: '*Call me Jane, call me plain, call me anything but call me again.*'

This project got the green light – in fact, it started shooting. But on the first day, one of Mr Rochester's Rottweilers went berserk and attacked Jane Eyre, practically chewing off her leg. Filming was stopped and the studio plunged into a $50 million lawsuit.

Another pair of producers picked up on the idea. They put into development a story where Jane Eyre is an au pair who has an affair with her boss, a New York bond broker. This was during the spate of Wall Street movies; Mr Rochester was holed up in a Park Avenue apartment with a mad ex-wife in the penthouse, and the whole block finally went up in flames. Tom Selleck was slated as the star; *Three Men and a Baby*, one of 1987's sleeper hits, had suddenly made him the nation's favourite caring father and this version of Jane Eyre was to end with the birth of his and Jane's baby.

At first draft stage, however, one of the writers had a mental breakdown, the producers were ousted in a studio coup and the project foundered. As independents, the producers moved to a new studio with another package. In this one, Jane Eyre was black. The movie was developed as a hard-hitting costume drama set in a nineteenth-century Virginia plantation. Jane, the daughter of a cotton-picker, worked as a maid in Mr Rochester's mansion. The producers had recently released a controversial rape picture, and in *Jane Eyre* Mr Rochester enjoyed *droit de seigneur* sexual relations with his servant. However, after being blinded by the Ku Klux Klan (a case of mistaken identity) he was rendered helplessly dependent; in a triumphant reversal, Jane nursed him and taught him how to become a warm and caring person. *'When you got no eyes'*, she said, *'all folks is the same colour.'* The marketing line went, *'He lost his sight but found his heart,'* and Whoopi Goldberg and Jack Nicholson were suggested for the starring roles. But that project, too, came to grief when the producers were arrested on a cocaine charge and all the studios dropped them.

I learnt this from reading *Variety* and *Screen International*. Over the past six months I had learnt a great deal about films. I had read every interview with Lila, of course. I had scanned the trades as eagerly as I had once scanned the *Guardian*. I had changed. Even my vocabulary had started to change. My past life seemed grubby, penurious and amateurish. What was the point of freezing rehearsal rooms, the Equity minimum and plays full of integrity that nobody came to see? What was the point of it all? For Christ's sake, where had integrity got me?

You slave your guts out at the Soho Poly, playing an incest victim in some obscure Czech drama to an audience of three, two of whom have just come in out of the rain. You agonise over interpretation, you slave over rehearsals, you get behind with your mortgage repayments and what happens? The chute opens and you're tipped into the garbage.

If this were a movie I'd have my comeuppance. If this were *Jane Eyre* I would win him round in the end. I would be Jane – quiet, mousy and subservient, but burning with hidden passion. As invisible as a stand-in, I would watch the glittering Lilas coming and going, bathed in the spotlight. I would bide my time, and I would get him in the end.

But life's not like that. That's why we go to the movies.

I was driven to the shoot, early the next morning. The driver wore Ray-Ban shades but he still looked about sixteen. He said he was writing a film script. He said the guy who serviced the limo fleet was writing a film script. He said everyone in LA was writing a film script.

Including Trev. Why the hell would anyone sign him up? I'd had diarrhoea that morning; I was damp with sweat. Would he be on the set? Would I see him? Would he try to avoid me – or, worse than that, much worse, would he just not bother?

I had made up my face with care; I had some pride left. When I looked in my compact, however, there were beads of perspiration on my nose. The round, powdery mirror jogged in my hand. Like a camera close-up, it presented me with my own fractured self – eyes, lips. It gave me the most attention I would get all day. I wore jeans, Reeboks and a pink knitted t-shirt I had bought in Bloomies – carefully casual, don't-give-a-fuck clothes. But nobody noticed what a stand-in wore, anyway. I had prepared myself for this moment. In London I had re-streaked my mousy hair; it was nearly as blonde as Lila's. Despite my preparations, however, I suddenly felt flustered. Soon I was going to see them; soon I would be giving the most painful performance of my life.

We drove for miles. The radio burbled on about the traffic build-up: '. . . *a non-injury accident at Cienega and Sunset . . . this news brought to you by Gourmet Pride . . .*' Sitting in the back of the car, I looked at the driver's slender neck and sticking-out ears.

195

'Lila's a bit old, isn't she,' I asked, 'to be playing Jane Eyre?'

He shrugged. In his earlobe, a diamond caught the sun. 'She's the element,' he replied.

Spoken like an executive! Everyone in LA, I was to discover, spoke like an executive. 'Element' meant the selling point, the big name – a big director, a big star. You needed one, to raise the money for a picture. Or two smaller stars who were like half-an-element each.

Lila was a big element, at the moment. Her career had had its ups and downs. There had been a low point in the mid-eighties, when bimbo roles were going to younger actresses, but her career had revived. Her last three films had done terrific business; the *Sexbusters* try-outs had been successful, it was being released in the spring, and Lila Dune was becoming a hot property. See – I could sound like an executive, too.

If I weren't so nervous, I would be giggling. In this re-make of *Jane Eyre*, tailored especially for Lila, Mr Rochester was a reclusive multimillionaire and Jane Eyre was his ward's shrink. *Lila* a *shrink*!

Wasn't that mad? But no madder than anything else. I felt car-sick; I clicked my compact shut and closed my eyes. New York was a deranged city, but this place was far worse. Despite its sunny, bland exterior the whole place was insane. We were in movieland now. I had been drawn here, helplessly, like a planet drawn into the magnetic field of the stars. Did you know that attendance at the Philadelphia Museum of Art has soared? But nobody goes in, they just run up and down the steps, because that's what Sylvester Stallone did in *Rocky*.

If we were in the movies, I'd have screwdrivers for hands. I could drill a hole through Trev's heart. Watch the film! Watch the blood spurting!

Three

The shoot was somewhere out beyond Bel Air, in a gated estate full of mansions. Some were colonnaded; some were turreted like French chateaux. In the sunshine they looked as false as movie-sets themselves, each one the back-lot of someone's demented imagination. The streets were wide and deserted, but real people must be living behind those gates, behind those rows of cypress trees that made mausoleums of the homes. I glimpsed garages filled with four fat cars. I couldn't believe there could be so many people in the world with so much money. It must have been garbage day; outside each gate were eight or nine bumper plastic sacks; I counted them as we passed. The appetite of it all! I thought of Lila; she lay spreadeagled like a map of America; she opened her red lips and sucked it all in: praise, attention, pop-corn, Fudge-Covered Oreos, sex-sex-sex. She munched it all, wetly, pausing only briefly to spit out a pip: me.

Mr Rochester's house was straight from the Yorkshire Moors – well, the Hollywood equivalent. It was weirdly appropriate, a rough-stone, Gothic pile. It was apparently owned by the Vice-President of Sanyo USA. Outside it, the street was lined with trucks, trailers and the usual film-crew collection of Merc convertibles, Golf convertibles and Cherokee jeeps.

'*Advancing on to the lawn, I looked up and surveyed the front of the mansion,*' said Jane. '*It was three stories high, of proportions not vast, though considerable: a gentleman's manorhouse, not a nobleman's seat. Its grey front stood out well from the background of a rookery, whose cawing tenants were now on the wing . . .*'

There were plenty of cawing tenants today. People were

milling around, yelling greetings to each other. I spotted Irma, her hair cropped Führer-short, scuttling along with some files under her arm. Riggers were busy setting up the shot – an exterior scene at the gates. I couldn't see any sign of Lila or Trev.

Before going on stage I've always done my breathing exercises. It calms and clears me. Ten deep breaths, ten indrawn draughts of oxygen. You feel it hissing down to your fingertips, your toes.

I had prepared myself in the car. I had closed my eyes and filled my lungs. Today I needed every ounce of discipline. Cool, calm and detached, I wandered over to the catering trailer. Ostensibly I was inspecting the goods on offer, but out of the corner of my eye I clocked everybody. My heart was hammering. A girl stood beside me. She was vacuously pretty – I guessed, correctly, that she was an assistant in make-up. I gestured at the table. It was laden with muesli, croissants, fresh fruit, and six electric blenders.

'You're so generous here,' I cooed, heaping some melon cubes into a blender and whizzing myself a drink. 'In England you'd be lucky to get a chip butty.'

She adored my accent. She said, 'My sister's dating Tracy Ullman's driver. Isn't she fabulously talented? You seen her TV show?'

I shook my head and took a sip of the frothy drink. 'Seen any of the cast yet?' I asked casually.

She shook her head. 'Sonny's been making-up Lila, and there's nobody else here yet.'

'I hear that she plays a shrink,' I said. I knew the script by heart, of course. The production office had sent me a copy two weeks earlier. But I wanted to hear anything I could.

'The little girl's been screwed up,' she said. 'Adèle. See, her guardian, that's Mr Rochester, he gives her everything in the world but time. Like a lot of Daddies. Like *my* Daddy, you know. He didn't give me, like, *quality* time.'

I smiled. 'Mr Rochester's words, exactly.' I wiped froth from my upper lip. 'Ever read the book-of-the-movie?'

'Also, like, he's a billionaire. He's real rich. And he's

shit-scared of somebody kidnapping his little girl. So he's overprotective. That's what Bikky told me, in wardrobe. She knows the screenwriter.'

I froze. 'Which one? The English one?'

She shook her head. 'He's just come to do a polish. Like, on account of being English, I guess, and boffing the star.'

I turned away, and pretended to inspect a long trailer with a row of doors and steps. There's a joke you hear on film sets – Ever heard of the Polish actress who fucks the scriptwriter?

Maybe he was here, in her trailer. I had spotted Irma going into it – a big, beige star waggon; a socking great thing with black windows, parked down the road.

I stood for a moment, lost amongst men in shorts who wandered around with their jabbering walkie-talkies. I thought about Charlotte Brontë turning in her grave, and my own heaving emotions. I wondered how the hell I was going to get through this.

Then a girl from the production office came up and introduced herself. She was called Chelsea, like somebody in an airport novel. Like everybody else she looked unnervingly young, suntanned and healthy, with strong white teeth. She addressed me coolly. I suspected that they resented me being flown over, on Lila's whim, to work on the movie. Stars were so damn demanding and difficult. I knew I had to charm her – to charm them all.

'Fabulous script,' I murmured. 'Inspired casting.'

She led me over to the First AD, a muscular preoccupied man called Mort. She introduced me to the various members of the camera crew who weren't otherwise occupied. They were lining up the first shot, at the gates of Mr Rochester's house. It was Jane Eyre's arrival for her first appointment with Adèle. She was to have a conversation over the intercom before the gates swung open to reveal a guard and a couple of Alsatian dogs.

I hung around, waiting for Lila, while a track was laid along the street. There was the sound of hammering. Most of the crew already knew each other, from working on other movies, but there was still a first-day-at-school atmosphere. It was hot by now, and I was sweating. Through the open gates I could see the dog-handler brushing one of the Alsatians. Two Mexican extras, who were playing gardeners, sat on the lawn, smoking.

Just then, I heard a familiar laugh. I didn't turn round straight away. I gazed at the plaque on the gate, counting the holes in the brass speaking panel of the intercom. Her voice grew nearer. Still I didn't turn round. I studied the notice, nailed to the gate: ARMED RESPONSE. You saw this on a lot of gates in LA.

I turned, smiling. Lila was walking towards me. *I swung round, raised the machine gun to my shoulder and riddled her with bullets; her flesh exploded.* I didn't look at her. She was with a man. He was bearded, and wore a loose shirt, baggy trousers and espadrilles. An Indian scarf was knotted around his neck; I guessed he was the director, Hutt Sanbourn.

She threw her arms around me and kissed me on the cheek. I smelt her perfume. 'Jules sweetheart, it's great to see you! How're ya doing? Why didn't you return my calls?'

'I had to go back to England,' I replied.

She looked quite different. For a start, she was dressed for the part of Jane Eyre, Psychiatrist. She wore a severe grey suit, with a white blouse and high heels. Quite governessy, actually. Her hair was pulled back in a sleek chignon. But it was more than that. She had lost weight. Her features looked somehow larger and clearer; the beautiful bone structure of her face was revealed. She looked calmer. Happier. My insides folded over in despair.

Swivelling around, she said, 'Notice anything?' She gave me a radiant smile. 'So long, impulse eating. So long, frigging Fritos. I've lost twenty frigging pounds!'

I looked at her tanned, glowing face. She didn't notice that I had lost weight too, for the opposite reason. I looked at her wide mouth. Trev had kissed it now. Not mine – *hers*. Curdled with fascination, I imagined his face sliding down the body I had glimpsed in Saks. I pictured him drooling and nuzzling her groin. In the States they call it *snacking on the carpet*.

'How'd you like it?' She was asking me something.

'What?' I asked.

She was asking me if I liked my hotel. By this time Hutt, the director, had his arm around her and was including me in his first-day bonhomie. People were always nice to me when I was with Lila. I was her appendage, her creature. Her gofer ('go-fer-this, go-fer-that'). I was simply included in his encouraging grin.

'We need you over here, Miss Dune,' he said to her. 'We've moved your mark. You get out of your car, over there, and then come over to the gate here and speak into the machine.'

I was speaking to her.

'Huh?' She asked.

I cleared my throat. 'Is Trev here?'

She shook her head. 'He's gone to the horse races with his dealer.' She laughed. 'He's the only guy left in LA who still does drugs. He's just crazy!' She glowed indulgently. 'He's already totalled his car.'

I didn't see Trev that day, nor the next. It seemed insane, for him to do a polish on a film script. Surely no company would hire somebody with a track record of one play in a pub theatre? Not unless, as Lila would put it, they were total *dorks*. He was – obviously like me – simply here because she had swung it. He was simply her toyboy.

The first couple of days, there wasn't much time to speak to Lila. We were shooting exteriors in the grounds of Mr Rochester's mansion. There was a scene between Jane and Adèle, where the little girl was hostile and withdrawn, refusing to speak to her. 'You're like all the rest,' she told Jane. 'You'll go away, just like the others.' There was another scene between Mr Rochester and Jane. They were strolling through his garden – first a crane shot, then a two-shot and close-ups. Though they were talking about Adèle's progress in therapy,

201

their own powerful attraction to each other was emerging from the sub-text.

I watched carefully. Lila, of course, was totally miscast as Jane. Joan Fontaine was, too. They were both too beautiful. It should have been me playing Jane. Me, the perennial outsider, plainly and neatly dressed '*for I had no article of attire that was not made with extreme simplicity.*' Me who, in the book-of-the-movie, tried to please as much as her want of beauty would permit. '*I sometimes regretted that I was not handsomer; I sometimes wished to have rosy cheeks, a straight nose, and small cherry mouth.*' Or, to be accurate; a snub, kittenish nose and wide, luscious lips.

But this was a modern Jane Eyre, a career woman. She had not married because she had devoted herself to her profession, furthering her career in a tough, competitive, male-orientated world. A hundred years ago they were called spinsters; now they were called singles. Instead of teaching Adèle school lessons she taught her self-awareness; instead of the three Rs it was the one, big I. Me-me-me. The script revealed, in fact, that it was Mr Rochester who was most in need of therapy. He was a billionaire who had not only barricaded his house but his own feelings. His first wife, a heroin addict, was locked away upstairs, but when she finally overdosed, burned the house down and blinded Mr Rochester, he was emotionally liberated and got it together with Jane.

Insane, wasn't it? But no more insane than anything else. No more insane than a movie about a man with screwdrivers for hands. When we broke for lunch the next day I sat on the Thornfield lawn. Even the grass in California felt unreal; it was spongy, thatched and plasticky, like a hair transplant. I leafed through *Hollywood Reporter*. It had an item about some TV game show that was being developed; it was called *Divorce*. '*Separated couples will compete for custody of their children. Says the producer: "We're aiming for a family show, with laughter and tears."*'

Lila was eating with the director, Hutt. During the afternoon, when she wasn't on the set, she was busy with wardrobe, publicity and a long rehearsal with the child who played Adèle. I didn't have a chance to talk to her.

I dreaded talking to her, of course. Whatever she said would be too painful to bear. Whether she told me this was just a brief fling or the love of her life I would be equally devastated. But I was as magnetised as a mongoose, edging around a cobra: I kept making little sallies, though I knew that each bite would be poisonous.

The last shot that afternoon was beside the pool. While Adèle splashed in the water, Mr Rochester mixed Jane a tequila and told her how Adèle was the daughter of an old girlfriend of his, a Broadway dancer who had abandoned her child and run away with a rock drummer. The set-up took some time. I sat at the poolside table with Mr Rochester's stand-in, a pleasant, middle-aged actor called Ivan. He said he was an ex-alcoholic. We chatted aimlessly for a while, as the camera crew busied themselves around us. It was still humid, though the sun was sinking. I scratched a mosquito bite on my ankle. Ivan told me that he had an apartment in Venice and worked out on Muscle Beach. I steered the conversation around to the subject of Lila.

'She looks terrific, doesn't she,' I said, 'now she's lost weight.'

'She's making it with some English guy,' he said. 'They're crazy about each other. This guy I live with, he valet-parks at Spago's and he saw them there last night. He said they couldn't keep their hands off each other.'

I replied politely, 'Really?'

'They got into her car and started necking like teenagers.'

I paused. 'Tiny bit undignified at her age, isn't it?'

'Seen her car?' he said. 'It's full of traffic violations.'

I laughed, lightly. I watched a beetle that was making its way across the flagstones. I waited until it nearly reached the grass, then I moved my foot and squashed it.

Lila didn't avoid me. She just looked radiant, preoccupied and busy. In short, too happy to notice my existence. It was obvious that she had no idea of any connection, beyond casual friendship, between Trev and myself. She was lousy at dissembling; she was one of the most ingenuous people I had ever met. Besides, I had studied her for so long that I could read every expression on her face.

She was, quite simply, transformed. She had no need of me any more, she was emotionally too absorbed. I watched her joking with Mr Rochester as they replaced us, sitting in our chairs beside the pool. She laughed as a mike was dropped down her blouse. Make-up – the vacuously pretty girl – dusted her face with a brush; Hair – a coffee-coloured guy with a pigtail – pulled back a loose strand of her chignon and pinned it up. She wore loose slacks, a matching blouse and a wide belt that emphasised her slender waist. She scratched her ankle. Maybe my mosquito had bitten her, maybe it gorged on our mixed blood. Perhaps she would fall ill with a blood infection and die.

The warning bell sounded. 'Quiet please! Background action . . .' Adèle slipped into the pool and threw a ball around in the water. A gardener pushed a wheelbarrow across the lawn. Up in the house, a maid closed a window.

'and . . . action!'

The scene began. Jane and Mr Rochester started talking. This time Lila had learnt her lines without my help. I watched as they cut, shot another take, cut, shot another. At each take the maid reappeared at the window, like a cuckoo in a clock. Standing there under the eucalyptus tree, I watched the shadows lengthening and felt desolate with fury and frustration.

What was I doing in this travesty of a book that I had loved? When I was a young girl, it had expressed all my secret dreams and yearnings. My father had taught *Jane Eyre*; the first copy I had read was his thumbed and annotated Everyman Classic. The margins were filled with pencilled speculations: *Why? See page 240*. His own wonderings were mingled with my awakening hopes.

Now Mr Rochester was drinking tequilas and smoking Pall Malls. In a cunning stroke of product placement, Adèle's Pepsi can was prominently displayed on the diving board. Jane Eyre arrived in a Chevrolet and talked about infantile rejection.

What the hell was happening? Everything was ruined, every bloody thing, even *Jane Eyre*. Five months ago I had stepped out into the street in my silver dress. I was a fairy godmother, who could make her own three wishes. Why, oh why, had I wished them to come true? If only I had stayed indoors that day, Trev would still love me.

Four

I went to Budget and rented a car. It was a little two-door Ford, the cheapest they had. I drove it around for a while, trying to get my bearings in this vast, sprawling non-city. Like all American conurbations, LA is laid out for imbeciles, on a grid-system, but the distances disorientated me. The whole 100 square miles was just a sliding glitter of cars. Half an hour passed and I scarcely saw another human being. It had been weird enough on foot; in a car I felt utterly disconnected. I drove past Wendyburgers and Pizza Huts and Fitness Centers, past a high school which had its coming events mounted on a huge plastic sign, like functions at a Holiday Inn. It all unrolled with the sunny gloss of a movie. In a car you are passive and sealed-off, released from responsibility; you sit in the driver's seat like you sit in the cinema. You can do anything and who's to know? Recently there had been a spate of freeway shootings – random killings in the traffic. There was a current joke going the rounds: 'Take cover honey, I'm changing lanes.' I drove up Santa Monica Boulevard, past the skyscraper towers of Century City. If I saw Trev in the street, I could riddle him with bullets, put my foot down and hey presto!

I had the LA map spread out on my knee. You can guess where I was going. It was the morning of the fourth day's filming and I wasn't needed until lunch. To get to Lila's place I had to turn left, drive through Beverly Hills, join Sunset Boulevard for a few blocks and then turn north up Doheny Drive.

Trev was living at Lila's house. There was a good chance, of course, that they would both be at home; by the doppelganger nature of my job, my free morning was also Lila's. But I was prepared to risk it, now I had transport. After all, I was only going to look.

Me, nervous? Calm as calm, I took a left and drove up Maple Drive, past white, hushed mansions set back on emerald lawns. In the sunshine they looked as implausible as houses in a dream. They looked like something in *The Wizard of Oz*. Their paintwork made my eyes ache. When had Trev moved in? Early December? Earlier than that? He must have flown over some time then. Were they just friends for a while, or was it instant combustion? *They can't keep their hands off each other*. Trev was a fast worker. How long had it taken, before they'd started balling? Bonking. Boffing.

My eyes hurt. In fact, I seemed to be crying. But you can do anything in a car, and nobody notices. I drove on, past rows of tall, alien trees which lined the road. Their shadows lay across the street like strips of black velvet; their trunks were as smooth and pale as human skin. When I closed my eyes I had dreamed this Technicolor landscape; at night, Lila's house had assumed so many shapes and sizes that it would be a shock to see the real thing. Would I recognise it, from one of my lurid nightmares? I re-wound my dreams, tasting them in my throat, watching Trev's head popping in and out of windows like a cuckoo in a cuckoo clock. In *Jane Eyre*, it all went up in flames.

Christ, it was hot. The radio said it was a record high for January. Sweat trickled down between my breasts; my t-shirt was stained damp down the front. *Gentlemen sleep on the damp patch*. Trev did, actually; as a lover he was surprisingly considerate. Have I told you that before?

I drove up Sunset, and turned left at Doheny. The street climbed steeply, winding up towards the canyons. *Laurel Canyon*, I'd said to Trev, *the starlet with the big tits who so admires your work*. Wasn't I a silly-billy? Fancy thinking a mere starlet would do.

Some of the houses were open to the street; others were

207

walled in. Luxuriant foliage frothed over the walls – bougain-villaea, some large leathery leaves I didn't recognise. I slowed down, searching for numbers. The houses were hidden behind electronic gates; I glimpsed the Armed Response plaques. Famous people lived here; people so rich and terrified that, like Mr Rochester, they hired armed bodyguards to take their children to school. They shoot film stars, don't they? Not just on celluloid. They had taken a pot shot in Rockefeller Plaza; there had been another incident, here in LA, a week or so ago. Some TV starlet; some maniac. But who could be frightened of me? Just a lone woman, in a car. I wasn't going to harm anyone, was I?

I had arrived. I slowed down, my heart knocking. Her house was hidden behind a blinding white wall and white metal gates. But that was the number, all right. I'd copied it from a letter I had found in her apartment.

I couldn't see much, the wall was too high. The street was deserted. On my left, a van was parked in a driveway; a team of gardeners, in green uniforms, was working silently. They descended on the houses like Vietnamese killer squads. One of them was clearing dead leaves with a sort of industrial blower. Otherwise there was no sign of life.

I switched off the engine. I could just see over the wall. I glimpsed a roof, and the top floor. It was Spanish-type. Those ribbed, terracotta roof tiles, mock fishing-village style. White walls; fancy ironwork grilles around the windows, the top of some arches. A profusion of blossoming, climbing plants. That was all I could see.

I climbed out of the car, closing the door quietly, and crossed the road. TOW-AWAY ZONE, said the sign. It was very hot; some insect was scraping away in the bushes, like a demented violinist. The street was swept so clean, it seemed no human had ever set foot here. I felt exposed.

I stood for a moment, watching the gates. I pictured them opening, with an electronic sigh; I pictured Trev driving out in a convertible. Lila was beside him, her blonde hair billowing.

My legs felt weak. I stood still as a deer, my head cocked, listening. Was that a voice? Far away, a telephone warbled, then stopped. Someone must have answered it. I smelt perfume – was it Lila's, or her flowers'? She had given me perfume, once. With my damp finger I had touched my pulse points. Trev was touching her now; a few yards away, at this very moment.

'You have a problem, ma'am?' I didn't hear the car; it must have driven up behind me. The first thing I registered was the voice. A police car had slid to a halt beside me. The window was open and a cop was speaking to me. He had a large, red face.

'You have a problem?' he asked, again.

I must have stuttered something. I can't remember. They must have thought I was crazy, standing in the street like that. What did they think? I was an assassin?

I hurried over to my car, started up the engine and drove away. I reached the bottom of Doheny, driving on the wrong side of the road. I only realised this when I pulled into Sunset Boulevard. Horns blared; cars slewed around me and somebody shouted.

I shrugged. For some reason I started giggling – a weird, high, chattering sound, like a marmoset.

I thought: I can't do anything. I can't walk. I can't park. I can't get out of my bloody car. I can't do a bloody thing.

In New York, men stood in the middle of the street, gibbering.

Do you remember the book? Jane Eyre is intensely jealous of Mr Rochester's fiancée, Blanche Ingram. Her first sight of Blanche is when the couple arrive at Thornfield on horseback.

Times had changed. Blanche wore Ralph Lauren now, and the scene was being shot on Santa Monica beach. Jane Eyre, whilst out jogging, sees Mr Rochester and Blanche horseback riding along the surf. In this updated version Blanche Ingram was a man-hunting divorcée who worked for Mr Rochester's oil corporation as a public relations consultant. Ruthlessly ambitious, she is after both his fortune and a place on the board of his multi-million-dollar conglomerate.

I arrived as the horses were being unloaded from their box. Lila strolled up to me. I blushed. How stupid of me – how could she know where I had been that morning? She was dressed in a dove-grey tracksuit – Jane Eyre wore dove-grey, remember? She was drinking Minute Maid orange juice straight from the carton.

'Hi, hon,' she said. 'Where've you been? Boy, am I pooped out.'

I didn't ask why. We stood there, watching the actress who played Blanche mounting a shiny black horse. It stamped its foot restlessly, and tossed its head.

Lila tossed the carton into a garbage pail. She didn't look pooped-out. She looked wonderful. Her hair was tied back in a ponytail; her cheeks glowed. Trev had a rejuvenating effect on older women; I could testify to that. No doubt he was a lot more fun than her exercise bike.

'Why're you staring?'

I jumped. She was looking at me.

'Nothing,' I said, and turned away.

The scene took a long time to shoot. Any scene involving animals is unpredictable, and in this case there were not only two horses but also Mr Rochester's dog, Pilot. This was a wolfhound which kept barking when the horses broke into a canter. Between each take they had to rake the beach clean of hoofprints. Hours seemed to pass as the horses cantered and Lila jogged.

Finally they set up reaction close-ups of Lila's face as she looked at the happy couple. Standing nearby, I watched her more attentively than any camera. Nobody, not even the director, watched her as I did. Hutt Sanbourn was actually quite a sensitive man, and had a reputation as an enabling director, who didn't impose his ego on actors but who coaxed out of them their own interpretations. I could see that he found it unrewarding, working with Lila. The camera was her confidante, she loved it, but there was no depth to her performance. As she watched the lovers riding by her face was blank. Her head turned, following their progress as if she were a spectator at a Wimbledon tennis match. All she did was to blink several times, and wrinkle her snub nose. Hutt was frustrated, I could see that.

'Let's go for it one more time,' he said, 'OK, Miss Dune?'

If only *I* could step in! I could show her; I could show them all. Watch me! I wanted to shout. Want to see rage, despair and humiliating jealousy? Want to see a real performance, from the heart?

In disgust I moved away, and went to pour myself a coffee. I'd had no lunch, but I wasn't hungry. What did Lila know about helplessness? What the hell did she know about jealousy? It was laughable.

I couldn't bear to watch her. I sat on the steps of the make-up trailer, looking at the sea. The waves looked swollen and oily.

Somebody laughed. In the trailer they were telling jokes about the guys who drove the trucks. I rummaged in my bag for my cigarettes. The beach was the only place in California where you were allowed to smoke.

'How can you tell if a teamster is dead?'

'The doughnut falls out of his hand.'

They laughed again. I gazed at the sand, pitted with hoof-prints.

'How does a teamster ask a woman to have sex?'

'Back it up, back it up.'

Feeling around for my matches, my hand closed around something spiky and metal. It was a key-ring. I took it out.

I knew what it was, of course. It was the keys to Lila's apartment; I had never given them back to her.

I sat there for a moment, looking at the sunlight on the water. Way across the beach, far away, a black guy was doing Tai Chi exercises; he slowly extended first an arm and then a leg.

I don't know how long I sat there. I remember the sun beating down, and the knobbly feel of the keys in my hand. I gripped them; they dug into my skin. They were surprisingly heavy. I was going to give the keys back to her, that was why I had put them in my bag. I really was. Why on earth would I want to keep them?

Afterwards you remember those turning points. Looking back, I can think of at least three. One was when Eric stepped out of that sweet-shop in London, smoking his cheroot. Another was that moment in Saks, when Lila happened to see a zit. And the other was when I got up to give Lila back her keys.

They had finished shooting. A handful of people had gathered, and Lila was signing her autograph for a young girl carrying roller-skates. She said something and everybody laughed, unctuously. Ten to one it wasn't funny. Then she left them and walked towards her trailer, looking at her watch. I went up to her, the keys in my hand.

'He's late,' she said. 'The rat.'

'Who?'

'Tee. He said he'd be here by four.' Impulsively, she linked my arm. 'Know something? I owe you a hell of a lot. You're my Cupid, know that?' She squeezed my arm. 'When you introduced us, that moment, I knew it was something special. Like, the chemistry there! Pow!' She pulled the band out of her ponytail and shook her hair loose. 'We didn't do anything for a while, I think it was too strong for us. You know, it's never happened to me before, not like that, and know why? Because I wasn't ready for it. I wasn't mature enough. That's why I kept having these no-hope relationships with older men. And I want to thank you because it's you who's helped me.'

I must have replied, because she was going on talking. I watched the horses being led into their box; one of them stopped, lifted its tail, and deposited a load of steaming dung on the sand.

'. . . you taught me how to be myself, to liberate myself. To be independent, I guess. That's something I've always admired in you, and I learnt from you . . .'

Jabber-jabber. I watched the smoke rising from the dung.

212

'. . . see, before I've always felt I was like kind of a vacuum. I learnt my lines but I had nothing to say, I had no real identity inside. But you gave me confidence. I just want to tell you that. And now I can respect myself, I can really give myself emotionally to a man . . .'

How long was she going to blather on, the stupid bitch? The sea blurred and danced, like a mirage, in front of my eyes. Nothing was safe. I turned away, so she couldn't see my face.

The unit was packing up. The catering guy was pulling the plastic sacks out of the garbage pails and dragging them into his van. All those styrofoam cups; all that rubbish. They used you, then, when they didn't need you any more they threw you away like an old Kleenex. That's what they did.

When I had recovered myself I turned round. Lila had gone into her trailer and closed the door. I gazed at the beige, ribbed aluminium and the metal handle. She hadn't registered anything. Happiness made her blind and ruthless. She hadn't bothered to ask me anything about myself, about how I had met Trev. She hadn't listened to me at all, or even noticed my face.

I put her keys back into my handbag. I didn't know why. I just felt too angry to give them to her. Maybe I wanted to hold on to something powerful, to keep it in reserve like the last, hidden bullet for a gun.

I closed my handbag with a click. That was the third turning point.

I met Trev a few minutes later. At first I didn't hear the sound of his car, the camera equipment was being loaded into a truck nearby and there was too much banging and shouting. Everyone seemed to be in high spirits that day; maybe because we were beside the sea. But then one of the grips, a guy called Shorty, turned and pointed.

A car was speeding towards us across the sand. It was a black, open Porsche. It slewed to a halt, skidding around sideways. Sand spurted. I heard the thump of pop music. There was a final, throaty rev of the engine and it stopped.

A man jumped out. He wore dark glasses, a plaid work-shirt and jeans.

It's curious. For weeks you imagine something happening; you play it over and over in your mind, in various locations. You rehearse it endlessly, your heart pounding in anticipation. And yet, when it happens, it's still utterly unexpected. You can never be prepared; it happens so fast that you can't catch up with yourself.

I moved behind the equipment truck, so he couldn't see me. He sprinted past, towards Lila's trailer. He looked smaller than I remembered; his hair was longer and my God he'd pulled it back in a ponytail. The trailer door opened and Lila came out. She half-tripped down the steps, regained her balance and flung herself into his arms.

I fumbled in my bag for a cigarette. My hands wouldn't work properly; my legs buckled, they felt as weak as string.

Maybe I didn't stagger at all. Maybe I looked perfectly normal. I heard my name being called.

'Hey, Jules!'

The two of them were walking towards me. They rose and fell, as if I were dreaming them. Trev's face was deeply tanned. I couldn't see his eyes, they were hidden by his shades. His stubble was thicker.

Lila was talking. '. . . you guys . . .' I heard. '. . . getting you together at last . . .'

Trev's hand seemed to be stretched out, waiting. I looked at it for a moment. What was it doing there?

I shook it. His skin was warm and dry. Wasn't he nervous at all?

'How're you doing?' he asked. His voice was just right – polite, friendly. 'Long time no see.'

'I'm fine,' I said.

'So you finally made it to sunny LA,' he said.

'So did you.'

'Been keeping well?' He asked.

'Fine.'

'Like the tan.' He spoke to me like an acquaintance.

There was a silence. The catering truck roared into life and drove away.

I said, 'I thought that was a hamster on the back of your neck.'

He grinned, and fingered his ponytail. 'It's just in development,' he said. 'It's soon to be a major hair design experience, we're very excited about it.'

There was another silence. He stood there, the smug shit, his fingers laced with Lila's. Above us the seagulls circled, mewling.

'I've been telling people what a great actress you are,' he said. 'We went to this party last night, at George Lucas's.'

'How kind of you,' I said.

He turned to Lila. 'I saw Jules on the stage, in London. She was fantastic.'

We paused. The gulls swooped down, jabbing at some spilled garbage.

'I see you're still forgetting to shave,' I said pleasantly.

'Not kidding,' laughed Lila. 'My skin feels like it's been rubbing against a cheese grater.'

Trev cleared his throat. I couldn't look at him. I kept my eyes on his workboots.

'Well,' he said. 'It's great to meet you again.'

Lila nudged him. 'Hey, dorkhead, is that all you can say? If it wasn't for Jules – ' She turned to me. 'We're going to take you out for dinner, real soon.' She turned back to Trev, nuzzling him. 'Aren't we, hon?'

'Sure,' he said.

They moved away.

'Be seeing you,' he said. 'Take care.'

I remember that I walked along Ocean Avenue, afterwards. It was dark. The blood-red sun had long since sunk behind the rim of the sea. The film unit had gone; it was as if they had never been. The beach had been returned to the night.

All I could see was a glow of phosphorescence on the water. It was getting chilly. The pedestrian signal chirruped me to cross, but I wandered over to a bench in the little strip of park. The bench was concrete, and painted with an advertisement. DRUGS. BANKRUPTCY. DIVORCE. BARNEY TOVEY, ATTORNEY-AT-LAW.

I sat down on the cold concrete, between BANKRUPTCY and DIVORCE. On the other side of the street was a row of restaurants, lit for the evening. In some of them I could see the kitchens; white chefs moved around, behind plate glass windows, stirring sauces. In Los Angeles you didn't go to the theatre, you watched your dinner cooking instead. *We're going to take you out for dinner real soon.* Somewhere Trev and Lila would be stuffing themselves with food, greedily. Eating each other.

I had lost count of the number of cigarettes I had smoked. The wide street, busy with traffic, separated me from the restaurants. Once you are an outcast, you suddenly notice that you are not alone. Santa Monica was full of bums. Like cockroaches, they came out at night. They panhandled the streets, their faces looming in the headlights; they weaved amongst the cars, pushing supermarket carts crammed with their belongings.

I sat there, numbly. Behind me, I heard something flapping. A man was shaking out a piece of plastic bedding. I realised, with surprise, that it was eight-thirty. Along the stretch of park, in the shadows, people were settling down for the night. They lay amongst the yuccas, muttering their grievances to the stars. Wrapped in ghostly grey plastic they looked like cocoons. The sound mixer had told me he had worked on *Cocoon* 2 – or did he mean *Cocoon*, too?

I wandered around for ages, vaguely looking for my car. I had forgotten where I had parked it. Fixed to a palm tree was a sign: *Bluff Subject to Slide: Use Park At Your Own Risk*. The concrete steps down to the beach were cracked and broken. Out here on the West Coast nothing was stable; all my old certainties had shifted, from under my feet. I was in the desert now. They had stitched it over with plastic grass but it didn't fool me.

Next thing I knew the phone was warbling. I jerked awake. I was in bed in my hotel room. It was midnight.

'Jules?'

It was Trev.

'Listen, Jules,' he whispered. 'I'm sorry about this afternoon, I felt such a shit. I want to explain everything. You're not working Thursday afternoon, are you? How about a nice cup of tea at the Four Seasons? Four o'clock, OK?'

Five

You start a love affair in the Warwick because it's so private. And you break it off in the Plaza, because it's so public you can't beat each other up. Somebody had told me that, once. The Four Seasons Hotel at teatime seemed about as public as you could get. Who could start a fight amongst dainty cups of Earl Grey? He'd planned it all out, the bastard.

I dressed that morning with great deliberation. My face looked pinched; unhappiness had desexed me; it had aged me alarmingly. I couldn't bear to hear what he had to say.

I stood in the middle of the carpet. I felt utterly exhausted, and I hadn't even met him yet. There were ten hours to go. What if he told me that the thing with Lila wasn't serious, he was just using her to get into the movie business? Could I believe that? What if he told me that this was just a mad fling, and that he'd come back to me in the end?

I felt sick. I pushed some more bangles onto my wrist, and brushed my hair. For the hundredth time I asked myself: what would Lila do if I told her the truth, that Trev and I had been lovers for the past two years? How would she react? Would she be outraged, that he had lied to her and that, by doing so, he had shown himself capable of lying to her again? Would she be sorry for me and break it off? Or would she just say to me, '*Tough shit, cookie-face. That's the way it crumbles*'? They had both betrayed me terribly.

At seven o'clock I drove to the location. We were shooting a scene on Rodeo Drive. Jane Eyre goes into a jeweller's shop to get her watch-strap mended. Whilst she is standing at the counter Mr Rochester and Blanche drive up in his Jaguar XJ-S convertible, park outside, enter the shop and choose an

218

engagement ring. You might think it sounds unlikely for a shrink to get her watch-strap repaired in Van Clees & Arpels, but there you go.

It was a complex scene to light, because the shop was an Aladdin's cave of precious jewels. They winked at me; they hurt my eyes. I stood for hours at the counter, resting my hands on its glass top. Jon, the cinematographer, shouted instructions to Andy, the gaffer, and his scurrying crew. They darted around, pulling clothes-pegs off their t-shirts and pinning up screens and filters.

'I'm getting a kick off that necklace, move it to the left . . . Lose that piece of white paper, next to the cash register . . .'

I'm losing you, the love of my life.

I stood there, numb as a cow waiting at the slaughter-house.

'So you're an actress, then?' Trev, wandering around my living room, picking up books and inspecting them. His jeans were torn at the knee. 'Should I know you then?'

'Only if you want to.'

His grin, flashing.

A light-meter was held in front of my face, impertinently close. Why were they doing this to me? Maybe I should speak into it. Christ it was hot. I was suffocating.

'Fancy a drink? I've got the van outside.'

Assumed indifference. My heart hammering. 'OK. Just a quick one.'

I was locked in limbo. Around me, bejewelled clocks were displayed in their illuminated niches. Their hands had stopped. On the other side of the counter stood the actor who played the shop assistant. He was chatting to me, from far away. The words came out differently.

'Let me guess. You're a gin and tonic.'

'Pint of bitter.'

'Ah, the woman of my dreams! I've been searching for you all my life.'

Around me they banged and hammered; the whirr of a Black & Decker drilled into my skull. *I didn't even like beer. I only drank it so I could have the same liquid inside me as was inside this guy who had delivered my chimney pots. Wasn't I foolish?*

'You OK?'

A face loomed up, close.

They sat me down for a while. They thought I was ill. Lila seemed to be there now. She was particularly skittish that morning; she exuded such sexual gratification I could smell it. She flirted with Grant, the focus-puller. She always flirted with focus-pullers, I had noticed it for months. They were out front with her, in front of the camera; they were the willing accomplices in her sensual relationship with the lens. Revolting, wasn't it?

The warning bell rang; it made me jump. They went for a take. Lila spoke her lines to the shop assistant, lifting her watch and showing it to him. Somebody seemed to have brought me a glass of water; they must have done, because I was holding it in my hand. At the back of the shop, faces were clustered around the video monitor. They were lit an eerie, misty blue.

Trev, walking round that restaurant, his napkin over his arm. 'Are you ready to order, sir?' Walking from table to table, in his black suit.

Me, watching him. My hand clapped to my mouth, giggling into my fingers.

The door opened and the camera dollied round as Lila turned to stare at Mr Rochester and Blanche. They entered the shop arm-in-arm and laughing. Members of the crew watched, poised and hushed like doctors gathered around an operating table.

When we broke for lunch I couldn't eat. I went into the make-up trailer to fix my face. Sonny was sitting in there, eating a toasted muffin and watching *I Love Lucy* on his portable TV. He was an amenable guy; he sat me down in front of the mirror and got out his powders and brushes.

'Got a date? he asked. 'Someone special?'

I smiled mysteriously. He didn't just touch up my face, he

had his professional pride. He gave me the full works: sooty eyes, sculptured cheekbones. Forgotten in the corner, Lucille Ball yacked at Desi Arnaz.

'You have a fabulous face,' he said. 'Plenty of character. It doesn't jump out at you all at once. Kind of releases its secrets, slowly. I've been longing to get my little paws on it.'

He stood back and looked at me proudly, like a cook inspecting a perfectly risen soufflé.

'I can always recognise my work,' he said. 'Some extras, they don't wash it off for days, they just touch it up each morning. I met one on Melrose, once. She said, "I'm taking care of my investment."'

I thanked him and left, walking down Rodeo Drive. I wasn't needed that afternoon, they were shooting scenes with Mr Rochester and Adèle. I had three hours before I had to be at the hotel.

I felt weak with dread; it came in waves, flooding me and then retreating, leaving me drained. Rodeo Drive was flanked with stores – Armani, Valentino, Christian Dior. Parked Rolls-Royce Corniches and Range Rovers gleamed in the sunshine. Their drivers were propped against them like dolls. Flowers blossomed in tubs; they looked as perfect as plastic. The whole street had a toytown unreality. When I was a little girl I dreaded the dentist because in those days it hurt like hell. The hours before my appointment had the same glazed artificiality; my impending pain set me apart from the passers-by, who went about their business sealed off from my terror, as silent, colourful and innocent as fish in an aquarium.

I walked down Olympic Boulevard and went into the Nieman Marcus department store. It was full of rich women with time to kill. I wandered around, my face stiff and hot under its mask of cosmetics. Maybe Trev wouldn't recognise me; maybe he would fall in love with me, all over again.

I went up to lingerie. Everything was made out of silk and ostrich feathers and cost about $3,000. Maybe Lila shopped here. Blonde women fingered the underwear; they had stretched, wolfish faces like Joan Rivers. *'Sure she had plastic surgery; I cut up all her credit cards.'* Soon Lila would be due for her first nip-and-tuck. Even a film star couldn't stop the clock. She had a Polish granny with loose skin on her hands. She and I had giggled together like sisters in the changing rooms.

Next to lingerie there was a roped-off snack bar called The Fresh Market. More paper-thin women sat there, toying with low-sodium salads. I sat down. A server approached. He was a small, swarthy man; his name-badge said *Jesus*.

'And what would you like today?' he asked.

I thought: *a miracle*. If Trev were sitting next to me, he would grin and say to him, *'How about a couple of loaves, with fishes on the side?'*

Suddenly I missed him, desperately. I missed his jokes.

Jesus stood there, fiddling with his order pad. He looked embarrassed. That's because I was crying again. At least I wasn't making a noise; I managed to do it almost silently.

Wasn't I stupid? All that lovely make-up ruined.

I waited until ten past four before I went into the Four Seasons Hotel. I did have some pride.

The hotel was not far from Rodeo Drive, on Burton and Doheny. I had spent the afternoon wandering around in the sunshine, feeling nauseous. I knew Trev so well; I could guess exactly what he was going to say. And yet I didn't know him at all. Not now. I had re-run so many different conversations that I felt dizzy. My rehearsals had confused me.

The Four Seasons was a luxury hotel surrounded by foliage. I had imagined so many versions of it that the reality gave me a jolt. As I arrived, gardeners were planting ornamental cabbages in the flowerbeds. Stretch limos were sighing to a halt outside the lobby; bellhops were scurrying around, valet-parking cars. There was a brass plaque beside the door, warning me that Trev was inside. *DANGER. This Area Contains Chemicals Known to the State of California to cause Cancer, Birth Defects and other Reproductive Harm.* Funny, wasn't it, that there was a law forbidding smoking, but no law forbidding the possession of an armoury of automatic machine-guns and Kalashnikov rifles with which to blow people's brains out. Trev's brains, for a start. Insane place, America. It drove me insane, in the end.

The lobby was all marble floors, carved stone tables and huge, spotlit bowls of lilies. A Vivaldi lute concerto played over the sound system. Trev obviously believed in disposing of me in style.

I went into the Rest Room, brushed my hair and inspected my tense, glistening face. I put on some lipstick and returned to the lobby. My heart thumped. To my left was an ornate drawing room, all creamy silk settees, mirrors and obelisks. It was empty, except for a sign pointing to the *Microsoft Strategy Briefing*. Where was he?

I asked the concierge for instructions and he directed me across the lobby. On weightless legs I walked through an archway and into the bar area. I glanced around. No sign of Trev. He hadn't arrived yet.

I sat down at a table. It was an elegant room with a grand piano, recessed lighting and trompe l'oeil murals. A waiter came up and I ordered a pot of Darjeeling tea for two.

I lifted my wrist to look at my watch. My hand was trembling. It was 4.15. A brochure on the table informed me that I was in *an oasis of privacy and calm, where my every moment would be cushioned and pleasured by the incomparable Four Seasons service.*

There was only a handful of people in the room. At the next table sat an intense-looking Jewish woman and two young men.

'It's a relationship picture,' she was saying, 'and I've added the environmental issues.'

Should Trev find me casually reading my book or gazing into space? The young men were telling the woman how much they admired her work, and how she could give this project a lot of edge. They said it was very much a go project now. Her cloudy black hair was tied up in a spotted ribbon; she wore a black trouser suit and white Reeboks. She said that since she'd had children her writing had a stronger dramatic centre.

'Having my two kids, it's like, a reality base,' she said.

It was 4.20. The tea arrived and the lute concerto started replaying its loop all over again. Trev was always late; how many times in the past had I waited for him impatiently? How many times had my suspicions stirred? I'd never let him know, of course. I opened my Maya Angelou novel and pretended to read, but the print danced in front of my eyes.

A phone warbled. I jumped. The woman opened her tote bag and pulled out her phone. For a mad moment I thought Trev was calling. She'd pass the phone over, saying, *'It's for you.'*

She was speaking into the phone. 'I'm still in my meeting, Max. Why don't you call Nicky Stein and ask him over to play? Put Fiona on . . .'

It was 4.25. A man came into the bar; I froze. But it wasn't Trev. The man walked through to the garden.

'Fiona?' said the woman. 'Go into my office, press button 6 on my phone, that'll connect you to the Steins, and ask Nicky if he wants to come over and play.' She put the phone back into her tote bag and said to the men: 'I'm a high-tech housewife.' They laughed. She said, 'I'll give this project some serio-comic thought.'

They started talking about their favourite Monty Python sketches. People in LA were always talking about their favourite Monty Python sketches. She liked the Silly Walks and they liked the Dead Parrot. It was 4.40. This was a designated smoking area and I had smoked three cigarettes, threatening reproductive damage to both my neighbours and myself. I had drunk two cups of tea, the cup chattering like teeth against the saucer.

I gazed at the large, leather-bound folder that contained my bill. It was as heavy as a library book. At five o'clock I finally admitted that he wasn't coming, the low-life, snivelling little coward. So I paid up and left.

Trev phoned me late that night, when I was in bed.

'Where the hell were you?' I asked.

'I'm sorry,' he said. 'Honest.'

'Why didn't you come?'

'I meant to,' he said. 'Honest. Straight up.'

'Think I liked just sitting there?'

'Look, I've got to be quick.' He paused, lowering his voice. 'I started out. I got into the car and everything. Then I thought: what's the point?'

'What's the *point*?'

'Where would it get us? We'd have all these recriminations. You'd just get upset.'

'Upset?' I gasped. 'My God, your grasp of vocabulary . . .' I took a breath. 'Look, we've got to talk.'

'You wouldn't want to hear it.'

'What do you mean?'

'You just wouldn't.'

'Go on,' I said. 'Try me.'

'Look, we knew it wouldn't work out in the end.'

'What the hell do you mean?'

'You know what I mean,' he said.

'No. What?'

I heard him taking a breath. He had prepared this. 'When I realised that you put your career first, that it was more important than your life with me – '

'You lying creep!' I yelled. '*You* suggested I came to America – '

'You were always too intellectual for me, you knew that. Come on. If you're honest. Listen, Jules, you'll find someone more your level. You're incredibly attractive – '

'Christ almighty! The condescension!'

'It's *you* who were condescending,' he said. 'You were always analysing me, you made me feel inferior – '

'That's a lie!' I shouted.

'Now I've found someone who's not superior, who just loves me – '

'When did you two get together?'

'Look, I didn't ask to come out. I want you to know that.'

225

His voice was spuriously sincere. 'Her office contacted me. What could I do?'

'You could've *told* me!' I yelled. 'When did it all start? Before you went to Scotland?'

He sighed. 'That's why I thought we shouldn't meet. What's the point? You'd just shout and scream – '

'I wouldn't!'

'Look, Jules. I'll always be grateful to you, you know that, but let's have no hard feelings – '

'No hard feelings?'

'Maybe when it's all over we can still be friends – '

'*Friends*? You lying shit! You bastard! You never even told her about us!'

'I can't talk to you, if you're going to be like this,' he said, and put the phone down.

I jumped out of bed, rummaged in my bag for my address book and found Lila's number. In that moment of fury I suddenly didn't give a damn if she knew the truth. What the hell. She'd see what kind of a creep he was.

I dialled but I only got the engaged signal. The bastard must have taken the phone off the hook.

Six

I behaved perfectly normally the next day. The rest of the
cast was performing, but boy could *I* act! I was pleasant
to everybody, you would have been proud of me. I chatted
between takes, I shared a joke with Scott, one of the grips,
and I listened patiently while the continuity girl told me how
to make a marbled vegetable terrine. We were filming up in
the Will Rodgers State Historic Park, a beautiful mountainous
region north-west of LA. The sun shone. We were shooting
a sensitive and relevant scene where Jane Eyre, wearing a
fetching period costume of bikini top and tight white shorts,
is hiking. She's in tears, on account of the Blanche Ingram
business. And what do you know? By chance she happens
to meet Mr Rochester, who is fishing and who happens to
be landing a twenty-pound salmon, brought in fresh that day
from Gelson's Fish Counter.

I've always prided myself on my self-control. That stupid
outburst on the phone – Jules shouldn't have done that. She
had sat there, shaking, in her pastel hotel room; she had sniv-
elled into her Kleenex. How could she have been so stupid?
She wouldn't do *that* again.

Phaedra was the first film where a woman really cried. Do
you remember it? Melina Mercouri, and her mascara ran
down her face. She looked mannish and ugly; she looked real.

I watched Lila. She had taken my place on an outcrop of
rock. She stood there, being shot in profile. The wind blew
her hair; on her cheeks were glycerine tears. She looked as
bland and glamorous as a shampoo ad. No Mercouri, she.
The stupid bitch couldn't act to save her life. What did she
know about grief?

Trev wasn't around. At lunch-break, trestle tables were set out in the car park, a stretch of tarmac with a Scenic View. I sat down next to Chelsea, the girl from the production office. She was pulling giant prawns apart with her fingernails.

'Where's the English guy?' I asked casually. 'What's-his-name?'

'Trevor Parsons? He's back in the office, doing re-writes.'

'So he's not coming up today?'

She shook her head. 'We've nailed him to his desk.'

I didn't know whether to be relieved or disappointed. I gazed down at the city; smudged with smog, it stretched to the horizon.

'He's working on the big sex scene between Jane and Mr Rochester,' she said, chewing. 'Know what? I didn't understand, at first, why they brought him in. He had no experience. Hutt was really antsy about it.'

'Antsy?'

'Ants in his pants. But Trevor's fabulous! Everyone's really pleased with what he's coming up with. His work, it has a lot of energy. Kind of moody and erotic. Hutt says it reminds him of the early Sam Shepard.' She sucked her fingers, one by one. 'Kind of looks like him too, don't you think? Right down to the Calvin Klein work-shirts. Who's betting he's left a few broken hearts in England.'

'Who's betting,' I said, gazing at a bottle of mineral water. At the far end of the table Lila laughed.

How could Trev have attacked me like that? *'Lila's not superior, she doesn't analyse me, she just loves me.'* She was a working-class, uneducated woman, that's all. Obviously he couldn't cope with anything more subtle and challenging than that. He couldn't cope with an intelligent woman like myself. He wasn't man enough for that. He wasn't even man enough to meet me at the Four Seasons.

I wasn't going to cry. Not now – not any more. No Mercouri Mascara Runs for me.

We broke early that day, at four. I had to talk to Trev. Calmly

228

and reasonably. I had to salvage what was left of my pride. He wasn't going to get away with it. Did he really think I could be fobbed off that easily, after two years?

Lila was staying behind; a journalist from *Redbook* was interviewing her. No doubt she was telling her all about her wonderful new relationship with the priapic Trevor Parsons, and how great he was in the sack. Pow! The chemistry between them! How she'd really gotten the confidence to give herself emotionally. How every woman needs a toyboy; a lot more fun than a face-lift and twice as efficacious!

I got into my car and drove down the winding mountain road, fast. The sun was sinking; it was suddenly chilly. Night fell quickly, here. Didn't the stupid cow realise he was using her, just as he'd used me? *I* wasn't going to tell her, nope siree! Let her find out for herself! I was driving through the residential area now. The road was cracked from landslips, but vast mansions stood on either side. They had stable blocks and servants' blocks, towers and turrets. Up above the smog line, these properties were worth millions. Heady stuff for a boy like Trev, who had grown up in a house with an outside toilet. First step, me. Second, Hollywood. *'Their properties and possessions are seen as reflections of their core being,'* I had read in a magazine. *'Affluent Americans today enjoy a standard of living that matches the splendour of the medieval popes.'*

I slewed into Sunset Boulevard. It was thick with rush-hour traffic. Recklessly I weaved through the cars; I was heading for the Hyatt Hotel. The production office had taken over a couple of suites on the second floor; Trev had a desk there.

I had planned exactly what I would do. I would go in, ostensibly to pick up a copy of the next week's shooting schedule. I would saunter into Trev's office, express surprise that he was there, and casually suggest we went for a drink at Barney's Beanery. This was a big, dark, macho bar – Trev's sort of place, with pool tables, thousands of different kinds of beer and signs that said things like *'A Fool and his money are soon Partying'*. I had gone there, a few nights before, for the production runner's birthday drinks.

I parked outside the Hyatt and brushed my hair. How could the bastard cut me dead, in mid-conversation? I slammed the car door shut, like a cop, and strode towards the hotel. I had rehearsed several speeches and finally decided on this one. I know what you mean, Trev – see, I've fallen in love too! Couldn't tell you on the phone. I wanted to, though; I wanted to share it with you. Pow! The chemistry. It's amazing, the sex is astonishing, quite unlike anything I've ever known. Isn't it wonderful when it really happens? I met him in New York; he's called Clayton and I met him in a restaurant in Greenwich Village. Now he's followed me out to LA because we can't bear to be apart. Maybe we'll all make a foursome some time. I'm so happy! For me, and for you.

I took the elevator up to the second floor and knocked on the door of the production office. It was empty except for one of the secretaries, a girl called Mary-Beth. She was on the phone. 'He'll be here for the dailies,' she said, looking at her watch. 'He's coming in from New York, with the composer.' The other phone rang; she darted to it and started talking to Cy, the location manager.

There were three doors leading out of the office. Two were closed. I breathed deeply, doing my pre-performance exercises.

Mary-Beth looked up. 'You OK?'

I nodded. 'Which is Trevor Parsons's office?'

She pointed. 'Over there. But you just missed him.' She smiled indulgently; Chelsea had smiled like that when she'd spoken about Trev. He obviously had a debilitating effect upon Californian women. 'He says it's their anniversary.'

'Their what?'

'It's four months since he met Lila. He's gone back to her place; he's planning some surprise dinner.'

I shrugged. 'I see.' I paused. 'Well, I'll just leave him a note.'

Stung, I hurried into his office. Their anniversary! When had he remembered *our* anniversary? Bloody never. On our first anniversary I'd booked us dinner at Orso's, but he had forgotten all about it and gone out on the booze with a mate of his, some builder. I'd had to cancel the restaurant. He'd crept into my bed at two in the morning, giggling, 'Got plastered with a plasterer.'

I sat down at his desk. In front of me was a silver-framed snapshot of Lila and a box of typing paper. His old Olympia typewriter sat there; he had obviously brought it over from England. He was deeply superstitious about his typewriter; he refused to work on any other one. In fact, I had bought him an electronic Olivetti but he had never used it. He could only work on his heavy old manual one; he'd bought it from Look Back in Ongar.

I sat down and slotted in a sheet of paper. At first, I thought I would simply write him a note. I sat there for a moment. But what on earth could I say?

So I did something else instead. Maybe it seems insane, to you. It seemed insane to me, later. But I had to do something to release my feelings.

I tapped out a letter to Lila on the heavy old keys. I had to bang down on the keys, hard, with my forefinger.

Dearest Lila
I know I'm a lousy coward, but believe me it's easier this way,
I've been trying to find the words to tell you that I don't think
we should see each other any more.

I stopped to inspect it. I was grunting with my exertions. I went on.

I've found somebody else. You suspected it, I denied it. I'm
sorry. This time it's the real thing. I've never felt like this
before. Maybe, when it's all healed, we can still be friends. I
hope so. And let's remember the good times.
All the best for the future. Chin up and take care.

I pulled it out of the typewriter and re-read it. A bit abrupt, but there you go. I signed it *Tee*, copying his writing. I folded it up and put it into my handbag. Then I left the office and went back to my hotel.

I honestly don't know why I did it. For comfort, perhaps. When I was typing it, actually, it did comfort me. Just momentarily; mildly. It assuaged my feelings.

Maybe I was superstitious. Once it was typed, maybe it would come true. It was like putting pins into a wax figure and making a wish. LA was riddled with superstition, with Tarot-readings and palm-readings, with horoscope hot-lines and miracle cures. It was Lila's sort of town. It dealt with magic. It was built on shifting sands and the San Andreas Fault; it was built on the illusions of celluloid, the stuff of dreams and delusions. Maybe the place was seeping through to me.

I was embarrassed at myself. It seemed such a pathetic thing to do. But I didn't throw the letter away. I hid it in my suitcase.

Seven

Pride stopped me approaching Trev again. In a way I was glad that he hadn't been at the production office; I might have broken down and made a fool of myself. The only way I could salvage my dignity was to play it cool and unconcerned. I would bide my time and work out a more effective plan of revenge.

It was bloody torture. The next week we moved to the sound-stage, at the studios, to shoot interiors at Mr Rochester's house. Trev appeared and I had to watch him canoodling with Lila in front of everybody. They giggled like teenagers. I caught Irma's eye, once; she was watching me. I think she guessed something was up between Trev and me; she was much sharper than Lila. But she had never liked me, so why should she care? She could see that Lila was slipping away from me, too, and I could detect a certain satisfaction on her sallow face.

Trev and Lila were the flavour of the month. Hollywood loves romance and there was something irresistible about a film star's infatuation with an unknown young English writer who had the impish grin of a new Steve McQueen. Toyboys were all the rage; Joan Collins had one, Stephanie Beacham had one. They were every woman's antidote to ageing. Whenever I read a gossip column, Trev and Lila's names sprung from the page. *'I've lost 20 Pounds and 20 years!'* trilled Lila. *'She's got a fantastic sense of humour,'* said Trev. *'He's given me new stability,'* she breathed. *'She's the most beautiful woman I've ever met,'* said Trev. *'It's like Christmas every morning!'* she gushed. *'I want to go for every experience and live life in its quintessential form,'* said Trev. Grinning inanely from flashlight snapshots, Trev was variously described as a drop-out, a builder, an antiques runner and a radical writer whose outspoken beliefs enraged the stuffy British establishment.

They had met in London, and since then had been in daily contact on the phone – '*our hour-long Indian love-calls*,' said Lila – before he flew out to join her. Apparently he was also writing a novel. It was called *Heavy Petting in Hornchurch* and was bold, erotic and autobiographical. The synopsis had been sent to Bantam Books amidst rumours of a six-figure advance.

Could I really believe it? Was he really writing a novel, and, if so, would I feature? Could I really believe that '*We're too happy to consider marriage*' when the *Hollywood Reporter* claimed that '*Wedding bells might be in the air*'?

Where was my Trev in all this? Did he really say 'quintessential'? Could he possibly? I despised myself for my weakness, for my demeaning, slavish passion. I wanted my old Trev back – feckless, unreliable, charming – the love of my life. Alone in my hotel room I could admit it; just to myself.

I thought of his play, *Use Me*. He had certainly used me, with a vengeance. Things that I had said started appearing in his re-writes. Jane Eyre told Mr Rochester a psychiatrist joke that I had told Trev long ago. She brought him some cuttings from her African violets, just as I had done once. Mr Rochester liked Ry Cooder and she gave him a cassette which he already had in his collection, so he hid the original in his jacket pocket and she felt it when they were kissing. Trev had ruthlessly cannibalised our most tender and playful moments; he had exposed them to the world. Worse, far worse – he had stolen them from me and given them to Lila. It was Lila who spoke my lines now, and caressed the back of Mr Rochester's neck. It was Lila who told him, just as I had told Trev, that he had the sexiest bum she had ever known. Except Lila called it 'ass'.

The most painful moment came during one of their love scenes. In the script, Jane has been evicted from her apartment building – developers are converting it into luxury condos – and she moves into the guest wing of Mr Rochester's house.

It is here that she slowly falls in love with him, even though he is having a relationship with Blanche Ingram. (At night, when Jane lies in bed and hears a distant cry from Mrs Rochester, she presumes it is Blanche in the throes of orgasm.) However, Mr Rochester finds himself irresistibly drawn towards his ward's shy therapist and they become lovers. In one scene he pretends that he is blind. He comes up behind her and feels her all over, making guesses on who she might be.

I went cold, when I read this. The day before we were due to shoot it I spoke to the director, Hutt.

'Surely it's a bit sick, isn't it, when later he's blinded for real?'

But Hutt said, 'We've given it some thought, Jules. We've discussed it together and we've come to the conclusion that it's kind of moving – being already an established motif in their relationship it makes his real disability all the more powerful when it occurs.'

Who was a mere stand-in, to object?

The next day I stood on the set of Mr Rochester's bedroom – a lavish, mock-baronial affair complete with four-poster bed and hunting trophies, just like the Ralph Lauren shop. Trev was there, leaning against the dressing table and joking with one of the grips. I wanted to shout: clear the set!

While they set up the lights I positioned myself with Ivan, the other stand-in. He pressed himself against my back; I smelt the tuna on his breath, from lunch.

I tried to pretend I was relaxed. 'Sorry I'm not a bloke,' I whispered, and he laughed.

We didn't have to perform the action – his hands running over my body. We didn't have to speak the lines. We just stood there, while Trev blew the smoke off his coffee mug and watched me cruelly exposed.

When they were ready, I was ushered away and Lila appeared on the set. She wore peach-coloured silk underwear; Mr Rochester wore a black, monogrammed bathrobe. Twenty years earlier they had been lovers, real-life lovers, whilst filming *Flames of Love*, and they acted this steamy scene with some conviction.

I watched Rochester, his eyes closed, pressing himself against Lila and running his fingers over her face. '. . . mmm . . . soft young mouth . . . warm lips . . . you're the checkout girl at the A&P.'

'Nope,' murmured Lila, her head flung back. She moistened her lips with her tongue.

The crew held its collective breath; everybody watched as she wriggled her shimmering, silky body; she parted her red lips and my words came out of her mouth.

He ran his hand lightly over her breasts; she started breathing heavily. His hand caressed her thigh.

'. . . ah . . . dancer's thighs . . . you've just arrived in town, all dewy-eyed . . . you're auditioning for *Fame 6* . . .'

The atmosphere was electric. Nobody stirred. Finally the scene climaxed in a close-up of her face as his hand slid to her crotch.

'ah . . . now I can guess,' he muttered hoarsely.

Followed by the camera, they stumbled onto the bed. Lila wrapped her legs around him.

She murmured, 'Know what you are? Shrink-wrapped.' This was Trev's joke.

When they cut there was a moment's silence, then the crew burst into spontaneous applause. I turned and looked at Trev. He was clapping too.

'Print that,' said Hutt. 'Hose down the crew.' He strode across to Lila and hugged her. 'Where did you find that, honey?' he asked. 'It was sensational!'

I had to get out. When they broke for tea I made for the exit, tripping over the cables and hurrying past the extras who had arrived for the next scene and were stuffing themselves with Danish pastries.

Outside it was quiet. There was a sharp, golden light; the sound-stage buildings looked as huge and faceless as cliffs and their shadows lay solid across the road. They looked like factories; people could be making carburettors in there. An electric buggy, loaded with documents, passed with a sigh.

I walked across to the back lot. I walked down the main street of a Wild West town: wooden façades on both sides of me. They were propped up at the rear. Through their sightless windows was the empty sky. Nothing was secure any more; nothing could be trusted. Touch it and it would all collapse. Lila re-staged my most intimate secrets in front of a horny film crew and, eventually, a horny audience of millions. With the willing help of Trev she had appropriated my past and taken it for herself. How could he just stand by and watch?

I walked into another part of the lot and found myself in small-town America. There were white picket fences and white clapboard houses, their porches shaded by trees. How innocent it all looked! At any moment James Stewart would saunter towards me, strolling out of *It's a Wonderful Life*. He'd be loose-limbed and engaging; maybe he'd be whistling. Doris Day would pop her head out of one of those windows, its chequered curtains blowing in the breeze; she would call her invisible children in for milk and cookies.

Our lives seemed so sunny and secure, but it was all as flimsy as a stage-set. Poke it and it keeled over. I pushed open a gate, walked up to a house and peered through the window. There was no mother inside, baking me cookies. There was nothing. Not even walls. It was as echoing as a warehouse. Just emptiness and some Coke cans, swept into the corner. Nobody was waiting for me, their arms open. I had no lines to speak.

The only way I could sabotage Lila was through her work. That was where her weakness lay. The only power left to me lay in my superior ability as an actress.

First of all, however, I needed Hutt Sanbourn on my side. He was the director and he held us in his hands. Up until now he had scarcely noticed me. I was simply a piece of furniture to be shunted around; he would then stroll on, like the owner of a house, and size me up to see whether the removal men had put me in the correct position. I think he had realised, from my various observations, that I was a great deal more intelligent than most stand-ins. Most actresses, in fact. But I needed to get to work on him.

My first thought was to try and seduce him, but I was too low-spirited for that. My confidence had taken a battering. Besides, I was outclassed. He had recently married his third wife, a gorgeous Finnish starlet. I had to try other means.

I had an opportunity to talk to him the next day, during lunchbreak. For once Hutt was alone. Nobody hassled or importuned him; nobody rushed up with urgent messages, proffering him the phone. He was leaning against a wall, leafing through the script and eating a BLT in an abstracted manner; a wisp of lettuce had got caught in his beard. He was a big man, running to fat. He wore red espadrilles, loose grey trousers and a grey checked shirt; he looked casual and approachable.

I told him how much I had admired one of his earlier films, a psychological thriller set in the Bronx. 'It reminded me of Chabrol in his heyday,' I said. 'Subtle and playful and unnerving.'

He was pleased, I could see that. The film had bombed at the box office. I flattered him, just as I had flattered the director of *Bump*. We talked about the European cinema and agreed that Truffaut's *Day for Night* was the best film ever shot about movie-making.

'I'd love to work in Europe,' he said, wiping some mayonnaise off his lip. 'In the present climate it's almost impossible to get a high-quality product made in Hollywood. There's no stability or continuity.'

I commiserated with him. 'It must be so frustrating.' I meant: working with people like Lila.

He said that very few actresses were trained on the stage, like me. 'It must be kind of frustrating for you, too,' he said.

I shrugged. 'It's a learning experience.'

'See, they don't have the reserves to draw on. They don't

have the background or the depth. They come in, raw, from the boonies. From modelling.'

We watched Lila. She was standing with her business manager, inspecting the salads.

'From Miss New Jersey Dairy Products,' I said.

'That where she started?'

I nodded. I popped a grape into my mouth and told him how I had worked for the RSC, up at Stratford.

He looked at me respectfully. 'No shit?'

'In Trev's Golden Period.'

'Trev?'

'Trevor Nunn.'

'What roles did you play?' he asked.

'Imogen. Hedda Gabler. A wonderful role for a woman. That was at The Other Place. An absolutely electrifying chamber production.'

Just as I was getting into my stride, he was called away. Maybe it was a good thing. He might have started to cross-question me.

But directors don't. All directors have tunnel-vision; they have to, in order to get their jobs done. I watched him talking to the line producer. I had achieved my goal. I had charmed and flattered him; I had impressed him with my deep theatrical roots.

And for the first time he had noticed me as a person. I would work on that.

Eight

I started undermining Lila's performance. This wasn't a difficult task. She hadn't understood the character of Jane Eyre at all, she hadn't inhabited her. During the fortnight of location shooting this had been apparent, I was sure, to Hutt, who had frequently looked somewhat underwhelmed by her interpretation. But those had been breezy exteriors, with few close-ups and little dialogue. Now we were sealed into the intimacy of the sound-stage, knuckling down for the bulk of the shooting, with long and complex emotional scenes ahead of us.

Lila simply couldn't act a woman who feels plain and neglected. Her only ploy was to take her glasses off and put them on again. She had no experience to draw upon, and she lacked the talent and imagination to think herself into the role. When had *she* been overlooked? When had *she* felt invisible?

The day after I had spoken to Hutt, the director, we were scheduled to start shooting the party scene. It was a typical Californian get-together. The men – Colonel Dent, Mr Eshton, Sir George Lynn and various other tanned freeloaders – play pool and talk real-estate values. The women – Blanche, Mrs Eshton, Louisa, Mary and Amy – drink Napa Valley Chardonnay and discuss their exercise routines. Jane Eyre, a mere lodger, feels uncomfortable. She is both an outsider and a career professional. Unlike the other women there, she is not making her living out of alimony. She is also deeply jealous of Blanche.

The party was held in Mr Rochester's den – a mahogany-panelled set, with a pool table and deep leather chairs. Jane Eyre, looking awkward, is offering a plate of taco shells to the guests. In rehearsal Lila played Jane like a gracious hostess. Her only sign of insecurity was a worried look at herself in the mirror, a quick tidy of her hair and a glance at Blanche.

I watched her with contempt. Newly-risen from Trev's bed, she positively glowed with triumph and gratification. Didn't she understand how Jane would behave? *I* knew, of course. *I'd* show them! I had plenty of experience upon which to draw. If a person feels excluded, they console themselves with food. If nobody is talking to them, they occupy themselves with displacement activities – sifting through the host's record collection, inspecting his books, anything.

Lila was taking ages in make-up, so Hutt called, 'Let's run it through. Jules – try the moves.'

So I began. I stepped in front of the camera. I performed my own interpretation and added my own bits of business. I went over to Mr Rochester's CD collection, picked up a couple and turned them over in my hand with exaggerated interest before I put them down. I paused, and gazed aggressively at the guests – for when we are vulnerable we become hostile. Standing around the pool table, the extras watched me with surprise. I leafed through a copy of *Newsweek*, pretending to read it, just as I had pretended to read magazines when I was a teenager and nobody had asked me to dance. I dredged up the most painful memories; they took me over. I stuffed taco shells into my mouth, I sat down and started pulling bits of thread out of my sweater. I fiddled with the gold chain around my neck. I breathed fast; that old, forgotten adrenalin fired up in my veins, like a boiler bursting into life after the dormant months of summer.

When I had finished there was a moment's silence. Then Hutt stepped forward. Frowning at me, he tugged at this beard.

'Jules, can we talk?'

Heart pounding, I followed him like an errant schoolgirl following the headmaster. We stepped through into Jane's bedroom.

He said, 'Know who I saw just then?'

'Who?' I whispered.

'I saw Jane. For the first time, it was Jane Eyre out there. I don't know why you did it, Jules, but it was a turning point for me. I just want to share that with you.'

He gave me a quick hug, just as he had hugged Lila. I smelt his musk-oil aftershave. And then he left me, abruptly.

They changed the marks and altered the camera angles. When Lila returned, Hutt took her aside. 'This way, it just looks right,' he said.

I strained to hear. 'You didn't like what I did?' Lila demanded.

'It was great. But let's try it this way, hon.'

And she did. When they shot the scene, she incorporated my bits of business. It improved the scene out of all recognition; it lifted it and gave it psychological truth. She didn't act as well as I did – that was apparent to everyone. Also apparent was my own contribution to her performance. Delighted with her, Hutt moved in closer and shot tight on her face.

Over the next few days I avoided Lila. I went behind the set and sought sanctuary with the noddies and extras – or background artistes, as they prefer to be called. For fifty dollars a day they had mouthed party noises. Now they sat around, leafing through magazine articles about aromatherapy. Some of them had brought their plastic recliners with them and they lay there with their feet up, reading Sidney Sheldon novels. I have always identified with extras – I was hardly better than one myself. They are simply camera-fodder. Nobody knows their names; they appear on the set for a day, maybe two. Strangers to the sealed-off family of the cast and crew, with its running gags, its emotional undercurrents and its growing cohesion, they are ignored until needed. Meanwhile, they stuff themselves with the unit catering, slipping melon slices into doggie bags; they steal bits of birthday cake, because it's always somebody's birthday on a film unit. They whinge about wardrobe and how they have to bring along their own shoes; they all seem to have a relative in hospital, with shingles. They hardly know the name of the film.

Just at that moment, such detachment was a relief. I had more plans, you see, and I needed to think about them. I sat on a props settee and leafed through *Variety*. There was an ad for a company that supplied synthetic blood for the movies; it supplied sixteen kinds, ranging from bright-red Accident, through Congealed to Brown Scab.

I nibbled a slice of pizza and talked to one of the pool players. I didn't catch his name. He told me that his daughter was getting a divorce. Then he told me how much it cost to add an earthquake clause to his house insurance cover.

'You listen to me, honey,' he said, wagging his finger. 'One day this whole goddam city's going to be swallowed down its own ass.'

I swallowed my pizza and imagined Lila and Trev stark naked and struggling, being hurled down a fissure like a Bosch painting. Tongues of flame licked out of the San Andreas Fault. Whose Fault was that? I heard their screams. I watched their bare, thrashing limbs.

I knew I was heading in a dangerous direction, but I couldn't stop myself. Some demon inside me pushed me on. '*O judgment! Thou art fled to brutish beasts/ And men have lost their reason.*' Emboldened by my earlier success, I upstaged Lila's rehearsals, and several more times Hutt suggested that she incorporate my reaction when they came to shoot the scene.

I knew, partly, why I did it. I wanted to trip Lila up; to disconcert her and threaten her performance. I wanted to show her up. But I also wanted her to notice me. Pathetic, wasn't it? I felt like a child, showing off in the playground.

That Thursday, I hardly saw her. She was having lunch somewhere with her agent, Roly; he had flown over for a few days and had spent the morning on the set. When she reappeared, she seemed perfectly normal. That woman was so bloody smug and myopic. Happy, I guess. She was obviously too dense to notice how Hutt was starting to rely on me, using my moves and suggestions. Or maybe she was more secure in her acting ability than I had thought.

We worked hard all that afternoon, shooting some lines of dialogue between Jane and Mr Mason. I felt strangely powerful, standing there in the lights. I felt that something momentous was about to happen. The crew seemed quick-fingered and alert, darting here and there; the extras seemed as restless as horses before a storm. There was something going on, something brewing.

When we wrapped for the day I collected my things and went out to the parking lot. Dusk had fallen but the air still felt stuffy. I walked past the numbered bays which were reserved for the studio executives. Beyond them I saw Roly, climbing into a Lincoln Continental.

'Hi,' I said, walking up to him. 'Remember me?'

'Sure I remember you. It's Jules, that right?'

I nodded. 'You like the picture?'

'Sure,' he said. How could an agent say anything else? 'Great story.'

Roly real name was Lester Rollins. He had the hottest client list in New York. Squat and balding, with a plug-ugly face, he glistened in the gloaming. His skin had a waxy, unhealthy pallor, as if he had been hidden for too long under a stone. In fact he was one of the most repulsive men I had ever met. That's what I thought, when I first saw him. But he did fascinate me, even then. There was something soft and female about him, as if in a former life he had lived in a harem. He wore a grey suit, and a white shirt that stretched tight over his belly.

Maybe I wasn't so fascinated, yet. But I was curious. He had discovered Lila when she was unknown; he had guided her through twenty pictures and two marriages; he was involved in a part of her life about which I knew nothing. He was her confidant.

'You've been trained on the stage?' he asked.

I nodded. 'I went to RADA.'

'I could tell, by the way you were working today.'

'Did it show?'

'You shouldn't stay too long in that job,' he said, gesturing back at the factory building.

'I don't intend to,' I replied.

He climbed into the car, and the driver started up the engine.

I started questioning Trev's re-writes, too. That was my other plan of action. Maybe I could even get him thrown off the project. After all, why should the shitty little opportunist get away with it? Why should shagging Lila turn him overnight into Britain's answer to David Mamet? Once, long ago, I had been so supportive. I had helped and encouraged him, chatting up my contacts in the theatre on his behalf. Loving him, I had persuaded myself that his work was terrific. Now I could see it clearly. He had brought a certain raw energy to the screenplay, but like Lila he hadn't a clue about Jane's motivation and character. This was one of the tasks he'd been brought in to point up, and in my opinion he had failed dismally.

I said as much to Hutt. Not in those words, of course; I wasn't a complete fool. Hutt and I had become pals, chiefly because he was besotted with the theatre and I was the only person with whom he could discuss his long-held dream of mounting an off off-Broadway production of *Huis-Clos*. It's a truth, universally acknowledged, that all the people directing off off-Broadway want to go to Hollywood and become famous film directors, whilst famous film directors in Hollywood all want to go off off-Broadway and have lots of integrity.

Anyway, I told him I was reading a biography of Sartre. I wasn't, but I went out and bought one. He asked if he could borrow it; I said I would drop it off one evening.

He was staying at the Château Marmont Hotel, an eccentric-looking pile in West Hollywood. As its name implied, it was a phoney French lookalike, complete with turrets. I had been there before, because I had heard that European film crews booked in there and one evening, when

245

I was feeling particularly desperate, I had driven there in the hope of repeating my Warwick experience and picking up somebody for a night of obliterating sex. However, I'd discovered that the hotel didn't have a bar, so I had gone home again.

I drove there on Monday evening, passing along the luridly-lit Strip with its loitering male hookers. The air was heavy and thundery. I arrived at the Marmont, crossed its wood-panelled lobby, all antlers and sconces, and took the elevator up to Hutt's suite. His secretary, a blonde woman called Mercedes, showed me in. Hutt was on the phone. Everybody in LA is always on the phone. He was talking about somebody called John, whose marriage was just breaking up.

I looked around the room. Film people's hotel rooms are always the same. In marked contrast to arctic rehearsal rooms, they are always swelteringly hot. There are always masses of files and papers on the floor and a sheaf of numbers by the phone. There is always a lavish but half-eaten meal from room service. Hutt's Finnish wife, who was hugely pregnant, wandered in from the bedroom and nibbled a celery stick.

'Hutt,' I began hesitantly, 'something's bothering me about tomorrow's scene. The fortune-telling scene between Jane and Mr Rochester. In the scene Mr Rochester disguises himself as an old hippie. Jane believes every word he says.' I suggested gently that this wasn't true to Jane's character. Trev had rewritten this scene for Lila rather than Jane. Lila was an instinctive, credulous woman, a slave to her emotions. She put her trust in Tarot cards and fortune tellers. 'But Jane's not like that,' I said. 'She's a cool, intelligent shrink. She has a crystal-clear knowledge of her own psyche. She believes that truth isn't found in your horoscope, it's found in yourself.' I sat back, breathlessly. My nerves had made me pedantic.

Hutt tugged at his beard. Avoiding his eye, I gazed at the hunting print on the wall; hounds and horses streamed over a mythical English landscape.

'I hear what you're saying,' he said.

*

When I came out of the hotel, it was raining. The rain drummed like a war tattoo on the leathery leaves as I walked to my car. All over the city I sensed the plants opening up and drinking.

I too was gasping for life. This nowhere city had tried to rub out my existence but I was fighting back. I had argued not for Jane, but for myself. And I was going to bloody win.

There was trouble ahead, I knew that. I knew I was behaving dangerously, but wouldn't you? I remember that night so clearly. I ate in the hotel coffee shop; it was too wet to seek out somewhere else. Afterwards I hurried across the courtyard. The pool was goosepimpled with raindrops; the scent of damp concrete gave me a lurch of homesickness for England.

I went upstairs and scuttled along the walkway to my room. I hadn't seen the altered, ponytailed Trev for days; absence had hardened him into my enemy. I could hardly catch up with myself. For two years I had festered with imagined jealousies, but now it had become true, in this most unlikely, banner-headline manner. I couldn't entirely believe it. I suppose I was suffering from delayed shock. When my father died, it was weeks before it truly hit me. Even his funeral had passed in a glazed way which I couldn't connect to the real person. It was only later that I was poleaxed by his loss.

That night I stood under the shower and turned the water scalding hot. I still couldn't quite believe it, that Trev had left me. At odd moments, I still expected him to walk through the door. Whistling, he would saunter around the room, jangling his van keys and flipping through my magazines. He would lean against the bathroom doorway and grin at me as I stood in the shower. His eyebrows were raised, his eyes were running up and down my body. I wouldn't know if he found me hilarious or deeply desirable. Then he would lunge forward and kiss me, licking my face like a dog, getting his shoulders soaked. I would drop the soap and we would struggle, dragging the shower curtain with us, stumbling against the lavatory . . . giggling at first and then suddenly, blindingly, serious . . . Oh his mouth, his hands.

The atmosphere on the set was growing more tense, day by day. Trev didn't appear; he was probably avoiding me. Lila didn't speak to me. There were rumours that she was having problems with the part, and making things difficult for Hutt. I heard her shout, 'I'm not wearing these goddam glasses! They make me look like a fucking professor!' She spent a lot of time in her dressing room. One day a scene had to be abandoned because she said she was hyperventilating, and we lost half a day's filming. The next day the producers appeared and met with Hutt. Maybe she was going to have another of her nervous break-downs; she'd had enough of them in the past. After all, she was a highly unstable woman. How Trev put up with her, Christ knew. He should have stayed with somebody strong and intelligent like me. Maybe she was going to start hitting the bottle again. Maybe she would go AWOL and wake up in a Ramada Inn in Indianapolis. They'd lock her up in a loony bin, which was where she should have been all along.

I inspected my face in the bathroom mirror. I looked gaunt; my lips looked thinner. My tan had faded, from three weeks indoors on the sound stage. She didn't look like me any more; what glittering eyes she had! *Mirror mirror on the wall, who is the fairest of them all?* Shakily, I spread lipstick around my mouth, until it was smeared crimson.

The weather had turned colder. At night I walked for miles, briskly, humming tunes from the sixties. At the hotel I chatted to the night captain. We were friendly; he had seen me come and go a lot, these past evenings.

'So how're your kids doing?' he asked.

'Fine,' I replied. I'd told him that I had got two children back in London, a little boy and a little girl. It gave me a buzz, to talk about them. We'd discussed what gifts I should bring them back, from LA.

'Big day tomorrow,' I said. 'We're shooting the mad scene.'

'Mad scene?'

'Where Mr Rochester shows Jane his crazy wife.' I grinned. 'Can't wait.'

Nine

That night the earth didn't just move for Trev and Lila.
There was a tremor, too, north of Los Angeles. It was just
a minor one, some low number on the Richter Scale. Merely
a windowpane-rattler.

I heard about it on the radio as I drove to the studio. Each
morning I crossed the hills to Burbank. Sunset . . . Laurel . . .
Mulholland. Houses hung crazily over the canyons; film stars'
hideaways teetered on the edge of the precipices. Wooden
ranches and Moorish bungalows . . . high-tech glass boxes
with their jutting sun decks . . . did they really believe they
were safe? One two three . . . a big breath . . . I'll huff and
I'll puff and I'll blow them all down.

Below the smog line the sands would shift, the freeways
crack. The dry hills would shift and crash bang wallop! Too
bad, folks!

The sky was a hazy blue, as it is today. I'm sitting here in the
sunshine, trying to remember that morning as I drove past the
flimsy dwellings of that flimsy city. Non-city. Nowhere place.
Raymond Chandler said it had no more soul than a paper cup.
It's dissolved now; I can't grasp it. I couldn't grasp it then; it
slipped through my fingers.

Everyone was jumpy, that morning. I presumed it was
because of the earth tremor, Californians' regular but unpredictable brush with mortality. They were all scared stiff of the
Big One: their own Apocalypse that was, so far, locked away
in the rock, geology's best-kept secret. Even the laid-back Hutt
looked nervous.

Lila was in wardrobe, having her wedding dress fitted. We
were shooting the climax of the movie where Jane, in her

wedding dress, is dragged upstairs by Mr Rochester and confronted with his first wife, a gibbering, psychotic junkie.

I ate a bagel with the standby chippie. 'Lila's raising hell this morning,' he said. 'Must be the weather. She's been bawling out Hutt.'

He said he had been at a bar, the night before, when he had heard the news of the tremor. He said the bar was run by Dean Martin's old double. Or was it Robert Mitchum's? I can't remember now. The guy was an ageing alcoholic, I do remember that. Stuntmen, doubles, stand-ins – they all seemed to end up ageing alcoholics.

They had set up the shot, but nothing seemed to be happening. Mrs Rochester's room was furnished like a clinic – all white walls and an institutional bed. The actress who played her sat on the bed. Her hair was black and matted. She looked like the Wild Woman of Borneo.

Tempers were short. Hutt had disappeared somewhere. My stomach ached, for some reason, and when I poured myself a coffee my hand was trembling. Maybe it's another tremor, I thought. Maybe it's me who is perfectly sane, perfectly steady, and it's the rest of the world that's collapsing.

I lit a cigarette. Trev was around. I had seen his car in the parking lot. He must be in Lila's dressing room.

The minutes ticked by. Something was wrong. Even Bruce, one of the more Neanderthal grips, asked, 'Where the fuck is everybody?' The actress who played Grace Poole inspected her watch impatiently, like a staff nurse. She wore a starchy white uniform.

By 9.30 neither Hutt nor Lila had appeared. The atmosphere was edgy and yet oppressive. I suddenly had to get outside and breathe some fresh air. I hurried to the door.

Lila stood outside, arguing with Hutt. She wore an ivory satin wedding dress, but she had pulled off the veil.

'I don't give a flying fuck,' she said. 'I'm not working with that fruit any more.'

I dodged behind a truck, and listened.

'She's off her head,' hissed Lila. 'She's a fucking psychotic! Why don't they lock her up someplace?'

Just for a moment I thought she was talking about the mad Mrs Rochester, that she was psyching herself up for the scene and improvising some lines. I crouched behind the truck, trying to catch her words. Hutt was arguing with her, in a low voice, but I couldn't hear because a helicopter clattered overhead.

'. . . she scares the shit out of me . . . she acts so weird . . .'

The noise was so loud it seemed the sky was breaking. I leant against the door handle.

'. . . you notice, she never speaks to me now?' said Lila. 'We used to be pals, we used to have fun together.'

The clatters faded away. I heard her quite clearly now.

'You've seen what she's been doing, showing me up in front of everybody. What's gotten into her? This is the most important performance of my career and it's going down the goddam toilet! What's she trying to do, take over my goddam part? They all get too big for their boots, that's the problem . . .'

Hutt said something. I couldn't hear.

Lila was speaking. 'Tee says you've got to get her off the picture. He says she's damaging me – Hutt, I'm cracking up –'

'But Lila –'

'Last night he had to call the cops!'

'The *cops*?' said Hutt.

I felt dizzy. I pressed against the door, my eyes squeezed shut. I smelt the warm metal.

'She's been parking her car outside my house,' said Lila. 'Three times – Tee's seen her. She drives up at night and turns off the engine. She just sits there, in the dark. I've gone to bed by then but Tee's seen her. Hutt, it gives me the heebie-jeebies!'

'What happened last night?'

'When the cops arrived, she'd gone. What the hell's she think she's doing?'

There was a pause. The sun had come out; it beat down on my face. I hardly dared breathe.

How come he'd seen me? *I* hadn't seen *him*. Just lights in the windows; sometimes a shadow moving. That insect, scraping away in the bushes. The faint sound of a TV.

Hutt took Lila away. I only realised this, because there was a silence. I peered out from the truck and saw them hurrying towards the production office, a low building fringed with palm trees.

I didn't tell you, did I? That I had been driving there and parking outside her house? Well, why should I?

Anyway, it didn't seem worth mentioning.

At school, long ago, I stole some money from another girl's locker. They never found me out, but I remember the days passing, and how I waited for the headmistress's footsteps.

I didn't have to wait long, that February morning. At 10.35 I was chatting to Mr Rochester, who like everybody else had been hanging about for hours. We were discussing Jamie Lee Curtis, who was starring in some TV cop show. I'm glad to say that I was behaving perfectly normally.

I sensed Chelsea coming in, before I saw her. Then she was beside me, and whispering into my ear. 'Jules, could you go to the production office?'

How glazed and unreal it all seems now! I'm pretending it's a movie.

It's not quite right, of course. If it were a film, they would have re-scripted that part. The showdown would have exploded during the climax of the mad scene. Lila is suddenly grappling not with the mad Mrs Rochester but with her stand-in. *You've been spying on me!* She's clawing her hair and screaming at her. The stand-in punches back and starts screaming back *You've stolen my boyfriend!* Two blonde women are fighting like cats, spitting and shouting in front of a speechless crew. Hutt strides over. *Clear the set!* he shouts, his commands echoing through the ranks like a jungle call. *Clear the set!* . . . fainter and fainter. We're finally torn apart.

We sit back, panting, our breasts heaving. We're sweating like Raquel Welch in that thing where she wore the suede bikini . . . slippery cleavage, tousled hair . . .

I told you that they wanted to film my story, didn't I? CBS, I think. Well, that's the way they'll film it. I'll tell them it happened that way; it's more *filmic*, isn't it.

Life's not like that. But it's just as unreal. I remember the walk to the production office. The joints in my legs felt loose. I passed the rows of blinding cars, oh so many cars, everywhere rows and rows of them. I passed a hedge of oleanders, eternally in blossom. I stepped over a low fence and crossed the plasticky, woven grass. Here and there were little puddles, where it had been hosed. The door of the production office was open.

Walton, the production manager, was alone. He wore a crimson t-shirt with some lettering on it that I couldn't read. He didn't meet my eye; instead, he addressed the framed movie posters on the wall.

'. . . deeply regret . . . must let you go . . .'

I remember some of his words. Not all of them. I was sitting in an armchair, running my fingers over its ribbed wool.

'. . . it's not my decision, but you must appreciate . . . Miss Dune is our number one priority . . .'

He was talking to a poster of Al Pacino, who gazed back, droopy-lidded.

'. . . she feels threatened and insecure . . . we can't take that risk . . . she may be making a mistake, but without her there's no movie . . . you have real talent, there's a real future for you, but . . .'

His eyes shifted to Bruce Willis, a poor likeness. We both looked at the twin barrels of his rifle.

'. . . financial arrangements . . . reimbursed in full . . . call you tomorrow . . .'

So I was kicked off the picture. Mercedes, Hutt's blonde secretary, took over my place as Lila's stand-in, and in two days I was on a Continental Airlines plane, flying back to New York.

NEW YORK

One

Chances are, you've met a murderer. Maybe just briefly, in a swing door or in a queue at a check-out. Maybe you've sat next to one in the bus. Statistically you must have passed several in the street, during your lifetime. You didn't recognise them, did you? Their breath doesn't smell differently. They look just like you or me, in fact. I'm the same as you, just driven one stage further, to breaking point. I've met plenty of murderers. Pitiful specimens, most of them. But they've only killed once. Women don't make a habit of it, you see. They don't go into McDonalds and spatter the place with machine-gun fire, grinning like Manson as the skittle-bodies fall.

You think I behaved oddly, on occasion? No more oddly than you, if you look into your hearts. It's only hindsight that makes you glimpse a pattern and draw your own hasty and smug conclusions. You shape up a person's life to make sense of it all. I have plenty of time for hindsight now. It's my own private entertainment channel, non-subscription, and I can re-run it in my head as frequently as I like. Which is often. Pretty continuously, actually.

Those early weeks in February I didn't know who I hated more: Lila or Trev. Lila had stolen my lover, she had played earthquakes and collapsed my world. More than that, she had stolen something in me, and was too damn self-absorbed to notice. Film stars are egomaniacs, and Lila was a film star down to her painted, slightly-chipped fingernails. She hadn't even thanked me for visiting her bloody mother; she didn't even know anything about me. I was as irrelevant to her as a piece of india-rubber.

But then it was Trev who had persuaded her to get me thrown off the movie. It was Trev who had jilted me; who had blown his nose on me and thrown me away like an old tissue. Worst of all – worse than anything – he really didn't seem to care. He and Lila were two of a kind. They were instant amnesiacs. They lived for the moment, like beasts.

I sub-leased an apartment in New York. Hutt, probably prompted by guilt, had given me the number of his sister who was out of town and who needed someone to rent her place. It was down near the Village, on 14th Street and 6th: a huge, shabby apartment building with rusting windows and jutting air-conditioners. It seemed a suitable enough place to go crazy. New York is a place that drives you to extremes. If you're happy, it drives you ecstatic. If you're depressed, it drives you suicidal. If you're crazy – why, it drives you crazier!

You thought I would go back to England? Nope, siree! Not me. I lay on my bed, brooding. Way down below I heard the wailing police sirens. New York City sucked me in, all over again. I lay immobile for hours, like Robert De Niro in *Taxi Driver*, planning and plotting my revenge. The apartment was just a single room with a pull-down bed. A fat, old-fashioned radiator squatted under the window. It was my only companion. Occasionally it gargled, and at night it rattled as if it had bronchitis. My room was sweltering, but outside my window a thousand smoke-signals rose from the skyscrapers, from the Chippendale cleft of the AT&T building, from manholes in the icy streets.

I went out, some nights. You wouldn't believe some of the interesting people I met. One woman loomed up out of the dark. Her hair was threaded with bits of kitchen foil. She smiled at me and said, 'I'm an accident waiting to happen.'

Sometimes I took a bus. I didn't know where they were going, but then nor did most New Yorkers. The city teemed with mysterious buses from rogue bus companies; their windows were tinted black and they took routes of their own

258

devising, steaming through the streets and suddenly halting at unknown bus-stops. But at least they were warm and I was on the move. My spirits lifted, then. Most of the passengers seemed to be deranged.

'You talking to me, lady?' a man asked me, once.

'No,' I said.

'What's this guy Trev?'

I looked out of the window, concentrating on the neon lights. The man went on staring at me. Why did everybody behave so strangely?

I'll tell you where I liked to go. Atriums. Those glassed-in plazas. They were nice and warm, for one thing. The same temperature as LA. The same plants, too. I had three favourites: the IBM, the Citicorp and the Park Avenue. Anyone could go and sit in them for the whole day if they liked, as long as they didn't act weird. Well, really weird.

They were public spaces, you see. The property developers had to donate them to the city in return for building a socking great skyscraper on top of them. I liked to take my lunch to the IBM Plaza. I'd buy a kebab, at a stand in the street. There was an open space nearby, between the buildings. Frail, leafless saplings were planted there, against a concrete waterfall. It was a whole wall, running with water; it seemed like the building was crying. But it was too cold to sit on one of the spindly wire chairs and I would push through the revolving doors into the huge, hushed IBM.

Outside, the trees shivered soundlessly as the wind blew. Trucks slid past. Indoors it was as seasonless as California. I sat down at a table. Each table was occupied, territorially, by a single person. Some of them looked as if they had been there for weeks. The black men wore leather caps with ear flaps; they shuffled repeatedly through their collections of carrier bags, like a nervous tic. I took out my book but nowadays it was too difficult to read; it required such monumental concentration. How had I ever managed it? Big fat people sat there, too fat for anyone to love. They wore baseball caps and had Walkmen plugged into their ears. The bamboo trees looked as Chekhovian as ever; they hadn't shed their leaves. But the tubs had been replanted since I had last been there, in November. The chrysanthemums had gone, and now spears of daffodil foliage poked between papery house-plants; they poked out like the knives in Lotte Lenya's boots.

I had nobody to talk to. The ache tightened around my brain and constricted my rib-cage. Sometimes I could hardly breathe. I took Seconal pills, like Lila. I used to sit in the IBM atrium for ages. Opposite was a garage. At intervals its doors slid open and swallowed a car; in the afternoon the process would be reversed, with cars emerging. High achievers were driving home to their families. Bitterness corroded my bones, like acid. In my saner moments I knew I should go back to London, but something locked me. Fury, I suppose. And despair. In fact I could hardly move. How could I possibly make all those travel arrangements when I could hardly drag myself across the street?

I told you I plotted my revenge, but in fact I don't think I did anything much. For two weeks I simply existed, numbly. I moved through the streets sluggishly, like a blind catfish at the bottom of the ocean. The streets were full of skips, dust and sudden gaps as shocking as a missing tooth. On either side, buildings were bandaged as if they would bleed. Lorries full of rubble jammed the streets; hoardings were removed with a flourish, like theatre curtains, to reveal new granite lobbies swarming with workmen. They stripped off the masking tape like Elastoplast; it made you wince. It all happened so fast, no wonder people got confused. During those weeks a new building was going up outside my window; day by day it rose, blocking my last gasp of a view. Soon the sun would be shut out and I would be faced with windows full of stenographers, so close I could see their charm bracelets.

I suppose I was simply waiting for something to happen. Besides, how could I go back to England and face my mother and the few friends who thought I was in Hollywood? They presumed I was having a thrilling time working on a major motion picture.

In fact, I phoned my mother one evening and told her my latest news. 'We've been shooting on location in the desert,' I burbled. 'Gosh, it's hot! Been to lots of parties and you should see my tan.' I lay on my bed, gazing at a crack in the ceiling. It was a rent-controlled building and they were trying to kick out my landlady by letting the place fall to bits.

And then, one afternoon, my luck changed. I knew it would, sooner or later. I had got up at noon and decided to visit the Museum of Modern Art. This was to convince myself that I could still do something. I had been starting to panic, you see. I thought I would never be able to do anything, ever again, except take long baths and lie on my bed.

That day I managed to get dressed, eat something and take a bus uptown. I walked the last few blocks along Park Avenue, a street whose monolithic, fuck-the-rest-of-you apartment blocks made me feel as puny as a snail.

I never got to the museum. I simply ran out of steam. It seemed such an enormous effort, to go somewhere unfamiliar. Anyway, what was the good of a few daubs on canvas? Unhappiness makes Philistines of us. Everything seemed too meaningless to be bothered with, so I bought a magazine at a news-stand and, because it was bitterly cold, sought sanctuary in the Park Avenue Plaza.

This was an echoing place carved out of tawny marble. It was furnished with grown trees and rubber plants. Huge, shiny steel pillars supported the roof. There was a restaurant area and another, roped-off area set aside for the public. These tables were occupied by the usual mild psychotics. They gibbered like monkeys amongst the jungle of foliage. A security guard strolled past, static and babble issuing from his chest. Piped music played, from speakers hooked to the trees. Executives entered through the revolving doors and strode across the lobby, heading for the offices upstairs. They were blind to us. Some of them stood waiting for the elevators;

some of them rode up on the escalator, standing motionless as they slid towards the ceiling. They looked like the chosen people riding up to heaven and leaving the rest of us amongst our litter of paper cups.

It was then that I saw Roly, Lila's agent. He was just entering the building. I jumped up and pretended that I was just sauntering out of the restaurant area.

He wore a black fur coat, and was heading for the elevators. I passed him, casually, and stopped.

'Hi!' I said.

It took him a moment to recognise me. I'm sure I looked perfectly normal, but he wasn't expecting me to pop up like that. He shook my hand.

'Hi, how're you doing?' he said. 'I thought you were in LA.'

So he didn't know. I breathed a sigh of relief. Why should he know? Sacking a stand-in was hardly headline news.

I smiled. 'You told me I should get out of there and I took your advice. You work here?'

He shook his head. 'I have a meeting.'

Suddenly I said, 'Listen, Roly. I need to ask your advice about something. Can I take you out for a drink some time?'

He grunted with surprise. 'Sure. But wait. It's *you* who'll be *my* guest.'

He took off his gloves and fished a diary out of his inner pocket. I watched him leafing through it with his pudgy fingers.

Why had I said that? The words had sprung out of me. I hadn't spoken to anyone for days – weeks, in fact. Maybe I was just desperate for some company.

New Yorkers can be surprisingly polite. Hospitable, too – especially to the English. Roly looked up. 'In fact, I have a lunch cancellation on Friday. Now why don't I take you for lunch instead?'

I gibbered something in reply.

'It would be a pleasure,' he said gallantly. He gave me his card, and told me the address of the restaurant. Then he shook my hand, squeezing it like an uncle. The lift doors slid open, and he stepped in.

He took me to a plush little French restaurant up on 66th Street and Madison. They obviously knew him well there, and fussed over us. In fact, as I was to discover, he had a regular table. It was one of those old-fashioned places that still served consommé. My God, it even served melba toast. It turned out that he always ate the same thing – mushroom soup followed by broiled sole and potatoes. He was pernickety about food and had a delicate stomach. But he urged me to order the most lavish items on the menu – foie gras, lobster thermidor. He was as generous as a sugar daddy.

I had pulled myself together, washed my hair and dressed up in my one smart suit – a flecked tweed thing with a nipped-in waist and leather collar. The intended effect was that of a cool and successful professional. I asked his advice about my career.

'Would I be able to find any work in New York? I'd love to stay here.'

He put down his soup spoon. 'You British, you're the flavour of the month. Your shows, they do great business here. Not all, but who's counting? Trevor Nunn comes, he has Broadway at his feet.' He patted his lips with his napkin. 'Over here, we're all the time looking for new British products, new British faces. Emily Lloyd comes, she has Hollywood eating out of her hand.'

'I'm a bit older than Emily Lloyd. You think I'd get anywhere?'

He spread out his hands and shrugged. I cracked off a piece of melba toast and gazed at him.

'I watched you on the sound stage,' he said. 'Know what you have, Jules? I know it when I see it. I feel it, here.' He touched the back of his neck. 'My T spot.'

'T?'

'Talent.'

I blushed with pleasure. 'Really?'

'You have class, sweetheart. Something thoroughbred. You have a kind of energy that's very watchable. There's something dangerous there.'

I looked at his glistening face. Despite his resemblance to Charles Laughton, I could have hugged him. Just for a moment I imagined kissing his pursed, squashy little lips.

It was all happening so fast. He got down to business, settling himself more comfortably in his red velvet banquette.

'Who's your agent in London?'

'Maggie Fitch.'

He nodded. 'She's well respected over here.'

I longed for a cigarette. I knew, however, that he hated smoking – I had seen him chiding Lila – so I knotted my hands together under the table. Maggie had no office in New York, so he suggested she send some tapes of my work over to his agency, Belrose Creative Management, so he could see what I had done. Thanks to Lila I already had my Green Card, and I already belonged to SEG. If BCM signed me up Roly would see about getting me my SAG membership. He said that he knew, off-hand, of two parts that were coming up for English character actresses.

BCM . . . SAG . . . How casually he had spoken! Was he really going to take me on? I didn't dare inspect the words, yet. I would hoard them until I was alone. It was like stumbling over a bag of bank-notes in the street and delaying the moment until I counted them, one by one, with breathless disbelief.

Roly, who had a weak bladder, went to the men's room. I couldn't eat a dessert but he had ordered a large piece of cheesecake for himself. I sat there, stupefied. At the next table, two women were talking to each other.

'It's so darling to have a real fire,' said one. 'We bring in the logs from our place in Connecticut and Frank, our doorman, he sends them up in the freight elevator.'

Their wrists were weighed down with gold. They had the restless eyes and pampered, porcelain looks of major-league shoppers. No doubt they both lived in penthouses, like Lila.

I felt dizzy. Yesterday I had been down amongst the garbage, jilted and unemployed. On buses I had acquainted strangers with the sickening injustice of my emotional and professional life. The steel doors of the city had revolved around, closing me off.

And now, over one lunch hour, they had rolled open again. New York City's hottest agent had taken a shine to me, and now a ravishing waiter was sweeping crumbs from my tablecloth with a small, silver brush.

After lunch I wandered around, shellshocked. I remember standing outside Bergdorf Goodmans, gazing through the glass. *He's taken a shine to me*. I repeated the simple words, over and over. I couldn't think of any other way of putting it. *He's taken a shine to me*. The mannequins gazed back at me, equally incomprehending.

And it was true. He had. Weeks later he confessed that it was my suit that did it. He had found it deeply disturbing. He loved the idea of a cool, dominating woman with severe shoulders who bossed him about. Charlotte Rampling, whom he didn't represent, inflamed him. He dreamed of her hard, cat's face above him as she scolded him for his shameful impotence.

Saturday was exhilarating – one of those freezing, sunny New York days that charge you with electricity. The city looked beautiful. The skyscraper shone, razor-sharp; the metallic Chrysler building made my eyes prickle. Somebody wanted me! Somebody who could be vitally useful! I walked through Central Park, along my old familiar paths. The entire population of the city seemed to be outdoors that day. Brawny baseball players puffed like cattle; rollerskaters sped past, armoured like warriors with helmets and knee-guards. Divorced fathers tossed footballs into the air, having quality time with their sons.

I went back to the IMAGINE plaque and looked up,

through the leafless trees, to the top of Lila's building. The empty windows of her apartment shone in the sun. Imagine! I had lived there. For a brief moment I had become Lila; a dry cleaner had addressed me as Miss Dune. Imagine fiercely enough and anyone will believe you. Life was more bizarre than any movie. I had some unfinished business with Lila, and indeed with Trev, and now I had a good reason to stay I felt confident that I could work something out. They weren't going to get away with it. Boy-oh-boy, no!

I strode home on strong, muscular legs. I walked ten blocks, breathing in lungfuls of exhaust fumes. Cars passed me, clunking over the metal plates that held the streets together. These rusting panels were bolted down, like lids over the chaos beneath. The whole city pulsed with danger.

I had forgotten to eat any lunch. In LA it was breakfast time. Lila and Trev would just be waking up, clammy from sex. '*O my America!*' he'd be murmuring. '*My new-found land!*' He wouldn't, of course, but that would be the gist of it. They had stolen each other from me. I still had her keys in my handbag; at each step, they rattled. Even then, I guessed that one day I might use them.

A woman, loaded with carrier bags, was hailing a cab. It slewed to a halt, but I got to it first.

'Hey you!' she shouted. 'Whaddya think you're doing?'

'My boyfriend's been hurt,' I panted. 'He's in terrible trouble!'

'Jesus!' Her eyes widened. 'What's happened?'

'I've got to get to the hospital,' I replied. 'He's dying.'

I jumped into the cab, slamming the door. As it pulled away from the kerb I pressed my gloved hand against my mouth and started cackling.

When I got back to the apartment the phone was ringing. It was Roly. He invited me to accompany him, as his guest, to the opening night of a new play the next Tuesday.

Two

I nearly overslept. I had fallen asleep that afternoon, and dreamed that Trev's nose had grown into an elephant's trunk. Winking at me, he shook his head from side to side, his trunk swinging and thumping against the wall.

I woke up, sweating. It was dark. The TV was on; it was some cop show and a policeman was beating a cowering Hispanic, thump . . . thump . . . with a leather truncheon.

I was late. Panic-stricken, I switched off the TV, made up my face and zipped myself into my bronze dress. It was 6.15.

Roly was waiting for me in the lobby. He wore a dinner jacket and his fur coat; in fact, he looked remarkably debonair. A tubby, ageing dandy.

'My dear,' he said, 'you look ravishing.'

He gave me a corsage – a white rose – and pinned it to my dress. I felt like a favoured niece, being taken out for a night on the town.

Outside a limo waited for us, purring in anticipation. It wasn't a vulgar stretch; it was a Lincoln Town Car. I sat in the back with Roly, looking at his two plump thighs next to mine. I remembered sitting in that limo with Lila, on the way to the pub in Tottenham. I crossed my legs with a faint rasping sound. Roly smelt of expensive soap. As the car pushed its way through the traffic, he chatted. The second time with somebody it's always surprisingly different, have you found that? Tonight he seemed as familiar as a female schoolfriend. He obviously liked women, and gossip. He told me a wonderful story about Debra Winger and a sound mike.

Gazing at his chubby hands, I speculated about his sexual

orientation. I had phoned Maggie Fitch, some days earlier, to tell her my news. We had gone on to talk about Roly, and I had asked her about his private life. She'd told me that he had never been married, and that his proclivities were somewhat opaque. 'He's not gay; you can't keep that sort of thing a secret in New York,' she'd said. 'He certainly doesn't screw his clients, one would've heard about *that*. Besides, they'd have to be pretty desperate, wouldn't they? The general opinion, darling, is he's some kind of eunuch, but he likes to be seen with a pretty girl on his arm.' Now that I seemed to be hitting the big time she had been particularly forthcoming to me, with a lot of 'darlings'. She'd laughed, throatily. 'Maybe you can find out.'

So tonight I was the pretty girl – woman – on Roly's arm. At least I had dressed for the part. Outside the Music Box the street was jammed with limos, hooting and inching forward. They filled the street like an oil slick, moving slowly, black and shiny.

Flashbulbs popped as we entered the lobby of the theatre. I wriggled like Lila; he had taken *her* to a première too, I had seen them on the TV. Tonight it was my turn. Crowds milled around; I didn't recognise anybody, though people came up and greeted Roly. Later, when we were in our seats, he pointed out faces in the other rows.

'That's Frank Rich,' he said, smiling at him and lifting his hand. 'Over there, that's Clive Barnes. The Butchers of Broadway.'

I craned my neck to look at them. Maybe one day they would be sitting there, sharpening their knives and waiting to make or break *me*.

'Across there, in the third row, that's Al Hirschfeld,' said Roly. 'The world-famous caricaturist, with his wife Dolly. They always sit close to the stage so he can see to draw.' I leaned forward and glimpsed a grey-bearded man, as stately as a Velasquez portrait. Somebody was tapping his shoulder; he turned politely and greeted him.

I've always loved the buzz of first nights. Despite the

unknown faces I felt that I was coming home. It had been months since I had sat in a theatre. As the lights went down I wondered why Roly had chosen to bring me. Did he really find me attractive? Did he really think I had talent? Or was I simply a temporary replacement for Lila, who was still in LA?

The show was a vehicle for one of Roly's rising young TV comediennes. It was based on Dorothy Parker's writings and called *You Might as Well Live*. In fact, it turned out to be a somewhat arbitrarily linked series of sketches and poems, set to music. My mind wandered. During the later part of the show, as Dorothy Parker sank into alcoholism, despair and eventual suicide, I realised how relieved Trev would be if I simply overdosed. All his problems over! He would go around for a few days looking soulful – an uphill task – saying what a terrific actress I was and what a good friend. He and Lila would console each other, in public, with showbiz kisses. Forgetting our recent contretemps, Lila would witter along about how I'd been like a sister to her and given her confidence. Then they would forget all about me.

What a blissfully easy solution for both of them! What did they take me for – some kind of idiot?

'You feeling all right?'

Roly's voice startled me. He was looking at me anxiously. The audience was applauding, and the house lights coming up.

'Fine,' I replied.

He squeezed my hand. 'Enjoy the show?'

'Lovely,' I said. 'Especially the suicide.'

Afterwards there was a party. It was given by the producers in a private room at the Sherry-Netherland Hotel. I drank a lot of champagne. This waiter, carrying a tray of glasses, kept reappearing like a rerun videotape. When I closed my eyes I pictured him being rewound – marching backwards like clockwork into the crowd – and then coming forward again. It made me giggle.

269

I clung to Roly. He was shorter than me, and I imagined squashing his balding head against my breasts. I speculated with drunken, idle curiosity. In my bronze dress I was playing out my fantasy: the simpering starlet. It aroused me. My dress was slashed to the thigh; I remembered exposing myself, in the cubicle, to those two unknown Arabs. This made me giggle, too.

I'm sure the party was full of famous people, but I didn't recognise many of them. There were gay young actors wearing poloneck jumpers – powder-blue, pink and yellow. There were ageing, vivacious women with wonderful bone-structure. ('The only thing you can rely on not to let you down,' according to my great-aunt.) I heard Elaine Strich's gravelly voice but I couldn't see her. Nobody seemed to be drinking much, except me. Coral Browne was there, with her husband Vincent Price. He was immensely tall and benign; he was dressed in an immaculate tweed jacket like a Sunningdale colonel. I seemed to be standing beside him. His feet were so large that they made me giggle, all over again. He told me that they were size thirteen. Or maybe he was telling someone else.

People kept trying to take Roly away but he kept my arm tucked into his, and introduced me. I suddenly felt absurdly bound to him; it must have been the effect of all those strange faces. Everyone seemed to know everyone else; the New York theatre community is small enough anyway, but the devastation of AIDS had drawn it in on itself, even closer.

'The devastation of AIDS,' I intoned to myself solemnly, trying not to grin; trying to get the words right. My tongue lolled in my mouth.

People talked about Marsha and Ted and how somebody was flying in tomorrow from Paris. An elderly man nodded and smiled at me, as if he knew me; he had a lipstick print on his cheek.

'Scott's writing his memoirs,' said somebody. 'The chutzpah!'

'She's gone into the hospital, the poor sweetie,' said somebody else. 'For more tests.'

A small woman, dressed in black like a crow, asked me

about Mrs Thatcher and I must have gibbered a reply. Somebody else seemed to be talking to me about Kenneth Branagh, but I said that I had never met him. Had I? I couldn't remember. Somebody asked Roly what Lila was doing.

'They finish principal photography next week,' he replied. 'She'll be back mid-March.' Even in my drunken state, her name jolted me. For an hour or so – what was the time? I couldn't be bothered to lift my wrist. For a while, anyway, I had forgotten all about her. In fact I couldn't remember where I was. What were these embossed walls and chandeliers? I knew I should have eaten something, in fact I vaguely remembered Roly pressing a plate of food on me, but God knows where I had left it.

A woman's face loomed up. She wore glasses. 'When I saw you in the theatre,' she said, 'I thought it was Lila.'

The waiter reappeared. I put my empty glass very, very carefully on his tray. I felt weightless; the faces swam in front of me. It suddenly seemed as if Roly was the only person I knew in the world; I gripped his arm, as if I were drowning.

That night I seduced Roly. Well, half-seduced him. The trouble is, I can't remember much about it. I hadn't been so drunk since I was a student. Later, I realised I had dosed myself up on purpose, to fortify myself. I couldn't have managed it otherwise.

I had decided to seduce him, you see, that first day at lunch. It was lust and loneliness and curiosity. It was that same compulsion I had felt when I'd picked up that man in the Warwick bar. I wanted to explore Roly's strange, smooth flesh with my fingers. I wanted to have power over him, to control him. He fascinated me, and I sensed how I could use him. He was my only link to Lila. Early on, I had guessed that he was sexually inadequate; there was something about his limp hand-shake, something soft and unused about his body. And I knew that if I managed to arouse him, he would be mine.

I could start to manipulate him then. I had planned it all.

I can't remember getting into the car that evening, or

anything about the drive. I presume he was going to take me back to my apartment, but I must have got to work on him in the back seat because we ended up at his place. Maybe he just thought I was too drunk to look after myself; maybe he was just being gentlemanly.

I can't remember anything about the lobby or the elevator; we could have flown to this apartment, for all I knew. I was hardly conscious. I can't remember if he undressed me or if I undressed myself, though I remember now that he made me a cup of hot milk. There was something heavy on the bed, which I presume was his cat. I later found out that she always slept on his bed; he adored her. The sheets were crisp and the mattress so soft that I sank into the blackness. The fluid in my brain rocked to and fro. Even when I lay still, it rocked. If I moved, I would fall through space. He wore silk pyjamas; I think he kept them on throughout.

During my deepest slumber something damp and intimate happened. I think I started it, though I can't be sure. I think he resisted at first; but something did happen, because I remember his small, wet cock in my hand. It's always a surprise, isn't it, to touch that for the first time? Even when you're drunk, you remember how it felt.

I woke in the morning with a monumental hangover. I remembered Lila's obliterating binges. She too had woken up next to unknown men in alien bedrooms. My skull felt as if it would split.

'You ever done this with Lila?' I asked Roly. He was putting two eggs into a saucepan of boiling water. He had his back to me; he wore a striped, velvet bathrobe.

He didn't reply; he just shook his head. The eggs rattled against the spoon as he lowered them into the pan.

So Roly and I started an affair, though 'affair' was hardly an accurate term for our series of furtive, sweaty manoeuvres in the dark that were never mentioned during the daylight hours. Over the next few weeks we often met for lunch at his usual restaurant. He was the ordinary Roly, then; the recognisable, daytime one: a small, ugly, amusing and powerful man with a fund of fascinating anecdotes. He had been in the business for thirty years. I learnt a lot about the hierarchies at the TV networks, the shifting, volatile power struggles in Hollywood and the way the entertainment industry was changing. I heard some delicious gossip about famous people, which I repeat in this place to anyone who might be interested – some are, but not as many as you would think.

Most important of all, he told me about Lila. He was my lifeline to her, my secret link. I cracked my melba toast in half with assumed indifference as he told me things about her past which I hoarded up for future use. He kept me in touch with her current activities, because most days he spoke to her on the phone. I felt like a spy, toying with my salmon steak and pumping him with ostensibly innocent questions.

'She's completed shooting,' he said. 'She's back in town. Trevor's with her, he's buying himself some real estate. That guy, does he move fast!'

With the fee from *Jane Eyre* and the advance from another project – maybe a contribution from Lila, too – Trev was buying an apartment a few blocks from hers, on the Upper West Side. I was both enraged and cheered by this – enraged because he was raking it in, and cheered because it seemed that even Lila couldn't get him to live with her.

I wondered if Lila knew that I had joined BCM, her own agency. Maybe Roly hadn't told her. Maybe she didn't even know that I was still in New York City. I didn't want to meet either her or Trev – it would have been too painful – but I had a compulsion to hear about them. I felt like a muslim at Muharram, whipping myself with their news until my back was flayed and bleeding.

At the end of March Roly told me that Lila was forming her own production company, with Trevor as her partner.

'Sure I'm happy for her. Why not? Jane Fonda, Goldie Hawn, they all do it. Jessica Lange. Used to be quilting bees, now it's production companies. I see three women in a supermarket and I think – hey, they're forming a production company!'

We had stopped, on the way back from lunch, to buy some vitamin tablets. Roly was a compulsive hypochondriac, in a city of hypochondriacs, and thought he had a cold coming on.

'Did Lassie have a production company?' he asked. 'Sure!'

We left the pharmacy and walked along the pavement.

'What's happened to what's-his-name's apartment?' I asked casually. 'Trevor's?'

'He's moving in next week. Some Thai decorator's doing it up, really fancy. He should've asked me, I know this fantastic guy, he owes me a favour, he did up Daryl Hannah's place. I could've fixed it for him, a really good price, but you know Trevor.'

'Hardly,' I said. 'I hardly know him at all.'

Blowing his nose, Roly hailed me a cab. He pressed a ten-dollar bill into my hand for the fare – he was unfailingly generous – kissed me on the cheek and headed towards his office a couple of blocks away. The cab stopped at the lights and I watched him with surprising fondness – a portly, fur-coated little man who knotted his scarf more tightly around his neck and who walked with short, fussy steps. Phones were ringing for him in his house of deals – he once told me he had over a hundred calls a day. Million-dollar contracts awaited his signature. Studio executives grovelled to negotiate with him.

There he went, one of the most important men in the business. And my sexual slave.

He worshipped me, you see, because I humiliated him. During our twice-weekly, night-time sessions I grew to understand this other, secret Lester Rollins. His own sexuality was deeply shameful – his mother had repeatedly told him so. The more I chastised him, the more aroused he became. As time passed I learned more about him. He grew up in a household of women – his family came from Latvia and his father died when he was young – and his mother spanked him once when she found him masturbating. This had a profound effect on him. His mother's suffocating love disturbed him and he grew up locked into an unhealthily erotic relationship with her that had rendered him almost impotent with other women. They couldn't respond to his needs, which were admittedly rather specialised. I guessed that they had been alarmed by him; maybe they had tried to laugh him out of it. Worse still, perhaps they had tried to help him. He didn't want that, he wanted contempt. So, in the past, when occasionally visited by lust, he had simply used the services of high-class call girls.

And then along I came. At the beginning my motives were manipulative ones, but I grew fascinated by his soft flesh and his whimpering vulnerability. I know it sounds hard to believe, but it's true. Powerless for so long, I blossomed as a sexual dictator. *I* found it arousing too. He loved some high-heeled leather boots I had bought at Charles Jourdan. Wearing them, I straddled his pale and curiously female body; I rode his little cock until his body was slippery with sweat and he cried out with spasms of pleasure. Having been humiliated myself – boy, did I enjoy humiliating someone else! As I worked on his spreadeagled bulk I thought: *this* one for that bitch Lila, *this* one for that shit Trevor. That he was Lila's agent gave me a keener frisson. I don't know why. I didn't want to *think* why. But it did.

Frustrated as an actress for so long, I used my imagination to invent more baroque and adventurous games for us. A good whore is a good actress, after all, so why not vice versa? During my night-time visits I became the woman I had fantasised about, performing for her customers, exposing herself in shop cubicles, arousing a camera crew and an audience of millions. Inflamed, I watched myself. Sometimes I pretended to be Jane Fonda in *Klute*, tenderly pleasuring her elderly client. At last I was a successful actress, a true professional!

What he liked best was dressing up in his mother's clothes. She'd had exceptionally dowdy taste. Secretly I giggled, that a man could be in thrall to a woman who wore outsize

Crimplene shirtwaisters. In the back of his wardrobe he had stored various ample, matronly garments. They were lovingly pressed and folded, and locked away in a suitcase so his maid couldn't find them.

He needed to go through certain routines. I had to get them right or he became distressed and frustrated. First I had to stop him opening the suitcase.

'Lester!' I said. 'I've told you not to do that!'

The more angry I became, the more excited he grew. Then he would switch off the light – thank goodness for that, because once he was dressed up like Charley's Aunt it was wiser not to see him. He wore some high-heeled shoes, too, which I guessed hadn't belonged to his mother, they were far too smart. He must have bought them specially.

He liked me to touch him under his skirt. 'You've been a bad boy, haven't you,' I murmured. 'A dirty, bad boy.' As I chastised him, his breathing quickened. In my hand, his cock grew stiffer. Never *that* stiff, but stiffer. He liked to draw out these proceedings for as long as possible, so I made up little scenarios.

'Just because I'm in the kitchen, cooking your dinner, think I didn't know what you were doing? I heard you going into my bedroom; I heard my closet opening. So I turned off the radio, Lester, and I listened. How could you do something like that? . . .' Once I knew what he wanted, the words rolled off my tongue. It was like doing improvisations in drama class. Having a strong fantasy life myself, I could join him without great difficulty in his. Sometimes he simply tied on his mother's apron; naked except for her pinny, he played with himself whilst I spoke to him in the dark. I murmured to him until he was near breaking point, and then I pulled him roughly onto the bed and told him what I wanted him to do to me. He loved me bossing him around, and using him for my own pleasure.

Once or twice, when the mood slipped, I got it wrong. I suddenly lost concentration. One night he wanted me to spank him. He had smooth, surprisingly youthful buttocks. I didn't enjoy spanking him, it just seemed silly. He lay on top of me, weighing me down; my hand lay on his nylon-skirted rump, idly stroking it. I heard the crackle of static. My mind wandered and I remembered Trev's beautiful hard back. Suddenly I missed him painfully. What the hell was I doing here?

Disgusted with myself, I pushed Roly off and told him to hurt me. 'Seen the scar on my hand?' I muttered. 'I like it, I like being hurt. Scratch me! Make me bleed!' This confused him. Disconcerted, he withered.

He didn't say anything about it afterwards. In fact, he never mentioned our erotic activities once they were over. To some extent we are all sexually split – I certainly am – but in Roly's case his needs were so cut-off from the rest of his life that he refused to recognise them once they were satisfied.

He would take me out to dinner, maybe once a week, or he would pick me up at my apartment after he had been to some business function. We were seldom seen together in public. He was very discreet – he couldn't be seen canoodling with a client – and this suited me. I've always thrived on secrecy and I found it arousing, to be his night-time whore. Besides, it embarrassed me to be seen on the arm of such a small, fat, ugly man. Every relationship is a trading process, and showbusiness in particular throws up dramatic visual evidence of this – hideous old producers with young starlets, raddled old film stars with toyboys. I didn't want to be seen as yet another example of this coarse equation. It hurt my pride, and anyway my feelings for Roly were more complex than this.

The most important reason, however, was Lila. I didn't want Roly to mention me to her, and I guessed that he didn't. He had scores of clients on his books; I was just one amongst many, and he had probably forgotten my earlier connection with her. She certainly wouldn't ask, she was far too self-absorbed. Her life was busy and they had plenty of other things to talk about. Now I was Roly's mistress I was his secret.

So he would collect me in his hired limo and we would go

back to his apartment. He lived in Beekman Place, a highly respectable street near the East River. A lot of theatre people lived in the neighbourhood because it was within walking distance of Broadway.

'Irving Berlin lived here,' he said. 'His parents, they were like my parents. They were so poor, know what they did? They sold the samovar for the price of the brass. That's how poor.'

Like Berlin, Roly had flourished in the land of opportunity and he was now extremely rich. Beekman Place was hushed, and shaded by trees. Some of its apartment houses were built in the medieval style; they had gothic lobbies and stone carvings. I loved it there; it had the heavy, brooding atmosphere of serious money.

He would take me up to his apartment and pour me champagne, which he bought for me specially because he didn't drink. His refrigerator was like his fellow-hypochondriac Lila's, full of pills, suppositories and refills for his asthma inhaler. Plus his beloved cakes and pastries. He worried that I was too thin; like a Jewish mother he fed me up, watching me eat with anxious solicitude.

'Finish it up, sweetheart,' he said. 'Every crumb.'

His apartment was formal. There were stiff, brocaded curtains and a reproduction Wedgwood mantelpiece. In contrast to Trev's place, it was always spotlessly clean. There were Chinese vases; there was his bloated, pampered cat, which resented me, curled up in the best armchair. It was stuffy; he never opened the windows in case he caught a chill. It resembled the flat of a spinster aunt with a large private income. He had travelled a lot in the East, and had a collection of Javanese shadow-puppets displayed in a glass-fronted cabinet. He was a connoisseur, a collector; he treated me tenderly, as if I were a precious object that he was lucky enough to have found after decades of searching.

We would talk for a while. I would sit on the floor, between his legs, drinking Bollinger and stroking his knee.

'Tell me about the contract *I'm* going to get,' I murmured.

'Two million upfront,' he said.

'What's wrong with three?'

'So she wants three? So she has three.' He patted my head. 'Plus a weekly expense allowance.'

'How much?'

'Say, $15,000 when you're out of town. And you keep your wardrobe from the movie.'

'Go on,' I urged him greedily. He was like an uncle, telling me my favourite fairy story over and over again.

'Plus, the production company will pay for your hotel suite, a car for your exclusive use and a driver.'

'For my exclusive use too?' I murmured, running my hand along his thigh.

'You want this contract?'

'Sure.'

'You want this contract, you behave.' He kissed the top of my head. 'While on the set, you'll have a first-class motorhome dressing room with shower, double bed, refrigerator, stove, TV . . .' He stopped. 'You have wonderful shoulders, sweetheart, know that? Strong, muscular . . . Your shoulders, that's all I'm thinking about today. The phones are ringing and I'm just seeing your shoulders.'

'Get on with the contract.'

'VCR. Mobile phone. Air conditioning.'

'You've forgotten the stereo.'

'Stereo, sweetheart, anything you want. The moon! Nothing's too good for you.' He stroked my hair. 'Plus approval of the final script, your hair, makeup and any photographic likeness of you used on the videocassette package, the soundtrack album cover and theatre displays.'

'Go on!' My skin glowed. I felt fuller, riper. I was a movie star. 'Tell me more,' I said greedily.

'You'll also be consulted on the casting of your leading man and the initial United States ad campaign.' He stopped. 'Let's make ourselves more comfortable,' he whispered.

'Not yet! Go on!'

He sighed indulgently. 'She wants more? Sure she wants

more. Don't they all? OK, so your name will appear above the title in all advertisements.'

'What size?'

'At least 35 per cent of the artwork title and 100 per cent of the regular title. You'll attend all dailies, previews and premieres of the movie, with expenses and transportation paid for by the producers.' He shifted his legs, and stood up. 'Come on, sweetie.'

'Haven't you forgotten something?'

He smiled. 'Plus a complimentary video copy of the film and a piece of any profits from advertisements placed on those tapes.'

He pulled me to my feet. I smiled, inflamed by his story just as he, soon, was going to be inflamed by mine. Sometimes I would initiate it, getting up and pulling him to his feet. We would both yawn, exaggeratedly, as if we simply wanted to go to sleep.

Actually, sometimes we did. I never knew his age but I guessed he was in his early sixties. He'd had a tiring day; he was extremely unfit, and he wasn't used to frequent and vigorous sex. But usually we would pull open the curtains of our little theatre and our two-hander would begin. I was aroused by his power-talk; he by my sensual conniving. We both knew the script and the costume-changes; we both responded to the various improvisations. But when the curtain fell he would never mention the performance. As I said, sex was furtive and shameful. In fact he usually crept out of bed and slept in his spare room. He said he was a poor sleeper and didn't want to disturb me in the small hours by switching on his light and reading scripts.

In the morning I woke alone, the cat weighing down my feet. Roly didn't exactly hustle me away; he was too polite for that. Besides, he liked to watch me eat a good breakfast. But he was anxious to get rid of me before his maid arrived, at nine, and I made sure that I never met her. Which was lucky, as things turned out.

*

I felt as taut as a wire, those March weeks. As yet, no work had come my way. I went to a couple of auditions but didn't get the parts. Apart from the episodes with Roly I spoke to no one. Anyway, our night-time activities were so bizarre that they seemed unconnected to the rest of my life; they had the surreal insubstantiality of a dream. I had such powerful dreams, too, when I was sleeping; their violence shook me. I dreamed about girls at school; I had nightmares about my father. Sometimes I thought I should get back to England, before it was too late. My anger was growing, you see. It should have subsided, but it had gathered its own hot momentum. Inflamed by titbits about Lila and Trev, I seethed in my room. I felt like a boil, filling with poison.

By casual questioning, I had discovered the address of Trev's new apartment. It was a concrete high-rise behind the Dakota. Sometimes at night I took a bus there and stood outside, my neck straining, looking up at the lit windows and searching for his. Up in the sky, New Yorkers seldom close their blinds; a city of egoists, they don't believe that anyone else exists. Or maybe they are simply voyeurs. Watch their TV shows and you'll see what I mean. The curtains in Lila's apartment hadn't closed properly; she had obviously never bothered.

There was no sign of Trev in the windows I presumed were his. But his apartment might have been around the back. I felt uneasy, standing there in the underground garage entrance. It had a sign saying 'Active Driveway. Do Not Park!' I felt he might be creeping up behind me, ready to pounce. His fingers would dig into my eye sockets.

'Let me guess who it is,' he would mutter. He would press against my back, breathing into my hair. 'I know. You're some crazy nutcase . . .' His hands would grip my shoulders, hurting me. 'You're Chapman, ready to shoot.'

One day, near the end of March, I saw their photo in the paper. It was in the *Post* showbiz column. Lila clung, laughing, to Trev's arm. He had changed; he had the unmistakably sleek look of the rich. He had cut his hair, too. For a moment, in fact, I didn't recognise him.

'*Among the guests at the "Gaslight" premiere were Lila Dune and her constant companion, hunky British penman Trevor Parsons.*' They looked obliviously happy.

Gaslight. A re-make of the classic thriller had just been released. As I looked at the photo, something stirred in my brain.

Remember the original? Charles Boyer tricks Ingrid Bergman into thinking she is going mad. He lowers the gas jets; he hides her necklace. He works on her – oh so cleverly. He undermines her sanity.

It was the photo that did it.

My heart beat heavily as I picked up the phone book and looked up Linsky's number. Linsky's was a deli on Amsterdam Avenue where Lila ordered her groceries. She had told me about it; in fact, I had gone there myself. It sold a large selection of expensive, take-out items. I could picture them in front of me, in their spotlit earthenware dishes. I leafed through the pages and found the number: 787.2000.

I stood still for a moment, trying to compose myself. My throat had dried up; my bowels churned. I felt as if I were standing on a very high diving board, willing myself to move. The water glittered below me, miles away.

I took a deep breath. It was only stage fright, after all. I went over to the mirror.

I hadn't practised her voice for weeks now. I was rusty.

It's easier, speaking to your reflection. You ought to try it.

'Hi, this is Lila Dune,' I said. I tilted my head, just like she did, and looked at myself under my eyelashes. She could be so damned flirtatious, even with the phone. 'Hi, this is Lila Dune.' I smiled. She smiled.

It's fascinating. Once you start speaking in somebody else's voice your face subtly changes. Mine does, anyway. I'm an actress, you see; that's why.

My face looked fuller, softer. More sluttish. Pouting at Lila,

I moved my head slightly as I spoke. She did that. I knew her mannerisms so well; I had studied her with great attention – Lila, my PhD.

Actually, I felt quite calm. I shimmied over to the phone and dialled 787.2000. I looked at my watch; it was 2.30.

'Linsky's,' said a brusque voice.

'Hi,' I drawled. 'This is Lila Dune.'

His voice grew warmer. 'Hi, Miss Dune. How're you doing?'

'Fine. I have some people coming over to dinner tonight. You ready?'

There was a rustling sound. He must have been getting his pen. 'Ready to go, Miss Dune.' He repeated my name in that distinct way people speak when they're wanting other people to listen, and be impressed.

'Some of your fabulous seafood salad,' I said. 'For eight. Parma ham, two pounds, thinly sliced. Artichoke hearts in vinaigrette, you got any?'

'Sure.'

'Some pumpernickel,' I said. 'You got any Beluga?'

'Sure, Madam.'

'Four ounces. No, make that eight. Some sour cream . . .' I rattled off the list in my head; it grew, recklessly.

When I had finished, he said, 'Let's just check that.' He repeated my order.

'Great,' I said. 'When can you deliver it?'

'Right away, Miss Dune. Within the hour.'

'Thanks,' I said, and put down the phone.

It was then that I started trembling. My bowels had turned to liquid and I rushed to the bathroom.

I remember giggling. I sat on the lavatory, gazing at the towel rail and shuddering with laughter. What a hoot! Two hundred dollars' worth at least! Two hundred dollars' worth of dinner party turning up at her apartment!

But you ordered it, Miss Dune, said the gum-chewing delivery boy.

I wha-a-at? Lila stared at him.

You ordered it. Look. Here. Showing her the list.

I had to get out. I felt full of energy, like a wicked schoolgirl. I left the apartment and hurried down the street. A police siren wailed. What if they came and got me?

They couldn't, of course. I was a nobody. I was a ventriloquist.

I strode all the way to Battery Park. The wind whipped my face. I felt flushed and vigorous; I hadn't felt in such rude health for months. Buses thundered past me, rattling the metal plates that bolted the streets together. The whole city rocked and creaked on its loose joints but I had conquered it. I felt as powerful as a potentate. One press of a button and lo and behold! In a far country it was all chaos. This was fun! With my stick, I had broken open an ants' nest; its inmates teemed in confusion. *I wha-a-at?* echoed, far away, from Central Park West.

I was due to see Roly later that night. First, he was taking his contracts manager out for dinner. Half BCM's clients had been signed up for *Bonfire of the Vanities* – half of *everybody's* clients had been signed up for *Bonfire of the Vanities* – and Roly was celebrating. Unlike many agents, Roly was generous to his staff. He was always taking them out, sending them flowers when they were sick and remembering their children's barmitzvahs and birthdays.

He was always sending *me* flowers, too. When I got back there was a huge bunch of roses waiting for me in the lobby. Trev had never sent me flowers. Well, once he had nicked some forsythia from somebody's garden but it wasn't the same.

No, it wasn't. It was wonderful. He had wrapped them up in an old copy of *Exchange and Mart* and delivered them to me with a flourish. I had flung my arms around him and smothered him with kisses, rubbing my face against his stubbly cheek.

'*Feels like a goddam cheese grater,*' said Lila, droolingly.

She called him *Tee*. Wasn't that revolting!

Roly was particularly affectionate that night.

'You've changed my life,' he said, stroking my cheek. I was curled up in the armchair. 'Know that? You've made an old man very happy.'

'You're not so old,' I said abruptly. I turned away from his fat, jowly face. I hated it when he talked like that. Didn't he understand the rules?

'How's Lila?' I asked casually, addressing the ormolu clock on the mantelpiece. 'Heard anything from her today?'

He shook his head, and went on to tell me about some screening he had been to that afternoon, some new Michael Douglas picture. His words pattered like rain on a distant roof. Why should she have phoned him, anyway? Why should she have phoned her agent about a mysterious deli delivery? Ridiculous, wasn't it?

He was telling me about location problems on some rain-forest project, somewhere in Brazil. Inside my skirt, his hand was creeping up my thigh. His fingers were always slightly damp. They reached my stocking top.

Why couldn't he find out about Lila, for Christ's sake? Why did he think I was *here*?

'Everybody's working on a rainforest picture,' he chortled. 'Soon there'll be more film crews than Indians.'

Suddenly I pushed his hand away. I thought of *Gertie*. 'Don't talk like that!' I snapped. 'That's a stupid, cynical thing to say!'

A couple of days passed with no word about Lila. I decided to intensify my campaign. The idea had been brewing for some time; when I thought about it my skin prickled.

I bought some newspapers and magazines at the news-stand opposite and took them back to my apartment. Leafing through them, I wondered where I would plant my story. In *Spy*, *People*? In Liz Smith in the *News* or Suzy in the *Post*? In the *National Enquirer*?

Planning was half the fun. I lingered over the pages. '*Angry Zsa Zsa Flings Bread in Eatery*,' said one item. '*Guess What Kim Basinger Wears Under Nun's Habit!*' Celebrities smiled at me from flashlight photos. *'"Falcon Crest" Gal Panics Over Creepy Stalker,'* said another item, about a TV actress who was spooked by a series of threatening letters.

What a load of nutsos there were out there! One of them clung to every celebrity, like a limpet. Like a parasite. They clung on for dear life, sucking out the blood and discharging their poison. And nobody could see them! Clever, weren't they?

I decided on the *National Enquirer* because I was a coward; I didn't believe anyone would read it. My stomach had started fluttering, but I sat still for a moment and did my deep-breathing exercises. When I spoke I was admirably calm.

I asked for the celebrity items column. I used one of my favourite accents: Brooklyn. My name was Bernice.

Somebody called Mitch, or Rick, answered. I didn't get his name.

'I was sitting in a Greenwich Village eatery last night,' said Bernice. She told him the name and address of the Cajun place. 'It was late, there was only one other couple there. Imagine my surprise when I recognised the guy. Boy, was I in for a shock!'

Mitch, or whoever, asked, 'And who was that, Bernice?'

'Trevor Parsons! You know, who's been having a relationship with Lila Dune.'

His voice sharpened. 'Ah, yes.'

She paused, for effect. 'But it sure wasn't Lila Dune he was relating to, not last night! She was a petite redhead, in a dress that I assure you left nothing to the imagination! If what they'd been doing was shown on TV, why the lines would be jammed! I was kind of embarrassed myself. Kissing and cuddling, and a lot more than that.'

'Do you have a name for this person, Bernice?'

'Sure. I met her in the rest room, later, when she was putting back some of her lipstick. Her name's Susan. She told me. She said she'd met Trevor when they were shooting *Jane Eyre* and she was one of the background artistes. They couldn't date then, because he was staying at Lila Dune's lovely home.' I gave the address of Lila's place on Doheny Drive. 'They used to meet late at night, when Miss Dune was asleep. She always goes to bed early, apparently, when she has a call.'

'And could you give me your full name and address, Bernice?'

'Just call me a well-wisher,' I said, and hung up.

The story duly appeared in the next issue. Grinning, I read it in my local coffee shop. It was just a small item, pretty much as I had told it though peppered with exclamation marks. '*Psst! Wanna know where horny scribbler Trevor Parsons enjoys the hottest speciality on the menu?*' It was accompanied by a photo I hadn't seen before of Lila and Trev in evening dress.

Sniggering, I hurried out into the sunshine. It was a glorious spring day; I blinked in the glare. The driver of a passing truck whistled at me. I must have still been smiling.

I phoned the *National Enquirer* the following day. I cleared my throat and spoke in Irma's guttural Hungarian accent – another voice that I had perfected over the past few months.

'Zees is the private secretary of Miss Lila Dune. Your item deeply distressed Miss Dune and eet eez completely unfounded, a complete lie, she denies any truth in it whatsoever – '

The man interrupted. 'Thank you for calling us, but as we told you this morning – '

'Vat?'

'Maybe it was the publicist who called. Who was it, Curly?' There were muffled voices as he talked to someone else. He came back on the line. 'Yep, just checking. We've had a call from a representative of Miss Dune, we understand your position, if you hold on I'll put you through to – '

'Zat's OK,' I said, and replaced the receiver.

My hand was trembling. It took me a while to light my cigarette.

So she had seen it! Lila had read the item; she had been upset enough to get somebody to phone!

You plant these seeds. It's a miracle, isn't it? Those tiny, poisonous shoots appearing.

I had set events in motion and now I couldn't stop. I knew what it was like to be jealous, you see. I had suffered so much in the past. Why shouldn't Lila suffer now?

The next day I decided to phone Lila's private number. I planned it for the late afternoon, when both Fidelia and Irma would have gone home. Trev, I guessed, wouldn't be there either. Roly had told me that he had some urgent deadline; he had to finish his book. Nobody could possibly work in the vicinity of Lila, she would never let them. Trevor would be at his apartment.

I paused for a moment, my hand on the phone. Who was this girlfriend of Trev? I closed my eyes, let out my breath, paused, and breathed in Susan's. She was a composite of several extras I had met in LA. However, when I squeezed my eyes shut she thickened up. I could picture her now. She lay on her plastic recliner reading *True Confessions* and dreaming of her dream kitchen. Trev and she had gotten together in Le Dôme one lunchtime, when everybody else was out on location. After all, Trev was seldom on the set. He had plied her with spritzers and told her she had gorgeous tits and the relationship had blossomed. Now she had followed him to New York.

Moments later it was Susan who tsssk'd at a chipped nail and wrinkled her nose. Vowing to polish it later, she picked up the phone and dialled Lila's number.

It rang six times. Finally Lila answered, 'Hi?' She sounded sleepy.

Susan's high, whiney voice asked, 'Is Trev there?'

'Huh?'

Suddenly Susan said, 'Oh shit. Wrong number,' and quickly put down the receiver.

*

What was Lila thinking? She must have been uneasy by now. There was a story in the *National Enquirer* – hotly denied, no doubt, by Trev. There was a girl, phoning up – a secret girl-friend, who had dialled Lila's apartment by mistake, instead of Trev's.

Quickly I dialled Lila's number again. It was engaged. I knew it would be.

I put down the receiver. A deep sense of satisfaction spread through me, heavy as treacle. I knew exactly what she was doing – phoning Trevor to demand who the hell was that woman on the phone?

Now she knew what it felt like.

I poured myself a glass of white wine and drank it slowly, rolling it around my mouth. I gazed at the skeleton building opposite, rising to block my view. The offices on either side were emptying. Secretaries were returning to their blameless homes in Queens. They would pick up groceries on the way, in brown paper bags. They would kick off their shoes and surrender themselves to their TVs. Our buildings were so close, but I knew nothing about them and they were unaware of my existence.

Susan didn't exist either, except in my head. And now, in Lila's. We both believed in this phantom that I had created; she had thickened up for Lila just as she had thickened up for me, wasn't that fascinating? She was a performer in our own drama. Lila and I were strangely bound together by this figment of our jealousy. Where did reality begin? It's all in our heads: the most dangerous place on earth.

Roly didn't mention anything, the next time I saw him. Sony had taken over Columbia Pictures and he had been having dinner with some Japanese businessmen. He seemed very tired and lay on his bed whilst I massaged his pale, suety skin. He had fatty deposits around his hips, like a woman. Face down, he looked ludicrously unknown to me; he could have been a dead porpoise washed up on a beach. All day long he had been making and taking calls; he was in the middle of complex negotiations with Columbia, putting together some package with three of his clients – two stars and a director – and he was due to fly out to his LA office the next day. Why should he be interested in Lila's boyfriend's rumoured infidelities? His breathing grew rubbery and I realised that he had fallen asleep.

Once Roly was out of town, I felt bolder. I don't know why, but I did. The next morning I went to a call-box in the Citicorp Plaza and dialled the *Post*.

'I'd like to talk to somebody about the stories that have been circulating concerning Trevor Parsons and myself,' I said in Susan's die-away voice. 'I respect Lila Dune as an actress and as a human being, and I don't want to hurt her. But Trevvy and I have a very special relationship, and though he intends remaining business partners with Miss Dune, once the details of their production company are finalised he's invited me to move into his apartment. That's why he didn't move in with Miss Dune, you see, in the first place. We've gotten this fabulous Thai decorator to fix it up.' I gave the address of Trev's apartment and the name of his decorator.

I replaced the receiver, flashing a smile at a passing shopper. The lower level of the Citicorp was lined with shops. In the window of Doubleday's a book was displayed: *The Man Who Shot Greta Garbo*. Someone had tried to shoot Lila, hadn't they? So crude of them.

Dinosaurs stood in the lower level of the Citicorp. They were some sponsored display of fibreglass models. One of them had a long, arched neck; its piggy eyes were level with mine. I squinted at it playfully. Nobody else seemed to realise, but I knew. Underneath the city, beasts were breaking through like the rocks in Central Park. They reared up, under the buildings. The city creaked with their strainings. In the streets, metal plates were bolted vainly over them.

I sat down at a table, shaking. Nobody noticed, half the people there seemed to be afflicted with the DTs. I sat there, shaking with laughter.

*

All I meant, I'm sure, was to sow seeds of doubt and unease in her mind. I wanted to undermine her relationship with Trev and I knew I could do it because I was clever. I was also a superlative actress. You know that by now, don't you? I could become anyone I chose.

Lila was deeply susceptible – she went to an astrologer, for God's sake. She was incredibly insecure and rocky; she had freaked out often enough, in the past. I had heard more about this from Roly. One little push, and over she'd topple. Trev's charm lay in his shiftiness; women found him irresistible because they couldn't trust him. Or – more exactly – because he made them feel that only they could reform him.

I knew exactly what Lila was thinking: Where the hell was Trevor, all those days when he didn't turn up on location? Was he really writing? How did that girl know her own private number? Was this why Trev had bought a separate apartment – he was just using her, and he would dump her once he had set himself up?

This was all I meant to do, I'm sure. It's hard to see it clearly now. But I only meant a little harm.

I've never believed that Kennedy syndrome business. People remembering exactly what they were doing when the bomb-shell dropped; when the world changed. *I* don't remember what *I* was doing when Kennedy was shot.

But I remember that Monday in late April. The light was fading. I've always loved cities at twilight. In Los Angeles it was the most magical time. You didn't see many people, of course, just an increased activity along the freeways. But the flushed sky was beautiful, and there was the sense of a city stirring. Waiters stood in restaurants, combing their hair.

In New York, the streets swarmed. The setting sun hit the tops of the buildings, firing their windows. The Port Author-ity buses were packed; regiments of people stood, their arms extended like soldiers, hailing taxicabs. The grocery stores were illuminated like theatres. I had gone down Greenwich

Avenue to my local pharmacy, to buy some aspirin. My period had started and my stomach ached. But I was feeling surprisingly mellow, that evening. I remember that quite clearly. I was thinking about Lila and the times we had had together. I knew she wasn't thinking of me – like hell she was – but I was remembering the afternoon she had worn my jeans and we had sauntered along 3rd Avenue, our arms linked.

I hadn't heard from her for so long. Nor had I heard anything via Roly. Sometimes I didn't seethe; I just missed her painfully. I missed Trev all the time, of course. In fact I missed him more intensely as the weeks passed. I cried for him in the middle of the night, soaking my pillow. I missed his high spirits and his fitful companionship. I missed his sudden, obliterating lust. But my feelings for Lila fluctuated unexpectedly, as they did for my family, and I sometimes felt ashamed of the devious ways I had tried to damage her. I remembered her standing beside the phone booth in Leicester Square and gazing at me with her wide eyes. *'Boy, I sure as hell wouldn't want YOU for an enemy!'*

I went back to the apartment and unpacked some pasta that I had bought from Balducci's. I gazed at the limp, green tagliatelli; it lay on the draining board like something I had dredged from a pond. I remember thinking how sad it was, that I would be cooking it just for myself. Each month for decades my period had come, draining away my hopes.

Outside my windows the offices were lit for the cleaners. I was going to switch on the TV but I suddenly felt too weary. My life was slipping away from me. I couldn't even picture what I kept in the hall-way, in my Belsize Park flat.

And then, at 7.10, the phone rang. It was Roly.

'My dear,' he said. 'How're you doing?'

'Fine.'

He spoke in his office voice, suave and yet formal. It meant that his secretary was still there. He said that he'd had a call from some TV producer about a small part in a networked soap; they needed an English actress to play a tennis pro. 'Could you meet with them next week?'

My spirits lifted. Since joining BCM I had had several such meetings and they had all come to nothing. But in an actress's breast, hope springs eternal. It bloody well has to.

He told me the time and the place – somewhere downtown, in Tribeca. He told me the name of the guy and I scribbled it on a piece of paper. I remember taking a sip of vermouth and realising how much I enjoyed speaking to Roly on the phone. Like many unattractive men, he grew more alluring via the mouthpiece. One felt the pure pull of his personality.

I remember gazing at the worn, brown carpet and thinking about the terrible injustice of good looks. I was thinking about myself and Lila. God modelled us like putty, with careless abandon, and our only years on earth were determined by the whim of His thumbs. Maybe that was why I felt so bound to Roly, a walking example of life's insufferable chanciness. He and I had more in common than he realised.

I remember, very clearly, thinking this as I looked out of the window. The radiator rumbled, like my mother's stomach in church on Sunday. I thought of my parents and how, in their different ways, they had both expected great things of me. I was modelled by them as much as by a God in whom I no longer believed. One press of someone's thumbs and I could have become a Lila.

Roly was repeating some story Ellen Barkin had told him. They had bumped into each other the previous week in the First Class lounge at Kennedy. Then he told me about some catering cock-up at his nephew's barmitzvah. He was chatting to me at some length because he said he couldn't meet me that night. 'See, I have to go visit Lila.'

'Why?' I asked. 'What's happened?'

My mind raced. She was having a nervous breakdown. She had been toppled over by my stories in the papers. She was splitting up with Trev.

'You won't believe this,' he said. Just then another call came through for him.

'I'm sorry,' he told me. 'It's Jay. I'll have to take it.'

I don't know how many minutes passed before he came

back on the line. Only a couple, probably. I heard his faint voice. 'Talk with Alan Levine,' he said. 'He's their attorney. Sure Schulhof's seen the rough cut. His response was positive. I was led to believe we had a deal . . .'

I sat on the arm of the chair, my tumbler of vermouth on the table in front of me. During that moment, the apartment imprinted itself on my mind for ever; the two narrow windows, the brown carpet, the framed Edward Hopper print on the wall. The vase of dried flowers on the bookshelves. The illuminated kitchen doorway. My brain locked. All I could think was: *I've done it. She's finally freaked out.*

'. . . no, he has three others but they're all in turnaround,' said Roly, 'he's available, let's go with him.'

Finally he came back on the line.

'Sorry about that,' he said.

'What's happened to Lila?'

'Huh?'

I took a breath. 'You were telling me about Lila.'

'Oh. Sure,' he said. 'This is it.' He paused. 'She's pregnant. She's expecting Trevor's baby, isn't that a thing?'

I suppose I didn't reply, because after a moment he spoke again.

'Jules?' There was a pause. 'You still there?'

'Yes.'

'They're going to get married! How about that!'

Three

Some people here don't talk about what they have done. Others talk about it all the time, obsessively. They tell me more than I have ever wanted to know, and then they tell it to me all over again. A woman called Carletta follows me around like a dog. Her voice is low and monotonous; she mutters to my retreating back. I think she's got a crush on me. 'You have beautiful hair,' she says. She just loves my accent, and when I speak she gazes at my lips. Sometimes she reminds me of how I was, with Lila. She's my doppelganger. I can recognise her footsteps, without turning round. And I can never get away.

She talks all right, but she never tells me what I want to hear. Nobody does; not quite. What I want to know is when it happened. Not it: the deed. *It*: the decision. That's the most interesting moment, isn't it? The moment when everything changes. When your body changes chemically. It's as if you have had a transfusion, and there is suddenly someone else's blood in your veins.

It fascinates me, you see. In fact, it fascinates me a lot. I look at myself from a great distance. She's sitting in her apartment and she is changing in front of my eyes. One phone call did it.

The old Jules died and somebody else was born. She looked the same. White blouse, blue cardigan and jeans. Streaky blonde hair tied back in a band. She looked rather preppy that day. She moved around the apartment – look, she even did the washing-up, just like anybody else! Eventually she switched off the lights, one by one, and went to bed. But she didn't read. And her eyes remained open.

*

The next day I phoned the agency. I wanted the phone number of the TV producer, Abe Zacharias. I had forgotten to write it down the day before. Roly was in a meeting, so I spoke to his assistant, Larry.

He gave me the number. Then I asked him about Lila. I couldn't help it; I needed to confirm, from another source, that it was true. I had some sick compulsion to hear it again.

'Sure,' he said, 'but she's not announcing it to the press for a coupla days.'

'Why not?'

'Trevor's involved in some urgent project, he's working round the clock. He's holed up in his apartment and he doesn't want to be disturbed. Not by the press, not by anybody. He's writing some treatment he has to deliver Thursday.'

That day I lunched with Roly. I wore the fitted suit that he found so attractive. He noticed no difference in me. He talked about some deal he was putting together and his voice drifted past my nostrils like the scent of cooking. I smiled and nodded. My mind was being repeatedly scratched by a needle, playing the same tune over and over. *He's having a baby with her.* The record was stuck; by now the words had worn into nonsense, like a Yogic chant. *Om . . . om . . .*

'You're not eating, honey,' said Roly. 'You don't like it? Want me to send it back?'

I looked down at my *noisette d'agneau.* They were three small chops. Their bones had been removed; they were tightly curled like foetuses. They lay in their own thin liquor.

I paused, and said casually, 'I hear Trevor's working on a new project.'

Roly nodded. 'Lila told me about it. But it's a big secret.' He lifted his glass of water and took a sip. 'Even me, she doesn't tell the story to.'

'Really?'

He patted his lips with his napkin. 'Even me.'

*

Outside it was chilly. Standing under the canopy, Roly buttoned up my coat. He buttoned it so tightly around my neck that I could hardly breathe. We walked down the street, hunched against the wind. Outside a liquor shop, I paused. I thought: maybe I'm not sounding pleased enough about Lila. Will he think I'm strange?

So I said, 'I know! I'll buy a bottle of champagne for Lila and take it round to her place.'

He said something but I couldn't hear. Some truck had gridlocked, the traffic was at a standstill and the horns were deafening.

'What?' I shouted.

'If you're going tonight,' he said, 'make it early.'

'Why?'

'She's working for the next couple of days.'

'What?' I shouted. 'She's what?'

'She's filming. Guest appearance, just a couple of days.' He yelled at me closer. 'She has an early call, she goes to bed at nine. Dead to the world.'

Four

Jules took a cab back to her apartment. She slammed the door shut and dumped the bottle of champagne on the table. Her legs were trembling.

She sat down in the kitchen. She had to think, fast. The more she thought, the more flustered she felt. And yet paralysed. Such innocuous words, such an innocent arrangement! Lila drugged and asleep in her apartment; Trev alone in his. The two items of information had triggered off an idea so bold, so foolproof, that she could hardly believe it. Because it was magically simple. If she could keep her wits.

I can't remember what she did until twilight. Most of the time, I think, she sat immobile on the edge of the bed. At one point she jumped up, opened the closet and rummaged in her suitcase. At the bottom was the letter she had tapped out on Trev's typewriter. She took it out and put it in her handbag. She selected a book from the shelves and put it into her handbag too.

She must have sat still for a while, then. Everything had fallen into place. She didn't even dare think about it.

When she looked at her watch, for the hundredth time, it was 4.15. Some time later she made herself a cup of tea. Usually she didn't take it sweetened, but that day she loaded in three spoonfuls of sugar. It tasted like the tea they give you in hospital. Later that night, when I returned to the apartment, I found sugar spilt on the kitchen table; there was some sprinkled on the floor, too. What a state she must have been in!

At some point, too, she ran herself a bath. I suppose it

298

was something to do, before darkness came. She lay in the water for a long time, until it grew tepid. Then she dried herself thoroughly with the towel. With mild interest she looked at herself in the mirror and saw how thin she had become. Almost emaciated, really. Her hip-bones jutted out and her breasts had shrunk. She brushed her teeth, as if she were preparing for a long journey.

She sat down on the edge of the bed again. How insufferably hot it was! She could hardly breathe. So she got up and opened the window; then she sat down again. She smelt a faint scent of perfume. It must have wafted up fifteen floors, from trees down in the canyon of the streets. Spring had arrived; buds were swelling and bursting.

Jolly silly to open the window. She chided herself. Jolly silly, silly-billy. It was freezing! She got up and pulled down the window; it jammed, and she jerked it. Outside, the sunlight was creeping up the buildings opposite, as the sun itself sunk. She looked at her watch. It was ten past six.

She sat on the hard dining chair. She felt as if she were in a waiting room. In an hour she would have to leave. Words from a medieval poem that she had learnt in the sixth form rolled round her head.

> Fain would I wed a fair young man who day and night could
>   please me,
> When my mind or body grieved, that had the power to ease
>   me . . .

There was a curious, sour taste on her tongue, and her stomach ached. 'That had the power to ease me.' She mouthed the words silently. The room was so quiet. The next-door couple hadn't returned home from work yet. She knew their sounds so well: the murmur of their TV, the gurgle of their water pipes. For everybody else, this was just an ordinary Tuesday. Wasn't that peculiar?

> Maids are full of longing thoughts, that feed a sudden sickness.
> And that – for oft I've heard men say – is only cured by quickness.

She thought of her father. No thanks! She didn't think of her father.

She wondered why she felt no need for her breathing exercises. Before a performance she usually had an attack of nerves, but today she felt as cool as a cucumber. Silly expression, but she couldn't think of another one. She couldn't afford the effort.

It was twenty to seven. Outside the window, the shadow had inched up the building. Only seven floors of the office block remained in sunlight; she counted them. If she watched the solid block of shadow, she could swear she could see it moving. She ought to be getting ready to go – it was a long way to Central Park West, forty or fifty blocks. Something or other. It helped to feel careless about it. Insouciant. As if it were just a whim and, who knows? She might not go at all. Fooled you all! Silly-billies.

Ten to seven. She knew she ought to be going but she felt like a sack of turnips in her chair. She kept putting it off. The sounds of the city were much fainter than usual. What was happening, out there? Maybe she was sitting in her flat in London and it was all a dream. New York was four thousand miles away.

Maybe the neighbourhood was blocked off. When she emerged from the lobby the street would be silent. Just a wedge of police cars each end, their lights revolving. A semicircle of cops, closing in on her.

I think she brushed her teeth again. Later I found the toothpaste tube on the floor. The cap had rolled away. So unlike me!

At 7.30 she left the apartment, took the elevator downstairs and bought a pack of chocolate M&Ms in the supermarket. Then she hailed a cab.

The journey seemed to take a long time. The traffic, travelling uptown, was heavy, and for the first time in months she was landed with a loquacious cab driver. He was one of the old Jewish kind.

'So you came from London, huh? Me and my wife, we visited on vacation a coupla years ago. You know the Greville Hotel?'

She must have replied. The 6th Avenue buildings slid by, joltingly. The traffic jammed solid at each set of lights. A woman turned to stare into the cab. Jules sunk back in her seat.

All the passers-by were looking at her. They knew exactly where she was going and what she was planning to do. The plastic seat of the cab was scored down the centre; someone had sliced it with a knife.

'. . . the Observatory at Greenwich,' said the driver. 'Madame Tussauds . . .'

She gripped the bottle of Moët; her hand stuck to the paper bag. The cab swerved around a bus and lurched to a halt at the next set of traffic signals. People shuffled past the hood. They turned to look at her; their heads swung round, one by one.

'. . . Hampstead Heath . . . roast beef in, what's that place called? Lousy service, great view.'

'Jack Straw's Castle,' she said.

The cab sprung forward, bouncing over the potholes. The lights had all changed in its favour and suddenly the journey speeded up, alarmingly. Radio City flashed past, on her right, the Hilton Hotel on her left. She heard the piercing whistle of its doorman, hailing cabs. Or was it the cops?

Suddenly she panicked. Now she was nearing Lila's place she didn't want to get there. She could always go back. Nobody would ever know. She could simply stop the cab and get out. Then she could hail another one, go back to her apartment, put away the letter and the book. Switch on the TV and rejoin the human race.

The driver slammed on the brakes. She lurched forward. A man was standing in the middle of the road. He looked like an aborigine.

The cab driver leant out of the window and yelled, 'Wanna get killed?'

He revved up and steered violently around the man, who padded off on his bare feet.

'This city,' said the driver, shaking his head. 'This city, it's full of crazy people. You wouldn't believe it, some of the people I see. Cra-zee . . .'

The cab surged forward, flinging her against the back of the seat. They shot into Central Park, speeding along West Drive. Trees flashed past. She swayed sideways as it swerved around a bend. Two minutes, and they would be there.

'. . . should lock 'em up, where they belong . . .'

She felt nauseous, and closed her eyes. They were waiting for her in the lobby: Lila, Trevor, Roly and Irma. A burly cop stepped forward, handcuffs outstretched. *Just take it easy.* He clicked his tongue at her as if she were an animal. *Take it easy.* Lila stared; Trev grinned.

The cab juddered to a halt. She opened her eyes. They had arrived outside Lila's apartment building. The doorman was approaching, to open the cab door. He was the fat, friendly one.

As she climbed out, he recognised her. 'Well hi!' he said.

'Hi.'

'Good to see you again.'

Fumbling, she searched for some money in her purse. What if he saw something, inside her bag? Surely there was nothing unusual. Just a large, hardback book. She pulled out some dollar bills. She should have got them all ready beforehand; now she was trembling. Suddenly everything was happening too fast; her brain felt scrambled. She had planned it all out so carefully but now she felt horribly flustered, as if she had been thrust upon a stage with no previous rehearsals. Did it show?

She paid the cab driver; he thanked her and drove off. She had forgotten the champagne! No she hadn't – she was clutching it in her hand. Wasn't she silly?

She followed the doorman into the lobby. Unnervingly, it was just the same. Lacquered walls, shiny lampshades, a discreetly spotlit vase of mixed flowers.

'I've come to see Miss Dune,' she said.

The doorman lifted the phone, and dialled. What if Lila had company? Why on earth hadn't she thought of that?

The doorman put down the phone. 'Go right on up. You know the way.'

She walked across the lobby, stepped into the elevator and pressed the PH button. The doors slid shut. She was alone.

She closed her eyes and breathed deeply. It had happened before, after all. The clothes of the character slipped from your shoulders and suddenly you were naked. You broke into a sweat. You panicked. The only thing to do was to pause and catch up with yourself. You pick up the clothes and step into them. Simple as that.

She was a professional, wasn't she? By the time the lift arrived at the 31st floor, the PH floor, she had recovered herself. The doors slid open. Calmly she stepped across the vestibule and rang Lila's bell.

Five

Orson barked, and then stopped. For a moment, nothing happened. She cocked her head, listening. She heard the murmur of a voice.

She stood close to the door. There was somebody else in there. Lila was talking. She could hear her muffled voice, and then laughter.

Do you know what she felt, just then? Shock and disappointment, of course. Panic, that maybe it was Trev in there, and she would have to face him. Then, believe it or not, she felt profound relief. It spread through her like a blush.

She stood there, weakly. Through the door she heard footsteps approaching, crossing the marble floor. All she had to do was to give Lila the bottle of champagne, say 'congratulations' and leave. Simple as that!

She heard the lock being turned. The door opened and Lila stood there. For a moment, her face was blank.

'Jules, honey!' she said, kissing her on the cheek. 'I didn't get the name, when they called up. Come on in.' She hurried into the living room, speaking over her shoulder: 'I'll be through in a moment. Make yourself at home.'

She didn't have company. She was on the phone.

Jules went into the living room and sat down on the familiar white settee. The apartment looked exactly the same, except for some magazines spread around and several large vases of flowers.

Orson growled at her and then retreated under the glass table. Lila kicked off her shoes, curled herself in the armchair and picked up the phone.

'. . . hey, Carrie, why not drop by tomorrow? Matt's on

304

this picture, know that?' She laughed. 'Yeah, *Matt*! Whaddya know! Raised from the dead.'

She wore a fluffy yellow sweater and jeans. It was nearly two months since Jules had seen her. She looked pale; her face was scrubbed clean of make-up and her hair was pulled back in a knot. She looked very beautiful; pregnancy obviously suited her.

'. . . I said to my agent, real powerhouse casting, huh?' She laughed again. She stretched out her leg and inspected her bare, wriggling toes. 'Still, I'd do anything for Stan. We go back a long way.'

She looked up at Jules and mouthed that she was finishing. Jules gazed around the room. She had forgotten how vast it was. She didn't want to look at Lila. She needed to concentrate on how much she hated her. She hated her more than any woman in the world, and she was going to do her terrible harm.

'. . . we'll be breaking at one, see you then!' Lila put down the phone and uncurled herself from the armchair. 'Jesus, you look hot! You OK? Want me to take your coat?'

Jules took the champagne bottle out of its bag. 'I heard your news.' She beamed at her. 'Congratulations!'

'Isn't it just terrific? Course, I feel grungy in the mornings. Yuk! – but doesn't everyone? Wanna drink?' She lifted up the bottle. 'I've still quit, how about that? Longest ever. But you want some?'

No fear. She needed a clear head, tonight.

She followed Lila into the kitchen. Lila poured them two glasses of Paul Newman lemonade. 'Know we got the green light?' she said. 'For the pasta sauce? They sent me the label designs yesterday. Marinara, Pepperino, Vongole. Vongole's clams.'

They went back into the living room. Glass in hand, Jules wandered across to the window. The sun had set and the city was laid at her feet; she had forgotten the sensation. How high they were! Below the luminous sky, a million lights sparkled. Suddenly she felt profoundly sad.

'Know what?' said Lila's voice. 'You've lost a heck of a lot of weight, since I saw you. You can't afford it, hon. Your bod's flushing out those valuable minerals. I didn't recognise you at first.'

'Really?'

'I didn't know you were still in town, but Roly told me you'd signed up with them, so we have the same agent! How about that! It's really fabulous to see you again.'

She did sound genuinely pleased. No doubt she had long ago forgotten the fracas. She was not the type to harbour grudges, and besides she looked too blissfully happy to think about anyone else.

Jules stayed looking out of the window. She heard the click of a lighter. 'So you're still smoking?'

'Yeah, but I've cut right back. I'm taking real good care of myself, this time. Tee's told me to.'

Jules gazed at the rusting barbecue on the balcony. She needed a cigarette badly, but she didn't dare light one in case Lila noticed her hands shaking. She thought: I used to buy Lila cigarettes and store them in my room. I used to love her.

'With my history, I have to,' said Lila. 'See, I never thought I'd have a child, I thought I was too old. I thought it was too late. My tubes were all fucked up. This is the best present I've ever had.'

Her voice rattled on. Jules moved away from the window. It hurt, to talk to Lila. It made her head ache. She picked up a paperweight. It was a heavy, onyx one. How simple just to walk over and bash Lila's brains in! Save a lot of trouble.

'After Thursday I'm quitting work, I'm going to tuck myself up in here and take it easy.'

'You do that.'

'The nineties is the nurturing decade,' said Lila. 'I read it, someplace. *Vogue*.'

Jules sipped her lemonade. What an infantile drink. Typical, really. She needed something alcoholic, badly. Lila didn't know when to stop, did she? She had always been hopelessly

306

stupid. Her voice sounded like two bits of wire being rubbed together.

'Tee's changed my life, know that? I'm putting all those bad old days behind me. He's selling his apartment and moving in here, isn't that just dandy?'

'Is he?'

'He'll make a heap of money, the way he's fixing it up. It's fabulous. You should see it.'

Don't worry, she thought. *I will.*

'We're planning on a June wedding,' Lila went on, dreamily. 'He's taking me to Venice. This time, it's for keeps.'

Jules lowered her nose into a vase of crimson roses, and sniffed. 'Thought I saw something in the papers,' she murmured. 'About some, you know. Girl.'

'Oh, *that*. There's a lot of flaky women around. Sad cases, you know. The people out there, you wouldn't believe. You should see some of the letters I get. They've got nothing going for them, they're lonely. They're inadequate. It didn't threaten us.'

Jules breathed in the perfume. 'Didn't it?'

'Tee and I, we have a mutually respectful relationship. Say, did I tell you we're working together? A fabulous project – but it's hush-hush, nobody knows about it. Not even Roly. We're not telling anyone. Tee's working on the treatment now. He's so brilliant. I've been doing some research – see, he doesn't consider me just a bimbo! He respects my mind, too!' She laughed. 'We've formed this production company. Tee says it's not just for movies, it's for babies too!'

Would the woman never stop? Jules's throat felt tight. Her head throbbed. What the hell right did Lila have, to be rabbiting on like this?

Jules raised her head, wearily, from the roses. Lila stretched, and looked at her watch.

'Sweetheart,' she yawned. 'I have an early call tomorrow, and you know me! First I'm going to take a long, hot tub.'

'I must be going, anyway.' She walked across to Lila, leant

down and kissed her. She felt like Judas. Lila's cheek smelt of that perfume, the one she had given her. *Je Reviens*.

'Bye,' said Jules. 'I'll see myself out.'

She walked briskly to the door, turned and waved at Lila. Then she let herself out of the apartment.

She closed the door behind her, with a click.

She stood in the vestibule, her heart pounding. She was an animal now, on the run. She sniffed the air. Was this how a criminal felt?

It was an eerie, lonely feeling. Her temples throbbed and there was that sour taste in her mouth; it exhaled from the pit of her stomach. It must be fear. When she looked at the silk stripes of the wallpaper, they pulsed and blurred like Op Art.

She walked along the vestibule, past the elevator doors, towards the freight elevator. There were three other apartments on this penthouse floor; their doors remained closed.

She felt a lurch of exhilaration. Events were in motion now, and there was no turning back. She called the freight elevator. When it arrived, she rode in it down to the ground floor. Its doors opened to reveal the chilly little hallway at the side of the building, and the one-way exit door. Some garbage bags were piled up in the corner. What if the janitor came?

From her handbag she took out the big, hardback book. *Hollywood Wives*. Like Lila, her landlady was obviously not overburdened with intellect.

She pushed open the door, just slightly, and wedged it ajar with the book. She smelt the cold air from the street, and heard the sound of traffic. She pictured Lila's lover creeping out; a furtive TV personality, head bowed.

She stepped back into the freight elevator and pressed the button for the second floor. Any floor would do, really, for her to move over to the passenger lift.

The freight elevator rose and jolted to a halt. Its doors opened to reveal an identical vestibule to Lila's except the silky stripes were beige. Thank God there was nobody around.

She transferred to the passenger elevator and rode it down to the ground floor. It would have looked odd, to arrive from the direction of the freight elevator.

The doors slid open and she marched confidently across the lobby. Some residents had just arrived with a load of luggage; the younger doorman was taking it to the elevator. A man sat in one of the armchairs, maybe waiting for his date. They weren't people; they had been transformed into abstract figures called witnesses. They were seeing her leave the building.

The fat doorman was behind his desk. 'Have a good night, now,' he called.

'Night,' she called to him, cheerfully, and walked out into the sharp spring air. Going into the street was like stepping off stage, into the wings. You walk a few paces and then the character drains from you, leaving you limp.

It was 8.30. She had an hour to kill; that was what she had given herself. An hour, at the very most, for Lila to bathe, drug herself to the eyeballs with Mogadon and fall into a deep sleep.

She walked up to Columbus Avenue. The yuppie restaurants were lit; the people sitting inside them looked startlingly normal. She felt like another species, prowling along the pavement. How swiftly she had become an outcast, and how ridiculous when *she hadn't yet done anything criminal*. Her only act, so far, had been harmlessly eccentric – wedging a door open, just a few inches, with a Jackie Collins novel.

What if the janitor came down and closed the door?

She walked past the pasta shop, where they had filmed so many months before. It seemed to have taken place in another lifetime. So had her lunch with Roly, that very day. All the events that had preceded her moment of decision and her subsequent afternoon's plotting seemed locked away in another, sunnier country to which she was now denied access.

She wore flat, suede boots and her overcoat; she was as silent as a cat. Passing the darkened dry cleaner's, her little theatre of impersonation, she walked up towards the Natural History Museum. It loomed up, its columns massive in the street light. She walked a further couple of blocks, and then dared herself to look at her watch. It was ten to nine. She longed for a drink, but she didn't trust herself to enter a bar and perform the simple transaction. She might get it wrong, she might act in an abnormal manner. This would alarm herself more than anybody else; she was frightened of losing her grip. Besides, she couldn't possibly speak to anyone.

At random, she chose 85th Street. She turned up it and walked a few blocks, across Amsterdam Avenue and towards the Hudson. At the DON'T WALK signals she stopped, like an obedient citizen. Wasn't that quaint?

Just about now, Lila would be swallowing her sleeping pills. It was nearly nine o'clock. The whole business was starting to feel deeply unreal. During breaks in filming, the illusion drains away. You have to hold on to your concentration. You may be drinking coffee and schmoozing with the extras but in your head you must be still at work. Same thing backstage, in the interval, as the minutes tick by your character dissolves. She kept herself alert by thinking about Trevor. She had avoided passing his apartment building; she couldn't risk an attack of nerves. It was a cold night, but under her coat she was sweating. Now the moment was approaching she worked herself up into a fury. At least, I presume she did; I really can't remember. Those last twenty minutes are blank in my memory. Maybe she was too numb to think. I don't know. I don't hold myself responsible.

I remember how loud the traffic was, on Columbus. It battered at her ears. I remember someone slamming a car door and making her jump. In the lit windows people were watching her; they were lifting up their phones and dialling the police department. She didn't dare turn her head.

Then she looked at her watch. Christ, it was 9.25! Time moves in fits and starts, like the traffic. Suddenly she felt flustered, but she told herself to calm down. What did a few minutes' difference make, either way?

She strode back to the apartment building, her heart hammering. On the way, she pulled on her thin leather gloves. It unnerved her to do this; it meant business. The side doorway was so dark that for a moment she couldn't tell if the book was still there.

It was. She saw it jutting out, like a foot. She pushed the door wider, and stepped inside. It felt colder in here than in the street. She closed the door behind her, softly, and replaced the book in her handbag. Then she pressed the freight elevator button.

Nothing happened. The lift shaft was silent. There was no muffled stirring, no creak of pulleys.

She froze. It could only mean one thing. The elevator was in use. Somewhere, up in the building, goods were being loaded. Or unloaded.

She stared at the rusty, closed doors. She couldn't move. A smell of rotting fruit came from the garbage chute. Should she run for it?

Hours seemed to pass. She gazed at the single light bulb, hanging from the ceiling. And then, finally, she heard the machinery crank into action. The elevator was on its way down.

Like a rabbit, she was paralysed. In a moment the doors would open and somebody would be standing there. The janitor. A delivery boy.

The elevator stopped, with a sigh. After a moment's hesitation, the rusty doors slid open.

It was empty. There was nothing in it but a pile of boxes.

She stepped in and pressed the button to the PH floor. The elevator rose, crankingly. It was slower than the passenger one. 3 . . . 4 . . . 5 . . . At each floor it paused, as if it were going to stop. 16 . . . 17 . . . She was sweating; her blouse stuck to her backbone.

Finally the doors opened to the bare concrete walls of the penthouse floor. She made her way along the passage to the carpeted vestibule outside Lila's door.

Silence. She stood for a moment, close to the door, listening.

Not a sound. Then she took out the pack of M&Ms – why hadn't she done this in the safety of the elevator? Stupid stupid stupid.

She tore open the pack. It was difficult, in the gloves; she had to do it with her teeth. She dropped a few M&Ms into her hand. At the bottom of her bag, wedged under the book, she found Lila's keys. They rattled; she flinched. Surely she could be heard all over the building?

Before she inserted the key, she paused. A strange feeling seemed to stretch the skin, all over her body. The hallway enlarged, echoingly.

This was it. One twist of the key and she was a criminal. She was breaking into somebody's home. Once she opened the door, there was no turning back. She tried to make herself realise this, to truly digest it, but she simply felt numb.

Her hand moved, without her help. It inserted the large key, and turned it very gently in the lock. She had opened this door often enough, in the past. The big lock was easy; it glided open. The small one was trickier; you had to lean against the door to ease it.

She pushed against the door, twisting the key in the lock. Suddenly, behind the door, Orson barked.

He was very close. He scratched, on the other side of the door, and barked again.

Frantically she turned the key again. The door creaked open.

Orson snarled at her. She knelt down, nearly overbalancing, and held out the M&Ms in the palm of her hand.

Slobberingly, he ate them. She patted his head. 'Good Orson,' she whispered. 'Good boy.'

She wiped her slimy glove on her coat, and looked up. The lamp was on, in the lobby. This was for the dog; Lila had told her, long ago, that he hated the dark. Apart from that, the apartment seemed to be in darkness. It smelt, faintly, of Badedas. The living room door was ajar and she could see the glimmer of the white settee, and the night sky behind.

Lila's bedroom was to the right. Its door was ajar. She crept up to it and listened. Silence. Behind her there was a snuffling, damp sound as Orson licked up M&Ms from the marble floor. She heard his jaw clicking.

Thank God she knew every inch of this apartment. She paused, her hand on the doorknob; it was round and cool.

Think I didn't dare? Think I couldn't do it? As we used to say at school: you've got another think coming.

I have to admit, I nearly turned around and made a dash for it. For a moment I was gripped by pure terror. But Jules didn't move. She took a breath and pushed open the door, softly.

The room was in darkness, but the light from the hallway dimly illuminated the furniture. The bed was over by the window. Jules paused on the threshold. I'm watching her; she looks surprisingly shy and hesitant, as if she's in a hotel and gone into the wrong bedroom by mistake. Then she takes a step forward.

Lila was in bed. There was a glimmer of pale hair, on the pillow. On the bedside table, the clock glowed. It flipped from 21.39 to 21.40. If she held her breath, Jules could see the duvet gently rising and falling. Or maybe it was just her imagination.

How obedient of her! thought Jules. She gazed, almost fondly, at the humped duvet. A totally unexpected feeling swept over her: she was so taken aback that for a moment she couldn't identify it. Then she realised what it was: professional camaraderie. She grunted in surprise.

Lila knew the script. For once she wasn't taking the starring role. Content with a non-speaking – indeed, almost non-existent – part, she had relinquished the centre stage to her colleague. Jules knew her part perfectly, of course. She had been rehearsing it since God knew when. Only that afternoon? More like months, really. Ever since she had seen Trev stepping out of that limo.

She told herself: this is the performance of my life. She knew, now, that Lila wouldn't wake up. Lila would act according to the script. How suddenly easy it was!

Her stage-fright vanished. Lila lay motionless, curled on her side. Her eyes were blindfolded with an airline mask, as if she were taking a nap before going to a ball. When Jules kept still she could hear the deep, regular breathing, followed by a faint whistle as the air exhaled between Lila's lips. She had never seen Lila asleep before; ridiculously enough she felt the usual slight awkwardness, the sense of invasion. But no terror, not now.

She moved away and tiptoed across the dimly-lit set. She opened the walk-in closet. It was dark in there, and she didn't dare switch on the interior light. But she knew where Lila kept her sable coat; right at the back.

She smelt perfume and leather. Like a blind woman she felt her way through the clothes, running her gloved fingers over the fabric. Silky blouses, light as tissue . . . the supple leather of Lila's blue dress, she had tried it on herself once . . . The slippery satin of the Bill Blass . . . They smelt of Lila. As she touched them, she felt oddly aroused. She moved down the rack. Finally her fingers sank into fur, oh such soft fur. She lifted the sable coat off its hanger. It was unexpectedly heavy. The hanger clattered against its neighbour.

She froze. No sound from the bedroom.

Then she felt around, amongst the shoes. Lila had a large collection. '*Let me loose in a shoe store*,' she had said once, '*and I'm like a kid buying candy*.' Many of them were evening shoes, shoes for premières, for stepping in and out of cars. They came from atrociously expensive shops in Madison Avenue. In some way, they were more familiar to Jules than her own. Bunching up the coat, she knelt down and ran her hand over their shiny leather. She touched their high, spiky heels. Finally she selected a black pair with slingbacks, she recognised them by their feel, and emerged from the closet.

Lila hadn't stirred. The light from the hallway lay across the carpet. How quiet it was! Jules had forgotten that. It was so quiet, up here, that you couldn't even hear the traffic.

Jules laid the coat over a chair, which nearly tipped backwards. She caught it just in time. Orson had come in. He snuffled at her ankles; she gently nudged him away.

The blonde, shoulder-length wig glimmered on the dressing table. She sat down and pulled back her hair with clips; her gloves made her clumsy, but she did it. She lowered the wig onto her head. She was sitting in her dressing room backstage, preparing to go on. Her fingers barely shook. Lifting her head, she inspected her shadowy reflection in the mirror. Lila the imposter gazed back, smiling.

She picked up the crimson lipstick and, leaning closer so she could see her mouth, outlined her lips generously. Lila's fuller, riper mouth smiled back.

Swiftly she got to her feet, picked up the coat and shoes, and took one last look at Lila. She lay there like the Sleeping Beauty. Whatever her failings as an actress, she was playing this part to perfection. Orson jumped onto the bed. She didn't stir. Her clock bathed its surroundings in a greenish mist. It flipped: 21.55.

Jules looked for the handbag, but it didn't seem to be in the bedroom. She left, closing the door softly behind her, and tiptoed into the living room. Once there, she breathed freely.

In the half-light, it seemed as vast as a ballroom. She crossed the floor, almost skidding on one of the rugs, and searched for the handbag. Finally she found it, a dark bulk on the pale upholstery of the armchair. She bent down, the long hair swinging on either side of her face.

She couldn't touch the bag. Not for a moment. For some reason, it felt more of a violation than anything else. Opening somebody else's bag – it was as lawless as wetting the bed.

She touched the bag, then jerked back as if it had stung her. There was a noise in the kitchen. A muffled clatter, as if something was shifting its position.

It was only the ice-making machine. She reached out again for the handbag, lifted it up and clicked it open.

Inside, she felt the dark glasses. They were folded like an insect. She took them out. Then she inserted her hand, deeper.

The gun was surprisingly cold. Even through the gloves, she could feel it. Heavy, too. She lifted it out, gingerly. She ran her hand over the stubby metal shaft, and the safety catch. It was locked back. How curious, that it could blow off somebody's face! It felt as unconvincingly convincing as a stage prop.

Stage directions: she puts the loaded pistol into the pocket of the fur coat. Glancing around furtively, she takes off her own coat and boots and hides them behind the settee. She also hides her handbag. Then she puts on Lila's shoes and wraps herself in the fur coat. She leaves the room.

In the lobby, she selects a headscarf from the assortment lying in the copper bowl on the table. She ties it around her head: Lila's street disguise. She puts on the dark glasses, checks her appearance in the mirror, and exits.

Closing the door behind her, Jules felt a curious sensation. She was in an Italian Primitive painting; she was the soul, issuing forth, like an identical doll, from the mouth of a sinner. Around her, the colours glowed with an intensity that has never been recaptured. Lila, in a simple cobalt robe, had opened her mouth and her spirit had flown out from between her lips. Was it her soul? Or was it the devil?

Jules pocketed the keys and pressed the elevator button. It took an age to arrive.

Finally it came. The doors slid open. She stepped in and pressed the button for the ground-floor lobby. The elevator started to descend.

Adjusting her dark glasses, she glanced up at the indicator panel. Something was wrong. After a split second, she realised: the number 16 was lit up.

Her stomach lurched. She wrapped herself tightly in the coat and turned away to inspect the wall. The lift stopped on the 16th floor and the doors opened.

Out of the corner of her eye she could see a large, grizzled man. He wore a track suit and he was accompanied by an Airedale dog. He stepped in, nodding to her.

'Hi!' he said.

She nodded back, and turned away. He was obviously a resident, taking his dog for a run. She fixed her eyes on the veneered mahogany panelling. Suddenly she jumped. The dog was sniffing her leg.

The man jerked it away. 'Torts!' he said, 'lay off!' Then he addressed her. 'Sorry about that. He can smell yours.'

'What?' Christ, her voice was wrong! She hadn't practised.

'Your dog,' he said.

'Ah.'

They stood immobile as the elevator descended. 9 . . . 8 . . . She could smell his aftershave. He cleared his throat. She willed him not to speak again.

'Took my daughter to *Fields of Desire*,' he said. 'Beautiful picture.'

'Thanks,' she muttered.

. . . 4 . . . 3 . . .

He laughed. 'Now she wants to go and live in Wisconsin.'

The elevator slid silkily to a halt. The doors opened. The man stood back, to let her out.

'Bye,' she said.

'Take care,' he said.

The lobby was empty, except for the fat doorman. He was sitting behind his desk, watching TV. He jumped up as she headed for the door. It took such an age, to cross the marble floor. Her high heels beat a tattoo. She knew she was hurrying too fast, but the man with the dog was behind her.

The doorman held the door open for her.

'Night,' she said.

Shielding her face with her furry collar, she hurried out of the building.

She turned to the left, and walked briskly up Central Park West. Behind her, she heard the thud of footsteps. They gathered speed. She walked faster. The footsteps thudded nearer and the man passed her, dragging his dog behind him. He raised his hand, in a half-salute.

Her heartbeat returned to normal. *I've done it*, she thought. A wave of traffic, released from the lights, leapt past her. A

317

cab's loose hood bounced up and down. Across the street, the darkened park accompanied her like her tangled dreams. It was windy. The trees waved their branches against the lurid sky, as if trying to attract her attention.

The shoes pinched – Lila's feet were a half-size smaller than her own. But they helped to create Lila's provocative, wriggling walk. Shoes always help – hadn't Bette Davis said so? Or was it Audrey Hepburn?

For the first block she didn't meet anybody. Wooden barricades, topped with barbed wire, surrounded the next apartment building. She passed its lit entrance like an assassin at an airport, passing through the infra-red security system. The doorman didn't turn.

Crossing the next street, she stumbled on the kerb. In the dark glasses she couldn't see clearly. Lila couldn't, either. Shielded from the world's stare she stumbled, half-blinded by her ostentatious attempt at anonymity. Wear shades and you can guarantee speculation. Walking up the next block, she passed a young couple. They nudged each other. What were they saying? Who did they think they had seen?

Guess who we saw last night! They would tell their friends.

She turned the corner into 73rd Street. Halfway up it stood the building where Trevor lived. Wedged between brownstones, it was tall and modern. Its angled balconies jutted out like ashtrays. She had scanned it so often, standing in the shadowy entrance of the underground car park opposite. But tonight, it was as if she had never seen it before. It looked as temporary as a stage set. Even the cypresses in the tubs outside looked too good to be true. It awaited her entrance.

From across the road she could see the doorman, sitting behind his desk. He knew his part so well. Hadn't she rehearsed it with him, often enough, in her head? He only had a few lines, and let's hope he was going to get them right.

She paused, before making her entrance. It was all going just fine. Down the street, an extra emerged from one of the brownstones and climbed into a waiting cab.

And . . . action! Lila crossed the road and entered the lobby.

The doorman smiled and nodded. In fact, he seemed to have no lines at all.

She walked across the shiny floor. For a split second, she faltered. Ah! There were the elevators! She veered to the left and made her way towards them, past a sunken pool swarming with carp.

Trevor's apartment was 18C. That must mean that he lived on the 18th floor. She couldn't very well ask the doorman.

'Miss Dune?'

She swung round. The doorman was calling her.

'Shall I tell him you're on your way up?'

'Er. No thanks.' She smiled. 'I want to surprise him.'

The doorman grinned at her, across the lobby. She stepped into the elevator. Its doors closed behind her.

How very fast it was! Much faster than Lila's. Her ears crackled as the brushed-steel box hurled her up into the sky, like a space-ship. Before she could draw breath, the doors opened.

She stepped into a white corridor. There were five doors. 18A . . . 18B . . . She walked down to the end. 18C.

She stood outside the door, absolutely still, her head cocked. Was that the sound of a typewriter tapping? There was a roaring in her ears. For a moment she couldn't hear anything. Then her head cleared, and she pressed the bell.

Six

Silence. The typewriter stopped. Footsteps approached and the door opened.

Trevor stood there, dressed in a blue bathrobe. He was unshaven, and smoking a cigarette.

'Hi, hon,' she drawled.

His face lit up. 'Lila!'

He dropped his cigarette on the floor, and squashed it with his foot. He stepped forward, closed the door and put his arms around her.

'Couldn't keep away, Tee,' she murmured. 'My, do I feel horny tonight.'

He slipped his hand under her coat and kissed her. She tasted his saliva; she smelt his hair. Oh, those forgotten scents!

His stubble rasped against her skin. She pushed her tongue into his mouth and pressed her body against his. Below the knot of the bathrobe cord she felt the bump of his erection.

His fingers slid through the opening in her blouse and touched her bare breast. He pulled the coat off her shoulders.

Suddenly he jerked back. 'Jesus!' he yelped.

He pushed her away, roughly. She stumbled against the doorframe. Revolted, he wiped his lips. She wiped her mouth, too, and smiled at him. She was panting, hard.

'Who the fuck – ?' he started.

Watching his face, she removed her dark glasses.

His eyes clouded. Just for a moment he didn't recognise her. Wasn't that amazing? He didn't remember her. Then he stared.

'Jules?'

He blenched. *Trev.* He actually went pale.

'What the fuck are you doing?' he demanded. His voice was so high! He sounded like a schoolgirl.

'Don't see what you're making such a fuss about.' She spoke in her normal voice, low and reasonable. 'We're the same underneath, you know. Me and her. Just the same.'

He backed away from her, into the next room. It smelt of fresh paint. There was a work desk, but the rest of the furniture was draped in dust sheets. A step-ladder stood against the wall.

She followed him in and nodded towards the window. 'Nice view,' she said, conversationally.

'You're out of your mind,' he said.

'It's all trappings,' she said. 'All the other stuff. Coats, cars, money, all that shit. Fame and everything. Underneath we're just the same. Just women. That's all your fat dick knows about, doesn't it? That's the only thing that matters.'

His nose wrinkled, as if he smelt something rotting. 'You're totally round the bend.'

She smiled. '*She's* the one who's round the bend, not me. For starters, she's a liar. I've discovered quite a lot about Lila, recently. She should be locked up.'

'*She* should?'

She smiled at him, charmingly. 'Sorry you're so disappointed. Once – remember? Once, you wouldn't have been quite so disgusted. Shame, really.' She stood beside his desk. It was overflowing with papers.

Trevor stood beside one of the shrouded armchairs. The dust-sheet was spattered with paint. He fumbled in the pocket of his bathrobe and took out a pack of cigarettes.

She smiled, taking her time. It all depended on pauses. Every actor has discovered that secret.

'Shame, really,' she repeated, sliding her hand into her pocket. Feeling the gun, she clicked open the safety catch. In *Hedda* the gun had been larger, a Colt .44, but the mechanism was similar.

'Sit down,' he said. 'Have a cigarette. You're obviously in a bad way.'

'Shame you're such a shit, because the day you smarmed yourself into her arms you bought your death warrant.'

She took out the gun. Trev burst out laughing.

Finger poised against the trigger, she raised it so that it was pointing in his direction. It was so heavy that it strained her hand.

'What a totally crappy line!' he laughed. 'What're you out of, some B movie? Where did you learn that shit?'

He was shaking with laughter. She stared at him. The gun dangled in her hand.

He walked up to her. 'Leave the big scenes to the experts,' he said gently. He took the gun and put it on the desk. Patting her shoulder, he said, 'Calm down, you poor little bitch.'

Seven

That did it. Something clicked, inside my head. I sat down, heavily, in his office chair. It swivelled from side to side and I tried to steady it with my foot.

He squatted beside me, on his haunches, and gazed into my face like a doctor. 'Want a drink? You look as if you need one.'

He went into the kitchen. Slowly I unknotted the scarf and pulled it off. I was suddenly terribly tired. The wig felt crooked; I hadn't even fixed it on properly. From the kitchen there was the sighing clunk of a fridge door closing, and the rattle of glasses. I pulled off the wig, stuffed it into the pocket of the coat and unpinned my hair. It felt as stiff as cardboard; I clawed it down around my face with my clumsy, gloved hands. I hadn't even got a hairbrush.

I had never felt such a complete idiot in all my life. I dreaded him coming back. From the kitchen came the pop of a cork. How on earth had I even contemplated such a pitiful charade? Why hadn't somebody stopped me? I must have been out of my mind. For Christ's sake, I had never even fired a gun, not a real one. I didn't know how. I wasn't a murderer, any more than you are. Something about this place seemed to have unhinged me; working in the movies had obviously warped my sanity. How could I have dreamed up such a ludicrous scenario? It was utterly pathetic.

Sweltering in the coat, I gazed at the shrouded furniture. I wished I could just cover myself over and curl up in the corner. Nobody need ever see me again. My face burned with embarrassment. Trev's decorator had already painted one wall a deep red. There was a sheen on it, like oil in a puddle.

323

He padded in from the kitchen, carrying a bottle of white wine and two glasses. He put them down carefully on the floor. It was covered with dust-sheets, too.

'Could I have a cigarette?' I asked. 'Haven't got anything with me.' My teeth seemed to be chattering. Ridiculous, when I was so hot.

'Sure.' He passed me one, and flicked his lighter open. He still had his old favourite: the brass one filled with petrol. He leant towards me and lit my cigarette. 'Who knows about this?'

'Nobody.'

'Isn't Lila in on it? It's not something you cooked up together? A kind of joke?'

I shook my head. 'She was asleep.'

Sitting in the armchair, he stared at me. 'What?'

'I let myself into her flat. I've got a key.'

'*What?*'

'She didn't wake up.'

'Hey, hang on.' He raised his hand. 'Hang on a sec. You went into her flat, and dressed yourself up in her clothes?'

I wished he would shut up. Put like that, it sounded so childish.

He was too amazed to pass me the glass of wine. He just sat there, staring at me. His mouth hung open.

'You were going to come here,' he asked, 'and shoot me? Or pretend to shoot me, or something?'

I shrugged. 'Perhaps.'

My God, he was starting to grin!

'Can I have my wine?' I asked irritably.

He passed it over. He was still staring at me wonderingly, half-grinning. 'I don't believe this!' He pinched his arm. 'I must be dreaming.'

'Why the hell shouldn't I?' I tapped my cigarette into his overflowing ashtray. He was trying to work something out. I watched his face.

After a moment, he looked up. 'Let me just get this straight.

324

I'm a bit slow. You wanted people to think it was Lila? Is that it.'

I took a long drink of the wine. Christ, I needed it.

'If you shot me,' he went on, 'you'd let her take the blame?'

I shrugged my shoulders again. 'Not really.'

'What were you going to do? Go back to her place and wake her up?'

I shook my head. 'Change into my clothes and go home.'

'What about if somebody saw you?'

'There's a side door,' I said. I tried to sound dignified, but it didn't come out right. I wished I hadn't given him the details; they sounded so laborious.

He buried his face in his hands, rubbed his face hard, and looked up at me. His hair stood up, ruffled. 'Christ, Jules, I always knew you were odd, but I never realised you were a complete nutter.'

'I'm not!'

He sighed, and shook his head. 'Know something? This is the saddest thing I've ever heard. You ought to go and see somebody. Honest.'

'It's not sad!'

He tapped his ash on to the dust-sheet. 'They warned me about you.'

'Who did?'

'Martin. Reece. They said you were bonkers.'

'What the hell do you mean?'

'Come on!' he said. 'You've always been strange.'

'I'm not!'

'Why do you think you didn't have any friends?'

'I did! I have!'

'People didn't like you,' he said.

'They did!' I shouted.

'They always said there was something funny about you, but I didn't listen.'

'That's not true!'

'It's not your fault,' he said. 'I blame it on your old man.

325

You were always going on about him. How he was so cold, and all. How he didn't love you.'

I stubbed my cigarette out, viciously. I was suffocatingly hot but I didn't want to take off the coat. It seemed too intimate a gesture. I reached down for the bottle and tried to pour myself some more wine. It sloshed out, flooding the glass. I wiped my gloved hand on the coat and replaced the bottle on the floor. Look! Perfectly steadily.

There was a silence. Down in the street, a car hooted. We sat there. I looked at his hairy ankles. They were still tanned by the sun. Long ago, I had run my fingers over every inch of his body. It seemed inconceivable, now.

'I know you're upset,' he said. 'I don't blame you. Honest. I know I've behaved like a rat.'

'Why did you do it, then?' I asked.

'Look. I'll try and explain.' He gazed helplessly around the room, and then he began. 'When I met you I was dead impressed,' he said. He spoke in a reflective voice I had never heard before. 'I'd never met any birds like you. You had this terrific confidence – you didn't know you had it, nobody with an education knows they have it, they just take it for granted. Bleeding middle classes.' He looked up. His unshaven face looked sad; thoughtful, even. 'You had this Coutts cheque book. I'd never even *heard* of blooming Coutts. You went to the theatre and stuff. Remember when you talked about Pirandello and I thought you meant tyres? Christ, I felt a wally. You didn't notice all that because people don't. Not people like you. And when we went to see your mother it was all latticed windows and Harvey Nichols and funny stories about the cleaning lady.'

'My mother's a fool.'

'To tell the truth, I was pissed-off. I thought about *my* Mum, what she'd been through. But know something? I was kind of envious.'

'My father thought she was a fool too.' I paused, running my finger down the side of the typewriter. It was plated with nickel or something; there was an embossed pattern on it. 'They both screwed my brother up,' I said.

'I loved old, solid things,' said Trev. 'Real quality. I loved polishing the furniture in *Look Back in Ongar*.'

'But it was hideous!'

Smoke dimmed the room. There was a long silence. Then I heard him drawing breath, to speak.

'For the first few months,' he said, 'it was fine.'

'Just *fine*?'

'You were brainy. You knew things. You introduced me to people. I was dead chuffed. They went on about magical realism, not about how many pints they could put back.' He poured himself out some more wine, emptying the bottle. 'You being older, it was like having an education all over again. But a real one this time. That's how I was able to start writing. It's you that did it.'

'I'm so glad.'

'No, really. I mean it. Straight up.' He sipped his wine. 'It took a bit of time before I realised something was missing.'

'What do you mean?'

'Who was that bloke in *The Wizard of Oz*?' he asked. 'The one without a heart?'

'The tin man,' I said flatly. I drained my glass. 'Got any more to drink?'

He got up and went into the kitchen. I heard the click of a cupboard door.

I must go! I told myself urgently. I must get out! But I couldn't move. He came back into the room, holding a bottle of scotch.

'Run out of wine,' he said.

'Rich old you?'

'I'm trying to cut down on the booze.'

'What the hell do you mean?' I demanded. 'Something was missing?'

He poured some whisky into my wine glass. I remembered, with a stab, how he used to slosh drink into any available container – mugs, teacups – when we were together.

'It's not your fault,' he said. 'I blame it on your Dad.'

'Blame what?'

'That you can't feel anything.'

'That's not true!' I yelled. 'What the hell do *you* know?'

'It's like, you've spent all this time developing your mind and you've forgotten all about your heart. About how to be a human being.'

'What's this? Some kind of lecture?'

'It's what happens to intellectuals,' he said. 'You've got no spontaneity. That's what's so creepy. Like tonight. You've planned it all so carefully, it's kind of sick. Lila'd just storm in here and blow my brains out.'

I looked at him. 'Would she?' I sipped the whisky. It spread through my veins, burning; it spread to my fingertips. 'Would she?' I paused. 'You don't know me at all,' I said.

'It's, like, you're looking at yourself in a mirror all the time, you're watching yourself. It's like you're permanently masturbating.'

'Don't be disgusting!'

'Everything's a performance for yourself,' he said. 'Even when we were screwing it was like you'd learnt it in your bleeding drama class – '

'That's not true!' I yelled.

'I knew you'd put it about in the past, you told me enough times. Knee-trembles in bus shelters, all the grisly details. Like you were trying to prove something. You've always been such a blooming show-off. But why hadn't you had any real relationships?'

'I had!' I shouted.

'Martin put it better. I remember, we were sitting in the First Aid van, and he said you'd never be a really good actress because you weren't connected to your feelings.'

'I *am!*' I yelled. 'What's *this*, then? Aren't these feelings?'

'Oh, you're technically OK, everybody's agreed about that. But your acting is a sort of wank. A sort of look-at-me. Why do you think you never got any good parts?'

'That's not true!'

'Jules, you're thirty-eight!'

Actually I was thirty-nine. He had forgotten my latest birthday.

My head reeled. He lit another cigarette. I longed for one, but I wasn't going to demean myself by asking.

'The camera doesn't lie,' he said. 'I've learnt that, these last few months. I've learnt a lot of things. It sees the truth. That's why Lila's made it and you haven't.' He paused. 'It's nothing to do with luck or looks. Nothing you can try and analyse. It's to do with feelings. With being true to herself.'

'Talk about wanking! Who taught you to rabbit on like this, ghastly soft-brained American psychobabble? Lila?'

'You're incredibly superior about her. Her movies, everything. Ever asked yourself why?'

I didn't reply. He inspected his cigarette. I watched him, hunched in his blue bathrobe.

'I'm just trying to explain,' he said. 'Why I did what I did.' He lifted his head and looked up. Not at me; through me. When he spoke, his voice was soft. 'When we met, it was incredibly strong. The most physically strong sensation I've ever had.'

My heart lurched. 'Was it?' I thought he was talking about me.

'It was lust, really. For years I'd lusted after her.'

'Who?'

'Lila. Lots of others too, of course. Kim what'shername. Basinger. Who wouldn't? That's the point of them. I even used to pretend, sometimes, in the dark – '

'You said you didn't!'

'But the minute we met, in the pub, I knew I'd – like, found the person I'd been searching for all my life. Like, the other me. I'd heard about it but I'd never thought it would happen to me. We're very similar, see. We're sort of, like, related. Oh I can't explain it.'

I sat there, motionless, on the swivel chair. His face looked dreamy and composed.

'I thought she didn't feel the same way. How could she? She

was famous. What'd she see in a berk like me? She was older than me, she'd had two husbands. All that. But then she called me, soon after she got back to New York. We started talking on the phone, for hours . . .'

His voice went on. It was low, now, as if he were talking to himself. I suddenly realised that he was looking through me just like the directors I had worked with, who were only concerned with the lighting. I was simply a shape in a chair.

'She isn't clever like you. She's neurotic and insecure. I know all that. She has lots of faults but it doesn't matter. It's not like a balance sheet. I mean, I could make a long list of your qualities but it doesn't really make any difference, does it? Not really.' He talked about me as if I were something lying on the floor, an old pullover or something, that he had forgotten to put away in the cupboard. 'She's loveable, that's what's so special about her. She's herself. It's kind of difficult to explain.'

'Don't bother then.'

He carried on talking in that low, soft voice. 'My whole life has changed. It's amazing. I never knew it could be like this. Nothing in the world matters except her and yet I love the world more than I ever did. Christ, it sounds so bleeding pompous, doesn't it?'

'Yes.'

'I'm just trying to explain. I just hope other people get the chance to feel like I do . . . like we both do . . .'

My ears were roaring. I realised, quite clearly, that I was drunk. Maybe he wasn't really saying all this. He was saying something completely different. He was talking about me.

'. . . having this baby . . . the best thing that ever happened . . . I want to go and shout in the streets . . .'

My father's voice was in my ears. *How pitifully inadequate*, he had told me, *is the language of joy. Those tired old clichés, flogged into twitching life.*

Drone drone. The words rose and fell, in waves.

'She's funny, too. I've never met a woman who's really, naturally funny . . .'

330

In my ears the roaring grew louder. His voice was a sing-song, miles away.

'. . . know something? I love her so much I'd die for her . . . would you believe that? A bloke like me? . . .'

Shut up! I screamed, silently. *Shut up!* But on he went.

'. . . I want to be inside her skin . . . I'm jealous of the food when she puts it into her mouth. Even her horrible Carob Chips . . .'

Things that he had told me rolled round and round my drunken head. *'You're a lousy actress'* . . . *'you've got no friends'* . . . *'when you screw, it's like you're . . .'*

I looked at Trev. He was burbling on about some incident of vomit-making sentimentality between the two of them, I can't start to describe it.

And then, with shocking clarity, I realised the truth.

He had forgotten that I was there.

He had simply forgotten all about me. I didn't exist.

It was then that I grabbed the pistol, aimed it in his direction and squeezed the trigger.

Eight

I didn't think I had hit him. Not for a moment. I thought he was playing. Just like Trev, to fool me.

The gun had jerked out of my hand, as if it had a spring inside, and fallen on the floor. The noise had been shockingly loud; it still rang in my ears. I smelt Party Poppers; you know the moment, when you pull the string? But a stronger smell than that.

He was just pretending. The bullet had missed him – for Christ's sake, I couldn't shoot! It had landed harmlessly in a dust-sheet.

How embarrassing! That's all I felt. I felt terribly foolish.

He was still looking at me, you see. His face was tight – sort of pulled together – but his eyes were open. He had relaxed back in the armchair but that was only to survey me better.

I had wet my knickers. Wasn't that humiliating? Just a little. But he could tell. I hadn't wet my knickers since I was a child.

It's a funny thing. You see people being shot all the time, on TV. Staggering, gasping, clutching their innards. Sliding to the floor. You see it thousands of times but it's the one event that you never see in real life.

So it was sort of familiar. I watched, with a detached kind of curiosity, the stain spreading across the front of his towelling bathrobe. It was movie blood. How many kinds could you buy? I had forgotten. There wasn't a lot of blood; not at first.

I avoided looking at his face. I just sat there, damply, waiting for him to speak. I think he had made a little grunt, earlier.

I don't know how many minutes passed. But when I dared raise my eyes again, I could see that he was dead.

I had never seen a dead person before. But if you have, you'll know what I mean. It's unmistakable. The face changes. It's not just the colour, though that changes too. The face literally empties.

It was no longer Trevor, sitting there. It was an uninhabited body. A sort of mannequin, in a powder-blue bathrobe, with moccasins on its feet. It was as if the bones inside it had been rearranged. It looked somehow smaller, too.

I couldn't possibly touch his skin, to make sure. Not in a thousand years. *I've killed a man.* For a while, the words made no sense. They danced inanely, like a nursery rhyme.

Then, suddenly, I panicked. The neighbours had heard! Somebody must have heard. They were coming to batter on the door.

I jumped up and stumbled into the kitchen. I slammed the door shut and stood there, trembling. What the hell was I going to do? There was no escape. They were bound to find me.

My legs buckled and I slid to the floor. This seemed a stagey and melodramatic thing to do but I simply couldn't stand upright. I sat cowering, jammed against the units. They smelt of glue. A bag of carpenter's tools lay beside me. The floor was cold; it was made of granite or something. I don't know. I could feel it after a while through the fur coat. A red light glowed at me, from above the cooker.

Maybe I sat there for a quarter of an hour, I'm not sure. I sat scrunched up, my arms around my knees, burying my face in the fur. I willed Trevor to disappear. I kept expecting to hear a police siren down in the street, but for once I heard nothing. Nobody rang the bell or knocked on the door. Even in the kitchen I would have heard it.

Finally I climbed to my feet. On the draining board was the remains of his supper: an empty Budweiser can and a slightly smeared plate. He had left a piece of pizza crust. I wished he hadn't done that.

I turned away and opened the door, slowly. For one mad moment I thought he had got up and walked away. He'd hid in the bedroom. '*Fooled you!*' I could still smell the cordite in the air, mingled with our long-extinguished cigarettes.

It still sat there. I could see the top of its hair above the rim of the armchair.

Familiar, but utterly unlikely words rose in my throat. *Evidence. Clues*. I tried, laboriously, to connect these dime-novel clichés to myself. I felt I was hauling them in on a fishing-line. Flustered, I swivelled round, looking for signs of my visit. I had to move fast.

I took the wine glasses into the kitchen and rinsed them under the tap. I felt strange, washing them up in leather gloves, but what did people do in this situation? I emptied the ashtray into the bin. Would the butts be tested for saliva? I had never read about that. In fact, I hadn't read many whodunnits. I didn't like them.

I tried to keep myself under control. I thought: *Idiot. If you manage this properly they won't be looking for you anyway.*

It was hard, going back into the living room. I steered clear of the armchair, giving it a wide berth. I didn't dare look at it. I pinned back my hair, with shaking hands, took the wig out of my pocket and pulled it on. I felt like an old boozy actor in some preposterous stage-play, who had forgotten his cue. My leather gloves were soaking. I kept my eyes on the half-painted wall. All that trouble, doing up his apartment; all that effort, and money.

I wrapped the scarf around my head, picked up the pistol and put it in my pocket. Fumblingly I put on the dark glasses. Had I forgotten anything?

Then I checked myself in a mirror, left the room and let myself out of the apartment.

Nobody waited for me. The corridor was empty; the doors of the other apartments were closed. I pushed the elevator button. It arrived, swiftly. It was empty too. Nobody else called it while I descended. Superstitiously I took this as a hopeful sign.

There was nobody in the lobby except for the doorman. He sat behind his desk, watching TV. I tap-tapped across the marble. As I passed the pool the fish gaped at me, their mouths working. They looked as if they were trying to speak.

The doorman seemed to be opening the door for me.

'Good night,' he said. 'Go easy.'

'Night,' I mumbled.

Once outside, my head cleared. It seemed even colder. I hurried along the street. It was late, and a residential area. There was nobody around. I still felt numb. All I knew was that each step took me further away from the languorous mannequin in the bathrobe.

I retraced my steps down Central Park West. I crossed 72nd Street . . . 71st. Ahead of me I saw the lit canopy of Lila's apartment building. Ironically enough, I felt quite confident. Just at that moment. Nobody had stopped me yet. Cars passed and none of them slowed down.

I remember thinking this as I approached the entrance. A car stopped outside and a tall man got out. I slowed my steps. He went into the building.

I gave him a moment or two and then followed. The doors were open. Nestling my face in my collar, I went in.

A blast of warm air greeted me as I crossed the threshold. As I walked across the lobby, I turned to nod goodnight to the doorman.

It was another one.

My heart stopped. The shift had changed; a new lot came on at eleven. But this was a *new doorman*; I had never seen him before.

He stood behind the desk, writing something down: a young, coffee-coloured guy. Good-looking.

My steps faltered. He wasn't a doorman at all. He was a cop. He was writing down information about me.

I nodded to him and made my way towards the elevators. The tall man stepped in and the doors closed. I hesitated.

335

I could see the doorman coming out, from behind his desk. He was walking briskly towards me. I heard his shoes clack-clacking on the marble.

14 . . . 15 . . . 16 The elevator was rising without me. The other elevator seemed to be stuck at the 9th floor. I was trapped.

'Pardon me, Miss Dune.'

I swung round, as if he had stung me. He stood near, panting slightly. He had a notepad in his hand.

'Yeah?' I said. My voice croaked; I cleared my throat.

'Sorry to intrude on you,' he said.

21 . . . 22 . . . The light stopped at the 23rd floor.

'I wonder if I could ask you something,' he said.

The light started to descend. 22, 21. My mouth was dry; I couldn't speak.

'I'm a real fan of yours. Could you please sign me your autograph?'

A long moment passed. He was holding out something for me. It was a pen.

I must have looked odd. I simply couldn't move. My mind had locked. I knew I had to reply.

What on earth did her writing look like? Bloody Americans, they're always on the damn phone. They never write letters.

She had sent me that note, with the perfume. Big, childish, loopy writing.

'I'm kinda cold,' I said. 'Excuse my writing.'

I took the pen but simply couldn't write, in the glove. It seemed to have shrunk on my hand. I peeled it off. My skin did, indeed, look cold – mottled purple. I was shivering.

'Who shall I say?' I asked.

'Lorry.'

I paused. 'As in truck?'

'Pardon?' he asked.

'Truck – lorry?'

'I don't know, ma'am.'

Christ I was an idiot. No American actress would think of the word 'lorry'.

'Spell it,' I drawled.

'L-A-U-R-I-E.'

'Ah.' I wrote, '*Hi, Laurie!*' and signed it with a flourish *Lila Dune*.

'Wow. Thanks,' he said.

It was the strangest sensation, letting myself into Lila's apartment. Everything was exactly the same. I had been away nearly two hours but it was as if I had only stepped out for a moment. I couldn't believe that after all that had happened I would find Lila still sleeping, but when I checked the bedroom there she lay, motionless in the bed. Orson trotted up to me, tail wagging. He didn't bark, this time. In my chaotic state, he suddenly seemed my only companion.

He followed me into the living room. Through the windows, the faint glow of the city illuminated the same furniture in the same places. Nobody had been here. In the corner, the video recorder glowed. Its clock displayed 11.55.

With some difficulty I had pulled on my cold, damp gloves. This sign that I still possessed my wits reassured me, just slightly. I took out my handbag from behind the settee, and fed Orson the rest of the M&Ms. He snuffled around on the floor; it was nice, having a living creature near me. A *dog* didn't think I had done anything wrong. I paused, trying to remember my list of things to do.

Letter. Gun. Whisky.

Take your time, I told myself. *Keep your head clear.*

I took out the forged letter from Trev, folded it and hid it under the paperweight on the table. Wasn't that amazing, to remember? Lila wouldn't notice it there, but when the apartment was searched it would be found.

If the apartment was searched. What happened if Trevor wasn't dead, he was only fooling? He had waited until I had left, then he had jumped to his feet and called the police. I know it sounds stupid, but now I had left his apartment I simply couldn't believe what had happened. It was so utterly improbable.

337

The next moment I firmly believed that nothing had happened at all. I hadn't even shot him and missed. I would wake up in my apartment and realise that it had all been a dream. One of my violent ones. I would lie in bed, listening to the breakfast TV burbling next door and it would all drain from me like poison, leaving me innocent. I would lie there, filling up like a reservoir with the sweetest relief I had ever known.

I stood like a zombie in the middle of the room. My shoes still pinched; my knickers were still damp. I must have done something most peculiar, to wet my knickers. The coat still weighed on my shoulders.

Whisky. I darted to the kitchen, switched on the light and went across to the right-hand unit. Lila kept her liquor stores there. Americans always have stores, thank God. I opened the door and fished out a bottle of bourbon.

With a crack, I twisted open its cap and poured most of its contents down the sink. I turned on the tap and washed the sink clean.

'Want to know why I quit drinking? See, I do things I don't remember later.'

I straightened up and listened. Silence. Doing these things that I had planned was curiously soothing. It was like being on stage and returning to the script after a wild period of improvisation. I fetched a glass and poured a little bourbon into it. Then I took both the glass and the almost-empty bottle into the living room and hid them on the floor, behind the armchair. Lila wouldn't notice them there, in the morning. But somebody else would.

I took off the dark glasses and replaced them in her handbag. I took the gun out of my pocket – it gave me a shock, just feeling it again – and put it cautiously into her bag. I had locked its safety catch shut but I didn't trust it. Not now.

Then I slipped off the coat and shoes and tiptoed towards Lila's bedroom. Halfway there, I froze.

Down in the street I could hear a police siren. Not one – several. I couldn't hear the traffic but I could hear them. It was a whole cacophony.

338

I stood still, my heart pounding. The sounds stopped. Was that because they had turned the corner, or because they had stopped outside, their lights flashing?

The police were surrounding the building. At that very moment the elevator was rising to the PH floor.

There was no time to lose. I pulled off the wig and replaced it on its stand. I shrugged myself out of the coat and dumped it on the floor of the walk-in closet. I heard a sound, behind me. I swung round. Orson stood there, a glimmering white shape. His tail waved to and fro. Had he come to tell me they were here?

I emerged from the closet and took a last look at Lila. She lay, curled on her other side. She scarcely seemed to be breathing. Her digital clock glowed. 1.08.

Just then I felt a strange sensation. She was dead; just an empty husk. I had drawn her life from her. By pupating in her apartment, emerging from it dressed as her and killing Trevor, I had left the real Lila hollow. It was as if her duvet were an empty chrysalis. I had a ridiculous urge to prod her gently, and see if my finger fell through.

00.09. It flipped to 00.10. Suddenly I felt flustered. What else was I supposed to do? *Shoes.* I laid them gently on the floor at the end of her bed, as if she had just kicked them off. When she woke, this would confuse her further.

Then I left the room, put on my own coat and boots, picked up my handbag and went into the hallway. I dropped the scarf into the copper bowl.

I was just about to let myself out of the door when I realised: *keys.* They were still in the pocket of her coat.

The police were arriving. I knew they were. Somebody had dropped in, to visit Trev, and raised the alarm.

I hurried back into Lila's bedroom. At midnight? Somebody would visit at *midnight*? I tiptoed into the closet, knelt down and rummaged in the pocket of the coat. My fingers closed over the keys.

The bed creaked. Lila made a sound: a low, sighing groan. I stayed in the closet, crouched over the heap of fur. The mattress creaked again. It sounded as if she was getting out of bed.

The closet door was ajar. I stared at the greyish strip of light. I didn't dare move.

Five minutes must have passed. I could hear no sound from the bedroom. She had climbed out of bed and padded into the kitchen. When I crept out, the bed would be empty.

Finally I emerged. Lila had turned over, onto her back. Her masked face gazed at the ceiling. I knew her eyes were open, under the mask. I stood still, and listened. Her breathing was deep and regular. She was still asleep. You shouldn't sleep on your back; it gives you nightmares.

I fled. I let myself out of the apartment, double-locked the door and took the freight elevator down to the ground floor.

I pushed open the side-entrance door and looked up and down the street.

It was empty. Just two rows of parked cars. I slipped out like a shadow.

Released into the night air, I walked very fast. I walked four blocks before I peeled off my clammy gloves and threw them into a trash can.

I was going to walk all the way home. I felt safer out of doors; it cleared my head. Besides, a cab driver might remember me. But I suddenly felt sick, so I hailed a cab.

He looked Iranian or something. He didn't turn around when I climbed in and he was silent throughout our journey. It was as if I didn't exist. When I paid him, he didn't look at me; he just took the money and drove off. I thanked God for his rudeness.

There was nobody waiting at my apartment building. No cop cars. Nothing.

There was no porter on duty, either, in my building. At night they just locked the doors. I opened my bag and took out my keys.

Had I forgotten something? Had I left something of mine in Lila's apartment?

340

Incriminating evidence. I rode up in the elevator. The words applied to *me*. It was like hearing the words *malignant tumour*, so familiar in print, suddenly whispered into my ear by a doctor.

I let myself into my apartment, rushed into the bathroom and vomited violently down the toilet. I knelt there for a long time, my knees hurting on the cold tiles. Strings of mucus slid from my mouth; I watched them with vague curiosity.

What was I supposed to do now? What did people in my position do?

I didn't say the word 'murderer', even to myself.

Nine

I sat up most of the night, drinking tea and smoking. I felt
literally ill with fear. Like all clichés, you don't know how true
they are until they apply to you. It was the same sensation as
really bad flu. My own symptoms alarmed me. Time stood
still; I was jolted out of my normal life. My ordinary routines
seemed as distant and innocent as activities dimly remembered from childhood. Or from another life altogether. The
city went about its business below me, stirring as dawn broke,
and I was sealed off by my illness. The slightest noise that I
made – putting the cup down, getting to my feet – sounded
as loud as a pistol shot. My guts had turned to liquid; I had
diarrhoea and kept on having to go to the bathroom. The more
my body emptied, the more it ached.

What should I do? Buy an air ticket and fly back to
England? Far too suspicious. I was supposed to be living
here. A possible job was just coming up. How could I explain
it to my landlady and to Roly?

When would they find the body? When would the alarm
be raised?

He had decorators in; they would be arriving in the
morning.

Suspicions. *Body*. One of the strangest things was having to
apply this new vocabulary to myself. I still couldn't connect it
up, I didn't dare. I was still too numb. It didn't belong to me,
it belonged to books and films. Cosy, escapist stuff. A frisson
here and there, mounting to a climax. It wasn't supposed to
really happen. That was the point of it.

I re-ran the events over and over, but the more I did them
the more they slipped from my grasp. I tried to remember

342

the sequence and whether I had made any mistakes. Had I left anything in Its apartment? (I couldn't call him by name any more.) The conversation with the new doorman disturbed me, but he had seemed convinced. And nobody had come for me yet.

Nobody *would* come for me yet. I looked at my watch. 5.50. Nobody would have discovered anything. It seemed unbelievable, that I had been through all this and people were still sleeping. Even Lila, with her early call, wouldn't have woken yet.

It never would wake, now. I understood by now that It was dead. For several hours I had been like an amputee who still felt the phantom limb twitching. This was partly shock. Events hadn't happened the way I had planned. I hadn't meant to shoot It – not really. That was what I told myself. The débâcle had wrong-footed and flustered me. I had to catch up with myself. No doubt it would have been just as shocking if it had gone according to the rehearsal because nothing feels quite the same as you expected, once you're doing it. Events are always, joltingly, different.

At 6.0, or 6.30 at the latest, Lila would be woken by either her alarm clock or the studio phoning. Would she notice her shoes on the floor? Would she feel disorientated? I didn't think about her as a person at all, not now. I didn't think how she would react to the news of Its death. That part of me was locked.

I didn't think about It, either. Not in that way. It had ceased to be Trev. It had simply become a towelling-clad lump of silenced incriminating evidence. Murder depersonalises its victim, utterly. I had felt a passing tweak when I saw Its bit of pizza crust, and the effort It had put into doing up Its apartment. That was all. I couldn't afford to feel anything else. Besides, there wasn't space. I was simply consumed by fear.

When day broke I escaped from the apartment. I couldn't stay there any longer, trapped. I was too frightened of the phone or my doorbell ringing.

343

I spent most of the day at loose in the windy anonymity of the streets. Nobody could find me, there. It was a glorious spring day. I kept downtown, well away from Central Park West. In the Village, the trees were in blossom. My ears felt as highly-tuned as a bat's; I picked up signals nobody else heard. The slightest, imagined noise made me break out in sweat.

I bought myself a hot dog, though I wasn't hungry. I ate it simply to stop myself collapsing. At the news-stands I looked at the papers, but of course there was nothing in the headlines yet. Just some Wall Street scandal and a murder out in the Van Dyke Projects, in Bedford-Stuyvesant. Not his death; somebody else's. It seemed inconceivable, that Trevor's name might soon appear in print.

I paused outside Balducci's. Another Jules had gone in there and bought herself a take-away arugula and prosciutto salad. She existed in a past from which I was now completely excluded. I didn't dare stop anywhere for long. When I wandered into an art gallery in SoHo, full of dismembered bits of metal, the phone rang and I made my escape. When I passed the window of a coffee shop and a man turned to look at me I broke into a run. How stupid! It only made me more alarmed at myself. He had probably just fancied the look of me.

The whole city had changed overnight, as if it had been planted with invisible mines. The streets looked so innocuous, so deceptive, but I knew the truth. The whole place had been wired up. At school, when we played Prisoner's Base, our surroundings were transformed. The toilet block, the shrubbery – they were suddenly places of concealment and menace. Just looking at those bushes made my heart thump.

I sat for a few moments on a bench in Washington Square. I was flanked by old men, walking sticks planted between their legs, enjoying the sunshine. A woman passed, pushing a baby in a stroller. She glanced at me and leant over to tell the baby something. *See that lady? Know what she's just done?*

A black guy loitered, and caught the eye of another guy. They moved away together, murmuring. I told myself it was just a drugs deal but it didn't make it any better. Nothing

344

did. The usual chess games were set out, but today each player's pause was tense with significance. When they moved the pieces I knew they were signalling a message to the next table, and then the next. *Pawn to bishop. She's here. That's it, late thirties. 5 foot 6.* The hunched figures sat at the tables, pretending to concentrate. They looked like elderly immigrants but they didn't fool me. *Black, belted overcoat. Suede boots. She's getting up. She's heading for the kids' playground.* When I hurried past the slide, a little girl screamed.

I couldn't stay away for ever. At 2 o'clock I returned to the apartment. The doorman didn't step out with a message. I rode up to my apartment. As I fumbled for my key, I heard my phone ringing on the other side of the door. It was the police. I stood rooted to the spot. But why didn't they come here? The phone went on ringing. It seemed to be going on for a long time. I jammed my key into the lock, opened the door and rushed in. I picked up the phone. 'Hello?'

'Hi. Roly here.' I had forgotten all about Roly. He hadn't crossed my mind.

'Where've you've been, sweetheart? I've been trying to call you all day.'

I caught my breath. 'Just for a walk.'

'You OK? You sound kind of – '

'What's happened?' I gasped.

'I have some news for you,' he said.

There was a silence.

'Jules,' he said. 'You still there?'

I whispered, 'What news?'

'Abe Zacharias has to fly to LA next week. He has to rearrange his schedule. Can you meet with him tomorrow? At three?'

I put down the receiver. It was slippery in my hand.

That phone call had a disorientating effect. It made the whole thing return to unreality, all over again. If nothing had been discovered yet, maybe nothing had happened.

I made myself some tea, pulled down the blinds and undressed. I was suddenly very sleepy. In fact, I could hardly keep my eyes open. I realised that I was still hungover; that was why I felt so ill.

I climbed into bed and slipped between the sheets. It simply hadn't happened. After all, nothing had changed in the apartment. *Hollywood Wives* was back in its position on the bookshelf. How was even *I* to know that it had ever been removed? There was no sign that I had been out the previous night. No bloodstained clothing; no muddy shoes.

The whole thing had just been a series of fleeting, vivid projections in my head, as insubstantial as a film. Haunting, of course, but it had been powerful stuff. I would sleep, deeply, and other dreams would arrive to take its place.

It was dark. Something was ringing. At first I thought it was the doorbell.

I stumbled out of bed and started for the door. Then I realised that it was the phone.

I lifted the receiver. I glanced, puzzled, at my watch. It was 8.15. What day of the week was it?

For a moment I didn't recognise the voice on the line. It sounded so different.

'Jules,' said Roly.

'Hi.'

'My dear, I have some terrible news.'

There was a silence.

'You there?' he asked.

'Yes.'

'It's Trevor Parsons. He's been shot.'

'*Shot?*' I gasped. I sounded perfect. Then I asked, 'Is he dead?'

Clever, wasn't I?

'Yeah.'

'When did they find him?' I shut my mouth. That was the wrong question. Was I mad?

Roly didn't seem to notice. He sounded too upset. 'I don't

know all the details. Somebody came to his apartment, I've been with the police all afternoon, we had to find Lila, they been shooting somewhere up in Long Island. Jules, it's chaos here. Reporters, TV . . . sweetheart, it's terrible.' I heard phones ringing. Someone was calling him. 'Don't *you* worry, you look after yourself, my precious. Maybe I won't be able to see you tonight. I'll call you later.'

I put the phone down. My first feeling was pure terror. *It's actually happened.*

Then I thought: maybe Roly was phoning me to check that I was at home. The police had asked him, so I wouldn't smell a rat. Should I get the hell out?

Then I re-ran my lines. How had I performed, on my first test? Not too well. I had sounded surprised and shocked – fine. But then I had asked that slightly strange question. Not *too* strange. I hadn't asked: Did the decorators find him? Nothing really stupid.

I gave myself notes, like a director. It calmed me down, to think of Jules as somebody else.

It didn't calm me down. Not really. Just then I rushed to the bathroom and vomited violently, yet again.

Ten

The next day, Thursday, Lila was arrested. To be exact, she was taken in for questioning.

Roly told me. Thank God it was over the phone, so he didn't see my face. My performance was radio rather than TV. Actually I didn't have much chance to speak at all. He was distraught and the words poured out.

He had been at the precinct station all morning – he, Irma and various people. Lila's mother had arrived and was trying to see her. The entire news media was there; the place was staked out.

'She was seen going to his place,' he jabbered. He was speaking from a call box; I heard the buzz of voices in the background. 'She went there that night. Tuesday. They have witnesses. Do you believe this? They've traced the bullet. It matches her hand-gun. She had a hand-gun, see, in her purse.'

'Did she?' I asked in a surprised voice.

'It was no secret. We all knew about it, she showed it to just about everyone. Who'd believe it? Isn't it all just terrible? Her lawyer's in there with her, I'm waiting for him to come out. Sweetheart, I have some more calls to make.'

'What did she say?' I asked.

'Huh?'

'What did Lila say?'

'I just saw her for maybe five minutes. She's hysterical. Well wouldn't you be? She says she didn't do it. She says she was in bed asleep.'

*

I made myself some scrambled eggs for lunch, but I couldn't swallow them; they clogged up my mouth.

However much you prepare yourself for news, it can still throw you into chaos. Words like *Irma* and *her mother* were surprisingly shocking. They threw me off course. I imagined the two of them, sitting sobbing in some dingy waiting room. *Lawyer* gave me another jolt. Suddenly it was official.

I even thought, for a split-second: why isn't Trev visiting her? Wasn't I stupid!

I tried to reassure myself. I said: it's all going according to plan. But I felt so buffeted, I could hardly remember what the plan was. Had they found the bottle, or had Fidelia unwittingly cleared it away before the police arrived? Had they found the letter? Was there anything I had overlooked?

I had visited Lila that night. The doormen had seen me come and go. At some point, maybe the next time I spoke to Roly, I had to mention this. Otherwise it would seem a curious omission, to say the least. To sound innocent I had to volunteer the information. *I saw her that night! Gosh! It must have been just before it happened!*

I would certainly be questioned by the police, sooner or later. I had better start rehearsing now; I needed to be word-perfect. A wide-eyed look; a breathless voice.

I washed up my plate, looking out at the office block opposite. Sun shone through the windows, illuminating the snowy white blouses of the secretaries. They looked Walt-Disney-innocent; they looked like virgins.

As I stood there, a thought struck me. I hadn't put it into words before that moment. I remember gazing at the row of spider-plants along the window-ledge, and the plastic bottle of washing-up liquid. They had the carefully-spaced look of stage props. As I did so, I thought: *From now on, I will be acting all the time.*

It was true. *Unless they find me out, I'll be acting for the rest of my life.*

That was what a criminal did. Act. *All the time*.

I decided to walk to Tribeca; it wasn't far. On the way to my meeting I stopped at a news-stand. It was no longer a news-stand; it was a heavily disguised, unexploded bomb. I approached it cautiously.

There was nothing on the front page of the *Times*, though I didn't dare unfold it. All I saw were Budget Deficits and the Iran-Contras. But the *Post* had it: a double column on the front page. *FILM STAR'S LOVER SLAIN*.

I bought the paper. The man didn't even glance at me.

> *The father of film star Lila Dune's expected love-child was*
> *found shot dead yesterday morning in his glam 73rd Street*
> *condo. Painter Joseph Carillo discovered the body at*
> *12.30. London-born writer Trevor Parsons, 28, was*
> *slain by a single bullet. 19th Precinct police spokesman,*
> *Lt. Frank Gozzoli, said: 'We are treating this case as*
> *homicide.' Cops rushed to Long Island, where Lila*
> *Dune was filming in the Rittner-Morowitz comedy*
> *'Three Can Play'. When informed of her lover's slaying*
> *she screamed, 'No! No! It's not true!'*

'You play tennis?' asked Abe Zacharias. 'You play it well?'

I smiled modestly. 'I was the Junior Tennis Champion at school.'

He raised his eyebrows. 'No shit?'

Of course it was shit. It was a lie. But I could play well enough. Any middle-class, athletic girl brought up in Sussex knows how to hit a ball across a net.

He seemed to be talking about doubles.

'I play singles and doubles,' I said.

He lifted his hand. 'You've misunderstood me,' he said. 'We use doubles in the show.'

I tried to gather my wits. He went droning on. He was a swarthy, humourless man in his early thirties. TV producers, I had noticed, were getting younger. We sat on leather settees drinking Badoit water; the pink, rag-rolled walls of his office enclosed us like a womb. I told myself: I'm safe here.

'You seen our show?'

He was asking me a question. I had meant to watch it the day before but somehow or other it had just slipped my mind.

The phone rang. I jumped. He answered it, speaking in a low voice and looking at me.

He put it down. It rang again. I knew it was the police.

'I'm in a meeting,' he said down the phone.

The other person talked for a long time. All Zacharias did was nod, at intervals. His eyes were on me. *Keep her there, talking, while we surround the building. Act natural.*

'Yep. Sure. You got it.' He put the phone down.

There was a knock on the door. I froze. Another man came in. He was even younger. He was introduced to me but I didn't catch his name. He was disguised as another producer but I knew he came from the Homicide Bureau. He hadn't shaved; he had been up all night, trying to track me down.

They started talking to me about Samantha Seymour. Who the hell was she? I kept quiet. *You have a right to remain silent. Anything you say can and will be used in a court of law.*

Samantha Seymour was the English tennis pro in their show, *The Best People*. That's what they pretended, anyway. She appeared in six episodes. They told me the plot.

'. . . when Karl rejects Nancy, she takes her revenge . . .'

'. . . confrontation between Dwight and Jade . . .'

'. . . major surgery . . .'

The words boomed like airport tannoys, calling out unknown names and destinations.

'. . . Adam's blackmail demand . . .'

'. . . Abbie's near-fatal car crash . . .'

'. . . Tourmaline's half-sister . . .'

I gazed at the walls. Their pinky-purplish mottling reminded me of my father's hands, when they were cold. He used to take my hand in his; just when we were crossing the road.

*

351

Back in my apartment I phoned Roly. Apparently the producers of *The Best People* had already called him; they were favourably impressed. Ironic, wasn't it? The one time I hadn't been trying at all. There was a moral there somewhere.

'What's happened to Lila?' I asked.

'They've taken her downtown to Foley Square. To be arraigned.'

'I was thinking,' I said. 'I must've been the last person to see her. I was there, that night.'

I knew they would get to me, sooner or later. *It's simply a routine enquiry*, I told myself. I had researched my part with a great deal more thoroughness than I had researched Samantha Seymour. I knew exactly what I had done that Tuesday evening – oh, so long ago. The evening when so many lives had been changed, for ever. I had marked out my actions and learnt my lines. Reality slipped away as my character gained flesh and plausibility. I did my usual exercises, asking myself questions. What exactly did I have for dinner? Did I take a bath? What book did I read? (I had decided against TV, they might ask me which programme.) They were the sort of questions I had told Lila to ask herself all those months ago, on the set of *Bump*. Questions designed to thicken up a new persona. This time, however, there was a certain raw urgency to my self-examination. It was like suddenly having to use my Grade One Lifesaver skills after being thrown into the North Sea.

I repeated to myself: *Remember, they won't be suspicious*. There was nothing to link myself with any of this. Nobody knew my connection with Trevor, and my connection with Lila was by now of the most tenuous kind. I had gone to ground for so many weeks that I had all but disappeared from her life and that of her entourage. My only slight worry was the way I had questioned Roly about her, but the police weren't to know that. *He* didn't think there was anything suspicious about it. After all, I gossiped with him about most of his glitzier clients.

They weren't interested in me. They were interested in Lila.

What she was doing that night; how she behaved. That was all.

Sure enough, that evening I had a visitor. He was a detective; a young, freckly, red-haired guy called McConnell. He wore a tweed jacket and grey trousers; he looked as if he had borrowed his father's clothes to lend himself *gravitas*. Nothing is as you expect it; the shock can put you off-balance. I had visualised a pair of slack-bellied, gum-chewing cops. But then I had only seen this sort of thing on the TV.

'Nice place you've got,' he said conversationally, glancing around. 'Nice location.'

'I rent it from a friend. But she's not supposed to sub-lease so – oops!' I clapped my hand to my mouth. 'Shouldn't have told you that.'

He smiled.

I said, 'It's such terrible news. I can't believe it. Do sit down. Would you like a cup of tea?'

'Thank you.'

I went into the kitchen and put on the saucepan of water. 'Americans don't have kettles, do they,' I called out. 'One of the many funny things I've discovered. Would you like a biscuit – sorry, cookie?' I brought in the tin. 'I'm always making mistakes.'

'How long have you been here?' he asked. 'In New York City?'

Don't lie. Not about this stuff. They can check up on it. 'Since October.'

'You like it?'

I nodded. 'Sure. It's an exciting place, the Big Apple.' I shivered. 'But violent, too.'

'My grandparents came from your side,' he said. 'Scotland.'

'Really?'

'Kirkcaldy. You been there?'

I shook my head, setting out the sugar bowl and the milk jug. 'But I've heard the countryside's very beautiful.'

Absurdly, I suddenly felt like my mother. This was just the way she talked.

I went into the kitchen and poured the boiling water into the tea cups. I felt totally unreal, as if we were both playing in some drawing-room drama at Windsor Rep. We both looked such imposters.

When I returned, he had taken out a notebook. I put the teacups down on the table. 'Sorry there's no teapot,' I said. 'They'd have *that* in Kirkcaldy.'

'You saw Miss Dune on Tuesday night, am I right?' he asked.

My eyes widened. 'When exactly did she do it? If she did it. The whole thing is so extraordinary!' I sat down. 'I went round to visit her, oh at about eight. Thereabouts. I didn't look at my watch.'

He scribbled in his notebook. 'You know her well?'

'Not really. Of course I admired her work. I mean – *admire* her work. I'd met her on a couple of films. We'd rather lost touch. But when I heard she was pregnant I was thrilled! I knew how much she wanted a child. So I couldn't help myself – I rushed round with a bottle of champagne.'

'What happened, exactly?'

I shrugged. 'Nothing unusual. She seemed very . . .' I paused. 'Revved-up.'

'How do you mean?' He hadn't eaten his biscuits. 'Was her behaviour unusual?'

'She's very changeable, you know. Very volatile. I just thought she was excited about the baby.'

'What did you talk about?'

'Not much.' I said. 'I hadn't seen her for such a long time, you see. We'd lost touch.'

'Did you see her consume any alcohol?'

I shook my head. 'We had lemonade. She said she hadn't had a drink for a while now – it has a really bad effect on her.'

He looked up. 'What do you mean by that?'

I took a sip of my tea, flinching; it scalded my lips. 'I

354

don't know. Just something I heard. Other people would know better than I do.'

I watched his bent, gingery head as he wrote. Through the wall I heard the murmur of my neighbour's TV; it seemed loud, tonight. The window was open and I heard the clatter of their dishes in the kitchen.

'Did she talk about Mr Parsons?' he asked.

'Mr Parsons?' I shook my head. 'Not really. Well, just a bit.'

'What did she say?'

I paused. 'I can't really remember. I'm sure it was nothing bad. She didn't mention any of that business.'

He looked up sharply, his pen poised. 'What business was that?'

'Would you like another biscuit?' I offered him the tin. 'Cookie.'

'What business was that, Miss Sampson?'

'I'm sure she'd forgotten all about it. It was so . . . tacky.' I paused. Through the wall came a muffled burst of studio laughter. 'Didn't you read about it, in the papers? I'm sure there wasn't any truth in it.' I gazed at him, wide-eyed. 'I mean, who could possibly fall for somebody else when they had Lila Dune?'

He looked at me speculatively. The teabag lay in his tea like a drowned mammal.

'Shall I?' I picked up the string and pulled it out.

I realised, with some apprehension, that he was reasonably intelligent. At first he had seemed too young to be any good at his job, but that was probably just a sign of my own age.

'Can you remember anything else?' he asked. 'What happened next?'

'She said she was going to bed. She had an early call and she was going to take a pill. So I left her – Oh, I don't know. Haven't a clue. Maybe eight-fifteen. Eight-thirty. I wasn't there long.'

'And there's nothing else you remember? Nothing unusual?'

355

I sat, thinking. I desperately wanted a cigarette but I didn't dare get one out and light it. I looked at my handbag, lying on the floor near his feet. *Lila's keys were in there!* Just inches from his shoes.

I shook my head. 'I just came home, fixed myself some dinner and read my book.'

He got to his feet. 'Thank you, Miss Sampson. You've been very helpful. If you think of anything else – anything at all – just call me, or one of my colleagues.'

He gave me his card. My careful rehearsed alibi was not going to be needed. That was because he wasn't interested in me, of course. Only in Lila. As per usual. This time, however, I felt airy with relief.

I went round to see Roly, later that evening. He was terribly distressed. He collapsed on the settee; I knelt beside him and stroked his damp jowls. He was perspiring heavily.

'I've just called Ralph,' he said. This was Ralph Kahn, Lila's lawyer. 'You won't believe this. They found a letter from Trevor, calling the whole thing off.'

'Calling it off?'

'Saying he didn't want to see her any more.'

'No!'

'He says this to her, and she's going to have his *baby*! What kind of a man is that?' He threw up his hands. 'Then they found all these books.'

I jerked back. 'What?'

'Books on homicide, they found. A whole pile of them. In her apartment.'

I stared at him. 'What do you mean?'

'Me, *I* didn't believe it either. All those books she had – unsolved murders, transcripts of trials, that type of thing. She says it's for this project they were working on, her and Trevor, but it's kind of hard to believe. I mean, she ain't no Vassar graduate. We all know that. Sweetheart, I don't know what I *think* any more.'

I stroked his bald head. It was as smooth as the polished

356

knob at the top of the banisters. I used to grip the banisters, as a child, and gaze at the drop below.

'Shall I fix us a hot drink?' I asked.

I went into the kitchen and poured some milk into a saucepan. He wanted hot milk, because his stomach was playing up.

When I turned round his cat was standing there, staring at me with her yellow eyes. I thought: *if animals could talk.* I poured some milk into a saucer for her but she turned around and walked out of the room. She held her fluffy tail high, revealing the pink knot of her anus.

Roly seemed to have shrunk. He sat, huddled, in the formal splendour of his room. He usually switched on the lamps, to make it cosy; tonight he hadn't bothered. I sat down next to him in the gloom. I knew the reason for his distress; he himself had doubts about Lila. Absurdly, I suddenly felt sorry for him.

'She's been acting kind of strange recently,' he said. 'I didn't tell you, honey. But why not, now?' With his teaspoon, he lifted the skin off his milk. It rose like a tiny tent. 'These things been happening, things she couldn't remember she'd done.'

'What things?' I asked.

'Some item of clothing, she found it in her closet. Fidelia swears she didn't pick it up at the dry cleaner's, and Lila can't remember collecting it either. Irma said that really spooked her. Maybe she's mistaken, who knows? And there was some other misunderstanding. About a grocery delivery.'

'Really?'

He nodded. 'Like, she's been experiencing blackouts. Irma was really concerned. See, there've been . . . problems in the past. But Lila, she worked hard on them, we thought she'd come through that.' He sighed.

I turned away. Behind the glass, the shadow puppets looked more spiky and alive than he was. If I half-closed my eyes I could imagine their joints moving.

'And then, the items in the papers didn't help,' he said.

'Trevor denied there was any truth in them, but who's believing who in all this? Jules, it's crazy!'

I put my arm around his plump shoulders. 'It's absolutely terrible,' I said. 'It's crazy.'

Shortly after that I went home. Roly was exhausted; he was going to go to bed. I was glad to leave. It was a strain, performing all the time. I had a splitting headache.

It was a wild, wet night. I hailed a wreck of a cab. Its driver told me he came from Haiti. Dolls hung from his rear-view mirror; whenever he braked violently, they danced. He said he practised voodoo.

'I'm in communication, through this,' he said, tapping his CB radio. 'I'm in communication with people all over the country.'

Both the hood and the trunk lids were loose; as we bounced over the potholes they slammed like doors. I thought we would be stopped by the police.

I went over the scene with Roly. The discovery of the books had shocked me; I hadn't known they existed. Lila herself seemed to be conspiring in her own downfall. What a stroke of luck! It was uncanny.

Everything conspired. My earlier efforts at her disorientation had damaged her credibility further, wasn't that handy? At the time I had only meant to confuse her, and to infect her with the jealousy I myself had experienced with Trevor. I had simply meant to undermine their relationship. For once, everything was working in my favour.

Outside my apartment, the cab jerked to a halt. The dolls swung, wildly. For the third night running there was nobody waiting for me. I gave the driver a large tip, for luck.

As I rode up in the elevator I pictured Lila as a wax voodoo figure, punctured with pins. All these weeks I had been pushing them in, one by one. Magic, wasn't it?

Headlines scream. That's a cliché, isn't it? My father wouldn't have liked it. The next morning, Friday, the headlines

358

screamed at me from every news-stand. '*FILM STAR AR-RESTED*,' screamed the *Post*. '*DUNE CHARGED WITH LOVER'S SLAYING*,' screamed the *News*. It even made the front page of the *Times*. I bought all the papers, took them back to my apartment and spread them over the carpet. I crouched on the floor like an animal, reading them. I couldn't hold them up; my hands were shaking.

> *In a sensational move, cops swooped at dawn on the Central Park West home of film star Lila Dune and charged her with the murder of her lover Trevor Parsons, found shot dead Wednesday. Doorman Courtney Wilson, 26, said: 'They dragged her from the building. She was screaming.' In tears, her maid Fidelia Hernandez, 43, said: 'It's all a mistake. Miss Dune wouldn't hurt a fly.'*

There wasn't a lot of information; not as much as Roly had told me. The printed page made it concrete, and curiously separate. Now it was a newspaper story I was finally excluded. Instead of some bizarre and dreamlike costume drama in which I was somehow involved it had simply happened to Lila. All of a sudden I could believe that now.

I remember sitting up, in a fug of cigarette smoke, and realising with utter clarity: *I'm not the stand-in any longer.*

It's Lila's turn. It's Lila who's the stand-in now.

They held Lila for 24 hours. She was arraigned, and formally charged with murder. She pleaded not guilty. Bail was set at $200,000. All the networks were down at Foley Square – WNBC, WCBS. I think it was on *Good Morning New York* and the *Today* programme.

My moods seesawed wildly. One moment I felt secure, the next terrified. I couldn't believe that the wheels were turning without me and that I seemed to be getting away with it. Maybe this was just a carefully orchestrated charade, designed to lure me into complacency.

I looked out of my window. In the office block, the secretaries sat at their screens. They read their displays; then they turned, slowly, to stare at me. Down in the street, when I went out, I saw a hot-dog stand being pushed to the corner of 6th Avenue. The man opened up the metal plates, unfolding them like a magician unfolding his box of tricks. They had stationed him there to spy on me.

That Friday afternoon she was released. I sat huddled in my apartment and watched it on *Live At Five*. Outside the Criminal Courts there was a boiling scrum of reporters; they surged in the sunshine. It was only a mile or so away; if I sat still, I could almost hear the roar beyond my neighbouring buildings. I cocked my head, listening. Suddenly needing comfort, I stuffed myself with the cookies the detective hadn't touched; I gorged on them. On the screen I watched the TV cameras poised like heavy artillery. They all pointed at the steps. The anchor-woman, a Deborah Norville double with a glossy golden chignon, talked with ill-concealed excitement about '*the crime that has stunned the city's showbusiness community.*' The manoeuvres seemed totally unreal, simply a publicist's dream. New York City had come to a standstill; the very nation had ground to a halt. Well, that was how it seemed. After twenty years of second-league celebrity, Lila was all at once truly famous. One squeeze of the trigger and pow!

I watched the TV. She appeared on the steps, flanked by men in suits. She looked hunched and diminished in a blue coat; she wore the dark glasses which, I realised with surprise, I had myself worn. She looked as lost as a blind woman.

The reporters surged forward; she was hustled into a waiting limo. Momentarily engulfed with braying newsmen, it pushed through the crowd and sped away.

I switched off the TV. My sweater was sodden. I glanced up; I thought that the ceiling was leaking. Then I realised that I was drenched in sweat.

She had looked shattered. Sitting there in my clammy clothes, only I knew why. She was not just shocked by her arrest. She was shattered by Trevor's death. Funny how I had never thought of that. He was lost to her, for ever. She was alone now, like me.

I didn't think of Trev. That way madness lay. Nor did I think of Lila. She had ruined me; why the hell shouldn't I ruin her? I felt no remorse, not then. I just felt numb. I busied myself with preparations for departure. I felt like a fox slipping away while the hounds were busy elsewhere.

My contract was faxed to Roly's agency. I was signed up for six episodes of *The Best People*. Accommodation was arranged for me in Los Angeles. I didn't have a motorhome, a limo and videocassette rights, but it was a start. I couldn't get out of New York City fast enough. I phoned my mother. She hadn't heard the news about Trevor, I could tell by her voice. I asked her to check up on my flat when she next went to London. All my plants, my little babies, would probably be dead by now. I didn't trust my neighbours to water them. I told her my news. 'Goodness,' she exclaimed. 'We'll be reading about you in the papers soon!'

I paused. 'What do you mean?'

She laughed. 'You're a film star now!'

LOS ANGELES –
NEW YORK

One

I was away in Los Angeles for seven weeks, swallowed up in another world. LA teems with new identities, with people who have changed their names and reconstructed themselves. They are their own fabrications, their own plastic surgeons. God knows where they come from; they have no past. It's a city of outsiders. Their faces are comely but uninhabited; looking into their eyes is like looking through the windows of that clapboard house on the back lot. They are washed as clean as sand on the beach. I had met Trevor on the beach and look! The next day – no trace! Life is like filming. *Nothing really happened*. No trace; not even a cigarette butt.

It's a manufacturing city; people manufacture themselves. The media conspires in this, reinforcing lies and half-truths, colouring up film stars' childhoods and creating whole new personas. This suited me fine. I shed the past and reinvented myself. For my role as Samantha Seymour they cut and dyed my hair; it swung in a shiny chestnut bob. The weather was hot and we were shooting largely outdoors; I grew firm and tanned. I worked out in a gym and learnt a new vocabulary – *'Tummy-tucks', 'butt-burns', twist-stretchers', 'broomstick twisters'* – as if I were mastering a foreign language. Unknown muscles started to ache. My body felt like a refurbished machine, with a new network of nerves. I punished it.

I called myself Julie and rented a white Volkswagen Rabbit, like a singles swinger. I was given an apartment on La Brea and Melrose; I greeted the other inhabitants with a bland and sunny smile. I never opened a book; I could no longer read anything demanding, it made me nauseous. I just learnt, by heart, my new script.

'*It hurts, Tourmaline,*' I murmured at my new reflection in the mirror. '*All these years I've been hurting. Hiding and hurting.*'

I had been brought in to kill off two characters, my daughter and my ex-lover. This was because the two actors concerned had to leave the show. One was pregnant and the other's contract was being terminated because of some tax evasion scandal. *The Best People*'s ratings were at an all-time low and they needed two violent deaths to pick up the figures. So along came Samantha Seymour.

Are you sitting comfortably? Do you want to hear the story?

Shall we not bother? I can hardly remember it myself. I was an English tennis coach who had arrived on the West Coast to claim her long-lost daughter, Tourmaline. She was eighteen years old and had grown up unaware of my existence. She thought that her step-mother Liberty was her real mother, until I came along to her home to improve her tennis game.

'My life has been one long lie,' she said, gazing at me with her blue eyes. We were sitting in the grounds of her parents' estate. The lawns swelled like breasts, like the lawns at the Ortho contraceptive factory.

I put my arm around her. 'I was young then, honey,' I said. 'I was aiming to become a champion athlete – '

'Sorry, you guys!' called the director. 'We're still rolling. Take it from the top.'

We repeated our conversation. 'I had to work so hard,' I said. 'Excellence was all I believed in. I worked on my body, but the one part I forgot was my heart. It was like something was missing inside. And the hurting got worse. I had to come and see you . . .'

The words slipped from my lips, harmlessly. I spoke like a robot, but then so did everyone else. The other actors were as smooth and shiny and handsome as *Thunderbirds* puppets, and marginally less expensive. I moved through my scenes in a trance, mouthing my lines and repeating the one bit of business suggested by the director: reflectively running my fingers over the strings of my tennis racquet.

I was kept thankfully busy; there was no time to think. The pace was frenetic. They had to tape one episode every three days. I didn't socialise but then neither did anyone else, beyond back-slappings and 'How're ya doing?' They were too exhausted. Once or twice I heard people talking about Lila's arrest. 'Think he was screwing around? Think she really shot him?' When that happened I melted away.

Nights were the worst. Like Lila I took Seconal to make myself sleep, but it didn't work. I lay awake for hours, sweating, waiting for the phone to ring. Outside my window the constant hum of the traffic was periodically drowned by police sirens, wailing closer. They were coming to get me; it was only a matter of time.

Sometimes, half-asleep, I heard the engine of Trev's van. I recognised its special rattle. He had driven it across the States to find me; he was coming closer, down La Brea. When I drifted into sleep I saw him, slumped in the armchair. The crimson blood had spread over the bathrobe as if it were blotting paper. I tried to turn away but I couldn't. As I watched him, he opened one eye and winked.

I dreaded the insomnia, but I dreaded sleep more. Sometimes I was pulled, struggling nervelessly, back into my childhood. One night Lila was in my class at school. She passed a note to the teacher, Miss Hendricks, who looked at me for a moment. Then she lifted the phone that happened to be on her desk. Sure enough, down in the street the sirens started wailing.

I'd jerk awake, panic-struck. They were coming to get me. But sometimes, when I opened my eyes drowsily in the morning, I truly believed that nothing had happened. Trev was alive. He was living in New York a few blocks from Lila, and she was going to have his baby. Everything was the same. This feeling could last for a surprisingly long time, simply because I was so cut off that there was nothing to remind me of the past. I lay there in my rented apartment, the murmuring traffic out the front and the parking-lot out the back. In that spartan room I lay there numbly, waiting for the sensations to return to my body as one waits for one's gums to start tingling after a visit to the dentist. Sure enough, it happened. A sick sensation spread through my veins. It corroded me like acid. The feeling was fear. Maybe you have never felt it. I hope, for your sake, you haven't.

Roly phoned. 'How are you, sweetheart? How's it going? Have I been missing you!' He tried to tell me about Lila but I didn't want to hear, it knocked me off-balance. He wanted to fly out to visit but I put him off.

'I'm working flat out,' I said. 'I'm shattered. All I do is come home to sleep. Terribly boring.'

The thought of him made me nervous; I never wanted to see him again. Besides, I had started an affair with an optical effects guy called Lee. He was deeply stupid. He drove a black Trans-Am with flames painted on it. He had tattooed arms and he lived in a guest cottage on Coldwater Canyon. I didn't know much about him, except that when he was younger he earned a living sabotaging film shoots.

'Like, you hang out with actors,' he said. 'You get the location schedules and you set up there before they arrive. Like you're cutting down trees with a chain-saw, something real noisy.' He giggled. 'You say you have to finish the job so they pay you $500 just to get the fuck out.'

Thank God he wasn't into conversation; he discovered nothing about me, all those weeks. Such spaced-out self-absorption suited me fine. He was into bodies. We sat on his Navaho rug, the wind tinkling through the brass chimes he had hung up around the room, smoking dope and limbering up for sex. He was lean and small; in fact he physically resembled a West Coast version of Trev. Prior to marathon screwing Trev had recommended scrumpy and, if I remember, speed. Lee recommended Quaaludes, amyl nitrate and marijuana. Like many dope-heads, he listed the optimum intake with the solemn pedantry of a master chef listing the ingredients for his *specialité de la maison*. He closed his eyes and centred his bodily fluids or something by limb-burns and Ashanti chants. In their own way, his preparations were as dogged as Roly's.

I won't give you what Trev called *the grisly details*. They are obviously far too boring. But when I climaxed I forgot everything. I forgot Trevor; I forgot my permanent state of terror. Just for a moment, in the exploding darkness, I was released. And if I gazed long enough into the face of this almost-Trev, this weird and coarsened stand-in, Lee, I could feel my memories of the real Trev obscured and vandalised. It was like an old drawing defaced with a crude, child's crayon. Almost blocked out.

Once or twice, however, I had a fright. One evening I was sitting with Lee in Citrus. This was a restaurant on Melrose; one of the trendy, calico-umbrella kind. Lee was describing the plot of a picture he had worked on, *Bimbo Barbecue* or something. Maybe it was *Bimbo Bonfire*.

'We had this, like, smoke coming out of her eyes,' he said. 'It was amazing. Then she sort of collapsed and all this guk came out.'

Just then the waiter came up with the menus.

'I'd like to share some food notes with you,' he said, pointing at the evening's specialities. 'We have some bluefish, pan-roasted –' He stopped. He was staring at me. 'Hey, it's Jules!' He smiled. 'How're you doing?'

I gazed back, blankly.

'Your hair,' he said. 'I didn't recognise you.'

Still I didn't reply.

'*Jane Eyre*,' he said. 'Remember? I married you.'

'What?'

'I played the pastor.'

'Oh. Yes.'

'Hey, isn't it just something? About Lila?' he turned to Lee. 'Jules here, she was Lila Dune's stand-in on that picture.'

'No kidding?' said Lee, turning to look at me. He almost seemed interested.

'Think she did it?' hissed the waiter. 'Think she'll go down?'

'Excuse me,' I said. I pushed back my chair and stumbled across to the rest room.

In the fifth week we shot the murder. Tourmaline, enraged at her father's deception all those years, drives to his country club, jumps from her car and rushes at him, brandishing a pistol. As not only her mother but the resident tennis pro I try to stop her, wrestling with her and pulling her away but to no avail! They had to get him off the show.

It was a heavy, smoggy day. We were filming at the Brentwood Country Club. Tourmaline pushed me aside and strode across to her father. 'I hate you!' she shouted. 'All these years you've been deceiving me! You've betrayed me and everything I hold dear!'

She raised the pistol and pulled the trigger. There was the *crack* of a blank.

'Aargh!' Her father spluttered and staggered backwards, banging against a concrete urn. His eyes rolled. Finally he crumpled, clutching his chest. Blood (*No. 3 Normal Flowing Red Blood*) seeped between his fingers. He fell heavily onto the gravel.

'OK! Cut!' called the director.

The actor climbed to his feet, dusting himself off. 'That OK?'

'Fabulous, Jim!' called the director. 'I love you! Really convincing.'

I dreamed I was in my bedsitter in Hampstead, the place I lived in before I bought my flat, but it was larger and echoing. Outside the window was a row of chimney pots. I kept trying not to look at them because I knew somebody was hiding in them. Sure enough, my father's face rose slowly over the rim, like Ali Baba. He rose as slow and pale as the moon, and he was grinning too.

The days passed, bland and sunny. Back in London the licence had elapsed on my Renault. My rates were due to be paid. I suddenly remembered things like this, small tweaks from my past like a hand pulling at my skirt. Sometimes it made me panic, that my old life was slipping away. If I couldn't manage to pay my rates, how on earth did I think I could manage to deal with all this? At other times it comforted me, that I could still remember such small, homely tasks. I thought of phoning my mother, but she would have read the papers by now; she would start asking me questions in her thrilled, wondering voice. *'Trevor was your young man, wasn't he? What was he doing with her? Did you know? Are you upset?'*

I thought of phoning my friends, but they would ask the same things. Besides, *you haven't got any friends.*

But Trevor was dead now and his horrible words had died with him. I wasn't going to think about them. *He* couldn't any more, so why should I?

I didn't do anything. In a few weeks, I thought, I would be flying back to England for good. I would be making my final escape.

That was what I thought.

Roly flew over. I wished he hadn't; I didn't want to see him. On the other hand, I had to act normally. I couldn't risk any questions, anything untoward. I couldn't risk an emotional showdown. I was like an animal, edging around the danger zones, sniffing and testing the air. I had developed a new set of muscles and reflexes.

Roly had lost weight. The skin was looser on his face; it made him look older. More tired, too.

'This whole damn business,' he said, 'it's knocked the guts out of all of us.'

He took me to a dairy restaurant called The Milky Way. It was run by Steven Spielberg's mother; it was in the Jewish strip, out on Pica, I think. I can't remember. It was raining.

Inside it was dark and old-fashioned, with leather banquettes and posters of *ET* and *Indiana Jones* on the walls. Roly greeted Spielberg's mother, Leah, like an old friend, clasping her sorrowfully and kissing her. He had been coming here for years.

'It's been terrible,' he said. 'Terrible.'

She was a tiny, vivacious woman with cropped hair and white bobbysocks like a schoolgirl. She took our orders; we both asked for fried fish. For some ridiculous reason I suddenly felt safer than I had for weeks. The rain outside, and the rabbis and family groups inside, made me feel as if I were sitting in Golders Green.

'The show's going fine,' I said chattily. 'Dad was shot last week, and on Thursday Tourmaline's going to die in a car crash.'

He nodded abstractedly. 'It's going to help a whole lot that she's pregnant.'

'She's not,' I said. 'She's going to die.'

'Lila, is who I mean.'

'Ah.'

'Ralph assured us of that. What judge is going to look at a beautiful, pregnant woman and not feel some pity?' He raised his hands helplessly. 'What judge could do that?'

I sat there, fiddling with my napkin. Leah came over with some iced tea. I couldn't ask: *Is she pleading not guilty?* I couldn't get the words out. But he was telling me anyway.

'The defence, they're working on it,' he said. 'They're maybe going to plead extreme emotional disturbance. She did it when the balance of her mind was disturbed. She's undergoing this whole series of psychiatric tests right now.'

'Poor Lila,' I said, sipping my tea. 'We all knew she was off the wall, but *this* . . .'

Across the room, ET gazed at me. His goggle eyes were fixed on my face; when I moved, they followed me.

'I still can't believe it,' Roly said. 'She has everything to live for. She loves him, she goes and shoots him? Why would she do such a thing?'

'It does seem crazy.'

I took another sip of tea. The ice-cubes lay against my lips, freezing them. I gazed at ET over the rim.

'Have they decided a date yet?' I asked. 'For the trial?'

'October maybe. If they can fix an early slot.'

'What a shame!' I said. 'I'll be gone by then.'

He stared at me. 'Gone?'

'I have to go back to London for a bit. I have some things to sort out.'

This was a lie. I wasn't going to go for a bit. I had planned it all. I would go home, and then simply stay there.

'Only temporarily,' I said, touching his arm. 'Then I'll be back. Don't worry.'

'I guess you'll have to stay here, honey,' he said. 'In the States.'

'What?'

'They'll maybe get in touch with you.'

'Me? Why?'

'They may be calling you as a witness.'

Two

They interrupted the TV schedules for the trial. The entire population of New York seemed to be glued to their sets. There had been nothing so sensational since the Nussbaum case, but The People versus Lila Dunnacovicia was a lot more glamorous. A beautiful film star in the dock, accused of her lover's murder! It was better than any movie; it was real life!

I had flown back from LA. Thank God I wasn't called as a witness; they must have decided, quite rightly, that I had no useful information to offer either the prosecution or the defence.

I was flat-sitting for somebody in an apartment nine floors above my old one. I had been referred there by my ex-landlady, who had by now returned. In New York there is a network of flat-sitters who pay in cash for rent-controlled apartments. It suits everybody. It suited me. I couldn't have gone back to that place downstairs; I simply couldn't have stepped through the door. People say that when somebody dies it's all right if you stay with them; but if you go away and then return it's almost impossible to look at them again, they have become a corpse.

It was October 5 and fuggy. I had the air conditioners blowing full blast. This apartment was a fancier affair than the previous one; it had three rooms, uplighters and stippled walls. On the shelves was a bronze sculpture of supplicating hands. It faced the other way, too, away from Central Park. It faced downtown, and had an uninterrupted view of the power towers of Wall Street. They were as hazy as mirages in the smog. Somewhere down there, somewhere in the noise and

374

fumes, somewhere I hadn't dared go, Lila was sitting in a courtroom. The see-saw had swung; our positions were now reversed. I had risen way up into the sky, safe; I could hardly hear the sirens. The city was laid at my feet, just as it had been laid at Lila's feet in Central Park West. With my thumb I could squash the pitifully-purposeful dots scurrying in the street below.

I lowered the blinds to watch the TV; it felt guilt-inducing and unnatural, like watching Wimbledon in the afternoon. The light glowed through, as if I were underwater. I positioned myself in an Eames chair, cigarettes to hand, and switched to Channel 2. *Guiding Light* was being interrupted for Lila.

They weren't transmitting the trial in its entirety, just key segments. The picture bloomed onto the screen. Room 458 of the Criminal Courts was crammed and humming. Spectators filled the public benches, boxed in by blonde wooden partitions as if they were Puritans sitting in church. I was disappointed by the room; it was plain and modern. Next to the judge hung a limp American flag; behind him a marble panel stretched from floor to ceiling. IN GOD WE TRUST, it said. The camera panned round to Lila. Flanked by police officers and lawyers she sat, her face pale and blank as if she had been drugged. Her eyes didn't move. Her hair was pulled back and she wore a plain green suit that I hadn't seen before. I could hardly recognise her. It was like the first day on the set of *Jane Eyre*, when she had startled me with her transformation. In the bright TV lights she was playing a new role: the glazed homicide suspect.

The jury had been sworn in; the commentator explained that they had undergone the *voir dire* process of questioning. The camera panned over their faces, brown, white, old, young, like horses lined up at the starting post. The opening statements had been made by the prosecution and defence. The first witness was in the stand. It was Lt. Frank Gozzoli, of the 97th Precinct.

He described how he had arrived on the scene at 1.10 hours. He described the position of the body and the absence of a murder weapon. As he spoke the camera panned across the spectators in the public benches. I saw Roly. I saw Irma's stony, sallow face. She sat there, motionless. I saw Lila's mother, dressed in black as if for a funeral. I saw some familiar faces: an actor from *Bump*; somebody who looked like Norman Mailer. Members of the public craned round, celebrity-spotting. Even on the TV I could feel the buzz in the air, like a first night.

'There was no sign of a struggle,' said Gozzoli.

There was a break for ads. A freckle-faced boy clapped his hands in the sunshine and the screen rained Cornflakes.

Then the painter Joseph Carillo took the stand. He was a small, meaty man who looked both awed and excited by his surroundings. He told the court how, on the morning of 25 April, at 8.30, he and his two colleagues had arrived at Mr Parsons's apartment.

'I rang the bell but nothin' happened. We thought, maybe he's gone out to the coffee shop to get some breakfast so we go back to the office. At 9.30 we called him on the phone but nothin' happened again. We had a set of his keys in the office so we took those, picked up some more items on the way and got to his apartment at 12.30.'

'Can you tell the court what happened then?' asked the prosecutor, a tall, loose-limbed man whose name I hadn't caught.

'So we open the door. I call out, in case he's in the shower or someplace, but there's no reply. So we go into the big room and he's just sitting there. No question, he's dead. This big bloodstain on his chest.'

'So what did you do then?'

'What did we do? We get the hell out of that place, fast, and we tell the doorman to phone the cops.'

'One more question, Mr Carillo. You and your colleagues from Lotus Design Studio had been painting the lobby of his apartment the day before, is that right?'

'Sure.'

'Would the woodwork still be wet?'

376

He nodded. 'Kind of sticky, yep.'

The camera panned to an elderly, gnome-like couple sitting close together. They looked familiar, but it took me a moment to recognise them. My heart stopped. They were Trevor's parents, Ida and George. I wished they hadn't come.

As in any long-running soap, characters began to emerge. The prosecutor was called Rubinsky. His mobile, rubbery face reminded me of Walter Matthau. He wandered around in a casual manner – the whole process was surprisingly casual, compared to a British court. He wore a shirt, with the sleeves rolled up; he perched on tables, wrapping one long leg over the other, pushing his hands through his crinkly hair and suddenly jumping down and approaching the jury, his finger jabbing. I watched him with tense solicitude. Little did he know his vital importance to me, and how I urged on his performance with the proprietorial air of a playwright whose drama is being staged. Or, to be precise, whose drama might be changed by new characters, unexpected improvisations and alarming twists of plot.

A forensic expert was speaking. He listed the results of fibre tests, confirming that hairs found in the victim's apartment matched hairs on the defendant's sable coat. He listed some other items. Lipstick traces found on cigarette butts in the victim's garbage pail matched a lipstick found in the defendant's apartment.

'Is that all, Dr Zimmerman?'

'We found traces of dried paint on the defendant's sable coat. When taken away for analysis, these matched the paint on the woodwork of the victim's apartment. The lobby.'

'Which was still wet, I believe, at the time in question,' said Rubinsky.

A fingerprint expert – a small, colourless man who himself looked like a mass murderer – confirmed that though the drinking glasses in both apartments had been wiped, the defendant's prints had been found on countless surfaces in the victim's apartment, and that hers alone had been found on the murder weapon.

The defence attorney climbed to his feet and cross-examined him.

'Mr Thomas,' he said, 'would it surprise you if the defendant's prints *weren't* found in her fiancé's apartment? And, indeed, on her own property that she carried in her purse?'

'Yes,' he replied.

'Thank you,' he said, and sat down.

By the third day the trial had taken on a certain rhythm, a life of its own. I watched it with the compulsive regularity, with the growing loyalties and dislikes, of a soap-opera addict. It began to feel as if it had nothing to do with me, not personally. I was a Hollywood screenwriter whose concept had been taken over by the machinery of production.

Lila was acting a murderess, so she must have done it. I felt a spurious intimacy with these characters, denatured by the TV screen and transformed into performers. What was reality? *Rambo*, or shootings in the streets of Beirut? None of it threatened me as I sat there, chain-smoking.

Until I was jerked to my senses. I switched on the TV. A couple was being interviewed on the steps of the Criminal Court. It was Ida and George. Ida, a dumpy woman in her Sunday best, leaned forward and spoke into the microphone.

'He was a lovely boy. Bit of a tearaway but everybody loved him. His life was just beginning.' She stopped, and began to sob.

I sat there, frozen. Was she going to mention my name? But she hardly knew I existed. I had never met her. I only recognised her from a photograph.

George put his arm around his wife and stared belligerently at the camera. 'If he hadn't met that woman . . .' He meant Lila, not me.

'Nothing can bring our boy back to us,' sobbed his wife. 'We're just taking one day at a time.'

*

378

The state's next witnesses were the various doormen who had seen Lila enter and leave the two apartment buildings. The night captain of the 73rd Street Building, Donald O'Reilly, confirmed that Miss Dune had entered at around 10.15, the night in question, and left the building around 11.35.

'Did Mr Parsons have any other visitors that evening, the night of April 24?'

He shook his head. 'No.'

Then the coffee-coloured guy took the stand. I sat, watching him. My heart thumped. He gave his name, Courtney Wilson, and his home address. He said that the evening in question, April 24, it was his second night of duty in the job.

Rubinsky ambled up to him. 'I ask you to look around the court room and see if there's anyone you recognise?'

'Sure,' he said, and pointed to Lila. Then he added, 'Don't everyone?'

There was a murmur of laughter. Courtney Wilson seemed remarkably unintimidated by his surroundings; this was his moment of fame. Maybe some film producer would spot him.

'Just answer the question,' said the judge.

Courtney confirmed that Lila had entered the building that night, at around 11.45.

'Did you notice anything unusual?' asked Rubinsky.

He nodded. For a moment Courtney turned to the camera and looked at me. I shrank back in my chair. 'Sure,' he said. 'I smelt liquor on her breath.'

'You're sure of that?'

He nodded.

'How close were you?' asked Rubinsky.

'Like this close.' He demonstrated, with his hands. 'She signed her autograph for me, see. Least I said it was for me, but it was for my Dad. Laurie.'

The court tittered. He looked around, grinning. 'I'm not such a fan of her pictures. But I didn't tell her that. I said it was for me. So she's signing her name for me and I see that her hands are trembling. She seemed like she was upset – '

379

'Objection!' The defence attorney got to his feet.

'Sustained,' said the judge. He turned to Courtney. 'Just keep to the facts, Mr Wilson.'

I went for a walk. Down in the streets the air felt like damp cotton wool. It clogged my throat; I could hardly breathe. My t-shirt stuck to me.

I wandered sluggishly along the sidewalk. All these months Lila had been performing, instead of me. Now she was doing it for real. And I believed her too! Wasn't it just like Lila to be so damned brainless as to march out, in front of a whole bunch of witnesses, and shoot her lover dead? I always knew she was an airhead.

I passed a black guy, slumped in a doorway. He had white powder smeared on his cheeks and his hair was encrusted with what looked like dried spinach. He was giggling.

He turned to me and said something like, 'Wannabanabill-krannyman?'

I paused, and said to him quite distinctly, 'Six months ago I shot a man dead.'

He was still giggling. 'Howdyaganjang, man?' he said. He lay back and closed his eyes.

See? He didn't believe me either! I told you it hadn't happened.

That evening I switched on the TV and watched *The Best People*. I watched myself strolling across a tennis court, pulling my sweatband off and shaking my chestnut hair.

'I'm jolly well exhausted, Tourmaline,' I said in the Home Counties accent I had been instructed to use. 'Let's have ourselves a drink and a chin-wag.'

I gazed at this preposterous apparition. She wore a flirty white shirt. Who on earth was that?

The case was going badly for Lila. As the days passed the prosecution produced witness after witness to testify against her. A tearful Fidelia confirmed that she had found State's

Exhibit 8, the letter from Trevor, and had thrown it into the garbage. Prodded by Rubinsky, she confirmed a series of jealous rows, in one case violent, between Miss Dune and Mr Parsons, though adding that they'd been so happy too, didn't every couple have arguments, she did with *her* husband Mario, she couldn't believe that her employer would be capable of real violence.

'They were so much in love. They were going to get married! She was going to have a baby!'

A Dr Schluss from the Betty Ford Clinic explained the schizoid personality disorder that afflicted people with a drug or alcohol dependency. In a thick German accent he explained to the jury, as if they were children: 'They have a split personality, they are always two people. The one lies dormant within the other; it is only released by chemical stimulus. This hidden person then takes over . . .' He turned to look at me, through the TV screen. I gazed at him through my cigarette smoke. 'It makes the shy person bold, it makes the depressed person happy.' He paused, still staring at me. 'It makes the unaggressive person capable of great violence.'

I got up, abruptly, and went into the kitchen to make myself some coffee.

A middle-aged insurance salesman, Kirk Cooper, took the stand. He confirmed that in May 1987 he had met the defendant in a bar in Tulsa, Oklahoma, where she was filming the country-and-western picture *Cry Your Heart Out*.

'Sure she was loaded,' he said. 'She was smashed. So we had a few more drinks and she came back to my hotel room.' He paused, smiling smugly. 'I knew what happened next, but did she? No, sir. The next morning she wakes up and she says, "Who the fuck" – pardon me, "Who the hell are you? Where the hell am I?" I was kind of offended.' He looked at the jury, raising his hands helplessly. 'Kind of knocks a man's self-esteem, know what I mean? And who believed me, when I told them I'd had sex with Lila Dune?' Laughter rippled through the court. 'They said, "Oh sure you did."'

381

He winked. 'Except I'd kept her cigarette lighter. See, she'd left it behind.'

'Objection!' Ralph Kahn, the defence attorney stood up. He was small and unprepossessing. 'Your Honour, what's the relevance of this? If my client chose to forget, as she indeed might, a moment of indiscretion . . .' He gazed witheringly at Kirk Cooper. 'What does this prove, except that maybe she had taste?'

But Lila was slowly being dismantled in front of our eyes. Papers reported the events with ill-concealed relish. Much as they loved building up icons, it was even more fun to watch them tumble down. They hadn't had such a good time since the Trump split-up.

As Lila's background emerged it was revealed that, to put it kindly, she had a somewhat elastic view of the truth. She had invented some facts and falsified others. It was discovered, for instance, that she had lied about her age. She wasn't 39, but 43. Kahn stormed: 'So what woman doesn't? Isn't that her prerogative – especially if she's a star? What're we going to hear next? Testimony from her hairdresser that she lightens her hair? So that makes her a murderess?'

On the fifth day of the trial we were all in for a surprise. Fidelia had sobbed, 'She's going to have a baby!'

A police doctor, Dr Daniel Feinstein, was called to the witness stand. He confirmed that he had examined the defendant.

'What information did she give you, before the examination?' asked Rubinsky.

'She told me she was seven weeks pregnant.'

'And what did you discover, during your routine internal examination?'

He shook his head. 'That this was not the case.'

'Could you repeat that?'

'She wasn't pregnant.' He turned to the jury. 'She wasn't carrying a child.'

There was a hiss of indrawn breath, then a stunned silence. Lila sat there, her face wooden. Irma turned to stare at her.

I sat there, thinking hard. So she had pretended she was going to have a baby, the oldest trick in the book. *My* trick, in a sense, except I had planned to carry it through. She had feigned pregnancy to get Trevor to marry her. How sad!

If the court was in an uproar then, it was as nothing to what followed. After the lunch-time recess the court reconvened at 2.00. *As the World Turns* had been interrupted, so that the trial could be transmitted. Something was up.

I switched on the TV set. A balding man stood in the witness box. He had a drooping moustache, a Western shirt and a bootlace tie. He gave his name as Albert Standing. He ran a video store in Portland, Oregon.

'Can you describe your relationship to the defendant?' asked Rubinsky.

He looked across at Lila. She was staring at him, her mouth open.

He nodded. 'She was my wife.'

The spectators gasped.

'We were married in June 1963,' he said. 'She was 16, and I was near enough 18.'

There was a hush, while this information was digested by the court. The rows of reporters had their heads down, they were scribbling. I sat there, trying to work it out. Lila had *two* ex-husbands – Vince Quinn, the dragster-racer, and Bobby Del Ray, the night-club owner. I didn't understand. I gazed at the faces in the public benches. They were murmuring and whispering to each other; the hum rose to a roar.

'Silence in court!' snapped the judge.

Rubinsky said, 'The defendant was expecting a baby at the time, is that right?'

Standing nodded. 'We'd been dating a coupla months. She was still in school. So she quit, and we got married.'

He paused. People were craning their necks to look at Lila. She had bent her head; all that was visible was her blonde hair. I could see its dark roots.

'The labour was real bad,' he said. 'Both of them, they

nearly died. Then the little girl was born. We called her Jasmine.' He paused, and looked across at Lila. She didn't raise her head. 'We knew right away something was wrong. That she wasn't like the other babies.' He fell silent again. He was curiously dignified. The court waited. Someone cleared his throat. 'It was the oxygen, see. The cord had gotten around her neck, it had damaged her brain.' Suddenly he looked up and spoke to the public benches; he didn't know about addressing the jury. 'She was so young! It wasn't her fault!'

Rubinsky asked, 'Could you tell us about the events of December 3, 1963?'

'We were both of us just kids! Her friends, they were hanging out, going to parties. That's what she should've been doing. She was the prettiest girl you've ever seen.'

He stopped. He looked across at Lila; she lifted her face, briefly. He turned to the judge.

'You shouldn't have brought me here, sir,' he said. 'It was a long time ago. It don't make no sense to talk about it now.'

Rubinsky asked, 'Could you tell us what happened, that night?'

Standing paused, then he started speaking. He spoke softly, as if he were talking to himself. 'She yelled all the time, see. On and on. Like it was a chainsaw. Nothing stopped her, it drove us crazy. She didn't recognise us. Nothing. She just yelled.' He stopped.

The judge asked him gently, 'What happened?'

It came out hesitantly, the whole story. Lila had gone out for the evening, while he stayed home with their daughter. She had gone out with a bunch of guys and come home drunk. That night, when the baby had woken up, yelling, she had filled the basin and tried to drown her.

The baby survived. Lila wasn't convicted. In fact, she denied the whole thing. She simply couldn't remember doing it. She was put under psychiatric supervision for three years.

Jasmine was now aged 27. She had spent her life in a state mental institution; she wasn't even marginally well enough to be let loose, like most of her fellow-inmates, onto the streets of American cities. Lila had never visited her daughter. A few months after the incident she and Albert Standing had parted and finally divorced. He crossed the country, to Oregon, married again and started another life.

Below me, on one of the rooftops, a naked man was punching the air. He wore a blindfold; his body glistened. He was overshadowed by the rear of an apartment building. It was a menacing tangle of fire-escapes, rusting window frames and air-conditioners that jutted like teeth. Have you ever noticed how sinister New York buildings are, from the back? Beyond came the hooting of cars, stuck in some traffic jam.

I desperately needed a drink; I drained the vermouth bottle into a glass. A mile away, surgeons were slicing Lila open and I knew I should be running there shouting: *Don't! Stop it! Put away your knives!*

But I couldn't move; not enough to get out of the apartment. All at once I felt furious with Trevor, and with myself. I managed to get to my feet, pull his postcards out of my suitcase and stuff them into the garbage bin. I squashed them down with my foot, mashing them amongst the damp tea bags and lettuce leaves. '*Pissed*,' I read. '*Sassenack*.' The stupid bastard couldn't even spell.

Good fucking riddance, I thought, gazing at the chrome bin.

Lila had had a baby! Though the rest of us seemed to have died, one damaged grown-up was still alive. She had only been born to the world that afternoon. I wondered if Lila had told Trev about her existence. Maybe even *they* weren't that close.

Maybe they were. Who knew, now? It wasn't my business to ask. I lay on the bed, staring at the ceiling. Suddenly I felt weak with guilt. It was as if the mist had cleared, just for a minute, and revealed the forbidden vista. I knew I shouldn't let her be punished, that I should go to the police and confess, before it was too late.

But that seemed such a melodramatic and utterly bizarre

thing to do. As unhinged as a naked man punching the air. It simply seemed impossible. I would have to look up Precinct Station in the phone book – was that how they were listed? Find the nearest one, go there and ask for somebody. Who? And then blurt out my unbelievable story, like some pathetic fan, gatecrashing. Trying to muscle in on my heroine's notoriety. Trying, pitifully, to be her stand-in for real.

It all seemed far more ridiculous than Lila being tried for murder. *She's just a disturbed child*, Rodney had said, and now I could see why. It all made sense, now. Far more sense than the blurred and confused events of a certain night in April, when a towelling mannequin sat slumped in a chair and refused to rise to its feet.

Roly came round that evening. I wished he hadn't. I hated him coming to my apartment, it made me feel exposed.

'Sure you're OK, sweetheart?' he kept asking. 'You look terrible.'

'I'm fine,' I said, and gave him a slice of wholewheat apple pie.

'It doesn't look good,' he said. 'She hasn't got a hope in hell of winning this case. What's the defence got? Lack of motive. That's all they got. What else? You know what else? Lila says she didn't do it.' He threw up his hands. 'They got an *actress*, protesting her goddam *innocence*! She makes her goddam *career* telling lies!'

That night I lay awake, sweating. I told myself: movie stars don't go to prison. People like *me* did. Ordinary people. Lila was immune. She was enveloped in her own protective wrapping. People sensed it wherever she went. They swung round, to watch her. In traffic snarl-ups I kept close to a white Rolls-Royce because I knew it would find a way through. It drew me behind it like a magnet. Normal rules didn't apply to film stars. That was the point of them. They were magic.

Those children knew that, the summer before. They had all run away to catch a glimpse of Lila. They had deserted me, in my spurious Oxfam glamour. They didn't want my pretend fairy story, they wanted the real thing. Just as I did. And fairy stories always ended happily. That was the point.

Lila's attorney, Ralph Kahn, tried to persuade her to change her plea. He wanted to turn the whole thing around and go with the prosecution evidence. He urged her to change her plea to guilty of manslaughter, whilst of an unsound mind.

But she refused. 'Her mind's fouled up,' Roly told me, on the phone. 'We know she did it, *she* seems to know sometimes. Least, she's all confused. She woke up that morning and it was like she'd gone out. Her fur on the floor, all that. See, she hasn't got the mental stamina for what she's going through. The questions, the stuff about her daughter. The courtroom, the shock. If you're not cracking up by the beginning, you'll sure be cracking up by the end. That's what the process does to you.'

On the ninth day Lila took the stand. The entire city ground to a halt. That's what it seemed. There was a hush, down in the street. The air felt heavy with thunder. People had been queuing since dawn for seats in the court; the WCBS News that morning showed the crowd snaking down the steps.

I had stomach cramps. They gripped me, waves of them. Sometimes they were so painful that I yelped, as if I were in labour. Then they subsided for a few minutes before they renewed their attack.

I drank herb tea, the cup clattering when I lowered it onto the saucer. I switched on the TV and watched Lila being sworn in. She wore a white blouse. No jewellery; nothing. Her hair was pulled back from her pale face. She looked as if she had shrunk; she looked terribly nervous.

Rubitsky looked refreshed and urbane that morning. I could almost smell his cologne. Strolling to and fro, he questioned her about her relationship with Trevor, and whether there was any truth in the rumours that he was leaving her for another woman. She denied them, shaking her head. He asked her to describe the events of the evening of April 24th.

'I took a couple of Mogadon,' she said. Her voice was low and faltering. 'Double-strength. I get them from my doctor. I went to bed.'

'What time was this?'

'Around nine-thirty.'

'Nine-thirty,' he said. He ambled across to the stenographer, and back again. He appeared to be in deep thought. Like any good performer he was playing the room – timing his pauses, milking his audience. All at once I realised that it was Rubinsky who was the actor today, not Lila.

'Did you consume any alcohol?' he asked.

'No.'

'You sure of that?'

'I've quit,' she said.

He paused, and looked around the room. *So she's quit, huh? You believe that?* He turned to her. 'So you went to bed and went straight to sleep?'

'First I called Tee.'

'Mr Parsons?'

She nodded. 'I called him, to say goodnight.'

'And what did you say?'

'Just the usual things.' She paused. 'You know.'

'What things?'

She looked across at him. 'Just things. I wasn't going to see him for a while. Not till the next evening.' Her voice grew quieter. 'It seemed like a long time, that's all.'

'And what did he say?'

She was silent for a moment. 'The usual things,' she said, at last.

'Anything else?'

'He said the odour of the paint was giving him a headache. Then we said goodnight and I went to sleep.'

Rubinsky stopped his pacing. 'You went to sleep.'

She nodded.

'And then what happened?' he asked.

'I woke up the next morning, at six-thirty.'

Rubinsky raised his thick eyebrows. 'You didn't leave your apartment, during the night?'

She shook her head.

'Let me ask you again, Miss Dune. Take your time.'

'I didn't leave my apartment. Why should I?'

'Please remember, you're under oath.'

'I was asleep!'

'How do you account for the fact that the doorman of your building saw you leave at five after ten – '

'He didn't!'

'That the doorman in Mr Parsons's building saw you entering at 10.15 – '

'I didn't go there!'

'These two men have sworn, under oath – '

'I didn't go!' She stopped; she was shaking. 'I wanted to go, but I didn't.'

'You wanted to go?'

'I wanted to see him.' She lowered her head; she spoke to the floor. 'I missed him. A whole lot. I just wanted to see him. You ever felt that?' She looked up. 'But I didn't go.'

Rubinsky asked them to show her State's Exhibit 3, the gun. He asked her to identify it.

'You recognise this?'

She nodded. 'I guess so.'

'Please, just say yes or no.'

'Yes.'

'Does it belong to you?' he asked.

She nodded.

'How do you account for the fact that this gun – '

'Why should I shoot him?' she cried. 'You think I'm crazy? I loved the guy! Why for fuck's sake should I shoot him when I loved him? Maybe I've done some strange things but I'm not totally bananas! We loved each other, we were going to get married, I was going to have his baby – '

'Miss Dune, you know that's untrue – '

'Nobody believes me! Why don't you believe me?' She

389

stared at him, her face ravaged. It looked as if claws had been dragged down it. 'Why should I shoot him? I just want him back!' She burst into sobs, burying her face in her hands. 'I want him to come back!'

They found her guilty. There was simply overwhelming evidence to prove that she did it, when under the influence of alcohol. Nobody had believed her testimony, though the *News* applauded what it called *'the best performance of her career.'* Shame, it added, that she couldn't have won the Oscar which had so far eluded her.

Prior to sentencing, the judge said, 'There can't be one law for the rich and another for the poor, but I'll take into account the provocation and your mental condition at the time.' He sent her down for eight to twenty-five years.

Three

Afterwards I felt curiously light, as if a poisonous growth within me had been removed. I felt released and airy. I roamed the streets, a free woman. Nobody could get me now. For months a monstrous foetus had been sucking the life from my veins. Now, after a difficult labour, it had been pronounced dead at birth.

I cancelled my plans to return to London. Instead, I fixed things on the phone. I decided to stay in New York, for I had nothing to fear now. I had some trouble sleeping at night and I had to dose myself with Mogadon. I had rather strange dreams. But I told myself it would all improve with time. Lila had been sent to the Women's Correctional Facility at Bedford Hills to begin her sentence. It was all over.

Now I had been seen on *The Best People* – I had returned to the show for six more episodes – the job offers started coming in. My career looked set to gather some momentum. In a funny way I felt I was taking over from Lila, at BCM. A hundred rungs lower, but still taking over. Roly even put me up for a small part in a forthcoming movie which had been earmarked for Lila, though in her case, of course, it would have been called a cameo.

'How's your American accent, honey?' asked Roly.

'Terrific,' I replied, smiling. 'I could pass myself off as an American any day. Nobody would ever know.'

I didn't get the part, in fact. I was relieved; it would have been creepy, wouldn't it? But I was on my way up, no doubt about it.

And then, one day in November, I had a call. Would I like to appear on the *Marv Winfield Show*?

I had no idea what they were talking about. Probably you don't either. *Marv Winfield* was a short-lived, networked chat show created to dent the Carson ratings, a feat it failed to achieve during its brief run. This was principally due to its host. Apparently Winfield was a celebrated ex-football player, but his talents didn't extend to dynamic conversation.

Roly advised me to accept; it was good publicity. So I agreed.

It's a strange thing, about fate. Hindsight tells us we felt uneasy that morning; we had intimations. We try, this way, to make sense of the dizzying and random universe. But that day, when I went out into the hushed street in my silver Cinderella dress, I had no intimation that my life would change. The chance whim of the *Sexbusters* location manager, the chance blow from that unknown stand-in's husband which took her off the picture and changed my life – like the *Titanic*, I sailed gaily into the dark; I had no premonitions of the gathering forces of coincidence.

I felt nothing, the morning of the show. I felt nervous, of course, but I simply put it down to stage fright. The show was being taped in the morning and transmitted the following evening. I had no idea that events were already being set in motion, the invisible countdown beginning.

My fellow guests were a black multiple-rape victim called Macey and a man who imported New York's latest status pet, Vietnamese pot-bellied pigs. He said they were hygienic and affectionate. During the break he was hustled off, carrying a struggling piglet, and I took his place. The audience clapped. I wore a new silk jacket and slacks, and high heels. I sat down on a beige leather sofa whilst somebody dropped a mike down my blouse and Marv Winfield beamed at me. He was a large, amiable man and I had already been primed on the subject of our conversation: the Brits in Hollywood. I felt perfectly safe.

The cameras started rolling. We chatted about the soaps, and the success of Joan Collins and Stephanie Beacham.

'Would you consider yourself a glamorous person, Jules?' he asked.

I shook my head. 'I just consider myself an actress.'

'You've achieved great success in *The Best People*; how did you start your career?'

I told him about my early days at RADA, and my various stage roles, omitting to mention their obscure venues. We all create personas for ourselves, in front of an audience. Their presence and their rustling reactions shape us. I found the old Jules emerging – a dedicated, socially aware actress who struggled against Thatcher philistinism, devoting herself to her craft. Getting into my stride, I babbled on about community theatre and multi-cultural workshops.

'I did a lot of work with disturbed children,' I said. 'That gave me a wonderful training for working with Hollywood directors.'

The audience broke into laughter. Ah, music to my ears! I was starting to enjoy myself. I lifted my hand. 'Look – here's the scar where one of the kids bit me. Must have been a budding critic.' The laughter grew. 'The next Frank Rich.'

Winfield consulted his notes. 'You came here at first, I believe, as Lila Dune's stand-in,' he said.

I tensed. 'Yes.'

He grinned. 'How about telling us something about her?'

I shrugged. 'We hardly spoke a word. Stand-ins are nobodies. They're just gofers. She just got me to buy her cigarettes.'

Thank God our time was up. He wished me best luck in the future.

A limo drove me home. I took the elevator up to my almost-penthouse on the 24th floor. I thought: next stop, Central Park West. My skin tingled from the TV lights. The question about Lila had given me a jolt but there was nothing to worry about. I didn't even look like her any more.

I gazed at myself in the mirror. My hair was cut even

shorter now, just to my ears. I had had it re-dyed chestnut. I gazed at my reflection. It had been a curious sensation, talking about my life in England. It had felt as if I were talking about some distant cousin of mine, who I hadn't met for years. *'You look like her long-lost cousin. The family swot.'*

On impulse I went off that afternoon to a nail salon, down on 3rd Avenue, and had my hands done. Silk-wrap this time, like Lila. As I sat there, I thought of the show. I thought: a few words from me, and I could have sent their ratings through the roof. I closed my eyes and pictured the headlines. WINFIELD SENSATION! STAND-IN SLAYER CONFESSES!

'You OK?'

I opened my eyes. An oriental face gazed at me, puzzled. It was the nail girl.

The next week, something unsettling happened. I had spent the night with Roly. Though extinguished during Lila's trial, our sexual relationship had sluggishly revived. I blamed my lethargy on his overheated apartment, but he chose that night to talk.

'You've gotten really weird,' he said. 'Know that?' He was sitting, naked, on the end of the bed. His folds of fat reminded me of the piglet on the show.

'There's nothing wrong with me!' I said.

'Maybe you should go see somebody.'

I stared at him. 'What do you mean?'

'I know this guy – best in the business – '

'There's nothing the matter!'

'That's not what I hear,' he said.

I froze. 'Hear?' I whispered. 'From who?'

'From you.'

I paused. '*Me?*'

'At night.' He gestured to the other bedroom. 'I'm in there, I can hear you.'

There was a silence. 'What do you hear?' I finally asked.

'It's like – someone's pulling your guts out. I never heard anybody make a noise like that. I guess you're crying.'

A few minutes later, I left. No more sleepovers with *him*. I took a cab downtown, back to my place. I hurried across the lobby and took the elevator up to my apartment. I remember looking at my watch. It was 10.30.

The moment I stepped through the door I knew that somebody had been there. The air smelt different. It was the scent of another human being.

I stood there, unable to move. I stared at the dark shapes of the furniture. I heard my stomach rumbling with fear; it was startlingly loud. Then I switched on the light.

I searched the apartment. There was nobody hiding. Nothing appeared to be stolen – the video and stereo were still there. But somebody had visited. Things had been re-arranged. One of the desk drawers was half-open; in the closet my luggage had been re-stacked in a different order.

Somebody had tried to burgle me. That's what I thought, at the time. But if I had disturbed them, how come I hadn't bumped into them, leaving? How had they known I was coming home? And if they had broken in, why wasn't the door-lock damaged?

Maybe my landlords had come back from Europe. They had arranged to be away for six months but maybe they had returned home early, and had dropped in to collect something.

None of it made sense. Not then.

Four

I had landed a small part in a thriller, which was just starting shooting in New York. It was five days' work; I was to play an English physiotherapist who nurses the hero back to mobility after the Mafia had tried to kill him.

The Thursday after the break-in, November 23rd, I had a call from Roly. I presumed it was about this job, which I was due to start in a couple of days. But I was wrong.

'Sweetheart,' he said. 'I went up to Bedford Hills today, to visit Lila. She asked me to pass on a message.'

There was a silence.

Finally he said, 'You there?'

'Sure,' I said. I took a breath. 'What did she say?'

'She says she'd be really happy to see you.'

'*What?*'

'She wants you to go visit her.'

My first reaction was to rush to the bathroom and throw up. I knelt on the floor and gripped the lavatory bowl. I was being tossed on the sea, and I tried to grip the lifebelt. I knelt there for a long time, I didn't dare move.

Afterwards my throat felt eroded with acid; it felt raw, as if it had been rubbed with sandpaper, over and over. I gazed in the mirror at my bloodshot eyes. I looked crazy. I looked like one of the people I met in atriums.

What on earth was I going to do? I couldn't possibly go. How could I face her? What could I say? What was *she* going to say?

Going to prison is a sort of death. It happens so suddenly. You are plucked from your home, leaving it a *Marie Celeste* of

396

shockingly half-finished tasks. You are bundled away, locked up and silenced. Six weeks ago Lila had to all intents and purposes died. Now she had spoken, her voice threw me into confusion.

It took me hours to decide. At first I thought I wouldn't go, but I knew I was helpless. I couldn't resist her siren voice; it still had the power to summon me to her side. A blush rose to my face; wasn't that ridiculous?

After a struggle I decided I would go. Just for half an hour. It would look curious, if I didn't. Besides, Roly had told me her reason for wanting to see me.

'She says she's lonely. Nobody visits her except Irma and her Mom and they irritate the hell out of her,' he said. 'When I told her you were going to work on *Dead on Arrival* she said you had to go and see her and she'll give you all the dirt on the director. She worked with him on *Touch and Go.*' It sounded utterly innocent.

So the next afternoon I took the train from Grand Central Station. I was extremely nervous. But I wasn't suspicious; not at all.

The journey took an hour, up the Harlem Line of Metro North. I sat in an empty carriage. I concentrated on the names of the stations, counting them off. Bronxville . . . Scarsdale . . . White Plains. I willed the unwillable; for the number of stations to multiply rather than reduce, like a billowing, reversed spool of tape. I was a child going to the dentist; I cursed the remorseless, continual swallowing-up of time that was propelling me forward. The burnt-out hulks of Harlem had long since been left behind and I was out in commuter-land. The sun shone on white clapboard houses. They slid by, as blameless and unreal as those on the back lot. Nothing looks as innocent as an American suburb. I passed a drive-thru bank, disguised as a country cottage. I passed the Valhalla Animal Hospital, disguised as a church. There was no sign of life. The dormitory communities slumbered through the long, chilly afternoon. Just sometimes I passed pockets of marshy wilderness, as surprising as under-arm hair.

I arrived at Bedford Hills and got out. The station was empty. The main street of the little town was silent with parked cars. I walked past bow-fronted thrift shops run by commuters' wives. *Come to our Bake-In!* said a handwritten sign. I stopped outside *Jeni's Boutique and Gifte Shoppe*. All at once I had the strangest sensation. This town was just a façade; these boutiques were just erected for my visit. *Taffy's Bakery*, with its window display of muffins, was as phoney as the Dickensian corner shop where I had first glimpsed Lila that sultry day, over a year before. The town was simply a film set, to be dismantled when I departed.

I felt deeply uneasy. At that moment I nearly turned back, hurried to the station and made my escape. I nearly did. But Lila still pulled me. So I found a cab and it took me to the correctional facility, a mile away.

I'll never forget my first sight of the prison. Solid and brick-red, it looked like a Victorian power station. It was sunk in a valley, hemmed in by russet trees. Tall fences, topped with tangled sausages of barbed wire, surrounded the buildings. A sentry tower rose as high as a factory chimney.

I was directed to a peeling Portakabin. Inside, they frisked me for metal. There were notices on the walls, in Spanish and English. An officer searched my handbag and removed my street map, matches and bunch of keys. He put them aside, in a brown paper gunny-bag. I silently thanked God that I no longer carried the keys to Lila's apartment; I had hidden them back home. He wouldn't have recognised them but *I* would, and I needed my wits about me. I laid my hand on the desk and he stamped it with invisible ink, as if I were entering an exclusive night club to which the whole of New York was clamouring to gain entry. I was released, and walked through a huge wire gate, which was opened for me by another officer. I walked across a pen, through another gate up to the main entrance. My steps faltered. Suddenly my throat constricted; I was gripped with claustrophobia. *They've got me now*, I thought. *It's all an elaborate trick. I can't escape.*

Then I thought, *Don't behave oddly. Not now. They're all watching.*

In the entrance lobby, an enormously fat officer stood behind a desk. Her uniform strained over her vast belly and hips. A heavy bunch of keys hung from her belt, as if she were a jailer. She *was* a jailer. She was eating something from a tub, with a plastic spoon. Nearby was a heavy, barred gate.

I told her who I was visiting. 'Uh-huh,' she said, and lifted the phone.

She was telling them that the plan was working. The rabbit was in the trap.

I turned away, my heart thumping. A good-looking black woman, another visitor, stood waiting to be let through the gate. She glanced up at the surveillance mirror and fixed her hair.

The fat officer eased herself out from behind the desk, and inserted her key in the lock. The gate swung open. I held out my hand, under an infra-red light. Another officer escorted me down the corridor. Behind me I heard the gate clanging shut. It echoed. That's the sound you always hear in prison: gates clanging shut.

In the visiting room I spotted Lila at once, the only blonde woman amongst a mass of brown faces. But then you could always spot Lila, anywhere. She hurried over to me and kissed me on the cheek.

'Honey!' she said. 'It's great to see you!'

She dragged me to a chair and we sat down. I paused, glancing at her. I had expected all sorts of Lilas, but not this one. Her hair looked newly-washed and fluffy; it hung loose to her shoulders. Her face was flushed; her eyes bright. She looked wired up, as if she had been taking drugs. As if my visit was the most exciting thing that had ever happened to her.

'You look terrific,' I said.

Like the other inmates she wore a regulation, state-issued outfit: green slacks and a white blouse.

'Think so?' she asked. 'I think it's the pits. Remember that line from *Sexbusters*? "Honey, green's not your colour".'

'Our first scene,' I said. 'The first scene we did together.'

Just then I had the curious feeling that we were acting. At the time I blamed it on our unlikely surroundings, and the fact that, indeed, I was performing a part and would be doing so for the rest of my life. But she seemed phoney too; she seemed too animated.

To cover my confusion I rummaged in my bag and produced my gifts: Snicker bars, Pepperidge Farm Nantuckets, a pack of apricot kernels.

'Thanks,' she said, barely looking at them. They lay in her lap.

We were silent. Next to us, a couple was sitting close together, kissing. The man drew back, cleared the phlegm in his throat, and resumed. I heard a faint, slurping sound.

'Know who I miss?' said Lila. 'Orson.'

It was a large room, painted orange and yellow and lined with vending machines selling coffee and snacks. A rainbow mural had been painted on one of the walls. At one end was a sign saying CHILDREN'S CENTER; shouts came from the room beyond. At the other end was a raised desk. It was manned by officers, who surveyed the room. They were looking at me, I was sure of it.

The couple beside us hadn't said a word. They had stopped kissing; they sat side by side, like two ebony figurines. I knew I should be asking Lila how she was feeling, how she was getting on, what her day was like, but I simply couldn't bring myself to do it. It seemed such an intrusion. That might seem ridiculous, but that's how I felt.

So I said, 'Tell me about Lou Minke. What was he like on *Touch and Go*?'

She lit a cigarette and blew twin jets of smoke through her nostrils. 'I'm going to be straight with you,' she said. 'That's not the reason I wanted to see you.'

I didn't move.

She said, 'I've got something to tell you, Jules. It's been

bugging me for weeks. I've been trying to psyche myself up.'

I took a breath. 'What do you mean?' I asked.

She turned to look at me. 'I knew you'd been having a relationship with Tee. I knew it all the time.'

My heart stopped. It seemed like a full minute before it started again, hammering against my ribcage. She turned away from me and looked down at her hands; smoke wreathed up, between her fingers.

'That guy, he was a total son-of-a-bitch,' she said. 'I knew he was using me. He just wanted me for my goddam body. He used me like he used everyone, his fucking play said it all. I was just one more sucker.' She gazed at the shiny packages on her lap. Her voice was flat. 'Faking my pregnancy, what a jerk-off thing to do. But by that stage I'd do anything.' She looked up. 'Hon, you meant a heck of a lot to him, I had no idea. He always wanted you. He talked about you, about how you were so goddam intellectual, so goddam clever. That's why I had you thrown off the picture.' She took a drag of her cigarette. Her hands were shaking. 'I thought it was over. He was cured. He *said* it was over. Then I found out it wasn't.' She looked up. Her eyes were brimming with tears. 'You were still seeing him.'

'That's a lie!' I cried. 'I wasn't.'

'You might as well come clean,' she said.

'It's not true!'

'I know you were still screwing him. He told me, that night. That's why I shot him.'

I stared at her. 'What?'

'He told me everything.'

'What do you mean?' My head spun. *She'd* shot him?

She said, 'He said he only wanted me for the sex. But he wanted you for your mind.'

'He didn't!'

'Even though you were a lousy fuck.'

I stared. 'I'm not!'

'He said you screwed like a schoolmistress.'

401

'I didn't!' I protested. 'He always said I was terrific!'

I stopped. My brain felt scrambled. I realised that I'd said too much, but I couldn't work out what it was. I needed, desperately, to disentangle myself.

Lila shrugged, and tapped her ash on the floor. The couple next to us were holding hands. Nobody seemed to have noticed anything.

Finally I rallied. 'Sure,' I said. 'I did have a little fling with him. Ages ago. But that was way back in England. Anyway, who *hadn't* had a fling with Trev?' I tried to smile. 'He jumped anything that moved. No wonder you couldn't stand it any more.'

Lila nodded. She took my hand and squeezed my fingers. 'I just wanted to tell you why I did it.'

Why *she* did it? I kept my mouth shut.

'I went there that night and I told that motherfucker I was going to kill him.' Her voice was quiet. Her fingers kneaded mine. 'He didn't believe me. He laughed in my face. You believe that? He didn't think I could do it. But I squeezed the trigger and pow!' She pushed her hair off her face. 'Know something, hon? It was kind of a relief.' She leant towards me and kissed me on the cheek. Her lips were dry. 'I'm glad I told you. It's like this big weight's been lifted. We can be friends now, huh?'

I nodded, speechlessly.

The next morning I started work on *Dead on Arrival*. I still suspected nothing. Lila's revelations had sent me reeling, but I just presumed that she had finally cracked up. Prison had finished off what showbusiness had started. Whether it's the process of law or of the media, you finally get to believe what you're told. They hold up a distorting mirror of almost-lies, of persuasions and manipulations, and you start to believe that the reflection is your own face. It becomes your own truth; it reinvents you in its own warped image.

During breaks in the shooting my mind was busy. Trev must have told her, at some point, about us. That was all. The news had festered in her. She had seethed, just as I had seethed, with jealousy. Now he was gone, she realised how much she missed me, how much she had thrown away. How men could come and go, but it wasn't worth losing me, her great friend.

I felt exultant. Flattered too, of course. All this time, she had been thinking of me. Little old me. I had been in her heart, just as she had been in mine. At last we were truly close. I would visit her. She said she had few visitors. Obviously all those showbiz types just melted away at the first sign of trouble. Shallow, ruthless little shits. How lucky she was, to know a woman with good, solid British values. *I* wasn't like that; not me.

I had a marvellous day and turned in a terrific performance. I felt expiated. Blessed. Lila believed she had done it – even to myself, I could only call it *It*. If she believed it, so could I. There was nothing to worry about. Prison would be a deepening, ultimately rewarding experience for her. Though locked away, she would in a sense be released from the febrile imprisonment of her fame. She would gather strength from the real lives, the real struggles and tragedies of the ordinary people from whom she had been separated for so many years. She would be down amongst her public, at last. She belonged there.

And when she was released early, for good behaviour, she would emerge blinking into the sunshine to find me waiting.

No imposter now, I sat in a canvas chair marked ARTISTE. We were shooting a series of hospital scenes; I wore my white physio's outfit as if I were born to it. My career was just beginning; soon I would be a movie star. *Dead on Arrival* had all the signs of becoming a good picture; the director was sensitive, the story was gripping. It was a bleak, psychological thriller with a twist in the climax of each act. The female star, who I hadn't yet met, was an actress called Murielle Farnes whose work I admired.

As I sat, inhaling on my cigarette, a girl walked past me. She stopped, and came back.

'I liked what you did this morning,' she said.

'Really?' I replied. 'Thanks.'

She was mousy and instantly forgettable; she shuffled her feet.

'So who do you play?' I asked.

'I don't play anybody,' she said.

'What do you mean?'

She grinned ruefully. 'I'm just Miss Farnes's stand-in.'

I looked up at her and smiled. 'You just hang in there, kid,' I said.

Five

The next morning was freezing cold. The buildings looked
carved against the blue sky as I travelled to Brooklyn. It was
our second day's filming in the hospital; one of the climactic
scenes in the movie. The hero, with my support, is trying to
regain the use of his legs. He hobbles up and down his room,
telling me about his failed marriage. At this point, two hit men
burst in on us. Before they can kill him, however, a bunch
of cops come clattering down the corridor and there's a big
shoot-out.

The atmosphere was tense, that morning. It was a com-
plicated scene; there were a lot of moves to rehearse and
a whole lot of new actors on the set. They milled around
in their cops' uniforms, drinking Coke. Their leather gun-
holsters gleamed.

They had turned up the heating. I was sweating in my nylon
jacket. My stomach felt tight and gassy. I had dreamed about
my father, and this always dislocated the morning after. The
whole day, in fact. Images suddenly rose up, making me lose
my footing as if a stair had been removed.

'Miss Sampson, can you come over here?'

The coach instructed me how to support Oscar Blechman,
the actor. He leant against me, nearly toppling me over. The
sun shone through the blinds; my hands were slippery. My
feet slid on the polished floor.

I had the sensation that I was being watched, but when I
turned round all I saw was the black, homely face of the physio
coach. I hadn't caught her name. I hardly knew anybody's name.

'You got it?' she asked.

I nodded. Beyond the window, in the corridor, I saw one of

the cops pausing to look at me. He took a drag on his cigarette and walked on.

Oscar leaned heavily against me. I tried to rehearse my lines, silently, but I couldn't remember them. *I expect great things of you, Julia.* It was my father's voice. *Look at me!* I replied. *I'm acting in the movies! Aren't you pleased with your little girl now?*

'That's fine,' said the coach. 'Take his weight. That's it.'

How could I possibly support him and remember my lines, both at the same time? How did people do it? I was standing on a stage, the audience was waiting. The faces were upturned so hopefully. My father sat in the front row. I was standing there, naked, and when I opened my mouth no sounds came.

Through the door I saw the blue blur of a cop's uniform. It was crowded out there. Every time I saw the cops it gave me a jolt. Stupid, wasn't it?

They were only actors. This was only a rehearsal.

A camera was being manoeuvred into position. It trundled across the shiny floor. How cramped this room was! I could hardly move. Oscar lay back on the bed, his eyes closed. His jaws worked as he chewed his gum. His thick, grizzled hair reminded me of my father. He opened one eye and looked at me. Then he winked. *My father's head, rising from the chimney pot.*

'Can you come with me?'

I swung round. It was the make-up girl. Nothing too alarming, was it? She had a yellow ribbon in her hair. Wide-eyed, she gazed at my face.

'Jeez, you look hot.'

People moved back as I made my way to the door. What did she mean by that? The others were sweating, too, weren't they?

'I've forgotten my lines,' I said to her, giggling. 'Isn't that a thing?'

She didn't hear. I felt clumsy and foolish; in fact, I nearly tripped over a cable.

Out in the corridor, one of the cops scratched his nose with a beefy finger. He looked like Rod Steiger. He moved towards me and I flinched back. But he was only making his way to the water cooler.

'Where are we going?' I asked.

The girl, whose name I didn't know, led me towards the room set aside for make-up. But then the director blocked her way. He leant down and whispered something in her ear. It seemed to go on for a long time. She swung round and stared at me, frowning.

I turned, to move away, but a light blocked my path. I must have bumped into it; the metal column rocked.

A hand touched my arm. I swung round.

'Miss Julia Sampson?'

I looked at one of the cops, but it wasn't him talking. It was another man. He wore a tie and a navy blue jacket.

'Could you step this way?' he asked.

He was an actor, one I hadn't seen before. I suddenly realised, perfectly clearly, what he wanted to do. He wanted to hear my lines.

I followed him out to the lobby. 'I feel so stupid,' I twittered. 'So embarrassed.'

He stood at the top of the stairs. There weren't so many people out here.

'My big scene too!' I laughed.

He took something out of his inner pocket and showed it to me. He did it discreetly, like a pickpocket showing me a stolen watch.

'Detective John Ermelli,' he said.

I looked up. Another man had appeared beside him. Now where had *he* been all this time?

The first man took out a piece of card.

'You are under arrest for the murder of Trevor Parsons,' he said. 'You have the right to remain silent . . .'

The hand held my arm, gently but firmly. He seemed to be supporting me.

'Watch out!' I chortled. 'I'm the physio. *I* should be doing that!'

We seemed to be walking down the stairs, the three of us.

'. . . you can speak if you choose,' he said, 'but anything you say can and will be used against you in a court of law . . .'

'I don't know what to say!' I giggled. 'I've forgotten my lines!'

HERE

One

One of the showers is broken. They've blocked it off with a chair. I've reported it to the CO, that's the corrections officer, but nothing gets done. It's been out of order for days.

I had to wait in a queue for the other one. It's a laborious business here, keeping yourself clean. Everything's a laborious business. There's so many rules; so many lists. Shower lists, gym lists, yard lists. Bits of paper. 'You got your blue slip, lady?' 'Got your ID?' 'Got your buysheet signed? No? Go to the end of the line.'

I try to take two showers a day. The other inmates think there's something wrong with me. They think I'm Lady Macbeth. *'What, will these hands ne'er be clean?'*

They don't, actually. They don't even notice. Most women here, like I told you, they're pretty incurious. Some of them resemble the people I saw in atriums, mouthing at the rubber plants. They're like those film stars who simply learn their own lines in a script, scoring them with a luminous marker, Me-me-me, in orange.

This is even though Lila was locked up with them here, for several months. Even though both our cases made the headlines. I have to admit, there was some hostility towards me at the beginning, but it's mostly died down now. In some strange way, they're more interested in the stars on the TV. They watch the soaps; they call them their 'stories'. 'That bitch!' they say, jabbing their fingers at the screen. 'She's the worst!' They know them better than they know each other, than they know themselves. 'Go for it, Belle! Go get him!' Soaps, sitcoms, whatever. Roseanne Barr, it's like she's their nearest and dearest. It's a terrible, one-way intimacy. Once

411

you know them better than you know yourself, that's when the trouble starts. I should know. It's the most dangerous intimacy there is.

Perhaps my status would rise if Lila came to visit me. I've been here three months now, and she's only come once. I don't blame her, really. I read about her, of course. Her new toyboy; her new film. Roly comes; he's been surprisingly supportive, through all this. He's become a sort of father figure to me. My mother's been; she flew over to see me.

She sends me postcards, too. I've pinned them up in my cell. They're pretty picture postcards of England – rolling hills, churches, half-timbered pubs. That sort of thing. I know I sneered at them once: a never-never land preserved in aspic for American tourists; a Ralph Lauren theme park. But I find them comforting, now. That Britain, it exists for me. It has become a Kodachrome series of snapshots, like my childhood, fixed for ever.

My cell is 10 foot by 6½ but at least it's mine all mine. I wash its floor every day, with Joy liquid detergent. I have a bed, a metal locker, and a rail for my clothes which I've covered with a flowery curtain. Eight blouses, we're allowed. Two sweatshirts. Nothing with blue in it, even blue dots, because the COs wear blue and we might try to escape, ho ho. Six pairs of shoes. It's near enough all the clothes I had in Belsize Park, anyway. I've walked through those walk-in closets, those rows of Bill Blass, and right out the other side. Quick dissolve, and here I am!

I have a toilet. Like everybody else I cover it with a chair, and I've laid a patterned bathmat over that. We rig up our small euphemisms. They're not small here, they're necessary. Roly sends me books and I keep them stacked along the floor. I'm always on the lookout for pieces of wood; then I'll make shelves.

There's not much to read, on our unit. At the end of the corridor there's a recreation room, overlooked by a raised desk, it's called a 'bubble', where the COs sit. There are a few books in the rec, but they're mainly encyclopedias and religious tracts. There are scruffy armchairs, and ashtrays made from empty tuna cans. There's a TV, but with sixty women to one set everybody squabbles over what channel to watch. Yesterday I wanted to watch *The Philadelphia Story*, it was the afternoon movie, but all these women were glued to the shopping channel. The screen sparkled with '*a-designer-inspired diamondique necklet, only $90*'. They send off for things; they get the Penneys mail-order catalogue.

I have a window, in my cell. It's just a narrow strip, with glass slats that I can open on hinges like mouths. Through it can see a wall, a patch of grass and a strip of sky. It's timeless and seasonless here. During the spring, some blossoms lay strewn on the grass, blown in from the free trees. Of course I see the surrounding woods, when I walk from one building to the next. The trees are heavy now. I know their rises and dips so well, and the solid clots of the evergreens. I make up imaginary walks for myself, over the lip of the hill. In my mind I can make the woods go on for ever, I can dream up vast landscapes to explore, even though I know it's just commuter-land over there, and the bow-fronted toytown of Bedford Hills. Housewives must be walking in and out of Jeni's Boutique, as if it were the most natural thing in the world.

I've only seen this place twice, from the outside. The first time was when I came here to visit Lila. The second time was when they brought me here from Rikers Island, in the sheriff's car. I was shackled. Hands, waist, ankles. They do it to everyone. 'Sorry about this, lady,' said the officer. That's what they call us here, 'ladies'. I'm a lady for life. Well, fifteen-years-to-life. That's what they gave me. A longer sentence than Lila's, but that was to be expected.

Some of the inmates, they make their cells really homely. They stick up photos of their kids; blurred photos of birthday parties, year after year, from which they themselves have been excluded. They see their children grow in Polaroid snapshots. I'm glad, now, that I never had kids. They wallpaper their cells with mismatched floral strips. A white girl, down my corridor, she's in for homicide. She's painted this mural, a tree full of birds of paradise. She's really talented.

When we're banged up, at night, the door closes with an electronic sigh. They control it from the bubble. There's a tiny window, in the door. We have several counts a day, and one at night, to make sure we're still here. At night we have to put our hand against the glass as proof of our continuing existence. *Good night, sweet ladies.* Along the corridor there's a heavy gate that clangs shut. The clanging gates, they punctuate my dreams like that manhole cover down in the street, way back in New York.

The other noise at night, it comes from the next cell. There's a woman in there called Rita Salgado. Sometimes she throws her furniture around. She has seizures; she tries to mutilate herself. Sometimes they haul her off to the psychiatric wing. She killed her boyfriend, that's why she's here. 'I came in the room,' she says, 'this motherfucker's raping my daughter. Next thing, I was stabbing him in the neck with my kitchen scissors.'

She's in thrall to a big black dyke called Sadie, who's built like a meat-packer and has a whole harem of women here. In exchange for sex and cigarettes she offers them protection. All relationships are trade-offs, aren't they? Sadie has what's called a personality disorder, but then that's what they said about me.

Know what this shrink said, at my trial? He said I'm suffering from 'a severe schizoid personality with psychopathic tendencies. Denial of love at an early age has resulted in a blocking-off of the normal channels of emotion. This patient can neither give nor receive love. She has retreated into a powerful, at times uncontrollable, fantasy life. Playing a role triggers another personality that takes over her functioning self.'

I wanted to shout: But I'm an actress! That's what I'm supposed to do!

As I said, Rita mutilates herself. She tattoos herself with

414

pins and cigarette ash; she punishes her flesh. Her arms are a network of scars.

That's how they got me; my scar.

It happened like this. I've pieced it together from what I've been told, and the state's witnesses at my trial.

Courtney Wilson, the coffee-coloured doorman, was watching the *Marv Winfield Show*. He was sitting in the lobby at Central Park West, watching it on the portable TV, and he saw me on the screen. First he saw me holding up my hand. Then he heard that I had been Lila Dune's stand-in.

Something puzzled him. So when the day staff arrived, the next morning, he asked the captain if Miss Dune had a scar on her hand. The captain said she hadn't.

So off Courtney went to his father's apartment and he looked at the autograph. He went back to Central Park West and compared it with her signature on some service charge contract. The signatures didn't quite match.

He thought, maybe he was being fanciful. Maybe they'd laugh at him. Maybe her writing was different because she was upset. For Christ's sake, she'd just killed a guy! Her hand was shaking.

Finally, however, he went to the police. A handwriting expert was called in, who confirmed that the two signatures were not written by the same person.

From that moment, things moved fast. A detective came here, to Bedford Hills, to question Lila. How had I behaved, that night? What had I been wearing? Was there any way I could have gained access to her apartment?

Over and over, I've imagined Lila's reaction to this. The slow realisation; the sickening sense of my betrayal. At some point she must have remembered that I had never returned her keys. I don't want to think about it.

They searched my apartment, that evening when I was with Roly. They found the keys to Lila's place. I had kept them, you see. It might sound silly, but I couldn't throw them away. They were my prize, my medallion, for the best performance of my life. I needed to give myself some recognition. The police also found, bundled into the bottom of one of my suitcases, the blue denim blouse which Lila had described me wearing that evening. I hadn't been able to wear it again, or even touch it, actually. I had simply bundled it away. When they took it for analysis they discovered traces of the paint in Trevor's lobby. When the coat was half-off my shoulders he had pushed me against the door.

Ironic, isn't it? Undone by my moment of fame. Convicted by the TV screen. There's a moral there, somewhere.

The cops were smart. They near-enough reconstructed what had happened. They had the evidence, but no motive. During their search they had found no trace of any connection between Trev and myself – I had even thrown away his post-cards. Via the British police they could have investigated my life in London but there was a risk that I might get wind of it, and it was vitally important not to arouse my suspicions.

So they decided to use Lila. They got her to lure me to visit her, lure me with lies, and they hid a tape-recording device inside her blouse.

And I bumbled blindly into her net, just as she had bumbled blindly into mine.

I've had to stop for a while. First I've had to report for work, then I had lunch. We eat in this big brick mess hall. Lunch is ridiculously early, at twelve, as if we're in hospital. Remember, I wondered what had happened to rissoles? They're here; that's what. Today I ate baked franks, rissole potatoes and beans, followed by Jello. Kids' party food. After twenty minutes, whether you've finished or not, you have to get up, scrape your garbage into a bin, and leave. It's the rules. So's not having blue dots on your clothes, or more than one ring with a stone in it. We're locked into some insane, endlessly repeating production. Our director is a megalomaniac; he turns us into puppets. He pulls the strings, he choreographs our clanging entrances and exits. He's working on a mammoth production here, with a cast of eight hundred, and this one will run and run. A maximum security epic. There's no escape. Literally *no escape*. We are trapped in the present tense, we cannot get out to continue our lives. We're locked into the endless repeats of our past dramas, growing ever more stale with the telling. You, the audience, can get up and go home. Rummage for your car keys, step into the breezy and now unimaginable street. Decide to go this way, or that. Stop for a coffee.

A lot of the women here, they're philosophical about it. 'You play, you pay,' that's what they say. Jodie, who's becoming a friend, she says, 'This place, it's a warehouse. They're keeping us in storage. All they've gotta do is scrape the mould off us, from time to time.' Like most of the women, she's here for drug offences. She used to make $1,000 a day, selling crack. She earned nearly as much as Lila. When she's released, she'll start selling it all over again.

I've started drama workshops in the evenings. I've got groups of women to work together, exploring their feelings, using improvisation and role-reversal. 'Change places,' I tell them, 'and now begin all over again.' I'm a bit of an expert in that. I use some of the exercises from when I worked on an Afro-Asian project in Tottenham, in my community theatre days. At least I can do something. And if I get above myself, Serena, she's a huge, cheerful woman, she nudges me in the ribs. 'Listen, you whiteass honky cunt,' she chuckles. 'You just remember. You's just a number, same as us.'

Serena's training to be a cosmetologist. She does hair relaxing, cold wave, frosting. They used to be unfamiliar terms but I'm learning things, here. She's been longing to get her hands on my honky hair, which has reverted to mouse. She wants to dye it blonde. She says she'll do it for free if I can get Roly to send her Bette Midler's autograph.

Such things, she tells me about her past. Incest, rape, abandonment. It's like *The Color Purple* re-set in the Bronx. No wonder she likes to lose herself in her TV stories. I'm the other side, now. I can see what we have been manufacturing, behind the bright lights; those necessary dreams.

It's simpler on the TV screen, just as it's simpler in prison.

Locked in together, these women construct whole new families for themselves, replacing the families they never possessed. Someone is 'Mommy', someone else is 'Aunty', someone else is even 'Dad'. She might be the only Dad they have ever known; I'm not the only one with an absent father. We re-create each other, just as we re-create dramas of our pasts. And mine is no more, or less, believable than the rest.

I've been thinking a lot about Lila today. I'm at the commissary – we're allowed there once a fortnight – and I'm standing in line at the wire grille. You show your ID card and then you push your buysheet through, with the items marked. You write a disbursement, the money is deducted from your fund account. Like film stars we are imprisoned in a perpetual never-never land, a childish place free of responsibility.

I'm buying some packs of Winstons ($1.24), some roach disks for my cell ($3.10) and some raisin bran ($1.69) for my digestive system. By now I know the buysheet by heart, I hum the items as I wait.

Prolene Hair Food,
Pomade, Dixie Peach,
Hair Spray, Spritz,
Cocoa Oil Hair Cond.

The soap says *Caress* to me, the shampoo says *Agree*. The deodorants whisper to me *Sure* and *Secret*. The list of junk food always reminds me of Lila's hoards, stuffed away in her trailer and her cupboards at home. *Black Cherry Soda* (18¢), *Cinnamon Pop Tart* ($1.32), *Tootsie Roll Pops* (5¢). *'I'm a junk-food junkie,'* she said, smiling at me, the first time we met.

I'm standing here, behind the broad back of Aunty Carmel, and I've suddenly realised: Lila and I, we've both shared this. Nobody else has; nobody in the outside world. Even Trevor's body was shared by other women. But this place is ours; ours alone.

Two

The last time I saw Lila, it was when she came to visit me. It was way back in February, and I had recently arrived. I figured she would come, even if it was just to gloat. I figured she would be too curious to resist it.

Everyone's heads turned, when she entered the visiting room. She wasn't just a film star, she was an ex-inmate! She wore her red fox fur, dark glasses and high-heeled boots. She stopped to greet one of the COs as if she were a long-lost friend. Then she rushed up to various prisoners, hugging them.

'Hi Joanie, how're ya doing?' she called gaily, as if she were at a première.

I waited for her, shaky with nerves. Our positions were now reversed. It was me who wore the green slacks now, the white blouse and green pullover – you have to wear the regulation outfit, for visitors. Maybe it was the very same set of clothes she herself had worn; after all, we were near enough the same size. That's how the whole damn thing had begun.

She didn't greet me. She came over and sat down opposite me, on an orange, slatted chair.

'So how's it feel, huh?' she asked, taking off her dark glasses. Her face was heavily made-up; she looked nervous, too.

'So-so,' I said.

'Which unit you in?' she asked.

I told her.

She raised her eyebrows. 'You met Beverly yet?'

I nodded.

She smiled.

'She's in my corridor,' I said.

Lila's smiled broadened. 'She tried to get into your pants yet?'

I nodded.

She chuckled. 'You managed to protect your virtue?' she asked, bitchily.

'Yes.'

She took off her gloves, took out her Salems and lit one. 'Where're you working?' she asked, squinting through the smoke.

'In the Volunteers Services office,' I said. 'I just started.'

'Oh, real la-di-dah.'

'Filing and stuff,' I said. 'We're putting together packages for Puerto Rico Discovery Day.'

She nodded abstractedly and waved at Allie, a stylish ex-hooker. Allie waved back. It was as if Lila were visiting her old Sixth Form, at school.

'I'm thinking of starting some drama workshops,' I said. 'Maybe putting on a play. I've always wanted to direct.'

There was a pause.

'Worst thing's the squat'n'cough, right?' said Lila. That's when they strip-search you; you have to cough, so if you have hidden anything it falls out. 'Pretty bad, eh?' she asked.

I nodded.

'Even worse than having to kiss Sylvester Stallone,' she said. 'Till then, I thought *that* was the pits.'

She put the cigarette between her lips, rummaged in her bag and brought out a book. It was an early, proof copy of *Heavy Petting in Hornchurch* by Trevor Parsons. 'Where the fuck is Hornchurch, anyway?' she asked, passing the book to me. 'The publishers sent it. Wanna read it?'

'Thanks.' I took the book.

'I'm not in it,' she said. 'I flipped through it, then I read it slowly. There's nobody like me in it.' She took a drag of her cigarette. 'Nobody like you, either. It's all about a girl called Dawn. Know her?'

I shook my head. 'I saw her once. She worked in a wine bar.'

Lila indicated the book. 'It's full of dirty words,' she said, wrinkling her nose in distaste. 'I wouldn't let him do half those things with me.' She pulled some fluff off her coat and looked around. 'You notice, there's hardly any guys visit?'

I nodded. It was true. Mostly women came, bringing children to see their mothers.

'First sign of trouble, they all fuck off,' she said. 'Hightail it out of town.'

'Unless they're teamsters,' I said.

'Sure. Unless they're teamsters.'

'What did Jesus Christ say to the teamster?'

'I dunno,' she said. 'What?'

'Don't do anything till I get back.'

There was a silence.

She looked at me. 'Kinda sad, isn't it?' she said. 'I thought we were pals.'

'So did I.'

Under the make-up, I saw the lines around her mouth. Her lips seemed thinner. I realised that she was starting to look her age. Forty-three. Maybe forty-four by now.

'How could you do it to me, Jules?' she asked.

'I'm a severe schizoid,' I said.

'That's no excuse.'

I paused. 'I know.'

'Irma told me not to come. She said I'd get too upset. She hates your guts.'

'I thought you'd get off!' I blurted.

She stared at me. 'Why the hell should I?'

'Because . . .' I stopped. 'Just because.' I paused. 'You wouldn't understand.'

We relapsed into silence. I looked across the room. The COs sat in their bubble. When I first had a visitor – Roly – I got up to see him out. I had normal, hostess instincts then. But of course I couldn't see him out, could I? They clanged the gate shut in my face.

'I'm sorry,' I said. 'I don't know what to say. I'm sorry.'

421

'Sure, you're sorry.' She dropped her cigarette and ground it out, viciously, with her boot.

There was a silence. We both gazed at the flattened butt. It was splayed out sootily on the lino.

'The son-of-a-bitch never told me about you,' she said. 'It might have been different, then.'

'Might it?'

'Sure. What you take me for?' She shrugged. 'Maybe not. Who knows?'

I leant forward. 'How did you do it? When I came to visit you here. How did you know what to say?'

'My lawyer tried to tell me what to say. Like, to trap you. But I stopped him. I said I can do it fine. I'm not as dumb as people think. I'm a *woman*, for Chrissake! I know just what to say.'

'It was a terrific performance.'

She nodded smugly. 'They've nominated me for an Academy Award.'

There was another pause. The room hummed with voices. Next to us, a little girl stood with her head in her mother's lap.

Lila took out her pack of cigarettes. This time she passed one to me. 'You weren't so bad either,' she said. 'Prime-time news! Fame at last, huh?'

'Which bit did you see?'

'You standing in the witness box, socking it to them. Telling them every goddam detail of what you did. "So then I put on the wig, I put on the dark glasses and I quietly left the apartment." You had them there in the palm of your hand. You played the room.' She looked at me admiringly. 'Know what? You could've been one hell of an actress.'

'Could I?'

She nodded. We smoked for a while, in silence.

'Didn't see it all,' she said. 'I was sitting in the rec room and Beverly wanted to watch some garbage game show with Jaclyn Smith in it. Eek! *Jaclyn Smith!*'

She inhaled deeply and looked around. We were still edgy with each other. But the atmosphere had warmed, slightly.

The CO called out, 'Five minutes, ladies! The visitors' room will be closing in five minutes!'

Around us there was a stirring. The mother cupped her child's head in her hands, drawing her between her knees. People picked up their coats and put them on. We didn't, of course. We, the inmates. But they did.

Lila looked at me. 'Know something? Something really weird?'

'What?'

'Guess who was the stand-in this time?' She jabbed at her fur with a red fingernail. 'Me. *I* was your fucking stand-in. One helluva job, isn't it? Now I know what it's like.' She shivered, and ground out her cigarette. 'Kind of a creepy job, if you ask me.' She looked up. 'I did the set-up, honey, but you've got to act it now. And this show's going to run and run. For life.' She stood up.

'You play, you pay,' I said.

'You play *me*, you pay.'

Then she leaned forward and kissed me. I smelt her perfume, and the scent of tobacco on her breath.

'Bye,' she said. She turned around. 'Bye, ladies!'

Then she walked away, fast.

The tap-tap of high-heeled boots; the clang of a gate. Then the fainter clang of another gate, further down the corridor.

And she was gone.